THE HELMET'S HUNGER WAS A ROAR INSIDE HIM

Gath, his eyes red fire, screamed a harsh guttural howl and launched his body into the air. Robin turned in terror at the sound, presenting her face to the descending fangs of the bat. They came within a foot of her shuddering cheeks, and Gath's fingers tore into the creature, ripping it off course.

Gath and the huge bat hit the dirt and rolled into one of the fires. The fire spit sparks and embers, and smoke billowed up around him, concealing his actions.

Cobra raced up, shielding Robin behind her, and Jakar and Brown John joined them.

There was a short squeal from within the smoke, then it was cut short, and the bat's head tumbled out, torn from it's body at the neck.

Gath emerged from the smoke, eyes smoldering, body singed and smoking, and wearing blood like a blanket.

Also by James Silke
published by Tor Books

DEATH DEALER BOOK 1:
Prisoner of the Horned Helmet

FRANK FRAZETTA'S DEATH DEALER

BOOK 2

LORDS OF DESTRUCTION

JAMES SILKE

A TOM DOHERTY ASSOCIATES BOOK
NEW YORK

LORDS OF DESTRUCTION

Copyright © 1989 by James R. Silke
Artwork and Death Dealer character copyright © 1989 by Frank Frazetta

A TOR Book
Published by Tom Doherty Associates, Inc.
49 West 24 Street
New York, NY 10010

Cover art by Frank Frazetta

ISBN: 0-812-53821-5   Can. ISBN: 0-812-53822-6

Library of Congress Catalog Card Number: 88-51002

First edition: January 1989

Printed in the United States of America

0 9 8 7 6 5 4 3 2 1

One

THE INVADER

The sound of a horse and a jangle of armor came from the stand of fir and hemlock trees crowding the eastern edge of the murky slime. Then a single male rider, moving at a controlled and steady pace, appeared between the trees. Robed in shadows. Wearing darkness as naturally as the midnight sky.

A shaft of sunlight slashed through the needle cover and splashed across the mane of a thick-muscled black stallion, glittered on the blade of a huge axe riding a saddle scabbard and washed over the black chain mail covering the rider's body. A slight tug on the reins, and the stallion stopped facing a narrow trail of raised bald dirt crossing Noga Swamp, the sunlight a bar of gold across the man's sun-dark, handsome face.

Unruly, almost neck length black hair framed ruddy flesh stretched tautly across bold cheekbones and the bridge of his blunt nose. His lips were wide and flat, creased with a scar that ran to his square chin, and his eyes hid in deep clefts under a shallow forehead, casting black shadows. Enigmatic. Hard. The face of nature's child, as calm and steady as the sheltering pine and brother to the storm.

Wine bottles, dried meats and bread filled his saddlebags, and his belts carried a sheathed dagger

and sword, a coin pouch and a small earthen jar
drilled with air holes.

Two vultures landed silently on the limb of a
naked, fire-blackened mangrove tree, and craned
their wrinkled necks low, watching the stranger.
Their crops were stuffed, and their feathered bellies
ballooned over the branch. Good workers, as well
fed as graveyard worms.

Smelling the scent coming from the jar, they
suddenly cawed loudly.

The stallion reared slightly, snorting and stomping, and a scrap of dappled sunlight illuminated an
object hanging at the side of the rider's hip: a helmet
of black metal, with a spiked crest and horns that
curled down and back toward the masked face.

Cawing madly, the vultures spread their wings,
lifting heavily into the air, and winged their way up
in hasty retreat through a passage between the skele-
tal limbs of the mangroves.

The man who owned the horned helmet was no
stranger. He had invaded the forbidden lands before.

Reaching a safer perch at the heights of a tall fir,
the two vultures again settled side by side, and
looked down at the lone rider. Greedy hunger was
bright behind their eyes, not because they hoped to
feed on the large man, but because they were certain
they would dine heartily on the carnage that would
mark his trail.

The rider, Gath of Baal, gave the birds a routine
glance, and held the stallion steady just short of the
raised road. The caution in his eyes could have cut
steel.

The swamp's foliage and waters were totally
devoid of their customary serpentine shadows and
ominous clicking and hissing. There was no movement and no sound except for the faint songs of the

wind in the tree canopy, the cricket and the blue
bottle fly. Nature had used the swamp for a battlefield, and slaughtered the land as well as its inhabitants. The swamp was now one eighth the size it had
been when he had first crossed it, a shallow muddy
pond.

To the sides of the road, where the water touched
the edge of the forest, it was murky green and deep.
But in the main body, it became shallow and slimy,
then turned to dark wet mud. Beyond that, the
bottom was hard dry mud which had cracked and
pulled apart around the burnt and blackened bodies
of the mangrove trees.

On the opposite side of the swamp, tongues of
hard lava now curled and twisted down out of the
heights of Panga Pass, then spread out in widening
fans across the dry swamp bottom and dipped their
tips into the murky waters. There steam rose above
the edges of the pond. The recently molten rock was
still warm.

The skeletons of oversized lizards, crocodiles and
snakes were draped on the black limbs of the trees
and protruded from the dry mud bed. Bits of
charred skin danced on their burnt bones.

The land, once a sunless world of shadows roofed
by leaves, had been ravaged by rivers of molten lava
which boiled away the greater portion of the swamp
and set fire to the trees and undergrowth to leave a
grey, lifeless land exposed to sun, wind and eye. But
other, more unnatural forces, had also been at war.
Many of the dead creatures were headless and lay in
submissive coils and crouches, as if they had surrendered to execution.

Gath leaned forward, and the stallion started
down the road into the spilling sunlight, using center
trail in a manner that said no other had the right.
Both man and animal were stained with trail dust,

and moved with that easy grace only granted to those travelers accustomed to roads fashioned from mysteries and destruction. But their eyes were wary, hunting the strange, haunted devastation.

Up ahead, lava obliterated the trail through Panga Pass which the Barbarian had formerly taken. Now he would have to scout out a new trail, a task which would be difficult and time consuming. But this did not bother him. Instead it brought a dark smile to his face.

The Land of Smoking Skies lay somewhere to the west beyond the pass, and it was not simply one more mysterious, uncharted world so common to that distant time. It was a world ruled by the Master of Darkness and his armies of demon spawn, and for Gath, a world of compelling memories of unleashed evil which tugged at his soul, transforming his dark smile into one of flashing anticipation.

The demons of the Lord of Death had hunted him long enough. Now he was the hunter.

Gath was certain that the mysterious place he now longed to dominate, the place where he belonged, was up ahead at the mouth of the underworld. There he would stand guard and destroy the demons of the Master of Darkness as they came forth from the bowels of the earth. There he would find the satisfaction and fulfillment the helmet now demanded. To find it, he had to leave behind all he knew. His home in the rain forest called The Shades, and the only two people he had ever called friend, the lovely Robin Lakehair and the *bukko* Brown John. But he had no choice. The horned helmet's magic penetrated his blood and bones. It was rooted in them, and produced a hunger he could not resist.

Now the helmet was the only friend he had, and he was resolved to dominate its magic, make it the only one he needed.

His hand dropped to the headpiece and stroked its living steel. It made him the master of wherever he chose to stand, the equal of earthquake, thunder-cloud and lightning. With it mounted on his head, he would prevail against whoever he faced, and do it in the manner he had sworn he would long, long ago when he was a boy. By himself.

Two
THE NYMPH QUEEN

Far to the west of Noga Swamp, past the Land of Smoking Skies, across the great Barrier Mountains and beyond the vast sea of sand dunes called the Emptiness, lay a small ocean bordered by black-shadowed forests and shrouded in dense fog. It lay still, silent, then the sound of a horn echoed out of the gloom. Faint. Mysterious. Like the wailing moan of all that had died in the last year.

This was the Inland Sea, a slowly, steadily growing body of water which would one day be called the Mediterranean.

Only the sun and moon can remember what it looked like then, less than one-tenth the size it is now and confined to its southwestern extremity, only the meager beginning of what it would become.

In those barbaric days, the sea was landlocked. It was fed by falls cascading over a landbridge which linked the continents which would one day be called Spain and Africa. The source of the falls was the

Endless Sea, the Atlantic, to the west. Fed by the melting ice capping the northern continents, the Endless Sea was imperceptibly rising, cutting through the landbridge. In the far distant future it would push through and tear it down to link the two oceans with a passage called the Straits of Hercules, and bury the mountains and deserts and Great Forest Basin under its watery weight. But now it slowly spilled its icy waters into the tropical warm waters of the Inland Sea, content to send up billowing clouds of steam which hung over the western shore.

There the massive rock which would be called Gibraltar crouched like an animal with its paws extended to the south and its haunches bunched to the north. At that end, sheer cliffs of shale and limestone rose to the heights, supporting a castle constructed of black stone. Pyram, the lair of the Nymph Queen, the high priestess of Black Veshta, whose magic manufactured the demon spawn for the Master of Darkness.

The low piercing cry came from a horn mounted in the castle's east tower. It was a command.

The sound flooded over the blunt, thick ramparts and towers, swirled down through passageways and courtyards. Shutters banged against it. Doors were bolted, and behind them the inhabitants whimpered and covered their ears. But a few children ran through the ruins and perched on fallen walls overlooking the water, thrilled at the prospect of getting a glimpse of their legendary queen.

The horn announced the ritual feeding of the great Lord of Destruction who ruled the Inland Sea, and only the queen could feed him. When she did, the children would gaze down on her nymphet beauty and see why for the last months the horn had forbidden them to look at her. But soldiers quickly found them, drove them back into their homes and then hid themselves.

The horn continued to cry out, then abruptly stopped, and Pyram stood still and silent.

At the base of the cliffs was a large crescent-shaped cave. The blackened pylons of a pier extended from its shadows, thrusting up out of the turbulent waves like giant rotting teeth, their roots washed with clinging greenish-white foam. A moment passed, then a blood-red barge emerged, rode over the waves and pulled away from the end of the pier. It headed for the tip of a blunt rock protruding from the water about a half mile off shore. The sacred feeding area.

The barge's hull was a long narrow oval constructed of papyrus reeds. The bow and stern ends turned up, and were molded and painted in the shape of erect phalli. There were no masts or sails. Six oarsmen stood in stirrups on the stern deck plunging leaf-shaped oars into the surf with trained precision. They followed the beat of a pace drummer who sat under a thatched awning on the aft quarter. A weathered waterman stood behind him holding the tiller steady. Each had been deliberately made deaf and mute so they could not hear their queen's sacred voice, or speak of her sacred beauty.

At the prow, three elderly priests stood reverently, hands clasped in prayer. They were bald and bare-chested, their loose white skirts held in place by black ropes. The eldest, the high priest of Black Veshta, had three red circles painted on his shiny pate, and his foot rested on a brown-skinned girl who sprawled chained, naked and whimpering on the deck. She was blindfolded.

Tiyy, the Nymph Queen of Pyram, stood on the command deck, shivering like a leafy bush and smelling of Midnight Orchids. Her diminutive body was buried within a massive bear-fur robe, the hood hiding her head. Only her eyes showed within its shadows, large almonds under level eyebrows as thin as thread, and outlined in black kohl as wide as a child's finger. The upper lids were heavy half-moons blushed with pale indigo. The orbs were a flawless, translucent alabaster surrounding sky-blue irises, and the pupils were dilated, dark compelling doorways into a mind as predatory and cunning as the trapdoor spider.

A short thin man stood respectfully to the side of her throne chair. His black tunic was ragged and thick with trail dust. Where his flesh was exposed, it was greyish and smooth, almost slick, and blistered. Schraak, a serpent priest in the service of the Queen of Serpents. He had just arrived after an arduous, hurried journey from the Land of Smoking Skies with a message from the Master of Darkness, and the sweaty slime oozing from his worried cheeks said he had not brought good news.

When the barge neared the tip of black rock, and was too far away from the battlements for anyone spying there to see her features, Tiyy lowered her hood.

Her hair was dyed a bilious lemon-yellow and cut with flawless symmetry in the shape of a shoulder-length pyramid. Florid pink rouge thickly covered her cheeks, in an attempt to hide the wrinkles in her heart-shaped face, but without success. It was a face which undoubtedly had once been beautiful, but which now had no physical claim on the title Nymph. A withered sack of flesh and bone laced with lightning.

As the barge slid alongside the rock, she raised a commanding hand. The pace drummer stopped beating his drum. The oarsmen plunged their oars deep, holding them steady, and the barge slowed, came to a stop.

Tiyy advanced to the front of the command deck, and her robe fell partway open. Her face belonged to a woman in her eighties, but her throat was only slightly slack, and her bare round shoulders were as plump and firm as a girl's.

She removed a small leaden vial from her robes and thumbed it impatiently. It was thick and heavy, with a lead stopper tied to its narrow throat, and contained the magical black wine, Nagraa, which sustained the powers and forms of the Lord of Death's demon spawn.

The high priest joined her on the command deck, bowing low, and she handed him the vial without ceremony, saying, "Hurry! Hurry!"

The high priest scurried back to the prow, and his two assistants lifted the chained girl off the deck. She screamed and thrashed blindly, but they took little notice and forced her squirming body down on the deck, just short of the rail. One priest squeezed hard at the base of her gums, forcing her mouth open, while the high priest, holding the vial well away from his face, removed its lead stopper. A beam of black light shot forth from the mouth of the vial, accompanied by an almost human wail, and the blindfolded girl shrieked and thrashed, turning her head away. The priest forced her back into position, again pressuring her mouth open, and the high priest emptied the vial's fuming contents into it.

She gagged and kicked, screaming fitfully as the priests unchained her. Then the high priest plucked her off the deck as if she weighed no more than a cup of soup, and held her above his head. She screamed again, then passed out. He shook her until she regained consciousness, then heaved her out over the railing.

Her arms and legs windmilled helplessly against the air, and she hit the water, sending up a crowd of white watery spears, then sank from sight.

Tiyy, now standing at the side of the command deck, watched the water as Schraak moved up beside her. His eyes were white with shocked excitement, but the Nymph Queen showed no reaction.

The girl surfaced, thrashing and screaming. Her blindfold had been torn away, and she looked about with white startled eyes, then began to swim for the barge. One of the priests picked up a long blunt pole hanging on the deck railing and routinely drove her away from the barge. She screamed and grabbed hold of the pole. He shook her off easily and prodded her further off. She tried to swim for the rock, panicked after three strokes and began to thrash and scream mindlessly, churning the black-green waters to a white froth.

Tiyy watched intently. The blue of her eyes suddenly vivid behind their thick black lids. There was color in her smile.

Without turning to him, she said, "It begins well, Schraak. The girl has spirit. That is sure to bring him."

Three

THE WHITE LORD

Far below the blood-red barge, on the floor of the Inland Sea, a huge shadow drifted inside a greenish gloom enveloping a massive black rock. Looming behind weaving elkhorns and sea whips undulating on the sandy bottom, the dim mass came to a stop, as if hearing something other than the clicking of shrimp and the wet flutter of the sea whips. Ominous. Vague. Suddenly, as if yanked by a hook, it turned and shot forward, growing larger and darker.

A rainbow of fish of all sizes and shapes, swarming across pink coral beds in the shadow's path, burst apart in a chaos of color and fled through gently swaying sea fans. The clicking of the shrimp stopped, and a hush consumed the depths. Except for the enlarging shadow, there was a sudden void of life.

The mass of darkness, still within the murky gloom, crashed through a protruding arch of rock, dislodging a cascade of black boulders and swept up and out of the gloom, its pointed snout spearing up through the liquid-blue space.

Its underslung mouth was parted, displaying rows of jagged, saw-toothed teeth. Its round eyes were fixed with a cold death stare. Its sickle-shaped fin stood proud and regal on its back, the brutal crown of its primordial species. The sleek whitish barrel of its body pulsed with muscle and cartilage, driven by

the sweep of its crescent-shaped tail. An inevitable
force consumed with insatiable hunger.

Faster and faster it whipped upward, rising not
only from the depths of the sea but out of the
corridors of time. A great white shark. The culmination of one hundred and eighty million years of
breeding, and black magic.

A Lord of Destruction.

Near the surface, sunlight pierced the green-black
waters and glanced off the white blades of the shark's
teeth as its lower jaw opened and the upper protruded. Fifty feet above it, a small figure flailed
desperately, churning the surface to bubbles and
froth.

The shark thrust forward, like an ejaculation of
white death spewed by the bowels of the earth. The
suction-mouthed remora fish hitchhiking on its body
were ripped away.

Jaws spread, the shark hit the thrashing body of a
brown-skinned girl dead center. The impact drove
her torso deep into the mouth cavity, and a thrashing
leg thrust into the throat. The shark burst free of the
surface as the shrill scream of the girl sang in his
small brain.

The jaws snapped shut. The screaming stopped,
and bits of the girl fell away from the jaws, splashed
back into the sea. In a frenzy of feeding, the shark
devoured the scraps, churning the sea to a frothy red
foam and sending geysers of water thirty feet into the
air.

When it had finished, the shark circled, momentarily content, as it felt the sacred black wine spill
from the girl's butchered stomach to heat its own
belly. Then it faced the blood-red barge floating
beside the tip of black rock. On the command deck,
Tiyy, strangely wrinkled and wrapped in furs, smiled
down at him. Beside her stood a small smooth

stranger. The high priestess put a mouth harp to her lips and played it.

A painfully beautiful flow of notes vibrated across the water.

The shark convulsed angrily, rejecting the harp's musical command. But Tiyy continued to play, and the fish calmed, raised its pointed snout obediently, then dove, swept back down into the depths of the greenish gloom.

Reaching the floor of the ocean, it glided about the coralheads, rolled through the brown elkhorns and sea whips, touched bottom disturbing an ivory tongue of sand. There its gills expanded, as if savoring for the last time the cold fetid scents of home.

Four

ARRRGGG!

The Nymph Queen's royal barge swiftly returned to the sea cave, and Tiyy disembarked, strode into a shadowed rock tunnel siding the pier, with Schraak following at a respectful two strides.

Around them, the sound of the incoming tide crashed and thundered in the rock walls like the angry voice of a dark god, and Schraak shuddered with terror. He was a stranger to Pyram's underground world, but he knew it for what it was, the birthplace of horror. His body, however, enjoyed the dank air and odors of wet earth, and the deeper they went, the more his true nature came to show. His flesh became spongy and oozed a soothing slime.

Reaching a sizable cave holding a tide pool, Tiyy stopped at the edge of the rock ledge overlooking the water, and stared down into the swirling mass. Waiting. Awed and mystified, Schraak stood beside her, his quick small eyes searching his torchlit surroundings.

The pool was in one of the many natural caves which had been formed over the centuries by sea water eating into the cracks at the base of the limestone cliffs. Its submerged floor had a three-foot circular hole through which sea water spilled. It led down to more creeping water-filled passages, crawl holes and caves. These had been formed in the distant ages when the Inland Sea was much lower. Where the actual bottom of the underwater labyrinth lay was unknown.

Directly above the churning tide pool, stalactites, white, tan, rust-red, blue and grey, dripped from the ceiling of the cave forming a multitude of shapes: pillars, knobs, warts and cathedral arches. There were crazy, snakelike creepers formed by wind, cave pearls and rimstone which formed the ledge on which the Nymph Queen and Schraak stood. Here and there in the wall behind the ledge were crawl holes, some no bigger than a fork blade, and others large enough for the passage of a small man.

Sentries, crawling on hands and knees, emerged at the openings of three of the shadowed holes: worm soldiers belonging to the castle's underground garrison. Their umber flesh glistened wetly under sparse leather armor, and short curved blades grew from the stumps of their right hands. Small dark holes served them as ears, and their tooth-filled mouths hung open as they stared expectantly at the pool.

As the tide continued to rise, waves of sea water crashed through the large tunnel and spilled into the pool, sloshing up the rock walls and washing over the edge of the ledge. With the waves came thin spears of sunlight. They cut through the turbulent walls of water, turning them bright green and filling the cave with a foreboding glow.

Suddenly the cave darkened, and Schraak shuddered, backing away from the edge. Seeing what Schraak had seen, the sentries squirmed back into their crawl holes out of sight. But Tiyy held her place. Confident. Regal.

A huge dark shape was riding a wave, blocking out the light. Then it splashed into the pool, and sunlight again spilled in, giving shape and identity to the massive barrel of the great white shark's body. It whipped and writhed in the translucent green water, plunged down and vanished in the darkness of the pool's depths.

Nothing moved. Schraak inched back to the edge of the ledge, and the heads of the sentries slowly reemerged, revealing thin highlights of reflected sunlight between wet, spongy folds of flesh.

A tiny whirlpool, the size of a thumbnail, formed at the center of the pool. It spun in place, then suddenly widened. Its edges were a swirling froth of murky white, the center a black spinning hole. Slowly a silver-white helmet rose out of the inky maelstrom. It covered the head of a man.

Both helmet and neck cape followed the curve of bone and flesh like opalescent growth, and glittered metallically, parting over exposed pointed ears to flow into graceful depressions below wide blunt cheekbones. His large oval eyes opened slowly, a deep blue-grey and cold, with whites that were not white, but pale indigo. Intent. Humorless. Eyes possessed by death and the economical grace of controlled violence.

Tiyy smiled regally and said, "Welcome, Lord

Baskt, it has been a long time."

Schraak fell to his knees reverently, placing palms and forehead against the cold wet stone floor.

The Lord of Destruction floated toward the ledge and ascended the sunken steps. His armor was a dripping rainbow of color, subtle blue, pink and indigo plates that left a trail of color behind in the water. They rose and fell and slid slightly from side to side, accommodating his joints as he moved, and did so without the tinkle or clatter of metal. They were not metal, but hard cartilage growing out of muscle.

His corded arms were bare. Glistening saw-edged teeth protruded along the ridge formed by the bones of his forearms and from the backs of his knuckles. Standing on the ledge, his seven-foot bulk towered over his diminutive queen in a subtle whiplike crouch, as if ready to strike, his head low between his massive shoulders. Over his rounded back rose a dorsal fin.

The water coating the massive lord's body, instead of dripping off, clung to him adoringly. The whirlpool still spun and splashed, sending arms of water reaching over the ledge to bathe his legs. Then the water released its hold, drained off his body and submissively slid back into the pool. The whirlpool sucked it up, then quickly lost force and died, radiating ripples vanishing against the walls of the cave.

Baskt, taking no notice of Schraak as he rose uncertainly, dipped his head to his queen, giving her the bare minimum of respect. Then he put his hard wary eyes on her wrinkled face, staring intently at a mole on the side of her chin. There was a hair growing out of it thick enough to lace a sandal.

"Why do you stare?" she asked with irritable

sarcasm. "After three hundred years, don't I have the right to show my age?"

Her humor escaped his simple mind. "What's happened?" he asked, his voice demanding, arrogant.

In reply, she smiled and spread her arms, parting her fur robes. She was naked except for a thin paddle-shaped apron inlaid with precious jewels, a silver girdle studded with diamonds and a thin leopard-skin halter which barely covered the tips of her breasts. One was as round and firm as a fresh pear, the other a flaccid, leathery sack. It contrasted sharply with her brown-gold body, soft, curvaceous, carnal, that of a nubile seventeen-year-old.

Baskt stared at the decaying breast, and she said evenly, "I'm dying."

He straightened defiantly, unwilling to accept her announcement, because he was dependent, as were all other demon spawn, on the sacred black wine which only her magic could produce.

"Yes," Tiyy said, "you are right to be afraid. All of our lives, my kingdom, the master himself is in danger. But you are going to save us all." His eyes thinned with curiosity, and she nodded at Schraak. "This is Schraak. He has just arrived from the Land of Smoking Skies with a frightening tale. The horned helmet has been stolen by a Barbarian called Gath of Baal. With its help, he and Barbarian tribes of the Great Forest Basin have driven the Kitzakk Horde from their desert territory. Schraak's mistress, the Queen of Serpents, joined forces with the Kitzakks and tried to stop them, to retrieve the helmet. But she failed and then vanished. No one has seen or heard from her. Schraak, it appears, is the only survivor. He was buried alive in the underground chambers of the Kitzakk's desert capital, but his

wormlike nature allowed him to escape. He then
returned to the Land of Smoking Skies and told our
holy father what had happened. Our master ordered
him to come here and tell me. But as Schraak was
leaving, our lord became so enraged at this disas-
trous turn of events that he exploded, destroying his
altar . . . and silencing it."

Baskt's huge underslung jaw dropped partly open.
From the holy altar, and from it alone, could their
lord speak and instruct his servants. Without it, they
were all masterless. Doomed. He asked quietly, "But
you have the magic to build a new altar?"

"Yes," she said, "and only a month ago I could
have. But with the Queen of Serpents gone, there
have been no slave caravans from the Land of
Smoking Skies. The last was over a month ago.
Consequently, there have been no carefully selected
slave girls for me to feed upon, and I am losing
strength rapidly."

Arrogant pride flashed behind the lord's eyes.
"You don't need the slave caravans. I'll find the girls
for you."

"In the Inland Sea?" Her tone mocked him.

"No," he said, indignant. "I'll gather the
slavemasters. They'll find all you want, bring them
from the ends of the earth if they have to."

"Arrrggg!" she growled. "There is no time for that!
Besides," she turned to Schraak, "there is no need.
Schraak here knows where there is a girl who can
supply all my needs."

"One girl?" Baskt grunted in disbelief.

"Yes, my lord," Schraak said humbly, and bowed.
"She lives in the Great Forest Basin, in a village
called Weaver."

"A Barbarian," Baskt scoffed.

"Yes, my lord, but she is young, not more than
seventeen, and of a beauty that will amaze you. Her

Kaa is strong! Terribly strong! More than pure enough to feed your queen. My mistress, Cobra, the Queen of Serpents, she examined her herself."

Baskt, visibly impressed, shared a malignant smile of dark anticipation with his queen.

In that ancient world, the Kaa, the spirit, within all living things was still raw and powerful and untamed. Untainted and unweakened by fears a-roused by sophisticated technologies and religions, unchained by the stifling limitations of scientific reasoning. Some were so pure and strong that they could be extracted by magical formulas, and extraordinary powers of sorcery. A few were so rarefied that they could be given substance, be transformed into powders and potions, then be administered to human beings. In this manner one Kaa was joined with another, doubling the strength and frequently transforming both nature and body. Tiyy, having lain with the Master of Darkness, carried his demon seed within her, and it gave her the rare and extraordinary powers required for such thaumaturgy. In addition, within her underground laboratory she held a living source of power with which she could manipulate and control the strongest Kaa and bend it to her sinister will.

The Nymph Queen nodded at Schraak and said, "Schraak has seen the Barbarian girl and, if he wishes to earn the rewards I have promised him, he will remember her well enough to identify her for you. Her name is Robin Lakehair. Now, assemble as many soldiers as you think you will need. You'll leave immediately."

Baskt shook his head. "I need no help to steal a girl."

"I know," she snapped. "Nevertheless, you will take it. This thief who stole the helmet is somehow linked to the girl. He may be guarding her, and with the helmet his strength will rival your own." His grin grew with anticipation and she shook her head slowly. "No, Lord Baskt. If there is any way to avoid meeting this Barbarian, any way at all, you will do it. Understand? You will take no risks! None! This time, when you see a drop of water, you will harness your pride and not transform yourself into a shark just so everyone can see you do it. Your mission must be kept secret at all costs, or people will suspect what has happened to me."

He hesitated, and bowed belligerently, barely dipping his head.

"Good," she whispered, her voice feverish. "Now go! Fetch her! A few scraps of her meat, a bottle of her blood! That's all I need."

Five

THE HELMET

The border marker lay facedown in the dirt. A rectangle of stone of unremarkable color or size, its backside told Gath of Baal nothing.

He dismounted, turned it over using the toe of his boot. He could not read the words, but the crudely chiseled image of mountains and overhanging clouds told him he had reached the Land of Smoking Skies.

Five days had passed since he had left Noga Swamp, and each had been spent finding a new trail through diverted rivers, leveled mountains and up-

turned valleys and meadows. Now, just beyond the
marker, he faced a tongue of hard lava nearly twenty
feet in width. It receded, rising higher and higher,
toward a low conelike hill, the remnant of a volcano.
A meager spire of smoke rose out it, like a flag of
surrender. The remains of larger volcanos filled the
surrounding area beyond it, their tops cut off as if by
a giant knife. They rose off of low bald hills blackened by fire and radiating flows of hard lava. There
was no sign of life on the ground or in the air, and the
perpetual black clouds for which the Land of Smoking Skies was named had vanished.

Gath remounted his black stallion and rode up
onto the tongue of lava.

There was no sign of the many staircases which
had been carved out of the rocky cliffs. They were
either crushed or buried, and the shadowed mouths
of the mountains' many caves had vanished, either
swallowed by volcanic explosions or drowned by
spewing lava. The ground itself had been rearranged,
like a quilt kicked by sleeping feet. There was no
indication of which volcano had held the underground chambers of the Queen of Serpents with its
secret entrance to the living altar of her lord, the
Master of Darkness.

He halted at the crest of a rise, and his eyes
thinned.

The skeletons of men rose out of the lava flows,
some buried to their knees, others to their skulls.
More bodies were draped among the blackened
branches of burnt-out oaks and pine trees, their
bones picked clean by flying predators. There was no
armor on the skeletons, and no weapons lying about:
the booty, no doubt, of two-footed predators.

He turned one way, then the other, and saw a
distant ridge of black lava. Beyond it, in the far
distance, there was a patch of green forest that had

somehow escaped both lava and fire. He looked back at the dead volcanos, and his fingers drummed the head of his axe. A moment passed. He unbuckled the horned helmet from his belt and held it up with both hands.

Its living steel was warm against his calloused fingers, and the horns seemed to pulse and reach for him, daring him to defy its addictive power.

Snarling, he lifted the helmet over his head, as if to put it on as casually as he buckled his belt. But his blood and bones rebelled. The muscles in his forearms knotted and, with their veins bulging under sun-darkened flesh, resisted, instinctively afraid. They seemed to know that once the helmet covered his head there was every chance he could become its prisoner again, and could not remove it without the help of Robin Lakehair's magic.

His face glistened hotly in the shade cast by the headpiece, then his pride welled up defiantly, and slowly his arms forced the helmet down until its rim descended over his forehead. A primitive pleasure shone behind his reckless eyes, then they vanished behind the metal, and the helmet was in place.

His harsh breathing was noisy behind the mouth hole. The whites of his eyes glittered briefly behind the eye slits, then a fiery red glow replaced them.

The mark of the Death Dealer.

Six

FORKED TONGUES

Gath drew his axe and prodded the stallion into a trot. His helmeted head moving from side to side. Alert. Expecting trouble. Wanting it.

Veins corded and throbbed along his forearms, and steam drifted from the sleeves of his chain mail as his blood, growing hotter, coursed through him. His senses sharpened and expanded, sending vibrations into his scalp and hair, then into the metallic flesh of the helmet and through its horns into pointed tips.

He prodded his horse into a gallop and moved deep into the enveloping landscape, recklessly riding through narrow guts and gullies designed by nature for ambush. But he felt nothing save the chill of the air flowing past him, and heard nothing but wind and cawing vultures.

He was deep in the domain of the Lord of Death, crossing over earth and rock in which the heart of darkness was buried. Here sin, corruption and murder were the coin of existence. Here the power of evil rivaled earthquake and tornado. But he saw only a mysterious foreboding void.

He turned off the tongue of lava, galloped up the side of a huge crater and reined up at the crest of the cone. Rubble filled its center: the opposite side had collapsed inward and sealed the volcano. Here there was not even a thin spire of smoke to proclaim its former majesty.

He rode down into the crater, turning and twisting the stallion between massive boulders, churning up clouds of fine dust. Finding nothing but earth and lava, and sensing no danger, he galloped back to the crest of the crater and again reined up. The helmet throbbed against his head, hungering for battle, and frustration spit flames from the eye slits. But he sat still in his saddle, defying the headpiece's demands, and slowly the flames abated, the red glow died.

He spent the morning slowly and carefully searching the other craters, but found no cave entrances, no golden doors, no staircase cut out of lava, only the charred skeletons of lizards, pythons, adders and men with and without tails. Returning to the largest crater, he again searched the rubble filling the cone, and again found nothing. He remounted the crest and stood in his stirrups surveying the distant landscape.

Beyond the dead volcanos to the north and west, mountains rose in steep cliffs to jagged peaks half hidden by clouds. To the east and south, the direction in which the molten lava and its trailing cloud of dust had traveled, the hills were strewn with rocks and beds of dust, bisected and decorated by puddles and rivers of hard lava.

The entrance to the underworld was sealed. Hidden.

He sank back into the saddle, raging with frustration. Suddenly the red glow reappeared behind the eyes of the helmet, then black smoke spewed out, and he growled demonically. The stallion reared, whinnying, and Gath yanked on the reins, holding the stallion's head erect, his body quaking. The helmet's demon fire drained into his blood and groin, and the headpiece turned his head, its flaming eyes scanning the horizon to find a thin spire of smoke rising behind the distant ridge of black lava. He drove his spurs into the stallion, and it leapt forward, charged down the slope.

Gasping with blood lust, sweat draining down his arm to ride in glittering spider trails over the blade of his axe, Gath rode over hills, across tongues of lava and through a maze of towering boulders thrown about haphazardly by volcanic explosions. Folds of black lava undulated beyond the boulders, forming the ridge beyond which the smoke spire rose. A narrow rocky defile zigzagged through its left side. Gath plunged into the defile with the animal turning and twisting, then erupted into a clearing surrounded by rock walls thirty feet high, and reined up.

A campfire, surrounded by stones laid out in a ritualistic triangle, occupied the center of the clearing. Beside it, skeletons were stacked and strewn in a narrow stream of water flowing through the clearing. Some still carried chunks of meat and flesh, and the water was dark red. In the corners, armor and weapons pillaged from the dead made heaps against the rock walls. Three narrow, twisting gullies opened onto the clearing. They were filled with deep shade and crouched figures. More lurked in the clefts of the overhanging ridges, barely discernible against the black rock.

Gath, with a low rumble of satisfaction escaping the helmet's mouth hole, walked the stallion into the sunlight filling the middle of the clearing, and the helmet's horns pulsed with life, curving down in cruel challenge.

The shadowed creatures cringed and hissed with pink-red tongues protruding. They were forked.

Gath slowly turned the stallion in a tight circle, affording each of the creatures a chance to attack his back.

They hesitated, then lurched cautiously into the sunlight at the edges of the defiles and clefts. They wore ragged tatters of hunter-green tunics, the uniform of the Queen of Serpents' bodyguards, and belts hung with daggers and swords. But they ignored their weapons, and held their hands in front of them like claws, drawing back lips to expose fangs and teeth. Patches of scales clung to fuming sores in arms, jaws and thighs. Fingers and toes had fallen off. Noses had shrunken to hard black scales, ears had shriveled to bloody holes, and they were bald.

Gath reined the stallion to a halt and drew back warily as the creatures' fumes swirled about him. He gagged on the stench, and the creatures, some of them resorting to their bellies for propulsion, launched themselves at him.

The first attacker led with his mouth wide open and quickly discovered his mistake. Gath greeted him with his axe, and when the snakeman hit the ground, the upper half of his mouth was lying ten feet away from the lower half.

The axe buried itself in the meat of two more attackers, then five bodies hit Gath. They drove him out of his saddle, bore him to the ground with hissing squeals and buried him under snapping, swarming bodies.

Gath rolled across the ground crashing through the pile of skeletons, splashing in the blood-red water, ripping the bodies away. They came apart like half-baked dough, and greenish wet fumes and blood spattered helmet and chain mail. Fangs bit into his forearm, but broke off before doing damage. When he fought his way back to his feet, he no longer had his axe, but held a muscular arm by the wrist. He had pulled it out of a shoulder as easily as if it were a cherry on a cake. He hammered his assailants with the arm until they writhed on the ground like dying snakes, and in the process reduced the arm to a two-inch stump.

He threw it aside impatiently and moved for the creatures slithering on their bellies. His eyes held the hunger of a starved man.

He kicked at a head, removing it from its shoulders, and stepped on another. It exploded like a melon and he slipped on the pulp, crashed into a boulder headfirst. The rock, being made of harder stuff than the decaying demon spawn, left him in a dazed lump on the ground. The creatures slithered around to feed on him, and the stallion moved in among them, rearing up and stomping. The creatures coiled and hissed under the descending hooves, then began to jerk and fume in the throes of death.

The stallion backed away from the carnage, and Gath rose slowly. He moved onto the heap of skeletons, retrieved his axe from the bony rubble and stood leaning on it. The blade glistened with bloody streaks. Behind him, a red-orange glow filled the distant sky, tinting his black armor and matching the glow of his eyes. The same color tinted the flowing water. It was the only movement, a river of death.

The axe came back into Gath's hands, as two more figures emerged from one of the gullies. They also wore hunter-green and had forked tongues, but stood erect and held sword and spear in hand.

The horned helmet lowered its horns, growling in anticipation, and the creatures backed up a step, moving away from each other to attack from different angles. One hesitated, digging a small leaden vial from a belt pouch, and the other lunged for it. His partner lifted his sword in a short swing and cut off his friend's hand. Howling, the creature dropped to the ground with green blood spewing from the stump of his wrist.

Gath moved for the surviving snakeman, and he stuffed the vial back in its pouch, sank into a crouch with his sword playing in front of him. The helmet's eye slits replied with spitting fire, but Gath stopped in place. His body heaved as he once more brought the helmet under control, and the fire died in his eyes. He deliberately dropped his axe, then leaned in, feeding the snakeman's sword his helmet. The creature slashed, but the blade glanced off harmlessly. Suddenly Gath stepped inside the swing of the sword and, carefully measuring the force of his punch, hit the snakeman flush on the side of his head.

The creature went reeling back, leaving his sword behind, met a boulder with his face and fell back on the ground like a drop cloth.

Gath picked up his axe, moved to the snakeman and straddled him. When the stunned creature came to, he found the cutting edge of the axe poised on his Adam's apple and the menacing face of the horned helmet looking down at him. He held perfectly still, not daring to swallow.

"What has happened here?" Gath demanded.

An inarticulate hiss was the reply.

Gath leaned slightly on the axe, drawing a trickle of blood. The snakeman flinched with pain, and terror swam through his eyes as he blurted an answer. It was in a language Gath had never heard before.

"The entrance to the underworld?" Gath snarled.

The creature replied with a long, rapidly spoken and seemingly lucid flow of words, as if he understood Gath perfectly. But again he used the foreign language.

Gath lifted his axe angrily to pulp the creature's head, and the man fainted with a whimpering hiss.

Gath inspected the snakeman carefully, but found nothing that told him what he wished to know. He hesitated thoughtfully, then, without untying the jar with the holes drilled in it that dangled from his belt, lifted it, feeling its warmth, and gave it a shake. The captive in the tiny prison moved about vigorously, causing the jar to move on Gath's palm. Satisfied that it still lived, he lowered the jar and looked over the battlefield without satisfaction. The helmet, its hunger unfulfilled, still churned and boiled for satisfaction, and his pride still cried out for a worthy challenge. There had been no glory or honor in this day's work, only bloody labor.

Gath dragged the unconscious snakeman to his feet and threw him across the clearing beside the stallion. Then, tying him securely, he tossed him over the saddle facedown and walked the horse through a gully and out of the clearing.

In a nearby area was a flat spread of lava with a large irregular bowl-like depression in the middle. It was about fifty feet across and easily twenty feet deep at its lowest point. He dropped the reins and descended the steep incline of the bowl. About ten feet short of the lowest point, he set his axe on the ground, squatted and untied the earthen jar from his belt. He lifted it to his ear, listening, then held it in front and away from him. With the jar resting in one hand, he took hold of the cork and hesitated, did nothing for a long moment.

The helmet was hot and heavy against his head, sinking low and weaving back and forth as if trying to throw him down. He fought it back into place, and flames erupted angrily. He sat still, forcing them to abate, then firmed his grip on the cork, took a deep breath and, in one fluid movement, ripped the cork out and rolled the jar down the slope toward the bottom of the bowl.

Seven

THE SKINK

The jar spun around like a chubby dancer and rolled to a stop in the deepest depression. A moment passed, and a thick-scaled, shovel-like head peeked out of the open neck. Its heavy-lidded eyes blinked against the glare of daylight.

Gath, axe held across his thighs with both hands, rose into a crouch, as if facing a dragon instead of a tiny Skink snake.

The small creature probed the air with its tongue and wiggled partway out. Its brown wedge-like body had four tiny legs, no more than wrinkled memories degenerated from its primordial past. A short struggle and its puffy body popped free, fell on its smooth white chin.

The Skink gathered, and staggered about uncertainly, trying to burrow into the ground and hide. The lava was too hard. With a swimming motion, it hurried up the shallow incline, saw the axe and the man holding it and retreated. It tried to climb the steep sides of the bowl several times, but each time slid back to the bottom. Exhausted, it looked directly at Gath. The heavy lids lowered and the head tilted slightly. Waiting.

Gath took a step back.

The Skink spread its jaws wide, as if laughing silently, and yellow fumes issued forth, like a long vaporous tongue. They billowed and rolled, filling the bowl until the reptile was only a vague shadow within the yellow mist. Almost languorously, the creature rolled over, and its belly opened up like a lipless mouth. Hissing issued forth, faint and gentle, and a sharp wailing shriek. Then all sound and movement stopped, and the vapors hung heavy and thick, hiding whatever lay within.

The horns of Gath's helmet grew hot and slightly erect. A glow reappeared behind the eye slits. Excitement was spilling through him. He rolled his shoulders and advanced defiantly into the bowl, dispersing the smoke with the flat of his swinging blade until he reached the bottom.

Within the thinning vapors, a woman sprawled beside the jar, heaving with exhaustion. Her colorless tunic and faded brown cloak were ragged and rent with holes. She reclined on one hip and elbows, torso twisted away from Gath and face hidden between her arms. They were bare, an ivory white, and her legs were drawn up under her in artful disarray. Lush curves of breast, hip and thigh pressed through the torn openings in her garments, their poverty only enhancing the wealth of her voluptuous beauty.

Gath's eyes cast a hot light over the lovely sprawl, here and there invading its secret places.

When the smoke cleared, she lifted her head. Long straight black hair fell over face and shoulders. She parted it with three red-tipped fingers and looked up at Gath. Her face was the crowning jewel of her beauty. Bright red lips, creamy cheeks tinted with rose madder, grey-gold eyes set in thick black almond outlines flairing under arched brows. Regal. Deadly. Cobra, the Queen of Serpents.

She looked about furtively, then back at Gath, and asked breathlessly, "Where are we? What are you going to do with me?"

He did not reply.

"You're going to kill me, aren't you?"

"Probably," he said, as if it would take no more effort than folding a saddle blanket.

She hesitated, then spoke in a slow, precise voice. "That would be a mistake, Dark One. I can help you. And I won't give you any trouble. I've learned that lesson. I'll be whatever you want me to be, slave . . . cook . . . whore . . . anything."

"We'll see."

A careful smile lifted the corners of her lips, cold and bitter, and she drew her body into a sitting position, self-consciously arranging her rags about her. Just above her left ankle, the pale flesh of her calf had a greenish cast that grew darker at the anklebones, then became thick and crusted, and turned into scales covering her entire foot. Not the plain brown workmanlike scales of the Skink, but the glittering ice-blues and emerald-greens of the cobra. Seeing it, she gasped shrilly, and quickly drew the offending appendage under her, arranging her tattered cloak over it. Shame blotted her flushed cheeks.

There was no contempt or pity in Gath's harsh low voice. "Your cage has not been kind to you."

She dipped her head, more in surrender than agreement, and said submissively, "I regret that my appearance offends my new lord and master." A familiar stroking caress echoed in her tone, barely veiling the also familiar challenge. "Your prison was so small and cramped, and my strength has been diminished by a diet of dirt and beetles. But when it returns, the scales will go away, and you will no longer be reminded of my unnatural lineage. Until that time . . . if you will allow me . . . I will bathe and adjust my toilet to be as pleasing to your sight as possible."

She started to rise.

"Sit still!" he barked.

She sank back, eyes white with alarm.

He threw a leather thong to her. "Pick up the jar."

She did as she was told and sat obediently holding the jar in her lap.

He nodded at it. "Remove the mandrake root and tie it around your neck."

She smiled ironically. "Haven't lost your charm, have you, Dark One? Here I am, powerless and at your mercy, and wearing nothing but rags and shame, and still you would have me believe you fear me. I am flattered."

"Now!" A cold command.

She smashed the jar against the hard ground, and a piece of mandrake rolled free. She picked it up and, turning her head to hide her revulsion at its ugliness, used the thong to tie it in place. Finished, she took a deep breath and smiled suggestively over a naked shoulder, saying, "Now that my demonic nature is tamed by the root, perhaps you'll tell me what is it you want of me?"

He nodded at the crest of the bowl. "I just ran into a pack of your servants. They were dying, decaying and falling apart. Why aren't you?"

"Because their natures and strength are sustained by a far weaker sorcery than that which sustains me." Her voice was flat and precise. "They must have regular dosages of a black wine called Nagraa, and have undoubtedly run out of it."

"You don't need this wine?"

She shook her head. "The chosen few who are the consorts of the Master of Darkness are made of a sorcery that is strong and durable. For us the black wine is only a beverage, a pleasing stimulant."

He grunted impatiently, walked slowly around her studying her and said, "Follow me."

He moved up the incline, and she rose fluidly, followed obediently.

When the stallion saw them coming over the crest of the bowl, the horse reared excitedly, throwing the bound snakeman to the ground with a pained grunt. The impact loosened his ropes, and he wiggled free, rolled onto his knees, making obeisance to his queen.

Cobra stared in pity at his fuming joints, then surveyed the surrounding landscape with puzzled eyes. "What is this place?"

"The Land of Smoking Skies."

She looked at Gath in disbelief.

"You're not a hundred strides from your home," he added, his tone discouraging all argument.

She looked up at the cloudless sky. "But there's no smoke?"

"Your sacred volcanos are dead." He nodded at the snakeman. "Now talk to him, find out what's happened."

She didn't move. Fear cut deep into her smooth forehead, and she shuddered, looked off at the devastation. "Impossible," she whispered. "It's all gone. Everything . . . my people, my treasures, my whole kingdom!"

"Yes," he said. "Now talk to him. And find out where the entrance to your chambers is buried."

Her eyes questioned him, then understanding

showed in them, and she said, "So that's it. You're not satisfied with defeating my demons . . . with driving the Kitzakks from the desert and enslaving me. You still want revenge."

There was no reply.

She murmured softly, "You've grown reckless, Dark One."

"Ask him!"

"Of course," she said, her tone mockingly servile, "whatever my lord wishes."

Speaking in the snakeman's tongue, she questioned him at length, and he, trembling and stammering weakly, replied to each query. Finally, babbling in desperation and again pressing his cheek to the ground, he offered her the small leaden vial. She shook it, measuring the contents, and held it up to Gath.

"Black wine. It's his last bottle, and it's nearly empty. Apparently there have been no deliveries since the volcanos erupted."

"Bah!" Gath grunted. "What did he say about the entrance?" He slapped the vial out of her hand. It hit the ground with a clang, popping out the lead stopper, and rolled off spewing a faint shaft of black light from the mouth.

The reptilian stared in horror, whimpering. Suddenly, with a whiplike motion, he came off the ground with his mouth spread wide, striking at the Barbarian's leg. Gath turned his axe blade, and the snakeman, blind with fury, drove his chest against it. It brought him to a sudden crunching halt, his jaws snapping short of his target. Hissing and writhing, he tried to pry himself off of the blade, but could not, and Gath kicked him free. Flailing and hissing, he rolled across the ground, came to a stop and died with a shudder.

Her almond eyes narrow, Cobra glared at Gath.

His thick hand flew at her, caught her shoulder and drove her to the ground. "Now where is the entrance?"

Her arm parted the blanket of black hair that had fallen over her face, and she looked up at him. Her chin was smudged, and malevolent humor glittered on her grey-gold eyes. "So that's how it is," she purred. "You've worn it too long . . . the helmet's taking control."

"Don't worry about the helmet." His voice was low, coarse. "What did he say?"

"All right, I'll tell you," she said, drawing herself up to sit on a boulder. "But call in your little virgin to remove the helmet first." She looked off at the shadowed boulders, then back at the metal face of the helmet. "What you are about to hear requires a cool head."

"Talk!"

"All right," she said again, "but you are not going to like what you hear. Apparently, when my former lord was informed that you had defeated me and successfully stolen the helmet, he became enraged and began to roar and shake the mountain." She nodded at the dying snakeman. "According to this poor soldier, it continued to get worse, then all the volcanos started spitting flames and smoke, even those thought to be dead. Then they exploded . . . repeatedly . . . burning the forests and destroying everyone as they fled. When that stopped, a series of earthquakes began, tearing down the mountains and changing the courses of the streams and rivers. Only a scattered few survived. When the lava cooled, they returned to seek out the entrance and enter the altar room to ask what he wished of them. But as they entered the tunnels, the earth shook again and the crater collapsed, killing most of them in the tunnels . . . and burying the entrance. There were only a handful of survivors who you apparently have disposed of. Now there is no way to enter the mountain, or even to tell which mountain was mine. Not even I could find it."

"You lie."

She smiled bitterly. "I only wish that were true . . . but it isn't. The mountain is sealed. Everything I possessed is buried. Gone. And I am deserted, with no one to protect me . . . except the one who has ruined me . . . you."

He shook his head, once. "If your master is dead, the helmet's powers would have died with him."

She smiled briefly and said, "Now, Gath of Baal, you flatter yourself. You did not kill him. He has only temporarily retreated to the bowels of the earth, and when he returns, you will be in more danger than ever."

The eye slits glowed briefly in reply, and Gath said, "Come here." She rose, moved to him, and he added, "Remove the helmet."

The corners of her eyes smiled. "I thought that was a privilege reserved for your simpering virgin."

"She's not here."

Her mouth dropped open in shock. "You're not serious, you're . . . you're just testing my powers?"

He took hold of her wrists, lifting her hands to the helmet. She resisted, and a slightly mocking smile coiled in her cheeks as she purred, "So that's why you released me?" A faint echo of her old power rang in her voice. "You've left her, and now you need me. The helmet's killing you."

"You talk too much." He placed her hands on the horns of the helmet, but she stroked them instead of taking hold of them, and laughed lightly.

His blunt fingers crushed her hands around the horns, making her wince with pain. "Remove it, bitch!"

"No!" she said, her voice laden with defiant power.

He took hold of her throat, yanking her to him. But still she grinned, shaking her head. "It's no use threatening me. I can't remove it now."

"You've lost your powers?"

"It's not that. I used all my strength to restore myself, and I'm weak now, unstable. I must rest first, and eat." He held her slightly away, and she added, "I need bread, wine, berries, whatever you can find . . . and meat . . . fresh meat." He let go of her, and she smiled. "And since I now have something to bargain with, I want some proper clothing . . . and a bath."

Grumbling, he pushed her aside and mounted his stallion, slipping his axe into its scabbard. Looking down at her, he said, "There are some stacks of armor and weapons in a nearby culvert." He pointed it out. "There should be clothes among them, but they won't be what you're used to."

"I'll make them do," she said. "And the food?"

He nodded over a shoulder, saying, "There's a patch of forest over there . . . my guess is it's full of game."

She smiled. "Then by tonight . . . we should both be free of our prisons."

Without replying, he turned his horse away and walked it toward the black ridge.

Cobra watched him, holding her smile in place until he rode down into a depression and was out of sight. Then she let it drop, and raced to the fallen leaden vial. Snapping up both stopper and vial, she held them away so the beam of black light could not touch her, and inserted the stopper. She slipped the vial inside her cloak and breathed a sigh of relief. The black wine's magic had many uses and might help her prove her worth to her new lord if and when he needed her help. She rose and started after Gath.

When she caught sight of him, a rush of excitement flushed her cheeks, and she hurried to catch up. After three strides, she slowed abruptly, shocked by her actions. She was acting like a slave, and enjoying it.

Eight

THE HUNTED

Concealed by a boulder, Cobra stood knee-deep in the forest pool bathing. Moonlight filtered through the surrounding pines, dappling her creamy shoulders and back. The rest of her was as dark as the night, invisible against the forest shadows. Finishing, she waded quietly to the boulder and, bracing herself with her hands, raised up on her toes and peeked over the crest.

A campfire flickered in a small clearing beyond the boulder. The remains of a roasted deer were spitted over it. Beyond the fire, Gath sat against a thick oak. His weapons and armor were piled beside him, and he was naked except for loincloth and helmet. The headpiece hung heavily between his massive shoulders, and his burnished chest heaved impatiently.

Cobra stared in awe and wonder, marveling at the mere sight of him. Huge. Male. The most deadly force to walk the earth, and he needed her, was dependent on her. The knowledge made her senses

wilt with unruly pleasure. It was almost girlish, not
only enslaving her senses, but her mind and heart.

Realizing that a decidedly unqueenly blush had
risen to her cheeks, Cobra slipped back behind the
rock. She dipped her hands in the cold water and
held them to her hot cheeks, then did it again and
again until they cooled. She splashed her body with
water so that tiny droplets flickered on her flesh like
moving moonlit jewels, then waded out of the pool
into the firelight. There she stood drying herself with
her back to Gath, wearing her nudity with the same
audacious glitter with which midnight wears the
shooting star.

She could hear his helmet grate against its chain-
mail cowl, then his dry, harsh voice growled, "Hurry
it, bitch."

Stroking the drops of water off her body, she
asked, "Is it growing too heavy for you?"

"Just get over here."

"I'm coming," she said, but it sounded like a long,
time-consuming trip.

Piled at her feet were ragged garments and a small
dish of rose-tinted rouge she had made from talidda
and tamal berries gathered from the forest. She
applied the rouge to cheeks, lips and breasts using
her little finger, then tied her hair back with a scarlet
rag and dressed herself in silver loop earrings, indigo
robe and cloak and rawhide boots. She tied the robe
about her narrow waist with a scarlet rope, then
moved toward Gath.

The stallion, standing in the shadows of the oak,
moved restlessly as she approached, and she glided
to the animal, reached out a soft hand to its muzzle.
"Do I disturb you, pet?" She glanced down at Gath
and sidled toward him, deliberately stopping in front
of the fire so that it cast a red-orange halo around her

hair and shoulders, and her shadow over his body.

The helmet's eye slits glowed hot and menacing in the darkness. "What are you waiting for?" he snarled. "You've had what you asked for."

"Yes," she said evenly, "and I am strong now. But first, I want to say something. I can help you, Gath of Baal, help you in ways that no one else can. And I will take risks for you . . . risks that you can't even conceive of." She moved beside him and slowly sat down, straddling his thighs. Sensual. In control. His hands took hold of her hip and armpit, drawing her close, and she came willingly. Her hands slid along his arms to his shoulders, caressing them as if she had sculpted them herself, and her voice purred heatedly. "You see, even now I am tempted to risk making love to you before removing the helmet, if that is your desire?"

Flames spit from the eye slits, singeing her hair, and she ducked, but did not pull away.

"Don't hate me because you need me," she whispered. "It's not my fault . . . and I won't betray you. It will be our secret."

The helmet's flames licked her throat, and she flinched with pain, but still did not pull away. "Yes," she murmured, her voice breathless, "I'd take that risk, and cherish it. But I can give you more than momentary pleasure, Gath of Baal. I can find the Lord of Death's most powerful demon spawn for you, and my sorcery can help you conquer their kingdoms, take their wealth and power for yourself." She hesitated, then her fingers and words stroked him. "Let me help you Gath, and you can build an empire . . . one that will rival the underworld itself."

His fingers bit into her flesh. "You'd use me to rebuild your kingdom, is that it?"

"No," she protested firmly. "I want nothing for

myself . . . except to serve you and enjoy the game of
death, the pleasures of victory." She leaned forward
within his grasp, daring the helmet's flames. "I
hunger for them, just as you do."

"Remove it." A flat command.

She nodded and took hold of the horns. Flames
spit from the helmet, but she held on and called out
in a howling hiss to the Master of Darkness. She
dropped forward onto her knees and her back
arched, throwing her head back. Her eyes closed, and
she pulled. Pebbles bit painfully into her kneecaps.
Perspiration moistened her palms, and she tightened
her grip, knuckles turning white.

The helmet abruptly inched up, exposing his neck,
and Gath heaved beneath her, sensing impending
relief. She strained against the horns, pushing now,
and the helmet rose higher, the stubble of beard on
his chin appearing. Suddenly a flash of fiery pain
went through her neck, and the horns seemed
to grow within her grasp. She tried to hold on,
but her body suddenly emptied of strength, and
her arms dropped away lifelessly. The helmet
sank back in place, and she fell against his chest,
sobbing.

"I can't . . . I can't do it."

"Yes you can." he growled, and pushed her erect,
drawing her hands back to the horns. "I'll help you."

His fingers crushed her hands against the horns
and pushed, but she felt nothing, no pain, no
strength, only numbness from fingertip to elbow.

"Push!" he grunted.

"It's no use, I . . . I haven't the strength anymore.
I . . . I'm empty."

He dropped her hands and stared at her. The glow
had fled from his eyes. They were white and cold
with shock behind the eye slits, and she could see
why. Her eyes, reflected on the helmet's shimmering

metallic surface, glittered wetly with tears that were all too human.

"You've lost your powers." An accusation.

She nodded. "I'm sorry, I . . . I . . ." She stopped, not knowing what to say. Her nerves and emotions were jangled, and she suddenly had no appetite for blood, no hunger for the triumph of the clandestine kill, no queenly majesty, no carnal desire. All she felt was shame for having failed her lover.

The flat of his hand caught the side of her face and she hit the ground, rolled over on her back amid his weapons and glittering chain mail. When she looked up, he was on his hands and knees straddling her.

"You lied," he snarled.

"No," she pleaded. "I didn't know. I . . . I thought my powers would return, but . . ."

"You're dying?"

"No, no! I'll be all right. But I'm no longer the queen. I'm powerless, returning to my normal nature."

His eyes questioned her. "Normal?"

She nodded bitterly. "Soon I'll be nothing again. Just as I was when I first entered his service. A penniless, helpless woman!"

He hesitated, then asked, "Can you get your powers back?"

She shook her head. "Only the Nymph Queen of Pyram can do that, and her castle is many days from here. The helmet would kill you before we could reach it. Besides, she serves the Master of Darkness. She'd do everything in her power to kill you."

"Then you're useless."

"No," she protested, "I can still help you."

Ignoring her, he picked up his axe and stood over her, placing the cutting edge against her throat. She caught hold of it, trying to force it away. "Don't be a fool! You need me. Robin Lakehair is the only one

who can remove the helmet now, but she's in danger!
You've got to go to her before it's too late. Now!"

He glared at her, unrelenting.

"You've got to believe me!" she pleaded. "She's in
terrible danger."

He laughed at her.

"Then trust the helmet. If I were trying to deceive
you . . . if there were any threat to you in me at all,
the metal would sense it. But it doesn't. If it did,
there would be fire in your eyes and the horns would
be hot." He relaxed the pressure, and she added,
"Trust me, Gath. The Lakehair girl is your only
hope, and I can help you save her."

"How?"

"I lied to you. I didn't tell you everything the
soldier told me." She took a breath. "The Master of
Darkness, before destroying his altar, commanded
my servants to go to the Great Forest Basin and hunt
her down . . . kill her." Another breath. "Some of
those who survived hunt her now, and they are three,
four days' ride ahead of you."

A glow showed behind the helmet's eye slits, and
its horns pulsed with life, growing hot. He stepped
away from her.

She gathered slowly, feeling faint and weak, then
rose, bringing his chain mail with her. Offering it to
him, she said, "Apparently he thought it would be
the surest way of destroying you." Taking the chain
mail, Gath began to dress, and she added, "There's no
time to lose. The helmet is like a screaming infant.
The longer you feed it, the more it will demand, and
the stronger it will become." He thrust his arms into
the suit of mail and picked up his sword belt, began
to buckle it hurriedly. She watched him a moment,
then said, "Take me with you."

Continuing to dress, he said, "The helmet's hungers have entered my blood and bones and are drawing me to a new place . . . a land, or a country . . . it's not clear." His eyes met hers. "Do you know where it is?"

"No," she said openly, "but I can help you find it, if anyone can."

In reply, he pulled on a boot.

"Damn you," she snarled, "you can't leave me here!"

He put on the second boot.

"You fool," she growled. "You're still a clumsy forest lout, aren't you? Still too proud to breathe air from the sky because it doesn't come from your own magnificent self." Her eyes turned molten, and she shrieked recklessly, "You won't survive without help, can't you understand that? Nobody can. And I have the cunning that can hide your precious virgin. I can keep her safe and teach her to use her powers instead of squandering them! In time, I could even show her how to tame the helmet enough for you to remove it by yourself."

He looked at her, and a smile leapt onto her cheeks, unsteady, immature, but honest. "Think of that, Gath. Then you wouldn't need her . . . or me. You'd be free. That's what you really want . . . isn't it?"

A short time later, as the stallion galloped through the dark night, Cobra sat behind Gath clinging to his metal-clad chest and smiling with satisfaction. She felt strangely like a young girl again, one moment sublimely content, the next desperate and confused. Realizing this, she resolved not to let her feelings show, but to keep the cool composure which had come naturally to her when she was a queen. Consequently, she put her smile away and closed her eyes, resting her cheek against the Barbarian's back. After a while she believed she could feel his heat through the metal, and the smile, without her noticing, returned.

They were headed east, in the direction of the Valley of Miracles.

Nine
GUESSWORK

The two riders thundered through the morning sunlight at Pinwheel Crossing, veered onto Weaver Road and raced under the overhanging oaks and willows. Robes billowing, whips lashing and faces as sober as grave markers.

They had been on a dead run since leaving Rag Camp in the Valley of Miracles. At dawn, a traveling tinker had wheeled excitedly into the village and awakened them, telling them that he had seen a wagonload of suspicious-looking foreign mercenaries riding through the night toward the village of Weaver. The pair now headed for that village, eager to investigate the strangers and possibly prevent another murder. In the last seven days there had been five.

Each of the victims had been a young girl, well known for her beauty, who belonged to one of the Barbarian tribes occupying the western end of the Great Forest Basin. Each had disappeared, then been found deep in uninhabited parts of the forest with their bodies crushed and bitten by snakes and lizards. The behavior of the reptiles was easily explained. Weeks earlier there had been a series of volcanic explosions in the distant heart of the forbidden lands. Ever since, hordes of animals and creatures had been migrating into the basin in search of food. But the fact that reptiles did not selectively abduct pretty young girls added an unholy atmosphere to the growing mystery which, until this morning, had provided no clues or suspects.

Old Brown John led the two riders.

He was the *bukko*, the stagemaster and leader of the Grillards, a tribe of traveling performers whose home base was Rag Camp. In the spring he had convinced Gath of Baal to defend the Barbarian tribes, and together they had raised an army and defeated the marauding Kitzakk Horde. As a reward, the Council of Chiefs had confirmed upon him the kingship, at least in times of crisis, and now there was one.

The king was short, wiry, bandy-legged, and did not look like a king. He wore a bone-brown cloak with dark brown patches, the mark of his clan, brown boots and a belted short sword without decoration. His white hair fluttered in silky ringlets around his large ears, and his tangled white eyebrows arched low over alert brown eyes. He was a genial man who much preferred ordering about large-hipped, big-breasted dancing girls to solving crimes, and he would have much rather been traveling with the Grillard wagons which were now on the road, providing music and laughter to the forest tribes. But he was also a man of responsibility with the gift of foresight. He could see things coming, and within the murders he could sense a great and terrible impending tragedy. Consequently, he urged his already lathered horse on and, the performer showing, did so with gusto, noise and excessive gestures.

The second rider followed the *bukko* on a dappled grey stallion, sitting his saddle seemingly without effort, like the pea riding the pod. He was young, not more than twenty summers, and lean of body and face. A Kaven aristocrat, but without the pious rigidity and narrow-eyed greed common to that tribe of moneylenders. He was darkly handsome. Flowing chestnut hair, soft charcoal-grey eyes, prominent nose and sensitive lips. He wore soft leather jerkin, tights, boots and cloak, each item carrying its natural umber, sienna or ochre hue. A crossbow was slung across his back, and his belt carried pouches, two daggers and a quiver of steel bolts. The glint of their metal was slightly less deadly than the expression on his face. His name was Jakar, and his only living relative, his twin sister, had been the first to be murdered.

The two riders flew past the stand of apple trees marking the halfway point to Weaver, turned off the road taking a shortcut and dashed right and left between the trees with twigs and leaves slashing chests and cheeks. Retaking the road, they galloped on. Within the hour they reached Weaver.

The sun sat high in the morning sky, shining down on the hill that formed the village. Older women herded small groups of sheep in the clearing fronting the wooden palisade wall. Beyond it, thick steam billowed from huge wooden dye vats lined up on the rising tiers. There the Cytherian villagers moved about at their various tasks of weaving and dying. Above the vats, the steam gathered into a single spreading cloud, muting the deep earth-reds, rusts and siennas of the freshly dyed cloth hung out to dry on the heights. The stench of urine and lime was rich in the air.

Brown John and Jakar slowed as they crossed the

clearing, not wanting to alarm their suspects if they were still in the village, and moved to the Forest Gate. There they dismounted, and approached an old man sitting on the ground with his back against the palisade wall. He was whittling on a piece of wood. Marl, the gatekeeper.

He looked up with a smile of recognition at the king and nodded, saying, "Welcome, *bukko*. What brings you to Weaver on this fine day?"

"Nothing good, Marl," Brown John said flatly, and squatted facing him. "I'm investigating these vile murders and heard that some suspicious-looking foreign mercenaries were headed this way. You see them?"

"Haven't been no soldiers here, not today, least-ways. I been sittin' right here the whole time, and bein' as this is the only gate we leave open nowadays, I'd seen 'em sure."

Brown John frowned, glanced at Jakar, and the young nobleman said, "Perhaps they didn't look like mercenaries?"

Marl looked up, giving Jakar the same smile he gave the *bukko*. "Didn't see no strangers at all, lad, except for one, and he couldn't a been no soldier. Little bit of a man, and kind of emaciated."

"Is he here now?" asked the *bukko*.

"Nope. Left a little while ago. Wanted to see that pretty gal you made into a dancin' girl. Was real set on it, he was. So, since she doesn't live here anymore, I sent him on his way."

"Robin Lakehair?" Jakar asked. His tone was low and cultured, and he spoke without haste. But there was a tense concern in it. During the war with the Kitzakks, Brown John had seen the young nobleman among those men who had appointed themselves as Robin's bodyguards, and ever since Jakar had started helping him in the investigations, the *bukko* had observed him staring at Robin whenever the opportunity presented itself.

Marl, sensing the young man's interest in Robin, chuckled knowingly and said, "That's the one, and I'd feel the same way about her, if I was as young as you. Prettiest little thing I ever saw, and always was, ever since she was a mite."

"What was his interest in Robin?" Brown John asked briskly.

"Adores her, that's what his interest is. Worships the ground she walks on. And he's never laid eyes on her, or so he said. Came here all the way from Small Tree, just to thank her for her part in getting the Dark One to defend the forest, and save his tribe from the Kitzakk cages."

"A Kranik?"

"Don't think so. Every Kranik I ever saw was near naked, and this little fellah was fully clothed. Even wore a hood. He was dark-skinned like a Kranik, though. But slick and shiny, like he was wet or something. And he wasn't loud like them savages. Hardly opened his mouth when he spoke, wouldn't open his lips. I figured he had bad teeth. You could barely hear him."

The *bukko* and Jakar shared a thoughtful glance, and Brown John asked, "Where did you send him to find her? Rag Camp?"

"Nope! Sent him to Clear Pond, where I saw her perform day before yesterday. Why? Isn't she there now?"

"She's there," Brown John said, as Jakar leapt back into his saddle. Turning to him, the *bukko* said, "Hold on a minute, son. It's only a half hour ride. We'll get there well before he does." He turned back to Marl. "What else did this stranger say?"

"Well, he did ask an awful lot of questions about Robin. I figured he was like some of the folks here in the village who think she's possessed with some kind of unnatural magic or something. You know the ones I mean, those that made life so unpleasant for her here she had to leave."

"I know," said the *bukko*, encouraging him to continue.

"Anyway, he wanted to be absolutely sure he could identify her. I told him he wouldn't have any trouble, that she'd be in the opening number of today's performance, and would be the most beautiful thing he'd ever laid eyes on. That seemed to satisfy him."

Brown John nodded. "You're sure he was alone?"

"Was when he left here."

"Thank you, Marl," the *bukko* said, rising.

"You want to thank me, *bukko*, you just see that pretty little gal keeps on doin' what she's doing. She dances like the singing wind, she does."

They said goodbye, and Brown John mounted his mare, walked it over beside Jakar's stallion.

Jakar said, "Bad teeth?"

"Or forked tongue," Brown replied.

They headed off at a gallop, taking the forest road heading north toward Clear Pond.

As they rode, the older man glanced thoughtfully at Jakar. The young man's eyes were desperate now, but under control. Haunted. Carrying a cargo of bitterness and pain far greater than that which wrinkles the faces of the old and wise.

Brown John shouted over the din of horses' hooves. "You're right to be worried. Robin has enemies the likes of which you are too young to imagine . . . and they may have finally come for her."

"That doesn't explain my sister."

The *bukko* agreed, and they rode on, the colors of Weaver growing faint behind them. Then Jakar pointed up ahead at a clump of crushed bushes at the side of the road. They reined up beside them and examined the ground. There were muddy tracks of a heavy wagon and a group of riders coming out of the forest and heading up the road.

"They're fresh," said Jakar. "The mud's still wet."

The *bukko,* suddenly white of face and gasping, nodded. "Apparently this strange little man isn't alone."

"I count at least twenty. That's a lot of men for one girl."

"Not if she's important to them." Brown John spurred forward shouting, "Follow me! I know a shortcut!"

They plunged up the side of the mountains, crashing through shrubs and ducking the limbs of pines and oaks. Reaching a grassy meadow nestled among the tall trees, they galloped across and rejoined the road, heading for a distant tree-covered ridge rising in front of a sheer wall of jagged rock.

There were scattered travelers on the road, local tribesmen heading for the performance at Clear Pond. But no sign of the suspects.

Ten

A BIT OF FLUFF

Reaching the vicinity of Clear Pond, the two riders left the road again and galloped up through thick pines to the crest of a mountain spur. It was thick with trees and strewn with boulders and thin streams of water draining off the mountain. They could hear sounds coming from the base of the spur, the steady movement of the river and the garbled voices of those gathering for the performance.

They had not seen a wagon or riders on their ride, and now, as they searched through the shadowed trees, they found no fresh wagon tracks or ground cover crushed by horses' hooves.

Moving covertly, they walked their horses down between massive boulders and trees into a natural enclosure formed by towering rocks. Leaving their horses there, they continued covertly down a gully. The sounds of the river and the chatter of the gathering crowd grew louder, then the jangle of tambourine, the vibrating notes of harps and the wail of flutes being tuned.

Jakar and the *bukko* shared a worried glance. The performance was about to begin.

Reaching exposed ground, they dropped on all fours and scrambled forward to a cluster of large boulders set in a bed of brown needles. They climbed

53

the largest boulder and inched forward, looking over it.

Twenty feet beyond the rock, the Grillard wagons were parked among a thin spread of pines and oaks. Just beyond them the spur thrust bluntly out into the river forcing it to make a sharp turn, and forming the pond. The entertainers were moving animatedly among the trees on the crest of the spur, taking their positions. They moved with their normal excitement, indicating there had been no trouble and that they expected none.

Brown John and Jakar relaxed slightly, relieved, and the young nobleman could not repress a grin.

The wagons were all painted and decorated with florid pinks, yellows, purples and greens, and the Grillards themselves were adorned in an even more vivid fashion, in lemon-yellow feathers, rouged breasts, formidable codpieces and all manner of baubles, bangles and bells. The cumulative impression was that of an unreal world where color and laughter were the staples, instead of steady work and regular meals.

Brown John whispered, "We're in time."

Jakar nodded and started to edge back off the rock. "I'll go warn her."

"No! You stay here and keep out of sight. I want her safely hidden until I know who and what we're up against. And I know how to handle her. You don't."

The sounds of beating drums and tambourines rang through the trees in a musical fanfare, and the unseen audience on the opposite side of the river cheered excitedly, howling and whistling.

"It's starting," blurted Brown John, and slid back down the rock, scraping his hands and chest.

Jakar's grin was gone now. "Hurry, old man," he whispered. "Hurry!"

The *bukko*, holding his tunic above his knobby knees, ran and leapt through trees and rocks like a jackrabbit in heat, vanished behind shrubbery, then reappeared at the back of a large yellow house wagon. Gasping and puffing, he rose stiffly and walked carefully toward the wagon's door. He reached it without being seen, opened it and hurriedly climbed in, closing it behind him.

Jakar waited, taut and frowning with concern, then looked about sharply as drums boomed somewhere.

Above the tree canopy, showers of arrows soared into the sky directly above Clear Pond. Streamers trailed behind them forming a rainbow of greens that arched against the sky-blue void, then started down. Before they vanished beyond the trees, their arrowheads were whistling as air passed through them. The crowd cheered. The drums boomed. Tambourines, flutes and harps began a rousing song, and everyone, Grillards and audience, began to sing the bawdy lyrics of "The Women of Boo Bah Ben."

Jakar chuckled with youthful mockery and watched as five nubile girls burst out of an orange wagon and scattered through the trees toward a position upriver. They carried small wooden rafts with rope handles and wore just about enough scalelike jewels to clothe their natural jewels, not counting their backsides, which were marvelously naked. Their hair had been dyed a luxurious red-gold, in exact imitation of Robin Lakehair's.

Jakar rose slightly, making sure Robin was not among them, and the girls disappeared over the rim of rock. Lying down again, he looked back at the yellow wagon and held still.

Brown John, using the noise and commotion to cover his movements, had exited the wagon and was now racing through the trees toward Jakar. In his arms, wrapped in a blanket, was a small struggling body with tiny feet which kicked furiously.

Jakar climbed off the rock, and the old man raced past him without speaking, heading for the horses. Jakar peered between the rocks to see if he was being followed, saw no one and moved after him.

Just short of the horses, Brown John veered north toward the base of the sheer wall of jagged rock which showed slightly between the tall pines.

When they emerged from the forest, they were beside a fast-moving creek, one of the many which fed the river, and the sounds of the singing were vague, distant.

Brown John, gasping for breath, set the wrapped body down on a rock, then sat down beside it, peeling the blanket away from the head.

Robin Lakehair was gagged. Her short red-gold hair was in disarray, and the rouge on her cheeks and lips, as well as the thick lines of kohl outlining her big hazel eyes, was smeared. The eyes themselves were windows to a shocked body and mind, and angry. Nevertheless, as far as Jakar was concerned, her beauty radiated like sunlight striking through drops of morning dew, and the corners of his finely wrought lips turned up in a smile.

Brown John, between gasps, said, "I'm sorry about this, Robin. Terribly sorry. But I must leave the gag, just in case something might cause you to scream and reveal where you are. I'd explain why, but there's no time. I have to warn the others, and you have to hide." He looked up at Jakar. "I think you know Jakar . . . he'll stay with you."

Robin looked up with frightened eyes at Jakar and suddenly stopped thrashing, just stared.

Jakar bowed, with aristocratic reserve, and said, "It is a pleasure to serve you, my lady." Then, behind a slightly mocking smile that failed to hide his concern for her, he added, "But I must say, you surely manage to stir up a fuss."

Robin turned her eyes on the *bukko* and complained unintelligibly behind her gag, her eyes pleading.

"Just trust me," the old man said as he stood, "and go with Jakar. Your life may depend on it."

Jakar, forcing a light tone, said, "She's a pretty bit of fluff, isn't she?"

Brown John scowled at him. "That will be enough of that. You're going to have to keep your head about you now, lad, and if looking at her is going to make you behave like a popinjay, then don't look at her." Jakar blushed, and the *bukko* added, "Now listen to me. I am honor bound to protect Robin . . . and duty bound as well. My friend, Gath of Baal, depends on her, and the entire forest depends on him. Do you understand?"

Jakar nodded, once, deadly serious now.

"Good. Take her upstream to the falls." He pointed them out, explaining how to find a hidden chasm behind the falls, then added, "She'll be safe there. Now get moving. I'll find out what's going on and meet you there later."

Jakar watched the wiry old man dash down the boulder-strewn stream, thinking to himself that the *bukko* was taking a lot for granted, even for a king. But he liked him, and for reasons he could not explain, trusted him. He hesitated uncertainly, then put his soft charcoal eyes on Robin's consuming beauty and gathered her gently in his strong arms. She struggled slightly, then gave up, and a shiver swept through him as her softness came against his lean hard body. He felt color flooding into his sun-dark cheeks and tried to look away, but could not. For a moment their eyes met, then a smile warmed his thoughtful eyes as he spoke.

"Something tells me, fluff, that you are going to be a whole lot of trouble."

Eleven

REDHEADS

Brown John emerged from the bushes overhanging the creek and stepped onto the river bed.

It was thirty yards across, an undulating white bed of gravel and boulders carried down from the mountain by centuries of spring floods. Narrow slow-moving channels of water meandered through it, and twenty yards away, on the far side beyond nearly impassable boulders, the main channel flowed swiftly, churning its liquid-green body into white foam as it crashed against large rocks lining its sides and rising from it.

Gathering his torn, stained tunic above his knees, he scrambled across the gravel and splashed through a shallow channel, heading downriver toward faint sounds of drums.

He fell twice, the second dropping him into a deep channel. Its current swept him forward, bounced him off a large boulder and deposited him in the tangled branches of a dead pine tree which had fallen into the river. The sharp branches played with his face and back for a while, then he climbed onto the trunk and scrambled across it to the river bank.

Puffing, soaking wet and wearing a scowl that cut so deep into his wrinkled cheeks it could have supplied enough tragedy for an entire act of one of his own melodramas, he ran along a bald dirt footpath siding the river and saw his dancing girls in the distance.

They were far out on the river bed, tiny colorful figures against the white rocks. Their trim bodies were now wrapped in diaphanous yellow-green cloth, and they wore green-gold dragonfly wings on their naked backs. They stood beside the main channel where it narrowed into a funnel of white-water rapids for about twenty feet, then spewed out over a wide flat rock forming a natural slide which flowed around a bend in the river. Unseen beyond the bend was Clear Pond, and the waiting audience and musicians. But he could not hear them now. The crash and spill and roar of the rapids was deafening.

The girls looked anxiously toward the wagons on the spur, as if expecting Robin to join them any minute, and held their small rafts steady in the water, waiting to jump into them when they were cued. The sunlight glistened on their bouncing curls of red-gold hair, and at that distance they all looked remarkably like Robin Lakehair.

Realizing this, Brown John groaned with fresh panic, dropped his tunic and cupped his hands around his mouth, shouting, "Zail! Belle! Wait! Don't go in the water!"

The girls did not hear him.

Brown John, slipping and sliding and jumping, descended the sheer bank and started across the rocky bed, shouting, "Zail! Wait! Wait!"

The girls took no notice, and he ran recklessly forward, fell facedown, and boulders kissed his cheek, chest and shins. Slightly dazed, he climbed painfully onto his hands and knees and held still. The shrill clear notes of a horn were rising above the roar of the rapids. The cue.

Brown John jumped up and screamed, "Wait!"

The girls still did not hear him. Zail, the lead girl, kneeled on her raft and, hanging on to its rope handles, rode it, squealing and laughing, down the funnel of water. One by one the others followed, bobbing wildly and nearly spilling over as the water tossed their small rafts about and washed over their lovely bodies and laughing faces.

They swept onto the natural water slide, swirled around the bend in the river, and the unseen audience waiting at Clear Pond roared approval.

In reply, each girl raised an arm, unclenched a tiny fist, and streamers of glittering yellow and green unfurled behind them.

The audience applauded, and tambourines and drums caught the rhythm of the streaking beauties, turning the ride into a dance.

Brown John stood limply, his exhausted body heaving for breath. He could see Clear Pond now, and the girls were performing beautifully, just as he had trained them to. But without that extra sparkle he had planned on. Only Robin Lakehair had the skill, and nerve, to ride her raft in a standing position.

One by one the girls splashed into the large pond and rode the current, twirling their rafts and posing provocatively for the audience lining the shore.

Grillard strongmen, standing on a shelf of rock several feet under the water, waited where the pool widened. More shelves of rock rose out of the water behind them to form a natural stage which faced the audience on the opposite shore. The stage was

backed by boulders which rose like massive stepping-stones up the blunt face of the mountain spur.
More strongmen stood in a chainlike line which
wound its way across the stage, then up over the
boulders to a promontory rock out of which grew a
scrub oak.

Brown John knew the spot well. It was here that he
had first seen Robin Lakehair and asked her to help
him save the forest from the Kitzakks.

As the girls neared the waiting strongmen, they lay
down on their backs, crossed their arms across their
breasts and held themselves as rigid as arrows. The
first strongman plucked Zail off her raft, raised her
over his head and passed her to the next strongman.
In this manner she traveled across the stage and
up through the boulders to the promontory rock
where the two largest strongmen waited. As she began her ascent, her body was rolled over and over,
and her diaphanous wrap began to unravel color-
fully, much to the delight of the men in the audience.

When she reached the top, one of the strongmen
took hold of the end of her wrap while the other
raised her arrowlike body high over his head. With
a grunting heave, he threw her out over the deepest part of the pool a hundred feet below. Just before
she began to fall, the strongman holding her wrap gave
it a hard yank, and Zail spun around in mid-air.
The wrap swirled away from her body in a flurry
of colorful circles, and she dove out of their
center, naked except for the glittering yellow jewels
gracing breasts and groin, and plunged into the
water.

The crowd rose as one body and applauded,
whistled, wanting more, and one after the other the
girls obliged.

Brown John could not refrain from smiling, then suddenly his blood ran cold.

Two strongmen on the promontory had pitched forward and were flailing awkwardly in the air. One landed safely in the shallow water, but the other hit a rock with a loud grunt. He rolled several feet, then lay still. The audience gasped. The girls, now all in the pool, screamed. Then all movement stopped, and a hush fell over Clear Pond.

A huge man, nearly seven feet tall and massive, had emerged from behind the scrub oak and now stood poised on the promontory rock. A plain tattered cloak covered him, but his stance was proud, arrogant, regal. With a deliberate flourish, he removed his cloak and let it fall to his feet. His armor was smooth, a rainbow of plates fading from indigo at his shoulders to smoky blues to roses to white at his legs. A silver-white helmet graced his big-jawed head, and he stood in a whiplike stance. Rising off his back was a silver-grey stump, like the dorsal fin of a shark.

Brown John almost whimpered.

The audience gasped and edged back.

The Grillards, as if driven by unseen adversaries, fled off the spur and gathered together on the stage. Among them were Brown John's sons: Dirken, in his black tunic with its grave umber patches, and Bone, in his giant codpiece as red as his hair. They moved to the front of their tribe, facing the demon spawn standing above the stage, and stopped short.

A small hooded man with a smooth grey face had appeared beside the huge warrior and laughed mockingly. Suddenly he stopped and raised a fist, shouting in a language the *bukko* did not understand.

A dozen short, thick men promptly appeared

along the rim of the spur, and the shadows of more could be seen among the trees behind them. Their flesh was a greyish brown, and their faces had nostrils but no noses. Their tiny ears were pointed, and tufts of fur sprouted between the seams of their leather armor at their shoulders and elbows. Swords and quivers and knives rode their belts, and they held loaded crossbows in hairy hands.

The audience on the far bank, hushed and trembling, began to back away from the pond. Those in the rear of the crowd were already fleeing into the forest.

The Grillards gathered on the stage shifted anxiously in place with their eyes on the crossbows aimed at them, and raised their arms.

Brown John, stumbling forward in desperation, moved for the natural water slide.

Three of the noseless soldiers moved down off the spur onto the stage and, grunting and waving their crossbows at the Grillards, made a passage between them as the small smooth man, with surprising agility, bounded down the rocks. He strode between the Grillards and waded into the water until he stood among the bobbing faces of the terrified dancing girls.

He grinned, scratching his groin with both hands, and his lewd voice rang through the silence.

"My, my, you are the pretty ones! You're not going to make it difficult for me now, are you?" He chuckled. "Which of you is Robin Lakehair?"

The girls moaned and spoke all at once, saying Robin wasn't among them, that they didn't know where she was, and pleading not to be hurt. Then Zail shouted them to silence and brazenly and defiantly rose partway out of the water, taunting the small man with her half-naked beauty. "She's not

here, little man. You'll have to come back for tomorrow's show."

"Don't play with me, whore!" he snarled. He
waded close to Zail, examining her, and shoved her
back in the water, grunting, "You're too old." He
glared at the others and they whimpered, clutching
each other in fear. "Be smart, girl, I know you're
here," he growled. "So you might as well give
yourself up . . . and save your friends a whole lot of
pain."

The girls wailed and hugged each other, babbling
incoherently.

Grumbling, he waded as close to the girls as he
could without falling in the river, and leaned over
studying their upturned faces. "Damn! You're all so
bloody pretty, I can't remember what you looked
like." He straightened. "You have one last chance,
Robin Lakehair. Show yourself now, or these pretties
won't stay pretty much longer."

The girls screamed that Robin wasn't there,
and the Grillards on the stage shouted the same
thing.

The small man didn't listen to them. He grunted,
"What a waste," and waded back onto the stage. He
looked up at the huge man, lifting empty hands, and
shouted, "I'm sorry, Lord Baskt, but they won't
cooperate. And I can't pick her out. They're all
redheads."

Baskt nodded and strode to the edge of the promontory rock. There he gathered, and dove out over
the pond. He easily cleared the rocks below and
plunged down toward the water. There was a flash of
light and a roll of thunder just before he hit the
water, and it splashed in a flurry of geysers which
could only have been made by a man three times his
size.

What remained of the audience fled screaming into the forest.

The Grillards stood staring helplessly at the pond, holding each other.

Brown John, finally reaching the water slide, plunged in, and slid for the pond, his eyes fixed on the girls.

Their heads were turning and twisting as they watched something moving under the water. Then their eyes filled with horror, and they screamed.

A shark fin cut through the surface and moved toward them.

Screaming and flailing, the girls tried to swim and climb out of the water.

The fin slashed down into the water, vanished for a moment, then a pointed snout erupted from the liquid green, followed by the huge barreled body of a great white shark.

Two girls wading onto the stage saw it and fainted, falling backward into the water.

Brown John screamed, "No! No!" and hit a rock with head and shoulder. Nearly unconscious, he splashed into the pond and went under. The current caught him, brought him back to the surface, and gasping for air, he looked across the pond with dazed eyes.

The water seemed to be churning itself into geysers of white foam flecked with red streaks. There was screaming, a soaring crescent-shaped tail, flashes of huge teeth in an underslung jaw. Pieces of young girls were impaled on them.

The old man moaned pitifully, passed out, and the current carried him away.

Some time later, when he came to, his paunchy belly was hung up on a shelf of rock which formed part of the stage, and he was drowning in a foot of water. He raised his head out of the water, coughing and spitting repeatedly, and dragged himself onto dry rock. Gasping for air and shaking with exhaustion and terror, he looked around.

There was no sign of the shark. Clear Pond was void of sound and movement except for the flowing river, as if he had dreamed the entire thing. Then he saw them.

At the far end of the pond, where the river spread out and trickled through a man-made rock dam, the noseless, furry soldiers were wading in the shallows. They held pronged spears, stabbing them into the water. When the spears came back out, unidentifiable bits and pieces of bloody bone and flesh were stuck to the prongs. These they matter-of-factly removed and dropped in sacks slung over their shoulders, then went back to stabbing.

Brown John, snarling with fury, tried to rise, but dizzied and dropped back. He blinked his eyes and stared at the rock below him as a swirl of water washed under him. He lowered his head to drink, but stopped, and white showed around his shocked eyes.

The water was red with blood.

He tried to crawl away from it, as if it would contaminate him, and the effort drained his strength. He dropped facedown on a dry shelf of rock, and blackness filled his mind.

Twelve
GOODBYE

An hour later, Brown John sat huddled in a blanket facing his sons, Dirken and Bone, across a small fire. Around them, the Grillard women and children were gathered, faces tear-stained and bodies trembling and sobbing. Behind them, the men were noisily forming the colorful horse-drawn wagons into two lines on top of the spur. The wagons were loaded, ready for the trail.

"How many were there?" Brown John addressed the question to Dirken.

"I counted nine in the wagon when they rode off, seven on horseback, and I don't know how many in the forest standing lookout. But they weren't trying to hide. You could still see their dust when they were a mile from here."

"Heading which way?"

"Northwest. I'd say toward Small Tree."

"What are the filthy demon spawn after Robin for anyway?" growled Bone. "What good does it do them murderin' poor helpless girls?"

The women nodded and murmured, asking the same questions.

"I don't know," Brown John said evenly, "but I'm going to find out and put an end to it." He stood. "You two will take charge of the wagons." The

67

brothers nodded and he added, "You'll split up and leave this part of the forest. Folks around here are superstitious. They'll think you've got some curse on you now and will drive you away from their villages. So head east. Bone, you take the southern road. Dirken, you take the northern." He lowered his voice. "In a week or two, after everyone has had a chance to get over this, start looking for some new dancing girls."

"New girls?" Bone blurted in outrage. "You'll never replace . . ."

"You will!" his father cut him off. "And you'll use your heart and brains as well as that lizard hiding in your codpiece." He looked at Dirken. "You both know the code . . . we can't let this tragedy stop the wagons."

Dirken nodded. "What are you going to do?"

"What I have to," Brown John said. "The Council of Chiefs will no doubt want me to find Gath and have him deal with these brutes . . . and that may take some doing. I haven't seen him for weeks."

Bone and Dirken both stood, and Dirken, dark of face and mind, asked, "Did you hear about Robin?"

"She's disappeared!" Bone said it.

Brown John, without expression or emotion, said, "Don't worry about Robin. Just get our wagons as far away from here as fast as you can . . . in case they realize they don't have her, and come back."

They nodded, and the *bukko* hugged his sons, waved goodbye to the others, then mounted a horse that had been saddled for him. The saddlebags bulged with provisions, a wine jar, cheese, bread and meats wrapped in cloth. He headed up the spur, again waving goodbye, and the Grillards did the same, then began to climb on their wagons.

When he was out of sight, he looked around carefully to see if anyone was watching him, then moved into the concealing shadows of overhanging pines. He waited there, listening until he heard the sounds of the rolling wagons fade away. Then he rode back to where his mare and Jakar's stallion were hidden. Taking the two horses by their reins, he led them through the trees heading toward the sheer cliff of jagged rock. Reaching a thicket where the sound of waterfalls was loud, he dismounted and tied the horses to a tree, draped the saddlebags over a shoulder and hurried forward on foot.

Thirteen

TROUBLE

Panting and stumbling, the *bukko* came around an elderberry bush growing out of the creek bank and stopped, looking up.

In front of him, massive granite boulders, stacked upon and leaning against each other, rose up through a gorge to the distant heights of the sheer wall of jagged rock. Spilling waterfalls draped over and fell between the boulders. Some were mere trickles, others tumbled through gullies, churning themselves to white water, or spread out over flat rimrock and fell like living curtains, while the largest plunged in heavy torrents for hundreds of feet to crash into pools raising clouds of wet mist. There they again found passages through cracks and guts to form eddies that gathered and spilled again, down and down, until they destroyed their wet bodies on the boulders of the creek bed and tamely flowed toward the river far below.

To the southeast, the mountain was exposed rock. To the northwest, pines covered it almost to the crest. Here and there shafts of afternoon sunlight speared horizontally through gaps in the trees, and touched a pool or gush of white water to make them shimmer in the deep shade, like gorgets of wet light.

The water's roar obliterated all other sound.

The *bukko* wiped beads of spray away from his eyes and stared, the pain and tragedy and guilt slowly draining from him as nature's vital beauty flooded him with awe and wonder. He looked from side to side, searching the blurring mists. Seeing no sign of Robin or Jakar, and no cracked twig, crushed bush or muddy track that revealed they had passed this way, his brown eyes thinned with worry, and he started up the face of the falls.

A half hour later, soaking wet and exhausted, he was halfway up the steep gorge, standing uncertainly on top of a slippery round boulder. A torrent of water, as wide as a small house, fell beside him, and a flat-faced boulder, half again his height, blocked his passage. Groaning unheard in the wet din, he squeezed a booted foot in a narrow crack on the face of the bothersome rock. He set himself, then jumped up and stood in the crack, grabbing for the top of the boulder, and took hold of it. He hung on for a moment, gathering breath, then hauled himself up onto the rock. There he crouched proudly on his knees and elbows with his wet cheek against the cold rock, then rolled onto his side, and saw his naked foot, groaned again.

He got back onto his hands and knees and looked forlornly down at his boot stuck in the crack. It was out of reach. He removed his other boot, set it aside, stood, and examined the area. There still was no sign of Robin or Jakar.

He continued up the falls barefoot.

Reaching a large pool, he moved behind the wide waterfall to the narrow ledge protruding from the rock behind it. There he waited, peering through the waterfall to see if he was followed. But only nature's wonders shared his trail. With his face to the rock, he moved sideways along the ledge until he was a foot from the vertical corner of the flat-faced boulder. There the ledge narrowed sharply and ended. Directly in front of him, mist billowed from behind the corner of the boulder, caused by another waterfall dropping through a stone chasm. Gingerly, he looked down over a shoulder.

One step forward or to the side would undoubtedly provide a spectacular bit of drama he could never duplicate on a stage, and deposit him back where he had started, at the bottom of the falls, in more than several pieces.

Trembling, Brown John pressed his cheek against the slick rock. When the shudder passed, he cocked his knees for balance, spread his arms wide and flat against the rock and leaned toward the sharp corner with his free hand groping blindly around it. His fingers came to rest on a rough iron bar and gripped it tightly. He sighed with relief and suddenly lost his balance, falling forward.

With one hand gripping the iron bar and the other flailing wildly, his body rolled around the corner, and his feet came to rest on a substantial ledge on the opposite side.

A smile swept into his pink cheeks as exhilaration rushed through him, then it made him feel sick to his stomach, and his vision blurred. He sank down onto all fours, pressing back against the rock. When his vision cleared, he crawled along the ledge, then stood and passed under the waterfall, and wound through a jagged gut into a dry stone chasm rising to the top of the cliffs. Flat-faced boulders, cut by deep cracks, formed an irregular stone floor and three walls. In a corner was a small cave. Robin Lakehair sat in it, holding Jakar's cloak around her body and smiling with relief.

"Oh, Brown, it's you!" she sighed, and jumped up, ran to the *bukko*, embracing him. "Thank goodness! I was so frightened." She leaned back looking into his smiling eyes. "Are you all right?"

"Yes, yes," he murmured tiredly, "much better . . . now that I see you're safe."

He held her soft brown shoulders in trembling hands and studied her, trying to convince himself she was real; her small perfect fist clenching the cloak together between her breasts, the green and gold jewels glittering on a nut-brown shoulder, the smile blossoming around small straight nose and narrow full lips.

"You have no idea, child," he said weakly, "what a blessing it is for a man like myself, particularly on a mean day like this, to simply look at you."

She flushed with embarrassment and scolded him with her big warm eyes. "Oh, Brown, you flatter me too much. It's not right."

"It's not flattery today," he said behind a profound scowl. "It is a holy conviction bound to my flesh with the blood of those I dearly love."

She frowned with confusion, suddenly frightened by his tone. "What are you talking about?" she asked. "Are you quoting another play?"

He hesitated, looked up to see Jakar standing guard with his loaded crossbow on a shelf of rock fifteen feet above, then looked back at Robin. When he spoke, it was a whisper. "They're dead, Robin . . .

all your friends . . . Zail, Belle, all of them."

"No!" she gasped, and staggered back. Brown John nodded, and she cried, "But why? Why?" then collapsed crying.

Jakar, ashen-faced, asked, "Are they still hunting Robin?"

Brown John, suddenly feeling older, sat down, dropping the saddlebags beside him, and shook his head. "For now they've been drawn off her trail." He looked up at the young nobleman. "Apparently they knew Robin was a redhead. When they saw that the other girls also had red hair, it confused them, so they killed them all, thinking Robin was among them." He lowered his eyes to Robin's sobbing body. "She's safe now . . . providing they don't have some way of finding out they don't have what they came for."

"They'll find out," Jakar said fatalistically. He climbed down a root growing in a crack in the stone chasm, and sat down facing the *bukko,* his dark eyes demanding. "Now tell me what happened . . . everything."

"There's no need for that."

"Oh yes there is," Jakar said quietly, the glint of pain and hatred showing in his eyes.

Understanding showed in Brown John's eyes. Then, in precise words lacking his normal color and drama, he told Jakar and Robin what had happened at Clear Pond, finishing with, "I was simply too late."

A moment passed, and Robin, pale and tear-stained, rose slightly. Jakar, taking her gently by the elbow, helped her up, and spread her blanket on the ground for her to sit on.

"Thank you," she said weakly, and leaned back against the wall of the chasm, looking up into his eyes. "I'm sorry I've been so much trouble for you."

He shrugged it off, as if he would have done the same for any female, and squatted facing the *bukko*. "What now?" he asked.

"I don't know," said Brown John. "I haven't had time to think."

"Then you'd better start, *bukko*." The young nobleman's voice was low and uncompromising. "I know this filth called Baskt. He's a Lord of Destruction, the work of the Nymph Queen of Pyram, the high priestess of Black Veshta. And if she's sent him all the way from Pyram, then she might have sent others. Serpents, lizards, you name it."

"You think that's what killed your sister . . . the others?"

"It's a possibility." He indicated Robin with the back of his head. "So she could still be in danger. Right now."

Brown John nodded and glanced past Jakar's shoulder at the tears welling in Robin's eyes. "Don't blame yourself, child. There's nothing you could have done."

"But why are they hunting me?" she whimpered.

"I'm not sure." He sensed Jakar's hard eyes asking the same question, but did not look at him. "But you have enemies, you know that. It was not only the Kitzakks you helped defeat but the Queen of Serpents . . . and her master."

"But she's the only one who knew about me! And . . . and you captured her. She's Gath's prisoner now."

"Yes, but it's apparent others also knew."

She flinched, looked down at her hands for no reason and said softly, "Maybe . . . so there won't be anyone else hurt . . . I should give myself to them."

"Don't be ridiculous," Jakar blurted, and stood, moved off into a shadow.

"I'm only trying to help." She said it to his back.

Without turning, he said, "You can help by staying alive. When they come back, and they will," he made himself turn and look at her, "you can bait whatever trap the *bukko* here decides to set for them."

She blanched at his hard tone and looked at Brown John in shock.

"That may not be necessary," Brown John said quietly, calming her. "But there is also another reason why, at all costs, you must be kept hidden and safe." His eyes met Jakar's, then looked back at Robin. "Gath is the only one who can deal with these creatures, and when he does . . . he's going to need you with him."

Robin hesitated, and looked at Jakar. He was staring at her, his eyes soft now, suddenly kind and gentle. She shifted nervously, almost smiling, and he turned away, again faced Brown John.

"You're going to contact the Dark One? Ask his help?"

The *bukko* nodded.

"Then perhaps, since we are working together, you had better tell me what her link is with him."

"That, Lord Jakar, is between them."

"Can she control him?"

Brown John smiled, just a little, and shook his head. "No one controls him."

"Then who says he'll help? Or that we can trust him? He's half demon himself!"

"I do," said Brown John. He opened the saddlebags and spread out the food, handing the wine jar to Jakar. "Here. Cool down and feed yourself. There is going to be much to do and you are going to have to do most of it."

Jakar hesitated, then took the jar and drank. Brown John, with bread and cheese in hand, moved

to Robin and sat facing her, placing the food in her
hands.

"I'm really not hungry," she said.

"You will be," he replied. "Now listen to me. The
worst is over. Ended. And we both know what we
must do now . . . not let this calamity divert us from
our chosen path."

She nodded mindlessly, like a child who has heard
her parents tell her this a thousand times before.

"You're not listening," he said sharply, and she
looked up attentively. "That's better. Now, understand this: we have the advantage now. We know the
villain's intentions, and your part is cast. You are
now the virtuous heroine in flight, and it's a splendid
part, one on which the greatest artists of the stage
have made their careers."

"Brown John, don't," she pleaded. "Not now."

"Yes, now," he said. "Because everything depends
on how you play the next scenes. If you play them
with vigor and spirit, we have a chance. If you
don't . . . well, today has more than demonstrated
the consequences."

"Brown, please," she begged.

"No! The remorse and grief and guilt must end
here. Now! We've got to have our wits about us and
concentrate on what we're doing, not what's happened. If we don't, we're all lost."

He rose, moved back to the food and sat down,
began to eat. Jakar did the same, facing him, and
wearing a grimly amused smile. When he spoke, his
voice held the same amusement.

"I presume, from your ridiculous speech, that in
addition to your platitudes, you have some specific
action in mind."

Brown John nodded. "As soon as you finish eating, I want you to ride after these creatures. Your

horse is waiting at the bottom of the falls. When you catch up with them . . ."

"You don't have to tell me," Jakar interrupted darkly.

"Listen to me," snapped the *bukko,* sounding like a king. "You may be a nobleman, and I may be nothing but an outcast to you . . . but I see things others don't. And if you are truly serious about avenging your sister, you would be well advised to listen."

Jakar replied by staying silent and listening.

"Good," added Brown John, "that shows sense. Now, when you find the scum, you will stay out of their sight and follow them until you find where they are headed. Then when it turns dark, ride back to Rag Camp. Robin and I will be waiting there . . . hopefully with Gath of Baal."

"Is that all?" Jakar asked tersely.

"No!" the *bukko* said just as tersely. "You better get going now, before their trail turns cold."

Jakar rose, and Robin pulled his cloak from around her, handed it to him, saying, "Here, it may get cold."

He shook his head, moved to the narrow entry passage and smiled back at Robin. "I'll see you tonight, Trouble." Then he was gone.

Robin, unable to keep from smiling, gathered his cloak about her and began to eat. Brown John watched her a moment thoughtfully, then said, "Your timing is terrible, lass." She looked at him, confused, and he added, "We've got enough problems without you falling in love."

She took hold of her lip with her teeth, then said quietly, "I know."

"Then finish eating. You're going to need all your strength. We'll spend tonight in Rag Camp, then

tomorrow ride to Calling Rock and hope Gath
answers the horn."

She looked up between bites and asked, "Why
wouldn't he?"

"Because I've been going there and calling him for
days, ever since the first murder . . . and he hasn't
showed up." He smiled. "But I've got a feeling that's
going to change now."

Fourteen

STRANGE ALLIES

Well past the midnight hour, two riders galloped
through the Valley of Miracles. Reaching Rag Camp
at the northeastern corner, they reined up short of
the cool blue moonlight illuminating the clearing,
and studied it from concealing shadows cast by
surrounding apple trees. Their animals were flecked
with sweat and snorting steam.

The camp appeared deserted, and was silent except for the sounds of the river, Whitewater, flowing
under Stone Crossing, a massive rock at the far side
of the village.

One of the riders urged its horse forward and
walked the animal into the moonlight. Cobra, riding
a small mare purchased from an outlaw band in The
Shades, the rain forest to the west. She was gasping
with exhaustion, and her face was torn with fear as
she scanned the empty clearing. The Grillards were

apparently on the road. All that remained were four battered house wagons, no longer fit for the road, scattered along the eastern edge of the clearing, and a large red wagon on the opposite side. It was parked behind the stage commanding the center of the clearing, and there was a faint glow of candlelight in the second-story window.

She moved back to the other horse, took hold of its reins and led it across the clearing. The horse was Gath of Baal's black stallion, and he sat in the saddle. His huge body weaved unsteadily, and his helmeted head hung low between his shoulders, casting a red glow over his gnarled hands where they clutched the pommel.

Cobra guided the horses along the front of the stage and hesitated. Three horses were tethered to a railing at the side of the red wagon: a dappled grey stallion which appeared to have just returned from a long ride, another stallion, and a mare which had a brown saddle blanket with brown patches. Taking hope, she climbed lightly onto the stage and moved quickly to Gath, helping him out of his saddle.

"We're here," she whispered encouragingly. "Just a few more feet. I think the bukko's here, and he's sure to know where she is."

Without replying, Gath raised his head, and the sharp-tipped horns of his black helmet glimmered in the moonlight as Cobra headed for the wagon.

Gath moved after her, took three heavy-footed strides and fell facedown on the wooden planks with a loud metallic clang. Cobra rushed back and kneeled over him, trying to help him up as he clawed back to his hands and knees. He half rose, then a knee gave and dropped him on his back in front of her with another clang.

Cobra gave a sharp gasp, and her hands trembled as they hovered helplessly above his unconscious body. In the glare of the helmet's flames, the rose tint glowing on her creamy white cheeks was florid with fear. She looked around frantically.

There were sounds of activity in the wagons across the clearing, and the glimmer of candles being lit. Then the glow of orange candlelight in the second-story window of the red wagon above her grew bright, casting light on the horned helmet. She leapt up and stood over Gath, concealing him with her tattered cloak, and raised her arm so that the candle-light cast a shadow over her face.

The window opened, and a glowing lantern came out, followed by Brown John's tousled silvery head. "Who's there?" he demanded.

"Your friend, bukko," she said clearly, "and he is in need of your help."

"Friend? Help?" Brown John peered under the lamp suspiciously.

"Gath of Baal," Cobra whispered behind her arm.

The *bukko*'s mouth dropped open, and he smiled with delight, then quickly drew back inside, leaving the window open. The lantern's light cast wildly moving shadows across the interior of the second-story room, then faded to the accompaniment of hurried footsteps descending a staircase. A moment passed, the door of the red wagon burst open, and the lantern rushed out spilling light across the stage with Brown John striding behind it. He wore a bone-brown nightshirt which he held up above his slightly bowed legs.

He stopped short of Cobra, and she lowered her arm, allowing the lantern's orange light to splash on her face.

"You?" Brown John gasped, taking a step back.

Cobra's thin arched eyebrows drew down sharply, and her low resonant voice lashed at him. "This is no time for your theatricals, bukko. You're in no danger from me." She held up the mandrake root strung around her neck. "He set me free so I could help him. But I failed! I have no more powers."

Brown John laughed at her. "You don't seriously think I'll believe that, do you? Where is he?"

She stepped back holding her robe aside to reveal Gath to the *bukko,* but still shielding him from a small group of elderly Grillards gathering across the clearing. "Would I bring him here . . . like this . . . if I was lying? Use your head, old man. He needs the Lakehair girl."

Brown John, his face suddenly furrowed with fear, edged forward lowering the lantern to Gath, and winced as black smoke snarled from the eye slits amid sputtering flames.

"Holy Zard!" he gasped. "He put the helmet back on."

"Of course. Its powers are addictive, and his pride is more so. Now hurry!" Cobra urged him. She nodded at the group across the clearing: it had found torches and was starting for the stage. "Order them off! There is no telling what he might do to them in this condition. And take us to the girl! Hurry! Hurry!"

The *bukko* looked up, shocked by the almost girlish fear riding through the Queen of Serpents' black-rimmed almond eyes. He nodded and moved to the front of the stage. With one eye on Cobra, he shouted at the Grillards, telling them everything was all right. They came to a stop, lifting acknowledging hands, then turned and tiredly drifted apart, heading for different wagons.

Brown John rushed back to the door of his wagon

and stopped short seeing someone move in the shadows by the tethered horses at the side of the stage. Pointing at Cobra, he shouted at the shadowed figure, "Watch her! Don't let her get away."

The *bukko* dashed inside, and Cobra peered into the shadows. Standing in the blackest part of the darkness, obviously by choice, was an unusually handsome young man holding a loaded crossbow. He wore soft leather clothing and stood with regal assurance.

Cobra watched him defiantly as he watched her, and Robin Lakehair rushed out of the red wagon, raced past without seeing her. A harvest-gold cloak billowed behind the young girl, and a flimsy white nightgown conformed to her nubile body as snugly as a slick of water. Cobra edged further back into the shadows, and her eyes narrowed malevolently as she watched the girl drop beside Gath. Robin moaned pitifully, and her hands trembled as they hovered uncertainly beside the flaming helmet.

The *bukko* came out of the wagon, now holding a sword as well as a lantern, and placed the weapon's blade against Cobra's ribs.

She took no notice. Her eyes devoured Robin: firm budding breasts, the turn of ear, toss of red-gold curls, slim round arms and fingers. Young. Vibrant. Each part perfection, nostril, earlobe and fingernail. The girl's body radiated warmth and kindness, and Cobra knew her invisible glowing aura was still there. When she had possessed the powers of the Queen of Serpents, Cobra had been able to see the aura, but not now. Nevertheless, the knowledge of it, and the girl's rare beauty, made her eyes snarl with jealousy. But then the girl turned, saw her and shrieked shrilly, and that made Cobra smile.

Flinging a finger at Cobra, Robin shouted in

warning at Brown John, "It's her! It's her! She's alive."

"I know, Robin, I know," Brown John said in a calming voice. "But she'll be tame enough." He showed her his sword. "Now get that ugly metal pot off his head."

Robin nodded obediently. She glanced at Cobra warily, then scooted in close to the horned helmet so that one knee nearly touched the hot metal. She reached for its horns, hesitated and looked timidly at the *bukko,* mumbling with fear, "What . . . what if I can't do it anymore?"

"Are you afraid?" snarled Cobra accusingly.

"No! No!" Robin whimpered, "I'm not, but . . ."

"Then do it! Remove it! He's dying."

Brown John nodded agreement. "Do it, child. It's the only way you'll know if you still have the power."

Robin nodded again, and kept on nodding as she drew in a breath and leaned over Gath. She took hold of the horns, flinching at their heat, and pulled. The helmet twisted, but did not budge. She lowered her grip, this time using the weight of her body to help her. She tugged until she was panting and sweat drained from her temples. Suddenly black smoke billowed from the eye slits, swirling about her arms and startled face. She yanked her hands away and sat back choking and shaking with terror.

"I can't," she whimpered, "I can't do it anymore."

"Nonsense," snapped Cobra. "It's just wedged against the floor boards." She turned imperiously on Brown John and demanded, "Help her, you old mousebag. Lift his head."

Brown John obediently lowered his sword, realized what he was doing and put it back against her ribs. "Wait just a minute now, you're not in command here!"

"Arrggg!" growled Cobra. She brushed the sword away and dropped next to Gath on the opposite side from Robin. "Try again, girl! I'll lift his head."

Cobra forced her hands under the searing metal and flinched painfully, but held on and lifted Gath's helmeted head. Robin took hold of the horns, set herself and yanked hard. The helmet whipped off, and both women fell back, with the headpiece flying out of their blistered hands. Gath's head dropped hard to the stage, and the helmet rolled five feet off, came to rest with a horn stuck in the stage.

Cobra and Robin quickly rose to their knees, blowing on their fingers. Brown John, edging up behind them, lowered the lantern to Gath's head, and they all looked down uncertainly.

The flickering orange light still showed in his partially open eyes. It cast deep black shadows on his savage, chiseled face. His wild black hair and the thick eyebrows on the ridge of his blunt brow were singed and smoking, and the scar running from the left corner of his mouth to his chin was all but burnt away. His lips were parched and bleeding, and the dark sun-brown flesh was burnt raw on his nose, cheeks, jaw and forehead. Black charcoal crust rimmed the wounds. His eyes closed, and his head slowly fell sideways.

Whimpering with fear, Robin fell across his massive chest embracing him. "Oh, Gath, don't die. You can't."

Cobra, involuntarily nodding agreement, reached out a long-fingered hand and gently stroked his tangled burnt hair.

Robin raised her head and looked into Gath's eyes, her tears dropping on his chest and her voice breaking. "Please, Gath, we need you."

Cobra's eyes shifted curiously as she watched the

girl look up at the black sky where a single white jewel, the midnight star, glimmered brightly.

Robin spoke to it, saying, "I'll never leave you again. I swear it by the . . ." She stopped short, looked off at the shadow of the handsome young man and dropped back on Gath's chest sobbing.

Cobra looked down in defeat at the charred bits of black hair clinging to her fingers. She smiled with cold bitterness, then suddenly looked back at Gath.

His eyes flickered, then opened. He sat up and rolled over onto all fours in one erupting movement. His hand, having instinctively caught hold of the body lying across him by the shoulder, had thrown Robin down on her back beneath him, and the impact made her gasp harshly. He took no notice and held her body beneath his, straddling it with one great paw crushing her breast. He looked around, growling, with his head lowered like a trapped wolf. Then he hesitated, as if recognizing Brown John and Cobra, both of whom had jumped back, and looked down at Robin.

The hot glow came back into his eyes.

Robin, gasping in shame, pulled his hand away from her breast and drew it to her lips. "It's all right, Gath. It's me. Robin."

He growled and leapt to his feet, hauling her up by the neck, and she shrieked.

"It's Robin, Gath!" Both Cobra and Brown John shouted it.

Gath did not hear them. His head was lowered, and his eyes were on fire above his charred cheeks. He looked about the stage, grabbed up his helmet, shoved it in Robin's hands, then plucked her off her feet. Holding her under one arm, he jumped on his stallion and galloped off.

Cobra staggered after him, wanting to cry out and

stop him, but did not. She knew it was too late for words. But Brown John, standing beside her, shouted, "Wait, Gath! Come back! I've got to talk to you. Robin's in grave danger!"

Gath did not look back, and rode off with Robin clinging helplessly to his chest, vanished amid the apple trees.

"What's wrong with him?" asked Brown John.

"It's not him," Cobra replied, "it's the helmet."

He looked at her with sudden fear as the handsome young man galloped off on the dappled grey stallion in pursuit.

Brown John shouted after him, "Don't, Jakar! Come back! You don't know him. He could kill you!"

The rider did not stop or look back.

Cobra and Brown John watched the forest until they could no longer hear hoofbeats. Then Cobra looked off into the darkness as if it were her only friend. After a moment, she composed herself and smiled at the *bukko,* speaking in a low, ironic purr.

"I think, old man," she said, "the last time we met, you put me in a bottle."

"I remember it well," he said uneasily, then added, "I think I'll use a rope this time."

"There is no need," she said. But if your manliness requires a rope to arouse it, I will not fight you. On the contrary, I intend to cooperate with you in every way I am able." Her voice was solemn. "Whether we like it or not, we are allies now."

"Just how, may I ask, did you come by that plot?"

"You are obviously aware that the girl is in grave danger?"

"I am."

"And you presume Gath can deal with it?"

"Exactly."

"Are you aware of just how grave the danger is?"

He nodded. "A Lord of Destruction, Baskt, tried to kill her."

Cobra gasped with shock. "He was here?"

"Yes, at Clear Pond. The filth killed five of my girls thinking one of them was Robin."

All color left her face. "Then the danger is far worse than I thought. She knows . . . someone has told her everything." His eyes questioned her, and she answered them. "Tiyy, the Nymph Queen of Pyram. Baskt belongs to her." She took a breath. "Where is he now?"

"I had him followed, and he took Amber Road north, then headed west toward the Barrier Mountains."

"Did he," she hesitated, lowering her voice respectfully, "did he take the remains of your girls with him?" He nodded, and she relaxed slightly. "Then he's headed back to Pyram. That gives us some time. But as soon as Tiyy examines them, she'll know the Lakehair girl is not among them. She'll send him back. But it will take him better than two weeks."

"That won't do Robin any good. The bloody demon left his soldiers behind, to keep track of my Grillards, it seems. We could be being watched right now."

She looked off at the threatening darkness of the forest, listening to the whistle of the wind in the tree canopy, and said quietly, "Then the girl is our only hope."

"As I recall," Brown John said, getting her attention with the tip of his sword, "it wasn't so long ago that you wanted her dead yourself. In fact, wanted all of us dead."

Her pale cheeks lifted in an agreeing smile. "I know. But I am nothing but a woman now and, as such, I believe I am entitled to change my mind."

"A woman," he scoffed. "That you will have to
prove."

"In time, I am certain it will be all too apparent. In
the meantime, I suggest we work together. I know
Tiyy, and the nature of her powers. Perhaps you,
being a man of plots, can use the information I have
and fashion one to save us all . . . providing, of
course, that Gath doesn't kill the girl."

"Kill Robin?" He laughed. "You don't know
him."

"Oh, but I do, bukko . . . as well as you, if not
better. But it is not Gath we are concerned with, not
tonight . . . it's the helmet."

"But he's not wearing it now!"

"That no longer matters," she said, a rush of
childish fear pulsing through her voice. "It's part of
him now . . . perhaps the strongest part."

Fifteen

SAVAGE HEAT

The black stallion bolted out of the dark body of the
forest into a moonlit clearing beside the river,
Whitewater, bordering the eastern edge of the Valley
of Miracles. It pulled up, snorting steam and stomping the wild periwinkles and snapdragons to muddy
pulp, and Gath swung out of the saddle with Robin
in his arms. He dropped onto the mossy ground, and
she staggered free, fearfully averting her face and

clutching the horned helmet to her breasts.

He put a meaty hand on her shoulder, and turned her to him as easily as a swinging gate. She gasped. Singed, tangled hair hung beside his flushed face, brutish with raw wounds glittering wetly in the moonlight. She moaned and again looked away. Growling, he ripped the horned helmet out of her hands and threw it savagely aside.

It clanged against the trunk of an oak and tumbled across the moss, splashing to rest in the shallows of the river beside the startled horse. Cold water lapped against its hot metal, and steam rose, drifting around the stallion's head. He bolted back, snorting in complaint, and waded further out into the river to drink elsewhere.

Robin's shoulders twisted for release inside the grip of Gath's hands, and her eyes continued to avoid his.

"What's wrong?" she pleaded. "Why are you acting like this? Why . . . why did you bring me here? I'm . . ."

His thumb and fingers circled her throat. They were not gentle, and she gasped painfully. The sound encouraged him. He pushed her back against the sloping side of a boulder and pressed his metal-clad body against her pliant length, bending her slowly back. Blunt steel edges burrowed into her breasts and hipbones, and rock cut into the soft flesh of her back. She convulsed against him and cried out, an inarticulate, wailing plea.

The sound rang in his head like a mating call. His eyes narrowed, and he began to pant, lust mad, like a wolf fresh from the grip of death, frothing to defy its terrors in the forgetfulness of a sheet of flaming pleasure.

His hand gripped her jaw, turning her face to his, and his lips hungrily kissed her cool cheek, her open, gasping mouth, her throat. He pressed into her with chest and driving thigh, his lips and fingers probing and exploring the small body that twisted and cringed and shuddered like a mouse in the maw of a cat.

"No!" she screamed, beating at his shoulders. "Nooooo!"

Nothing in him could have resisted her wild song; the animal inside him had taken control.

He rolled her over, facedown. Taking hold of her clothing at the base of her back, he ripped both cloak and nightgown apart and fell heavily against her. His hands held her by armpits and shoulders. One of her closed eyes and a shuddering cheek were bright in a spill of moonlight.

He moved against her, his body heat mingling with hers despite the separating metal. Suddenly he held still, eyes transfixed by the moonlit cheek. It was so beautiful it hurt.

He snarled, and her red curls shuddered in the spill of moonlight. Her head rolled to the side as she moaned helplessly, and eye and cheek and lips again languished in the wan light.

Her beauty knifed into him, and his grip lost its rage. His fingers tenderly conformed to the soft sculpture of her back and shoulder. The savage heat in his blood cooled. The snarl on his face withdrew slowly.

Tears were welling from her eye, draining over her white cheek to gather in glistening drops on her lips. Their plump red flesh trembled fitfully as sobs racked her body.

The brutal glint faded from Gath's eyes, and he studied her uncertainly, like the wolf finding a human babe abandoned in the forest, sensing her helplessness and need.

His fingertips explored her lips, careful now to be gentle, and memories passed behind his eyes. Vivid memories of the first time he had seen Robin sleeping beneath the blackened thorn tree atop Calling Rock. Her lips had danced then in the fire's glow, to the song of her contented sighs and the night wind in the treetops. They had enchanted him, and brought back his childhood dreams for the first time since he could remember. But it was different now, and he withdrew his fingers as his flesh began to crawl and his neck hairs bristled.

Her lips were not dancing, but shuddering, and the song they moved to was that same song his lips had sung when, as a boy in Baal, he had been put to bed at night in his cage.

He released her and stepped back. His muscle and sinew contracted with self-revulsion, bending his huge frame.

Robin, still sobbing, placed her palms against the rock and pushed weakly, her head hanging. Her body lifted and she sagged back facing him with her hands outstretched, steadying herself against the boulder. Without raising her head, she wiped her tears away. Her body suddenly heaved for breath, and she staggered, but caught herself, again using both hands.

Gath watched her red-gold curls tremble, watched her breasts rise and fall against her cloak where his fingers had left dirty smudges. Lust again heated him, and he turned away, fighting off the demands the helmet had planted within him.

From the river bank, the helmet's black eyes watched him, mocking, as the shallow water washed in and out of the mouth hole.

He straightened, his pride returning, and strode to the helmet, stood over it. Frustrated rage, long caged

inside him, suddenly broke free, and he roared, a
sound echoing out of an ancient, howling age. His
boot caught the face of the helmet, drove it deep
under the water into the muddy bottom. Geysers of
water and mud and sparks erupted to his thighs, and
his body sank to one side. His leg was knee-deep in
river bottom. He yanked it out with a sucking sound,
and the water swirled around the hole, gulping and
bubbling, then flowed on.

He glared down at the tiny bubbles rising from the
unseen metal. His hard breathing slackened, and he
strode out into the deeper shallows to the stallion.
Leading the animal back into the mossy clearing
beside Robin, he removed his black cloak from a
saddlebag and wrapped it around her.

Her head lifted timidly, and she looked up under
long feathery lashes. Her eyes were vacant, hollow
corridors to shocked bone and blood and mind.

He gathered water from the river and held it up to
her lips with cupped hands. She stared at them a
moment, then brought her hands up to his, but
hesitated, not touching them. Looking into his eyes,
she asked, "Gath?"

The single word hung heavily on the night air.
When he answered it, his voice was thick and slow.

"Yes," he said, "it is Gath." That surprising
mystical tenderness which marked his soul even
more deeply than his savage strength was back in his
eyes and voice. "Forgive me."

Robin, voice trembling, whispered, "It was the
helmet, wasn't it? Not you."

He nodded. "It will never happen again." It was a
vow.

She took hold of his hands as if they were a bowl,
and held his fingertips to her lips, drinking slowly.
Two more times he fed her water. When his hands

had emptied the third time, she held their cool, wet fingers against her hot cheeks, and kissed his palms softly. As she did this, she spoke to him in a voice that trembled with surrender.

"You must forgive me," she said. "I should not have resisted. It was wrong of me. You saved my life . . . my people . . . everyone. I . . . I have no right to refuse you. I belong to you."

"No!" His low, coarse voice commanded her. "You saved my life . . . twice . . . I am the one who is in debt."

Her eyes widened, startled by his intensity.

"I will protect you, but I do not belong to you . . . or you to me."

"But I do," she protested. "I vowed myself to you . . . by the midnight star. This is written . . . isn't it?"

The surrender in her voice, her closeness and the smell of roses on her lips again stirred him. Heat flowed back into his wounded face, the brutal glint returned to his eyes. But as he spoke, he forced it back, his voice blunt.

"You were young and filled with victory . . . your vow means nothing."

"Nothing? But . . ."

"Nothing. We are bound by a mutual danger, that is all. I am your guardian . . . this is what is written."

A hesitant smile lifted her cheeks, as if with a sudden rush of relief.

He wanted to touch that smile, but turned away and strode to the river's edge. There he dropped his sword and dagger belts on the ground and ripped off boots, chain mail and padded undertunic. Clothed only in loincloth and moonlight, he waded out into hip-deep water, splashing his body, and steam furled from chest, shoulders and face. He dove into the water, stroked out into the strong rushing current and swam against it, defying it to wash him downriver. It could not.

When he came out of the river, he found Robin sitting on a rock beside his armor. She was wrapped in his cloak, and her own was spread across her lap. One of his daggers rested beside her. She had cut thongs on one side of the ripped seam and parallel eye slits on the opposite side. By overlapping the torn parts and passing the thongs through the eye slits and tying them off, she was mending the cloak.

Watching her, he kneeled in the shallows and scrubbed his face with water, removing the crusted ash and dirt and cleaning his wounds. Then he moved his massive bulk beside her and began to dress.

When she finished mending her cloak, she held it up and said, "This is the first way I learned to join cloth, when I was very little. The temple priestesses in Weaver taught it to us the first week of school. It's a very old and primitive method, but quite effective."

Pulling on a boot, he nodded without interest and said flatly, "You are in great danger, and I must find a place to hide you. I have angered the Master of Darkness, and to get at me, he has sent his demons to destroy you."

"I know," she said, holding her voice under control. "It's one of his sorceresses, a woman called Tiyy. She's the high priestess of the Black Veshta." His eyes questioned her, and she added, "It's true. Jakar, a . . . a young man helping Brown John, knows the demon she sent." Her voice suddenly filled with misery. "Oh, Gath, terrible things have been happening."

"What things?"

As he buckled on his belts, she told him all that had happened, ending her tale with the fact that Baskt had left soldiers behind to keep track of the Grillards, and that they could be nearby now.

He glanced at the shadows between the surrounding trees, more in anticipation than caution. "These soldiers are not the only danger you face. The Master of Darkness has sent the Queen of Serpents' creatures for you."

Her eyes widened, and she looked around, trembling. "You mean snakes and lizards? No wonder they're everywhere lately." She looked at him. "Then they did murder the girls, thinking they were me."

"Do not be afraid," he said quietly. "They have been deprived of the magic which feeds them, and are dying."

She nodded, and her trembling abated.

"Who is this Jakar?"

"Oh, yes," she said apologetically, "I should have explained. He's a Kaven nobleman, but also an orphan, like myself. His sister was one of the girls who was killed, and unlike the relatives of the other victims, he is not afraid to do something about it. He has sworn to help Brown John until the demons are destroyed, and he's been a big help. He knows all kinds of things, and has been just about everywhere."

Gath, studying her suddenly excited face, rolled his shoulders adjusting his chain mail, and moved to the river's edge. He reached deep into the water, came away with the horned helmet and washed it off in the river, shook it dry.

Robin held her breath as she watched him, and fear came back into her large eyes. "Please," she pleaded quietly, "don't put it on."

He turned to her, and their eyes met and held each other. His blunt facial bones were more chiseled since they had last seen each other, and the hollows of his cheeks were deeper, his shoulders thicker. She seemed to note each difference before she spoke.

"It's . . . it's done something to you. It's like I don't really know you anymore."

He moved to the stallion, unbuckled a saddlebag and forced the helmet inside. "You have nothing to fear. It's going to stay in here. You won't have to remove it again."

"Oh," she said. "I didn't mean that. That's no trouble. I just . . ."

She stopped short, seeing his dark eyes flash. "I will not spend my life at the end of your leash."

"Oh, Gath, I didn't . . ."

"I will destroy these demons that hunt you, because I have put you in danger. When that is finished, the serpent bitch, Cobra, will find a way to tame the helmet. Then you and I are finished."

She hesitated, then said quietly, "You've said that before. Not just once, but maybe three or four times." Her smile was slightly chiding.

"If Cobra fails, I will find another way." His expression became brutal. Blood trickled from a wound on his chin. "I will not be enchanted . . . not by the helmet, not by you."

She hesitated uncertainly and nodded, shyly removing his cloak. She put on her own, and handed him his, saying quietly, "I understand you want to be by yourself, but I'm glad you're here now. And I'll miss you if you go away. We went through horrible, frightening times together, but they were also wonderful." Her eyes became moist, and she smiled to hold back tears. "I'll . . . I'll never forget you, Gath. Never."

He looked at her a long time, absorbing her and the memories of her: of her healing the wounded wolf and healing him, of her bravely defying the dangers of The Shades to come to him and deliver Brown John's message about the Kitzakk invasion, of that time when the helmet was about to destroy him and the sight of her stopped it, and of that moment when he held her in his arms and kissed her wondrous lips.

When the memories were imprisoned again, he put his cloak back in his saddlebags and said, "Neither of us will forget."

The whack of an arrow striking into living meat, followed by hissing, came from within a bush to the right of Robin.

She shrieked, scattering back, and Gath, bursting forward, ripped his axe from its saddle scabbard. With his body cocked like a catapult and his axe weaving in front of him, he planted himself between Robin and the bush, his expression as cold as the steel of a butcher's knife.

Sixteen

BEHIND THE BUSH

A serpentine shadow whipped about within the bush, breaking branches and scattering leaves, then spilled out and thudded on the moss. A snake with a body as thick as a milk bucket. It was withered, oozing fumes between rotting scales, and wore brown, gold and black diamonds on its writhing torso, the natural jewelry of a Sadoulette python.

Gath's axe came down, splitting the snake in two parts. The two lengths thrashed about as if searching for each other. One wiggled across the moss, while the larger portion with the head crawled back into the bush to hide. But its poor condition gave it away. Thick green fumes flecked with sputtering blood spewed from the reptile's mouth and wounds.

Robin, peering over a raised arm, gasped in terror.

Gath grunted contemptuously, letting her know he had played with this kind of demon spawn before. He stuck his axe upright in the ground, two-handed the snake and swung it over his head, crushing its skull against a boulder.

Grunting annoyance, he tossed the body aside like a useless length of rope and stepped back.

The reptile rolled off the rock and plopped on the ground. There was a steel crossbow bolt in the snake's skull directly between the eyes.

Gath pulled his axe out of the ground, his wary eyes on the forest, hunting for whoever had fired the bolt. Robin cringed behind his shoulder, her large eyes wide with fear. Suddenly she gasped with shock and clutched her cloak tightly about her.

A shadowed figure had emerged from the forest shadows, just beyond the bush. Some fifteen strides beyond the figure, peering calmly between the black bodies of the trees, was a dappled grey stallion. The figure moved, and a young man wearing finely cut leather clothing advanced slowly into the moonlight, leveling a loaded crossbow at Gath.

"Oh, no!" whispered Robin breathlessly.

The young man bowed in reply, and in a formal but concerned tone, said to her, "I'm sorry, I came as fast as I could, but lost your trail in the dark."

"That's all right," she said hurriedly. "I appreciate your trying to help me. But there's no need. I'm in no danger."

"Perhaps," the young man said, doubt hard in his tone. "We'll let Brown John decide that. Now, move quickly and get on my horse before this large ape turns wild again." A low growl rumbled from Gath's mouth, and the intruder waved his crossbow at him. "Just stay put. I won't hurt you unless I have to."

"Don't, Jakar!" Robin moaned, stumbling forward. Gath lifted an arm and she stopped behind it, her eyes pleading. "Please, Jakar, I really do appreciate what you're trying to do, but it's not necessary. He won't harm me!"

"Just get on my horse, fluff."

"Jakar, please!" Robin begged. "Go away."

"I can't do that." He nodded at the dead snake. "This forest is full of these slimy demons, and they seem as eager to tear you apart as the large one here." His eyes met Gath's. "Now, if she is truly in no danger, kindly let her get on my horse."

Holding Robin in place, Gath studied the young man's hard, haunted eyes. Out of curiosity, he asked, "You are the Jakar that helps the bukko, Brown John?"

Jakar nodded.

"He sent you to follow me?"

"No. It was my idea."

Gath wiped blood from his chin with the back of his hand, glanced at it, turning his hand in the moonlight, then looked up at Jakar thoughtfully. "If you truly serve the bukko, ride back and tell him Robin has come to no harm, and that I am returning with her."

"Yes," urged Robin. "We're coming now."

Jakar lifted his crossbow, shaking his head behind it. "You're coming with me."

"Oh, Jakar, please," begged Robin. "You don't know what you're doing."

Gath, his head tilting to one side like a cat's, asked flatly, "Why do you argue? Do you wish to die?"

Jakar, without expression, replied, "I never gave it a thought."

Gath smiled. He liked the answer. "Go tell the bukko," he said, and turned his back on him.

Jakar's face flushed with angry pride, and he whispered harshly, "Don't turn your back on me, large one."

"Oh, no," moaned Robin. "Don't, please."

Gath casually dropped his axe back in its saddle scabbard, and began to rearrange the horned helmet inside the saddlebag, keeping his back to the young man.

"Turn around," Jakar threatened, "or . . ."

He stopped short as Gath's head slowly revolved, his brutal eyes glittering behind a metal shoulder. Jakar unconsciously took a step back, lost balance on the soft moss, and his crossbow dipped sideways. Gath whipped an arm around, like a bolt of jagged lightning in the moonlight, and threw the helmet.

Jakar's crossbow whipped back into place. The horned helmet hit it, splintering the weapon and dislodging the metal shaft into overhanging branches, then bounded off into nearby foliage.

Jakar looked down in shock at his broken weapon, threw it aside, drew his knife.

Robin screamed, "No!"

Jakar charged, more careful now and with agile movements. Gath let him come, his expression almost indifferent. Suddenly he stepped in, catching the knife blade on his chain mail, and drove a fist into the side of Jakar's head. Jakar dropped facedown in the moss and did not move.

Robin raced to him and sank beside his fallen body, shielding it with her own and sobbing, "Don't! Don't hurt him. Please." She looked up into Gath's hard eyes. "Please, Gath, don't. He . . . he doesn't know what he's doing. He's all mixed up. He's hurt, terribly hurt. He loved his sister deeply."

Gath said, "I won't hurt him." He retrieved his helmet, stuffed it back into the saddlebag. "Come, get in the saddle."

"But I can't leave him here. He's hurt."

Gath, without looking at her, buckled the saddlebag, saying harshly, "If you wish to help him, let him help himself. That will heal his pride far more quickly than your pity."

Robin hesitated. When Gath looked back at her, she nodded. "I know you're right, but I can't."

"I will not wait here for you to coddle him." His voice was impatient. "I must return to Rag Camp and talk with the serpent queen! Get in the saddle."

"No," she said. "I'm not going to leave him."

His eyes studied her thoughtfully, and the memories of their times together once more passed through his mind. Then he said, "He is your man, isn't he?"

Without looking at Gath, she shook her head. "I hardly know him."

"Perhaps," he said quietly. "But you wish to be as free of me as I do of you."

She lifted her wet eyes to his. "I didn't say that. You're the one who's always saying we're finished."

He nodded. "We will both be free." There was no compromise in his tone.

He strode to her, plucked Jakar out of her arms and threw him over the saddle of the dappled grey.

He put the broken crossbow in its saddle holster, mounted his stallion, drawing Robin up behind him, then led the grey into the dark forest, heading for Rag Camp.

Seventeen
THE PLOT THICKENS

Morning sunlight spilled over the crest of Stone Crossing and streamed in wide golden bars across Rag Camp, splashing over Brown John's huge house wagon. It now stood in the middle of the clearing, and was being prepared for the road. Three elderly Grillards were harnessing a team of four draft horses in thick padded collars to its shafts, while others were loading it with provisions, scraping off its bright red paint and nailing filthy totems to it. Disguising it.

Brown John stood to one side watching, his thumbs hooked in his belt. His body was rocking and his smile dancing, like a puppetmaster pulling strings.

He turned to Cobra, who stood behind him studying the edge of the forest with gloomy pessimism, and said lightheartedly, "Stop worrying, woman! Gath and Robin will come back. I can feel it in the air. Good times are coming now."

"Shhh, bukko," she said quietly. "Optimism makes me nauseous, particularly in the morning."

He laughed. "If you're afraid he won't go along

with our plans, don't be. He knows little about maps or sorcery or castles, and he'll listen to me . . . you can count on that."

"I am counting on it," she said frankly, and suddenly smiled. "Here they come."

Gath and Robin had emerged from the forest riding the black stallion. She sat behind the huge Barbarian, hanging on to him with one hand and using the other to wipe smudges off her cheeks. His scabbed face was slightly more beastlike than his bloody chain mail, and her cloak was filthy, badly torn.

Twenty paces behind them, Jakar followed on the dappled grey. He held the broken pieces of his crossbow, and there was a ragged bandage wrapped around his forehead, just above an expression of angry humiliation. But there was no surrender in his eyes, only bitter resolve, more than the *bukko* thought was healthy for one so young.

"Holy Zard!" Brown John exclaimed. "Look at them! You'd think Robin was playing the ravaged bride in *Up by Lamplight* and that both Jakar and Gath had done the ravaging. Well, this is no time to worry about it. They're safe, that's what counts." He turned to Cobra. "Leave it to me now."

"Of course," she said. "It's your plot." Her smile was flattering enough to make a three-legged chair behave like it had four.

Grinning as if he deserved such flattery, he moved to Robin as Gath reined up beside the water trough. "By Veshta, lass," he sighed, helping her down, "I am glad to see you." He glanced up at Gath. "And you too, friend."

Gath nodded behind an easy smile, and their eyes shared that silent trust and understanding which bonded them, both instantly seeing that each knew the gravity and size of the danger Robin now faced.

"What's the plot, old friend?" Gath asked from his saddle.

"We're going on the road again!" Brown John answered, his eyes becoming reckless. "But there will be no army to lead this time. It will just be the five of us." He took Robin by the elbow, guiding her toward the wagon. "And you, lass, must get suitably dressed. We leave as soon as possible."

"But where are we going?"

"That will all be explained later. All you have to understand is that from this moment on, we are no longer Grillards, but low, vulgar, outlawed traveling players. The very worst you could imagine! Whores and whoremasters." The glint in his eyes danced at the prospect. "So you must dress like it. Rags would be preferable, and don't wash. The filthier you are, the better."

She nodded, also liking the excitement of the idea. "And my hair?"

"We'll dye it once we're under way." He chuckled. "Butterfly, we're going to take the stage away from these demons, and your part is essential. Now hurry! Hurry!"

He opened the wagon door and pushed her stumbling up the iron rung steps and inside, closing it after her.

The *bukko* sighed and glanced back at the trough. Gath and Jakar had dismounted and were watering their horses, as Cobra watched. Jakar's ear was caked with blood, and it stained the water as he washed his face. Brown John moved to him and asked, "Are you all right, lad? Can you travel?"

"Don't worry about me," Jakar said.

"I'm not," Brown John said bluntly. "What I want to know is, are you able to drive a wagon? A big one?" Jakar glanced at the *bukko*'s huge house wagon and nodded. "Good!" the *bukko* exclaimed. "Then our cast is set."

Gath glanced at the large house wagon. Its red paint was nearly gone now, and the elderly Grillards were still loading it with provisions. "A long journey?" he asked.

"Yes," Brown John said flatly. "North to Small Tree, then directly west across the Barrier Mountains into the Forbidden Lands." He smiled. "We're going to hide Robin in the one place they will never think to look for her." He paused dramatically. "And steal the means to destroy her enemies."

Gath thought about that, then looked at the surrounding forest. "And the spies watching us now?"

"By the time we reach Small Tree," he looked at Cobra, "she will have devised a way to draw them out so you can get rid of them. After that, with proper disguises, no one will have any idea who we truly are. There will be dangers, of course, there always are in the Forbidden Lands. But those hunting Robin will never think to look for her there."

"Our destination?" Gath asked.

"The castle of the Nymph Queen . . . Pyram." Gath's eyes questioned him, and he added, "I know, nobody knows where Pyram is. Nobody, that is, except for the trusted agents of the Master of Darkness."

Gath and Jakar both turned to Cobra, and she nodded without expression.

"Actually," Brown John continued, "Cobra does not know the way herself. But she knows where we can obtain a map." He smiled knowingly at Cobra. "It's in a grotto, somewhere within the Barrier Mountains. More than that, she refuses to tell us . . . at least for now." He turned back to Gath. "She will only guide us to the map if we give our word she will be allowed to accompany us all the way to Pyram."

Gath, his hard eyes on Cobra, chuckled accusingly. "Just what is there in Pyram that she wants so much?"

"I'll answer that, bukko," Cobra said, her voice cold and flat. "Within Tiyy's castle there is a treasure, one of extraordinary proportions. If we are able to steal even a portion of it, and with your help I think there is more than a reasonable chance of that, then my share would provide me the means with which to regain my wealth . . . and power."

Gath hesitated, his eyes boring into hers, then turned to the *bukko*. "Just what are we going to steal, Brown?"

"The answer to all our problems, friend," Brown John replied. The glint behind his eyes was suddenly as reckless as a bouncing rubber ball descending a flight of stairs. "Pyram's is no ordinary treasure, but a fabled one. Gems not only worth a world's ransom, but spilling over with magical powers. Diamonds, rubies and sapphires which have been hidden from the sight of ordinary men for a thousand years . . . the jewels of the holy White Veshta, the Goddess of Light."

Gath glanced suspiciously at Cobra and she nodded. "They are there, Dark One. They have been there since long, long ago when my former master subdued the White Veshta and gave them to his favored consort, the Black Veshta. And I know where they are kept . . . I grew up in Pyram."

Brown John chuckled with relish. "You see, Gath, it's the perfect plot. We can't fail. And once we steal them, all we have to give her is two or three stones as payment for her part."

"As I said before, bukko," Cobra said flatly, "we

will discuss my payment after we have seen the
stones and measured their wealth and powers."

"Yes, of course," agreed Brown John, his eyes on
Gath. "But there is bound to be plenty for all."

Gath asked Cobra, "No one has seen the jewels?"

"No one . . . except for Tiyy, the Nymph Queen."

Gath studied her erect figure as the morning
sunlight sculpted her voluptuous body with brilliant
white-gold light, hiding nothing, yet enhancing her
mystery. Then, without looking at his friend, he said
in a matter-of-fact tone, "She's enchanted you,
Brown. Made you believe her lies."

"No! No!" the *bukko* protested. "This entire
scheme is my idea. I've known for years that the
sacred jewels were held in Pyram, and it was only by
chance that she mentioned she knew of a map
leading there."

"She says nothing by chance," Gath said, his eyes
holding Cobra's.

Brown John looked at the serpent woman warily,
then said, "Perhaps you're right. But it makes no
difference. If the map leads anyplace other than
Pyram, Jakar will tell us. He's seen it. From a great
distance, it's true, but there's no mistaking it, is
there, lad?" Jakar shook his head, and the *bukko*
added, "Besides, an opportunity like this simply
cannot be ignored, regardless of the risks. These
jewels are a veritable cornucopia of magical wonders. They have the power to turn the entire world
upside down, and then make it over in the manner it
should have been made in the first place. And
we . . . you and I, Gath of Baal," he held out upturned hands, "we can hold them in our hands . . .
set them free!"

Gath eyed him skeptically.

"I know it sounds mad," the old man said, his

tone deliberately mocking himself. "The road will be plagued with demons which only Black Veshta herself can imagine. But if you and I aren't the ones to jump off cliffs and attempt the impossible, then no one will. Besides, isn't this precisely what you want to do? Stealing the jewels would strike a blow at the Master of Darkness far greater than even you dreamed of. The jewels are the source of power with which the sorceress Tiyy, by corrupting their powers of light into those of darkness, creates her unholy demon spawn." Gath's eyes hardened, and the bukko added, "There's also a very personal reason for you to steal them."

He turned to Cobra expectantly, and she said, "Tiyy used the powers of the jewels to fashion the horned helmet . . . and the power that gives the helmet control over you is the same power that can remove it."

Gath's eyes smiled, and he said, "I suddenly like your plot, old friend."

"I thought you might," said the *bukko*. "But there is one danger we should discuss before beginning. Once this Nymph Queen finds out she has the wrong girl, she will undoubtedly send this sharkman back to find her. And since we are entering her domain on the road by which he will be returning, there is the chance we may meet him. In that event we should avoid him . . . but Cobra fears the helmet may not let you. In fact, she fears if you put the helmet back on, there will be no need for these demons to come after Robin . . . that you'll do their work for them." He hesitated, then added, "I, for one, don't think you'll give in to that headpiece, not for a minute! But I promised I'd question you."

Gath smiled, and glanced at Cobra, saying, "Have no fear, woman. I will do whatever I have to do." His tone carried the finality of a hammered nail.

"Then it begins," Brown John chortled, and Gath nodded.

On cue, the door of the red wagon swung open, and Robin tripped lightly down the steps. Seeing everyone look at her, she came to an embarrassed stop and covered her breasts with her arms. Then, laughing at herself, she lowered her arms and presented herself, turning in the morning sunlight. She wore a skirt of bright yellow rags low on narrow hips, a band of fuchsia cloth that conformed to high, firm breasts the way the skin of the pear conforms to the pear, and sunlight in her red-gold hair. There was no make-up on her face, except for the rouge of excitement.

Brown John murmured approvingly, "Well done, child, well done."

"Is . . . is it all right?" blurted Robin.

"Nearly perfect, child," extolled the *bukko*, "but bind your breasts in black. The fuchsia is too rich."

Robin, nodding, bounded back inside the wagon, closing the door behind her, and Brown John turned back to the others.

Cobra's eyes shimmered like becalmed molten gold, and her voice was low as she spoke to the stagemaster, "I don't mean to insult your theatrical skills, bukko, but if the girl is to succeed in drawing out these spies, she is going to have to play her new role, not with an entertainer's idea of the sins of the flesh, but with a sinner's . . . and I know the part."

"I am sure you do," agreed the *bukko*.

"Exactly, so I suggest you allow me to prepare all elements of her performance, including her wardrobe . . . just as we discussed."

"So we did," Brown John said reluctantly. "But you'd be smart to let her get involved. She's clever."

"She'll be involved, believe me." Cobra turned to Gath. "I presume, Dark One, that you agree to these arrangements, and will allow me to use the girl to draw these spies out . . . without interfering?"

Gath drank from the trough using his hands, then said, "If she's hurt, in any way . . ."

"Don't threaten me," Cobra interrupted, her voice a commanding purr. "It's useless. We are joined now like links of a chain, and you cannot change it. You want the jewels now as much as you wanted the helmet . . . even more. Because only they can set you free. And without me . . . you will never see them." She hesitated, then added, "Will you cooperate or not?"

Gath nodded, but the threat remained in his eyes.

"Don't worry," Cobra said lightly. "The trick she will perform is one any mountain girl can do. But she is not only going to have to dress the part of the whore . . . she's going to have to play it."

Eighteen

ON THE ROAD

The wagon, two days out of Rag Camp, rumbled north on Hog-Scald Road in the territory called Small Tree. Earlier, it had passed through the lands of the Kaven and Dowat tribes, and three times had met parties of Barhacha woodsmen on the road. But not a single member of these tribes had recognized the vehicle as their king's.

The carriage's wheels and shafts were now scraped

clean, and fetishes rattled on the bloated body: bones, gourds, beads, flapping rabbit ears and the pelts of leopard, tiger and lynx. They were nailed to the driver's box, the doorways, windows and sideboards, and mixed with them were bilious red and orange signs and numerals sacred to the deities of lechery, Zatt, Chuzz, Bajat and Yang.

All together, the wagon's appearance was not quite as civilized as a gorilla wearing a codpiece, and it moved with the grace of an armadillo making love to a fast duck.

Jakar sat in the box, holding the reins, and the *bukko* snoozed beside him.

Sounds of approaching horses joined the racket, and Jakar stood abruptly, glanced back across the flat roof.

Five riders had emerged from a forest trail, and were following the wagon, drawing closer and closer. A mangy bunch of freebooters, they carried crude spears and naked swords, and wore soiled leather armor. Blistering rashes on their bare arms and bald heads were crimson in the sunshine, and they were drinking in their saddles from wine jars. Coming close, they waved at Jakar and shouted crude words of welcome, then fell back, avoiding the wagon's dust.

Jakar acknowledged them with a wave and smile, sat back down and stared thoughtfully ahead. The riders appeared to be following for no other reason than the obvious one, that the wagon's occupants promised to provide a bawdy performance when it stopped for the night. On the other hand, the riders might be the demon spies the troupe had to destroy before it could leave the forest basin.

Jakar two-handed the reins, pulling back and slowing the horses as they rounded a bend and

headed down a long straight tree-lined lane. Forty
paces ahead, the broad back of the huge Barbarian
came into view, leading the way on his stallion.

Gath of Baal now wore a black bearskin, a weapon
belt, fur-trimmed boots and the shiny brass
armbands of a *macco*, a strongman. Both he and his
mount were stained with grease and trail dust, and
their black hair was matted and tangled with burrs
and bits of leaf. Jakar could not see Gath's face, but
he was certain that the large man's expression was
his normal one, about as tame as the bear who had
provided his new clothing.

The young nobleman glanced back at the following riders and nudged Brown John. The old man did
not respond. With entwined hands resting on his
paunch, he jiggled and tossed, lost to his dreams.

Both the *bukko* and Jakar now wore dusty, stained
tunics, sewn from rags, over their unwashed bodies.
Their belts, pouches and weapons were embroidered
with colored wooden beads, and loop earrings dangled amid greasy tangled hair. Coiled around Brown
John's neck was a coarse red whip, the scepter of the
traveling whoremaster.

Jakar nudged his king again, and shouted over the
clattering wheels and creaking body of the wagon,
"Time to wake up, bukko! Your plot just added a
whole new set of characters."

Brown John came awake with a start, and sat up
rubbing his eyes. "What's that? What did you say?"

"Take a look behind us."

The *bukko* yawned and stretched, then turned in
his seat and looked back at the following riders.

One of them howled wildly, pitched a wine jar
against a tree for no apparent reason. It crashed
loudly, drawing howls from the others. Not manlike
howls, but a high-pitched squealing.

Jakar put an eye on the startled *bukko*. "What do you think? Do we stop and let Gath murder them?"

Brown John scowled and faced to the front, saying patiently, "We can't go around killing people, lad, just because they look suspicious. We have to make sure we've got the right ones."

"I know," said Jakar lightly, "I just thought he might be hungry."

Brown John scolded him with his brown eyes, and nodded with the back of his head at the riders. "How long have they been there?"

"They just showed up." He put a wary eye on the old man. "If that's the bunch Robin is supposed to arouse, all she's going to need is a coat of oil and a tambourine!"

The *bukko* laughed easily and said, "There is more to it than that, lad, a great deal more. With the riffraff you find camped on the road, Robin's kind of beauty can be a detriment if not presented properly. It is too far out of their reach, and that offends them. Shames them. Makes them aware of their own sorry lives. They wouldn't pay an ave to look on Robin stark naked, and if they did, they'd only laugh with scorn at her inadequate breasts and buttocks, and demand their silver back."

"Is that right?" asked Jakar mockingly.

"Yes," the *bukko* said importantly. "The art, Jakar, is to make Robin appear as if she is one of them. The best of them, of course, and the most beautiful . . . but still one of them. Otherwise she is inaccessible, not only to their hands but to their minds and the secret passions in their hearts."

"I see, and you're going to let this serpent woman who was, and may still be, in league with the Master of Darkness decide just how accessible?"

"Precisely. She's dressing her now."

"You're taking quite a risk, aren't you?"

Brown John nodded firmly. "It's what I do best."

"Oh?" said Jakar with an arched eyebrow. "Well, from where I sit, Robin's the one taking the risk." That removed Brown John's proud expression, and Jakar added, "We'll make Upper Small by nightfall. With an early start tomorrow, we could reach the Barrier Mountains by mid-day. So, if we're going to kill anybody, we better do it tonight."

"I know," said Brown John. He glanced back thoughtfully at the bald-headed riders, then turned to Jakar. "You're right about Robin. She is taking the greater risk, and I appreciate your concern. Your presence is a great comfort to her."

"You misunderstand me, old man. Robin is nothing more to me than a tool. A beautiful and amusing one, but nevertheless a tool. I intend to cut as many of these demons' throats as possible, and apparently, by acting as bait, she can help me do it."

"Yes, of course," said Brown John. "I understand. Your feelings are motivated by the loss of your sister. But there is more at stake in this adventure now than revenge."

"Not for me."

The *bukko* hesitated at the hardness of his tone, then said, "I know how you feel, but you must not let your anger stop you from living." His voice softened with respect. "Jakar, your sister is gone now, and Robin is very much alive."

"Are you sure?" Jakar asked with cool mocking eyes. He nodded with an ear at the wagon. "Maybe you better find out just what they're up to."

"I will." Brown John stood behind his words, adding, "And rest assured, I will see she is not put in any danger."

He climbed back onto the roof and paused, once

more looking back at the drunken riders, then climbed down through the trapdoor, closing it behind him.

Jakar whipped the horses, and they lunged forward in their huge red collars, hauling their load faster and faster, and the wagon rolled and bounced precariously under him like a grotesque wooden whore. He laughed darkly to himself, his body relaxed, riding the pitch and bounce. The huge vehicle was acting as if it were eager to wreck its favors against every turn in the road, and crush its lovers, breaking its own heart in the process, and all for nothing more than love of the open road. And inside he felt just as reckless.

It was madness, yet mysteriously irresistible, and he shuddered. Now more things were at play which he did not understand and could not see. He could feel them as surely as he could feel the wind bite his cheeks. Not only in the girl and serpent woman but in Brown John.

Nineteen

PRIVATE
PERFORMANCE

The *bukko* descended the ladder and stood bracing
his hands against the walls of the second-story room
as the wagon tilted and shook its way around a
corner. Daylight seeped through the seams of shuttered windows, filling the room with moody grey
light. Baskets of provisions were stacked on the floor
and on the racks above his wall bed. In the corner,
vague whiffs of smoke rose out of the stairwell hole,
and the sound of voices.

He crossed to the hole, listened to the voices but
could not make out what they were saying. He
started down the narrow, enclosed staircase toward a
spill of orange candlelight on the floor below. Suddenly wheels squealed outside, combined with the
growl of grinding boards and thundering hooves,
and buried the voices in a cacophonous din. Just as
suddenly the din subsided, and he stopped short
only partway down. He could now hear Robin's firm
but muffled voice.

"But I don't want to take my clothes off! I won't! I
already feel cheap and dirty."

"Child," a female voice said in a low purr, as if
stroking a wildcat, "the time has come for you to put
your modesty behind you." The voice was Cobra's,
both indolent and authoritarian. "Now step out of

116

your tunic, your costume is ready."

"All right." Robin's voice was reluctant. "But I can put it on by myself. You don't have to help. I've worked with cloth and clothing nearly all my life." Robin's voice hesitated, then continued, "Besides, where is it? If it's so immodest, maybe I won't agree to wear it."

Brown John listened to sandaled feet crossing the room below, then the creak of tiny hinges, like those on a small ceremonial box, and more sounds of sandaled feet followed by Robin's gasp.

"Is . . . is that it?" the girl's shocked voice asked.

"Not all of it, but these are the essential elements." Cobra's voice was teasingly casual.

"Well, I won't do it," Robin's voice said defiantly. "I'm not going to dance wearing nothing but a few dabs of rouge and kohl."

The *bukko* smiled with amusement and sat down, listening to Cobra's chuckle drift up the stairwell. It was heavy with power, hypnotic. Her voice followed, redolent with the same qualities.

"Your body will be covered, child, have no fear of that. But first I must mark it with the required signs and numerals. Now come, make yourself naked. There is much to do and we are wasting time."

"But I don't trust you. What signs? What will they do to me?"

"Come, come, child, they won't harm you. Besides, did you not tell everyone that you would do anything . . . do whatever was asked of you, to help steal the sacred jewels?

"Yes, but . . ."

"Then disrobe."

"No!" Robin's voice blurted. "You tried to kill me when the Kitzakks held me prisoner! And you would have if that priest hadn't stopped you. And I think you want to kill me now. I can see it in your eyes."

Brown John rose into a crouch, his hand clutching the whip coiled around his neck, and listened intently. The women's voices were closer together now.

"You see correctly, butterfly," the sorceress said calmly, "but it is only a surface emotion. Come, stand next to me. Look deep, and tell me what you see."

"What am I supposed to see?"

"Just look!"

The sound of scuffling sandals, then the girl's voice came again. "I don't see . . ."

"Closer, put your face to mine." Cobra's voice was so close to Robin's it sounded as if their lips were touching.

Brown John descended three more steps, and turned an ear toward the bottom of the stairwell. Motionless. Intent.

"Now what do you see?" Cobra's voice asked.

"Fear!" The girl's voice was startled. Then she lost control, and her words tossed like leaves on a wind. "Fear! A . . . a terrible fear!"

"For what?" Two words as weighted with portent as the entire prologue of *Thirteen Knives at Hog-Scald*.

"For yourself, and . . ." Robin's voice gasped in confusion. "But I don't understand!"

"You see it now, don't you?" the woman's voice purred. "Here, I will remove the mandrake root." Her voice paused, then added, "And still you see it, don't you? I fear for you as much as I fear for myself."

"But . . . but why?"

Brown John's eyes asked the same question, and he felt suddenly out of control. Things were going too fast. He moved halfway down the stairwell until he could hear clearly as Cobra spoke.

"There is no mystery to it, girl. You are the one the Nymph Queen hunts, and if anything happens to you, all is lost! For me as well as your friends."

"I know that, but that's what confuses me. Why does she want to . . . to murder me instead of Gath?"

"Well, primarily, I would think, because you keep the helmet from overpowering Gath. But there are undoubtedly other reasons as well."

"What reasons?"

"They would only confuse you further if I tried to explain. Besides, there is no time. All you must understand is that I wish you no harm, and that you must trust me. Completely. Just as Brown John trusts me."

Brown John scowled. Cobra was taking him for granted.

"But why does he trust you?" Robin's voice asked tentatively.

"Because he knows, or rather senses, that I know more about you than you know yourself."

Brown John's mouth dropped open.

"But . . . but that's not possible."

"If you doubt me, look again into my eyes and see if I lie."

The sounds of pounding hooves and rattling wheels filled the void left by the momentarily silent voices, and the *bukko* slid down another step, his ear turned. He waited, and a whimpering gasp of recognition rose above the sounds. It was Robin's.

"You see," Cobra's voice said quietly, "I am not

playing false with you. I know you, butterfly, and I can help you do what must be done. Do you understand now?"

The *bukko* sat rigidly still, waiting. Why was the serpent woman trying to gain Robin's trust? What was she up to? When Robin's voice came again, it startled him. It was weak and timid, as if drawn out of her by sorcery.

She said, "Yes."

"You'll let me draw the signs, instruct you?"

"Yes." Weaker still.

"Then get undressed!" Cobra's voice no longer coaxed: it was in control.

"Yes," Robin's voice said obediently, then said it again. There was the sound of a cloak dropping to the floor, and sandals being kicked off, then her voice came a third time, startled now. "Why . . . why are you undressing?"

The old man's brown eyes widened until the whites showed all around, and sweat drained off his forehead. When Cobra's voice replied, it was cool and calming.

"Do not be alarmed. We are going to perform a routine transfer of knowledge, something every hill girl can do. All that is required is a belief in one's natural powers, and a strong Kaa. You have these, your gift of healing has proven it, and you have an exceptionally vulnerable and absorbing nature. When my flesh touches yours, it will instruct you, teach your senses how to arouse carnal pleasure in the men you dance for . . . and in yourself."

"Myself?" Robin's voice protested weakly.

"Yes." Cobra's voice was low and flat. Robin whimpered, and the woman continued with cold candor, "You must understand, butterfly. When you dance, you are going to have to perform in a way that is vile and repellent to you. You must allow feelings and sensations that you have suppressed to blossom, or you will not arouse these demon spawn and make them show themselves."

"But what if I can't?"

"You must!" Desperation had entered Cobra's voice, faint but shaking.

There was a moment of hesitation, and Brown John's breathing raced uncertainly. The serpent woman was up to something, and he was not sure he wanted to know what it was. Then Robin's trembling voice asked, "What's going to happen to me? How . . . how will these . . . these creatures show themselves? What kind of monsters are they? They're going to hurt me, aren't they?"

"I do not know their natures," Cobra's voice answered candidly. "Hopefully they will just circle you, like moths stupefied by torchlight. But I cannot promise it. Understand, I'll dance first and try to draw them out. If I can, you will not need to dance, but don't count on that."

"That's all I have to do, dance?"

"Yes, but this above all, Robin, you must understand." Her voice had quieted, and become deadly sober. "Whatever danger comes your way, tonight, tomorrow or next week, you must risk it. You must be willing to sacrifice yourself . . . at any moment . . . or the quest will fail."

"I don't understand."

"I cannot explain why, not to you or anyone else. The knowledge could tarnish you. You must simply understand that the risk and efforts you take to steal the sacred jewels must not be for your own gain, but for your friends. And you must take the risks and expend the effort silently, seeking no pity, no glory, no reward."

"But I don't want any. I only thought that their powers could not only free Gath but maybe cure Jakar of his grief and bitterness."

"Good," replied Cobra's voice, and Brown John thought he could hear her smile.

A moment passed, then Robin's voice asked, "Brown John doesn't know I'm in danger, does he?"

"No. He knows you take some risk, but he is confused as to its nature. He is a dreamer: he only sees things as he wishes to see them. I am sure he thinks that the only things at stake tonight are your theatrical scruples, and you must not let him, or Gath or the handsome young nobleman, think anything different. If they knew the risk, they would try to stop you."

Brown John held his breath, and visions of Jakar's threatening eyes and Gath's deadly axe coming at him passed across his mind. But he remained where he was. Motionless. Silent.

"I understand," Robin's voice replied. "Brown seems much older now, and somehow softer. I think he needs a woman."

Cobra's chuckle rang in the *bukko*'s ears, then her voice. "You are wiser, butterfly, than your years admit to. Now hurry, get those things off."

Brown John sagged back against the stairs. He was sweating, and his face was florid with humiliation. He pushed himself erect and started down the stairs. He came within two steps of the opening at the bottom of the stairwell and once more stopped short. He could hear the sounds of more clothing falling on the floor. He frowned in confusion and leaned forward listening. The wheels squealed again outside, and the boards heaved and groaned as the wagon bounced and tossed. Amid the noise there was a tinkle of warm laughter, then Cobra spoke.

"Child, you are indeed a wonder. Even more beautiful than when I saw you imprisoned in the Kitzakk priest's huge flask with the milk spilling over you. You've grown, filled out, and it becomes you. I wish I were not so jealous, so I could enjoy it more." She laughed again, with restrained warmth, then her voice purred invitingly. "Now stand close, let our bodies touch."

Brown John hesitated, a sudden rush of scruples making him think twice about what he was about to do. Then the rubber ball began to bounce again in his eyes, and he mischievously peered around the corner.

The two figures stood naked face-to-face in the dark shuttered room, flesh pressed against flesh. One body as carnal as the other was wholesome. One as white as warm cream, and the other the color of nutmeg and oiled, glistening in the smoky yellow light rising from the candles on the floor.

A rush of hot breath escaped the *bukko*'s lips, and fearing detection, he sank back out of sight into the stairwell. He was panting, and shaking his head, not in shame, but in wonder. The vision was chaotic. It confounded love and desire, and simultaneously unleashed disorder and order, and virtue and vice. It humbled him, and made him feel suddenly impotent, not as a man, but as a *bukko*. Never in all his days could his imagination have set two such extraordinary players on a stage. So, telling himself it was his professional duty to examine the vision in detail in order to instruct himself for further use, he again peered around the corner.

Robin stood perfectly still as the sorceress's voluptuous white body pressed against hers, and waves of heat appeared to unfold within the girl's flesh, like a flowering bud with petals a dozen shades of red.

Cobra slid her red-nailed hands over the girl's shoulders and down her back, pressing their breasts together.

Robin's hair had been dyed a reddish black, and oiled ringlets trembled about her flushed face, clinging wetly to cheeks and neck. Two buzzard feathers, tied with a thong to her hair, dangled rakishly beside one ear. A thick line of black kohl rimmed her large eyes, giving them a harsh, brazen quality the girl could not have managed on her own, and a scarlet arrow was painted on her forehead. It pointed down at her small nose, and its angularity had a touch of cruelty.

Brown John, using the cuff of his sleeve, dabbed at the sweat dripping off his face, and his eyes marveled at the sorceress's skill. Robin already seemed more accessible than he had ever seen her before, and the access was not to her heart, but to her flesh. It stirred him shamefully, but he did not turn away, and his eyes took in the whole room.

His chests were all open, and costumes of all description littered the floor. Some had been torn apart, others had obviously been discarded and were piled in the corners. A small firepot burned under a flask on the table which was littered with pastes, berries, herbs, the cadaver of a large featherless bird, jars of animal fat and a small leaden vial with a lead stopper which he did not recall seeing before.

Suddenly the girl pushed away from Cobra and stepped back, gasping for breath and trembling. Her body was flushed from ankle to forehead, and her eyes smoked with inner heat.

"Good," Cobra purred, "you begin to feel it."

Brown John unconsciously nodded agreement. He also felt it, and his eyes wandered over Cobra's naked curves. There was an ease and luxury to the serpent woman. Her breasts were pillowy, her belly a

soft bed, and her hips luxurious divans. Every part of
her suggested a place to lie down, but not to sleep. A
little bit more of that kind of thinking, and again he
had to look away.

When he looked back, Cobra had put her cloak
back on and squatted in front of Robin. She held a
jar of rouge in one hand. Dipping the tip of a small
finger in the paste, she used it as a brush and
carefully began to draw on the girl's inner thigh.

Brown John, suddenly ashamed and sweating profusely, withdrew his head. He took a deep breath and
started back up the stairs, moving silently. Behind
him, the voices came again, Robin's first.

"What dance will I perform?"

"One of the oldest, butterfly. The dance the
whores use to ward off the poxes and plagues of lust
common to their profession. It is called the Fire
Ceremony. I can teach it to you in no time."

"But will Brown John know it? He'll have to play
the drums."

The *bukko*, exhausted and wet and scowling,
stopped at the top of the stairs. Cobra's sarcastic
chuckle came first, then her voice.

"The bukko, child, knows a great deal more than
he chooses to tell innocent young girls like yourself. I
have no doubt that he knows the Fire Ceremony as
well as if he had invented it himself."

The pair laughed together at that, and Brown John
nodded agreement, crossing to the ladder. He put a
foot on the first rung and hesitated, listening to the
compelling rattle and shake of the wagon and the
thundering hooves. They all sang the same song, the
song of the open road. He was once again plunging
into the unknown, and realizing it, he grinned,
asking himself questions. What secrets was Cobra
withholding? Why was she so desperate to make
certain Robin's motives were so pure and virtuous?

What did she know about the sacred jewels that she wasn't telling them? And why was he allowing her to put Robin in danger? Did he truly believe the sacred jewels were worth risking her safety? Or were the jewels already enchanting him, filling his mind with wishful thinking and making him act like a foolish old man?

By the time he reached the roof, he was laughing quietly at himself. But when he saw a clearing up ahead amid tall pines, Upper Small where Robin would dance, he stopped short.

Twenty

UPPER SMALL

Cobra waited for her cue at the side of the wagon with Gath, spear in hand, standing beside her. Their bodies were enveloped in black cloaks and the blacker night, only the alert whites of their eyes showing as they watched Brown John start the performance.

The *bukko* stood between the wagon and a long, low campfire, juggling five flaming torches. Robin, covered by a long black cloak, and Jakar stood behind the *bukko* banging tambourines. He tossed one of the torches high into the air; it revolved brightly against the backdrop of towering trees surrounding the clearing, then lost force against the indigo sky and fell with a rush of light back into his hand, as nimbly as if it were attached with an elastic string.

The audience, gathered on the ground beyond the campfire, exhaled with pleasure, the orange firelight flickering on the booted legs, gnarled knees and brutish faces of those in the front rows. The bulk of the small crowd was lost in the receding darkness, except for an occasional glitter on the tip of spear or helmet. Not ten paces beyond the gathering, tall pines marked the edge of the clearing, and within the trees several small fires glowed, illuminating tethered horses and a pair of wagons.

Cobra, growing impatient, edged forward, sniffing the stench of male sweat, rank hair, leather, metal and horses coming from the audience. The scent of burning stone was mixed in them, and she whispered, "They're here."

"Where?" murmured Gath, and she lifted empty hands, not knowing.

When Brown John finished juggling, the crowd roared, and he took a long drink from a jar, making his cheeks balloon comically, then moved around the campfire to the audience. Suddenly he blew fluid from his mouth, simultaneously setting it on fire with a torch, and flames spewed over startled faces. Several men howled and cursed gruffly, much to the amusement of the others, and Brown John moved nimbly along the front of the audience blowing more flames at the laughing, cringing bodies, illuminating them.

They belonged to outlaw warriors and mercenaries, hardened roughs who were no doubt on their way to the endless civil wars that plagued the Atalan Outlands in the north. Many were young, with eager faces looking forward to their first battle and first foreign whore. Others had had plenty of both, and it

showed. Cruel scars laced cheeks and shoulders, and
eyes were drunk with wine and lust. Several camp
followers could be seen among the men, big-boned,
hardy women with small hope in their eyes and the
stains of food and men on their tattered tunics. At
the back, apart from the others, sat the five bald
riders who had followed the wagon earlier in the day.
When the *bukko*'s flames lighted their bodies, their
rashes showed brightly on faces and arms.

Cobra and Gath shared a sober glance and
watched Brown John set fire to three small stacks of
logs which had been placed about five feet from one
another. The wood quickly erupted with flames,
casting light throughout the small audience, and it
grunted with expectation, gathering around the fires.

When Brown John joined Robin and Jakar and the
three began to play a new tune, Cobra turned to Gath
and whispered, "Watch me closely."

He nodded, and she strode slowly out of the
shadows, drawing sounds of lewd expectations from
the audience. With haughty, deliberate movements
she took a position in front of the fire and withdrew a
tambourine, began to beat it lightly against a thigh,
her eyes holding her audience captive. Long black
hair framed the cool oval of her face, and her body
was an undefinable blackness against the firelight.
Carnal. Mysterious.

The crowd leaned forward, lowering big, meaty
faces toward her, and the sounds of scratching and
guttural anticipation mixed with the sounds of cricket and hoot owl.

Cobra tossed her shoulders, and her robe puddled
at her feet.

She wore a soldier's leather jerkin and a skirt of
leather thongs. The garments were black and rent
with ragged holes made by arrow, spear and fire.
Showing through the openings was creamy perfect

flesh trying vainly to hide itself, and the mercenaries' eyes widened.

With her hips grinding teasingly to the tune of tambourine and drum, she advanced into the audience, stepping through rawboned thighs, armored chests and rough hands. Her eyes boldly met their leering eyes and shamelessly explored their muscular necks, ears and shoulders, as if flirting, but actually hunting for scales, bits of unnatural fur or pointed ears.

A tremor of suspicion made her stomach churn as her smile came to rest on a squat, hairy freebooter, and she coyly lifted his lank hair away from his ear to see if it was pointed, and ran a finger inside his mouth to find if the tongue was forked. They were not. Nearing the first small fire, she pushed another soldier off balance to see if he sat on a tail, but he did not.

She twirled slowly around the first fire, and the *bukko*'s drum picked up the tempo. Faster she twirled, and her skirt lifted, exposing long curved legs. The men grunted with pleasure, and she spun wildly over the fire, lowering her dark crotch toward the flames in the cleansing ritual of the whore. The fire licked at her, and its light probed among the holes of her rent garment, illuminating the underside of a full breast, the curve of hip, arched throat and crooning lips.

Cobra danced over all three fires, inspecting each member of the audience, including the five bald riders. None of them showed any overt sign of being demon spawn, and her stomach churned nervously. There was only one way left for her to search deeper, and despite her shame, she decided to use it.

She picked out one of the largest louts, a big heavy-set brute missing one ear and wearing the cocky snarl of the braggart soldier. She extended her

booted foot toward him, implying that he could
undress it. The lout did not understand, but his
friends quickly explained it to him. Profoundly
flattered, he laughed with bravado and took hold of
the boot lovingly. Hand over hand, he slowly forced
it off and, with his leering eyes held captive by
Cobra's wicked smile, caressed her naked foot.

The men around him suddenly howled and
cursed, drawing away and touching their totems and
groins and stomachs with superstitious gestures. The
big lout looked at them, again not understanding
what was happening, and they pointed at the foot he
held, shouting incoherently. He chuckled, and not
looking at what he was doing, bent over and kissed
the hideous emerald-green and ice-blue scales.

At their touch, he dropped her foot, pulled away
howling and fled stumbling and staggering through
the laughing, hooting men.

Cobra, beating wildly on her tambourine and
flashing her leg invitingly, twirled among the laughing men, testing them to see who might be unafraid.
But they all drew away, wanting no contact with her
blighted foot. She laughed at them, bowing, then
passed among them as they cheered and tossed coins
into a helmet she removed from one of them. Then
the music of tambourine and drum began again, and
they turned toward it.

Robin now stood behind the main fire. A short
twisted rope of dark kamala leaves dangled from the
corner of her mouth, its tip glowing and emitting a
trail of smoke that angled skyward across rouged
cheek and buzzard feathers dangling from dark red
oiled hair. Her legs were spread wide, with hips
aggressively cocked. With a fist propped on hip-
bone, she tapped her tambourine against a snapping
bottom.

The men chuckled hotly and, taking her cue, began to clap in time.

Robin's skirt barely reached her thighs, faded black rags and strings and crow feathers, and a short-sleeved leopard-skin halter held her breasts snugly. She was barefoot and brown and oiled, and glowed in the flickering firelight, the smoke drifting across her face, the perfect cosmetic for her smile. Savage. Animal. Hot.

The audience hooted and whistled approval, and Cobra, now moving silently behind the back rows, watched it with hunting eyes.

The outlaws and freebooters chuckled and poked each other, but their eyes never left the girl. The five bald riders behaved no differently, but got up and moved closer, scratching their rashes nervously.

Cobra followed them, staying in the shadows, and her breathing quickened. Nausea spilled into her stomach. She looked at Gath, saw he had edged closer to Robin, and then spotted Jakar: he now squatted on the roof of the wagon and held something out of sight in his hands, his loaded crossbow. She put her eyes back on the girl.

Robin had discarded her twist of leaves, and was twirling over the long, low campfire with her legs spread and banging her tambourine wildly. The low flames stirred, and seemed to reach for her thighs and groin. She slowly lowered her hips, her bent legs driving, and threw back her head gasping at the heat.

Drawing her knife, Cobra stopped within reach of the backs of the bald riders. They were bouncing in place, scratching furiously and clapping all at once.

Robin spun faster and faster along the campfire, losing herself to the sensual stroking of the flames, then abandoned herself to them. Sweat broke out on her upper lip. Her red mouth parted; her breasts heaved. Her hips snapped and pumped, and the flames, unable to resist her invitation, shot up around her legs booming and crackling. She danced further along the low fire, and the flames followed, striking at the sky as she passed by.

Her thighs and buttocks were marked with lightning bolts, scarabs, claw marks and numerals, 3, 9 and 33. They were cruel on her soft, smooth flesh, and the hard-bitten outlaws and freebooters stared with open mouths, transfixed. The distance between their eyes and her body had become a sacred place. Inviolate. Magic.

Cobra shot a glance at Brown John. His smile was satanic with raw joy and power, and his hands were thumping his drum, raising a sensual racket. She glanced to the side of the wagon, and her stomach knotted, her body flinched.

A red glow now showed in Gath's eyes. Did it come from the firelight, or from within?

Cobra, trembling with fear, abruptly lifted her nose, scenting a suddenly strong odor of burning stone on the night air. She sniffed about, found the odor did not come from the bald riders and, gasping in sudden panic, raced around the audience toward the wagon as the smell grew stronger and stronger.

Reaching Gath, she whispered harshly, "They're close now, but I can't see them. You've got to . . ." She cut herself off with a sharp gasp, and pointed up.

The dark silhouettes of the overhanging pines were swaying fitfully, thrashing as if weighted down with something. Suddenly a small, dark object fell out of the darkness and hit the side of the wagon with a wet smack. They both jumped back, startled. Gath wiped the black smudge off the wagon with fingertips and sniffed them. His eyes became confused, and he put his fingers under Cobra's nose. She sniffed them and drew back abruptly.

"Bats!" she gasped, then screamed.

A huge black object soared out of the night into the firelight directly above Robin. A bat the size of a well-fed border dog, and wearing gold loop earrings. The audience howled, and the bat dove, hit Robin in the shoulder and knocked her staggering back through the flames. She screamed, fell and rolled away from the fire. Her flesh was singed, and her hair and rags were smoking. She covered her head with her bare arms, and the bat raked them with its claws as it swept over her again.

Gath bolted forward, a sweeping shadow.

Outlaws and freebooters rose as a body and scrambled for their horses and wagons, knocking each other down and cursing.

The giant bat caromed into the night, squealing.

Robin half rose, looking up, and screamed again.

Three dark shapes were falling through the firelight toward her. They had small, thick bodies with long arms, hairy shoulders and pointed ears protruding from dark leather armor and helmets. Their mouths were wide with lust-mad smiles, revealing needle-sharp fangs.

Gath planted a foot and threw his spear.

It caught the first bat soldier in mid-air, and the impact drove him back the way he had come. He squealed and windmilled in the air as if climbing an invisible wall.

Simultaneously, Jakar fired.

His bolt took a bat soldier in the shoulder, but did not stop him.

The two falling bodies hit Robin with thudding blows and drove her to the ground, facedown. For a moment they seemed confused, rolling her about, uncertain whether to maul her or savage her. She kicked and flailed, and they drew serrated knives, their snarling mixing with her screaming. Then Gath arrived.

His sword removed a furry arm just beneath the shoulder. The owner howled and rolled off Robin as his arm fell to the ground beside him, its hand dropping a knife. Simultaneously, the remaining bat soldier was removed by the crunching blow of Gath's body. The pair hit the ground tangled together, and the Barbarian gathered the furry body in his hands, rolled upright and threw it down on its back. Straddling the cringing figure, he drew back a bent arm and lunged down with a howl. Gath's elbow drove the bat soldier's head three inches into the dirt and pulped its skull.

Robin screamed and rolled away, covering her face with her hands. The backs of her legs and arms were splattered with blood as if she had a pox. She screamed again as two more bat soldiers, swords in hand, landed beside her, small eyes lewd and violent above hollow cheeks. She shuddered helplessly, and Gath came off the ground, grabbed both men by a shoulder before they could react and slammed them together headfirst. They dropped their weapons, staggered dizzily, and Gath gathered them in his arms, lifting them off the ground. They screamed and flailed to no avail. Gath's arms corded and bulged as he increased the pressure, and there was a series of dull snaps deep inside their meaty chests, then a splintering crack, and each let out a screech cut short because their mouths had filled with blood.

Gath threw them aside, his body cocked and eyes hunting for the large bat.

Jakar, still on the wagon's roof, crouched with his crossbow aimed at the dark sky.

Brown John, sword in hand, stood in front of the wagon staring with dazed eyes at the carnage. Everything had happened so fast he had missed the fight entirely.

Only Cobra, shielding Robin with her body, saw the huge bat swoosh out from under the wagon. She screamed a warning, and it knocked her down, buried its claws in the leopard-skin halter covering Robin's shoulder.

Screaming with pain, Robin twisted violently, and the bat's slashing fangs missed her neck, got tangled in her hair. She flailed at it with her arms as its weight bore her down, then Cobra came off the ground and threw herself heedlessly against it. Her body collided with the bat's chest and drove the creature off of Robin onto the ground. It thrashed and squealed, clawing and biting the woman's hands, and quickly flew off.

Gath dove at it, but it escaped under the wagon.

Cobra jumped up screaming, "Kill it! Kill it!"

Gath, Jakar and Brown John spread out around the wagon, but there was no sign of the creature. It had vanished into the enveloping darkness.

Robin hid behind Gath, her hands braced against his shoulder. It pulsed and dripped blood, and she backed away from him, shuddering and whimpering, eyes wide with terror. The bat dove out of the sky into the firelight, its hurtling body aimed at her, and she screamed, turned and ran.

Gath broke for Robin as she tripped on one of the small fires and fell, twenty feet away.

Jakar, his eyes as cold as death, followed the bat's flight with his crossbow and fired.

The bolt caught the bat in the gut. It squealed, flapped wildly off course for a brief moment, then dove again, fangs aimed at the back of Robin's neck as she rose onto hands and knees.

Cobra turned as white as a glacier: the impact would break the girl's neck.

Gath, his eyes now red fire, screamed a harsh guttural howl and launched his body into the air. Robin turned in terror at the sound, presenting her terrified face to the descending fangs of the bat. They came within a foot of her shuddering cheeks, and Gath's fingers tore into the creature, ripping it off course.

Gath and the huge bat hit the dirt and rolled into one of the fires. With his back squirming against the coals, Gath fought for a better grip on the screaming, clawing demon spawn. The fire spit sparks and embers, and smoke billowed up around him, concealing his actions.

Cobra raced up, shielding Robin behind her, and Jakar and Brown John joined them.

There was a long squeal from within the smoke, then it was cut short, and the bat's head tumbled out, torn off the body at the neck. Its furry pointed ears still wore the large loop earrings, and they clanged together musically before the head came to rest, propped between them. The eyes were wide open, and told a tale of terror far greater than any the creature itself could have inspired.

Then the source of that terror emerged from the smoke, eyes hot, body singed and smoking, and wearing blood like a blanket.

Robin turned away, crushing herself into Jakar's protective arms, pleading, "Hold me. Hold me."

He held her close, speaking quietly and comfortingly. "It's all right now, fluff, it's all right." His eyes were on Gath, and they were hard with respect.

Gath looked at Cobra, questioning her with his eyes, and she said breathlessly, "It's over. There're no more. I'm sure of it."

Gath nodded, looked at Robin and saw blood trickling from a cut in her scalp, and the dark bruised slashes across the backs of her arms. He growled, whipped around like a wounded animal and struck Cobra across the face.

She went down on her back, and her body arched with pain, her mind went dark.

Brown John leapt between her and Gath, shouting, "No, Gath! Leave her alone! It's my fault. I knew what the risks were, and I agreed to let Robin take them. And she wanted to, because she had to. It was the only way."

The two men's eyes locked, and held for a long moment, then Gath looked at Robin and she nodded, agreeing with the *bukko*.

Gath hesitated, then turned back to the *bukko* and whispered harshly, "Watch yourself, old man. If Robin is hurt again, you will pay as well."

He glared at Cobra as Brown John helped her up, then turned and strode into the darkness.

Brown John sighed with relief and turned to Robin. "Are you all right, lass?"

"It's nothing," she said. "I can take care of it."

Brown John nodded, and put his eyes on Jakar. "Stay with her. Don't let her out of your sight from now on, and see she washes those signs off."

Jakar led Robin to the wagon as Brown John turned to Cobra. Her bruised cheek throbbed, and tears welled in her eyes, but she did not let them fall. She smiled helplessly at the *bukko*, sighing softly, "Thank you, bukko . . . but you do not have to lie for me."

"It was no trouble," he said lightly. "Lying is my trade."

She smiled at that, because she knew he expected it. "I think we should get away from here as fast as possible. So, if you'll excuse me, I think I better attend to myself."

"Of course," he said, "and I apologize for Gath."

"There's no need. I expected his reaction."

"Then I apologize for myself, because I didn't."
He smiled. "Next time I'll be ready."

She dipped her head in gratitude, suddenly disturbed by his probing eyes, and hurried unsteadily toward the wagon to find her rouges and mirror.

Twenty-One

GROTTO OF THE BALD VESHTA

At dawn Brown John, sitting alone in the driver's box, turned the lumbering, squealing wagon off of Hog-Scald Road onto Boot Trail, and raced it through the thinning trees into the foothills of the Barrier Mountain Range.

They were covered with tall brown grass, and clusters of boulders were scattered about like the droppings of some constipated god. In the distance rose the jagged peaks of the bald desert mountains that separated the forest basin from the endless sand dunes beyond, and the known world from the unknown.

The wagon's destination was deep within that mysterious world, at the crossroads of Boot Trail and the Way of Chains where Cobra had told the *bukko* the map was hidden.

Simultaneously trying to hold the reins and eat his morning porridge from a bowl with one hand, Brown John whipped the horses with the pole whip with the other, and shouted encouragement at them. He was delighted. His players were finally taking the stage and, being a performer, he had to let it show even though no one was watching.

Two hours later, as the wagon rolled through the hot high desert, he was doing the same thing, but without the bowl and with Cobra sharing the driver's box.

She sat in regal repose, her voluptuous body gracefully turned in the seat, and one leg tucked under her. Her hands were folded in her lap, and her black hair flagged behind the clean-cut oval of her face as she let the wind cool her.

Brown John's smiling cheeks were flushed and he was bare-chested, with the upper portion of his tunic folded down under his belt, and his pudgy belly, despite his best efforts to restrain it, tending to hang over it.

Robin and Jakar rode inside the wagon, and Gath rode well ahead of it. A massive cut of meat and bone sweating in the sunshine, his chestnut flesh was naked except for leather loincloth, sword and dagger belts, glistening brass armbands and boots. Three times he had circled back through the foothills and searched their back trail, and each time he had returned to give Brown John the same report. He had seen no travelers on the road, and no animal among the rocks or bird in the sky that could have been following them.

Their disguise was complete, and their plot at play.

The *bukko* whipped the horses energetically, back-handed the sweat from his cheeks and glanced out of the corner of his eye at Cobra.

She now wore a plain sand-colored tunic. It was worn and patched, with short sleeves and skirt consisting of wide scallops and stringy threads which flapped about her bare legs and arms. The garment was of soft cotton and belted with a faded gold sash. Its collar was square, with a deep V cut between her swelling breasts and laced with leather thongs, as were the openings in the sides of the skirt, allowing more than pleasing glimpses of her curvaceous beauty as well as ventilation.

He looked back at the road and smiled to himself. For a former Queen of Serpents whose nature was undoubtedly still tainted by demon seed, if not corrupted by it, she looked not only surprisingly human and womanly but tempting. He rolled his head and shoulders to get the kinks out, thus allowing himself another peak at her bosom, and watched her breasts tussle and bounce. He had seen thousands of lovely bosoms, and not casually, but as a professional. He had examined them with care, measured and dressed and undressed them, and handled them on stage when the scene called for it. He had seen larger, higher, firmer breasts, but none so amazing to him. They seemed to have lives of their own. They continually tried to squeeze past the restraining leather thongs, or spill over the top of her bodice, and his palms itched to catch them.

Her head turned slowly, and her eyes looked at him, as a corner of her mouth lifted with a reserved smile. It said she understood his thoughts and did not mind. This sent a tremor of pleasure through the *bukko* that was tenfold greater than that which his hands had hoped to hold.

Chuckling to hide his reaction, Brown John said, "You are no normal adversary, woman. I keep forgetting I should be afraid of you."

"Good," she said lightly, "then perhaps we can not only share the same trail out of necessity, but as friends?"

He laughed. "You are dangerous, aren't you?"

"You flatter me," she said, "and I thank you. But it will gain you no advantage." Her smile lifted both corners of her inviting mouth, saying clearly that she did, however, have an exploitable weakness if he was interested.

Brown John chuckled and said, "Keep talking."

She laughed with delight, then in a level tone, said, "Despite what you say, I know you are not afraid of me. Neither of what I was or what I am. I like that." The reserved smile returned. "Men without fear have been few and far between in my life, therefore I am vulnerable to them." She grinned. "There, now you do have the advantage."

"Now you are really dangerous," he said.

Cobra laughed an easy relaxed laugh and said, "You, bukko, are neither a normal adversary nor an ordinary man. So, I will leave the choice to you. We can be adversaries or friends . . . I will enjoy either one."

Brown John, liking her reply a good deal more than he thought he should, said, "Maybe we better talk about the weather."

She laughed out loud, then sobered and put her gold eyes on his brown, saying, "Before we do that, I must warn you about this map. Once we reach the grotto and find it, I think it would be wisest if only I or the girl handles it."

His eyes became thoughtful, questioning her, but he saw only genuine concern in her eyes. "Perhaps you had better tell me about it."

"I will tell you all I know," she said candidly, "and I believe it is all that is known." She indicated the distant mountains. "At the crossroads of Boot Trail and the Way of Chains, there is a brothel called the Grotto of the Bald Veshta. Are you familiar with it?"

He nodded. "It was a soldiers' brothel when I was there. But that was over twenty years ago."

"It is still a soldiers' brothel," she said, "but long ago it was a sacred shrine to Black Veshta, who the local tribes call Bald Veshta. That's when the map was hidden there."

"It's been there all this time?"

"Yes. It's a small image of Black Veshta sculpted from dark stone and laden with magic. It's taboo. That's why it's not been touched. Black Veshta has forbidden any man to so much as put a finger on it, and promised to take cruel vengeance on any who do."

"So you think I shouldn't touch it," Brown John asked, with one frousy white eyebrow arching, "so I won't become contaminated?"

"It would seem to be prudent," she said with a chuckle, "since you would risk having your yang shrivel up and fall off if you do."

He laughed and said, "Blaughh! If I'm not afraid to put my hands on the jewels of the White Veshta, the Goddess of Light herself, then I am surely not going to hesitate when it comes to a puny little icon of a false bitch like Black Veshta."

"Your mind is set then?"

He nodded his frazzled white head.

"Then I will not argue the point further," she purred thoughtfully. "But I would have thought that a man of your profession, sensitivities and desires would have a greater respect for the deity which reigns over the glamour and passion of women."

"Oh, I have great respect," Brown John chuckled, "and admiration. Even adoration! But not for any goddess. It's the women I love, every last one of them. I find them all absolutely fascinating . . . and each and every one, in her own way, beautiful." He chuckled again and looked at her admiringly. "And my present company, despite her unnatural lineage, is no exception."

She shook her head with amused cynicism and said, "Bukko, you surely cut your dreams from bright cloth."

When the wagon pulled up at the crossroads, the sun was starting down the backside of the sky. Gath tethered his stallion to the wagon, then he and the *bukko* crossed the open clearing toward the brothel as Cobra, Robin and Jakar waited with the wagon.

Boot Trail, the Way of Chains and assorted footpaths and trails moved away from the clearing like crippled spokes of a wheel. The grotto, a series of caves pockmarking a wedgelike cliff of black rock, formed the hub. A wagon and several horses were tethered to a railing at the base of the grotto. A rough-hewn ladder rose to the first cave, where a guard sat with his legs straddling the ledge. Behind him rose a crude log building fronting the largest cave. Raucous laughter, the jangle of tambourines and the smell of musk and jasmine mixed with sweat drifted from it. Above the structure and to the sides, ladders led to higher caves, the highest being the one Cobra said held the map. There was no sign of guards near it.

Gath and the *bukko* climbed the entrance ladder, moved inside the log building and found what they expected to find.

Mercenaries sat at benches drinking wine, fondling their whores and haggling over the price of both. They were mostly spearmen and slingers, fodder which a warlord could feed cheaply to a civil war. At one table sat long-haired men in bits of armor. Recruiting captains. They were doing the laughing, as well as their share of the drinking, fondling and arguing. The whores were naked except for a sheen of perfumed oil and scraps of colored beads or sash. Among them was not one hair to cover head, armpits or groin.

Gath and Brown John sat down at an empty bench and did what everyone else was doing until everyone else was used to seeing them do it and stopped looking at them. Then they drifted through the back of the cave and up through the interior tunnels to the upper caves, giving the appearance that they were shopping among the girls lolling in the cribs dug out of the rock walls.

Reaching the next to highest cave, Gath sat on a rock and began to exchange stories with the three old whores relegated to this natural back room, while the *bukko* covertly climbed up the ladder and vanished inside the highest cave.

It was designed in the manner of all caves, carved and decorated by water and wind, about seven feet wide, thirty feet deep. A shaft of sunlight, passing through a hole cut through the rock ceiling, illuminated a black figurine standing on a small cleft carved out of the back wall.

Brown John smiled a smile that could not have been tamed with a stick, and cautiously looked back the way he had come. No sight or noise indicated he had been seen. He moved into the depths of the cave. There were many holes in the ceiling so that light, regardless of the sun's course across the sky, would illuminate the icon at regular intervals and awe superstitious visitors.

Reaching the figurine, he saw it was only slightly taller than his forearm was long, and covered with dust. The body was trim but voluptuous, and stood upright, knee-deep in a sandlike cone which spread out in waves to form the base. The arms were thrown back, and neck and back were arched so that the pelvis thrust forward, provocatively presenting the triangular temple of flesh for which the grotto was named. It was bald, as was the oval head.

Chuckling, and with the reckless glint in his eyes dancing, Brown John thrust a pudgy hand through the cascading sunlight and picked up the statuette. Holding it to his face, he examined its markings. There were tiny inscriptions in an ancient sign language, and carefully sculpted strings of beads draped over neck, breasts and belly. There was no doubt that they indicated trails, just as lines did on a map.

He laughed out loud, stopped short and quickly crept back to the front of the cave. Again there was no indication he had been detected. He stepped back into the concealment of the cave, thumbed the dust off of the figurine's breasts, and his smile once more roughed up his face, kicking his mouth wide and punching holes so deep in his cheeks that they ballooned.

Sounds of tinkling, flirtatious laughter came from within the cave, and he turned sharply, hiding the icon behind him. The sounds rose, filling the cave, but there was no one else in it. A wary shiver shot through him, but then he relaxed, telling himself that the sounds were coming from the cave directly below, and that in his eagerness he had simply not noticed them before. Then new sounds joined the laughter, a rising moaning and sighing, and the gasping of sexual pleasure. The sounds intensified, and he became aroused, began to perspire.

He held the icon at arm's length, suddenly afraid of its contamination, but unwilling to let go of it. The sounds continued to rise, then became vague and inarticulate, and he became hesitant, averting his head from the figure and peeking at it with one eye.

The black body was warm in his hand. It felt pliant, then alive, and his fingers relaxed, allowing the doll to squirm and turn, hiding itself modestly within his grasp.

He shook his head hard and blinked his eyes, trying to clear his mind and vision. He drew the icon closer, to see if it had truly come alive, but it hid within his pudgy fingers. He tried to unfold them, but did not have the strength or will. His eyelids grew heavy and slowly closed, as if relaxed in sleep.

There was only darkness in his mind, and his thoughts fled back through it to younger times, names passing by, names with laughing faces. Naso the rubber man, Dulcia the harpest, Podoo the dwarf, and Leto, Balmara, Connie and Lale. They were times of feathers and dancing, good times born of endless spaces and the open road, of yesterdays filled with tomorrows.

Slowly the faces faded, giving way to blistering sunshine which spilled out of the sky like warm syrup onto a field of tall brown grass. His mind's eye saw a small boy peering through the waving tips, a short stout boy of eleven with brown eyes. He scurried through the grass hiding himself, then stopped, raised up slightly and saw a girl of perhaps seventeen or eighteen moving through the grass some thirty feet away. She was running lazily, her arms outstretched, with her fingertips brushing the tips of the grass as she streamed past. Her raven-black hair was long and waving behind her in the glory of the golden sunlight, and her laughter was so light it weighed less than the air. Staying hidden, the lad followed her through the grass, then along a brook, trying to get a glimpse of her face, but could not. He ran faster, reaching the village before she did, and tried to casually intercept her. But he could not find her. Then, as he was about to give up and go home, he saw her standing in front of a large, brightly painted wagon with tall yellow wheels. She was talking to an old man and a dwarf, both of whom wore soiled tunics with large colored patches. He moved toward the wagon, trying to see her face, and just as it was about to come into view, she turned away and entered the wagon, closing the door behind her.

The boy waited until dusk, but she did not come out, so he raced home. But he was late for supper, so his father sent him to bed without his meat or milk. For a long time he stayed awake in the loft listening to the night, and was still awake when all others in the house slept. There was an ache in his heart and a trembling in his cheeks. He was thinking of the girl, and he could think of nothing else. She made him feel as he had never felt before, as if all things were now possible, and he was certain his small body was not nearly large enough to house the dreams of wonder and adventure that now soared within it. Later, he did sleep, and in his dreams he stormed castle walls, swung from vines and galloped to the rescue of a faceless dark-haired girl. The glory of her overwhelmed him, and when he came awake, he found himself crying and sobbing with such happiness that he had to hide his head under his pillow so that his parents would not hear.

The next day he returned to the place where the wagon had been parked. It was not there, and no one knew where it had gone, or if it would ever return. The boy fled back to the field of tall brown grass and hid there the rest of the day, alternately sobbing and dreaming, and certain he would never see her again.

Brown John came awake with a start, and found himself clutching the icon to his chest. He was still in the cave, and the sun still streamed down through the same hole, but he felt as if he had slept through a long night. He took a deep shuddering breath and looked down at the black doll far more carefully than he had earlier.

It appeared more normal now, just a crudely sculpted lump of black rock that was supposed to represent a strikingly good-looking goddess, but in actuality looked like nothing more than an over-weight, bald savage.

He chuckled, then in a gruff manly voice, said to the doll, "Behave, woman, I'm doing you a favor," and stuffed it inside his tunic.

It was dusk when Gath caught up with the wagon as it rolled west along the Way of Chains. Seeing him approach, Brown John reined up, halting the vehicle on the narrow cliffside trail. Cobra, sitting beside the *bukko*, turned in her seat to greet the Barbarian, and Robin and Jakar got out of the wagon.

Gath reined up on Cobra's side of the wagon and spoke to the *bukko*.

"Nobody has missed it! We are not followed."

The group expressed relief, and Brown John grinned with triumph at Cobra. "You see, Black Veshta has not been offended by my touch. In fact, I think she likes it."

Cobra smiled reservedly, and Gath, in a harsh impatient tone, asked, "Is it truly the map? Can you read it?"

"Indeed it is," said Brown John, grinning approval at Cobra. "She's gone over it carefully with me." He removed the black statuette from his tunic and pointed at a spot on the conelike base. "When we reach the end of the Way of Chains, we should be approximately here. Then we move northwest over dunes." His finger followed a line winding over the cone's undulating surface to the knees emerging from it. "Somewhere here, we'll find the river called Staboulle. It may have changed its course slightly, but we'll find it soon enough. Then we travel along the river, directly west." His finger rode up the depression between the icon's legs to the groin, and tapped the pubic region. "There, at the junction of the two rivers, is a caravansary, En Sakalda." His finger wandered over the belly. "From there, we take the Way of the Scorpion across a wilderness of lava beds called the Belly of Black Veshta until we come to a mountain range, the Breasts of Black Veshta, then take the pass between them." His finger slid between the cleavage to the throat. "About here we'll reach the Inland Sea, and the giant rock which supports Pyram."

Gath nodded his satisfaction and put his hard eyes on Cobra. The color promptly drained from her face, and she pulled away from him. His hand grabbed her by the upper arm and dragged her struggling and protesting out of the driver's box, threw her to the ground. She landed in an awkward sprawl, grunting painfully. Her body instinctively tried to rise, but her head sagged dizzily against the earth, blood draining from temple and lip.

The *bukko* leapt up in the box, shouting, "What

are you doing?" Jakar and Robin, startled and alarmed, moved to help Cobra, but Gath's glare stopped them.

"Get back in the wagon," he said, and turned to Brown John. "You ride ahead, I'll catch up."

"Hold on a moment!" Brown John blurted. "Let's not be hasty, Gath." He scrambled down from the driver's box and kneeled over Cobra, his hands cradling her heaving body. Then he looked up at Gath and added, "We still need her. She's the only one who can read the map, and we still need to know the distances and turns in the trail."

"We'll find a native to do that!"

"Perhaps, in time, we could. But it could cause delays, and since she's been tremendously helpful, and given us no indication that she can't be trusted, I think she deserves to be allowed to continue with us. Besides, we gave our word."

"Yes," said Robin, pushing forward.

Gath did not look at her. He said coldly, "She's a serpent. When it suits her, she will betray us."

He dismounted, and Brown John said, "Your point is well taken, friend, but it is also my point. Her nature can also be an asset to us. She has walked the very corridors of evil we seek to penetrate, she has looked upon the secrets within their shadows, and she knows their mysteries, the natures of Pyram's demon spawn, their disguises, forms, powers. We are going to need her help to find where the jewels are held. Besides, we have no time to find someone who can read the map."

Gath's eyes became wary.

Brown John held up the black doll. "According to this map, it could be, not four or five days, but eight or nine before we see the castle's walls. That means you'll have to control the hungers that headpiece has planted inside you twice as long as you thought."

"Do not worry about me, bukko."

"On the contrary, I must worry about everything."

Cobra half rose, and Brown John helped her to her feet. She straightened slightly and looked up under her arched eyes at Gath, blood spidering over her cheek. It was a more than appropriate cosmetic for the expression on her face. When she spoke, her voice was low and controlled.

"If you are going to kill me, Dark One, I suggest you use your hands. It will give the helmet far more pleasure . . . and give you an idea of how it will feel when the helmet's hungers overwhelm your pride and you put them around Robin's neck."

Robin gasped sharply and withdrew behind Jakar's shoulder, her eyes on Gath.

Gath again took no notice and said to Brown John, "You are growing soft, friend. A month ago, she would have killed us all if she'd had the chance."

"I agree," Brown John said evenly, "but she's changed. She's human now, just like the rest of us." His eyes held Gath's, refusing to release them. "Listen to me, friend. There is more to this quest than you or I understand. There are hidden powers at play, and if they have brought us this far, it would be madness to alter the cast now. Utter folly."

Gath stared coldly at Brown John for a moment, then nodded reluctantly. "I cannot follow your fancy twaddle, old friend, but if you believe it, I will accept that and allow her to live . . . under one condition." He removed a chain from his saddlebags and handed it to Brown John. "Keep her chained to your belt, night and day, or she dies."

Sometime later, as the wagon rolled down the western side of the mountains, the sand dunes came into view. Beyond them the sun was setting, flooding

the sky with sweeping blankets of oranges and pinks.
Cobra, sitting beside Brown John in the driver's box,
stared silently ahead, her beautiful face thrust regally
into the dying light. A chain was attached to the belt
spanning her narrow waist. It wound down over her
fleshly thigh and across the seat to an iron loop on
Brown John's belt. Her fingers fondled it idly as she
spoke over the steady din of hoofbeats and rumbling
wheels.

"You have a rare gift of twaddle, old man. I have
never heard such eloquent lies spoken with such
conviction."

"Are you sure they were lies?" he asked behind a
raised brow.

She smiled. "Whatever they were, your words
saved my life, and I would like to thank you for
them. But as I am no longer a queen, I have nothing
of value to reward you with. And as it has been a
very long time since I was a mere woman, I am not at
all certain of what you might enjoy . . . or expect."

Brown John looked at her, and she turned her
warm knowing eyes on him. "Perhaps, to maintain
our disguises as low, rude traveling players, I should
vulgarly offer you my body. It would be a cheap
enough payment."

He chuckled with delight and said, "That would
indeed be a generous offer, but there is no need to
even consider rewarding me. I expect nothing."

"I thought as much," she said in a tone implying
she was greatly disappointed, and the flattery of it
made his cheeks flush.

After a moment, he said, "I'm sorry he treated you
so roughly. There was no call for it."

"Do not be sorry," she said offhandedly. "As I told
you before, I expect as much . . . and I would not
have him any other way. He is a warrior. One more

death, more or less, is of small import to him. And . . . perhaps he is right, perhaps you should have killed me."

Brown John looked at her, and she looked off at the sunset, as if it marked the ends of the world. "This being a mere woman is strange and frightening to me, and I do not trust myself." She lifted the chain for him to see it. "You are wise to chain me, but I am sorry it is you who have to watch over me. I will try not to be a burden to you."

He shrugged and put his eyes back on the road. She waited until he looked back at her, then scolded him with her eyes. "I warned you not to touch it, but you would not listen. And now you are anchored with a woman, night and day, for how long, only Black Veshta knows." She laughed easily. "You are cursed, Brown, but it is your own fault."

He chuckled, then said, "That all depends on your point of view."

There were enough double meanings in his tone for a bedroom farce, and she turned away smiling her reserved smile so he could easily see it as he joyously whipped the horses forward.

Twenty-two

SPITFIRE

Tiyy stood waiting in the darkness of Pyram's underground tide pool. Behind her, at the far end of the entry passageway, faint red torchlight glowed, silhouetting her body, a furry black shadow crowned with a pyramid of wild, spiked hair. At the center of the pyramid, the whites of her eyes were thin almonds, as quarrelsome as hissing cats.

It was the hour before dawn, and the waves crashed and thundered unseen in the darkness, spilling into the pool. Vague bits of guttering torchlight graced spears of white foaming water, momentarily reflecting on a group of the Nymph Queen's household guards lined up at the back of the ledge. Their foppish scarlet uniforms had been replaced with buckskin and steel, and their weapons were no longer decorated. Huge, muscled, handsome louts with biceps for brains, she had handpicked them earlier that night and magically altered them into obedient weapons of flesh and bone.

When the water subsided, Tiyy removed a slim hand from her robe and beckoned with a finger at the orange glow behind her. The faltering sounds of sandals slapping the floor came from the far end of the passage, as someone started toward her, and she moved to the edge of the ledge, knowing even in the darkness exactly where it was. Cold water splashed over her sandaled feet, and the wet cold air made her cheeks tingle. She breathed deep, loving it, and parted her furs slightly so the air could stroke her throat and breasts and belly.

Across the pool, fog crept through the tunnel that linked the pool to the Inland Sea. It was banked just above the churning sea water, and within its formless tumbling body there was the grey glow of day's first light. The mist moved cautiously, like the fingers of a blind man exploring the face of a stranger, then suddenly burst forward as sea water filled the tunnel behind it. There was a flash of total darkness, then the light brightened and speared through a wave of green water laced with foam, and the huge white barrel of Baskt's body erupted from the face of the wave. Both water and fish arched out through the darkness above the pool, and crashed thunderously into it, sending geysers of water to the far corners of the shadowed cave.

Darkness again filled the tide pool, and the water quieted. The sound of slapping sandals stopped beside Tiyy, and she felt Schraak's small body brush against her fur. He was shifting with fear and uncertainty, and the white almonds of her eyes thinned with a smile.

After Schraak and Baskt had returned to Pyram with the bodies of the Grillard dancing girls, the aging Nymph Queen had commanded them to stay out of her sight until she returned from her laboratory. At that time she would send for them, and either reward them for their success or punish them for their failure. She had then closted herself in her laboratory, put on the sacred vestments of the high priestess of Black Veshta and consulted the secret sacerdotal writings of the ancients. When the formulas were selected and the priests had prepared the required rites, she had then transformed the girls' meat and bone and blood into salves that could be administered to her flesh, and potions that could feed her body and soul. Three days she had spent underground, and now she had summoned her two lords to give them what was due them. But the darkness hid her from their view, and they still had no idea of whether they had succeeded or failed.

Feeling kittenish, she stood silent in the darkness for a long moment, toying with them as if they were mice. Then she said sharply, "Now!"

Her word echoed around the cave, and the sounds of grunting men came from the darkness nearby, then the squeal of wood on wood, and she hummed with pleasure. Her guards were pulling the locking peg from the winch. There was a sudden clatter of chains, and the thud of counterweights bumping inside rock walls, then the squeal and rattle of the winch unwinding and a heavy iron door lowering somewhere inside the cave.

Schraak shivered at the sound, touching her furs, and she slapped his hands away, drawing a strangled whimper.

The rush of sea water momentarily subsided, and fog again entered, bringing the vague daylight. The mist now swirled through the grilles of an iron gate that was slowly descending from the roof of the sea tunnel to seal it off.

Schraak shrieked and fell to the floor with his forehead pressed against the wet stone. "Forgive me, great one! Forgive me," he whimpered.

Simultaneously, Baskt swirled violently within the confining pool and dove toward the sea tunnel. There was still a small opening below the descending gate offering escape. A wave crashed through the tunnel, and the shark plunged into it. There was a thudding crunch of meat and cartilage ramming rock and iron, and the cave shook, dust and pebbles falling away from the ceiling to drop noisily into the pool.

Tiyy chuckled with moody pleasure. The waves had subsided again, and the wan daylight revealed Baskt once more circling in the confining tide pool. His pointed grey snout was washed with blood, and serrated teeth dangled from his lip. He slashed one way and then the other, then dove deep and circled. A rusty iron grille door now sealed off the hole at the bottom of the pool. He bumped into it again and again, still seeking escape, then thrust upward. He burst up out of the water in front of Tiyy with his massive jaws spread wide. But she was out of reach, and he dropped back into the pool, splashing geysers of water to the ceiling.

Tiyy lifted a hand, gave a command with fluttering fingers, and long orchid nails glittered at the ends of smooth brown fingers.

The rumbling sounds of heavy iron wheelbarrows came from within the entry passage, grew louder quickly, and Tiyy crossed like a shadow to the far end of the ledge with the small smooth man crawling after her. There she stood waiting in the blackest shadow.

Slowly, almost imperceptibly, a glimmer of orange light adorned her face, warming the whites of heavy-lidded sloping eyes, caressing florid pink cheeks and blood-red lips.

The light came from the entry passageway where a deep red glow grew brighter and brighter as the rumbling of the wheelbarrows grew louder and louder. Then the first barrow appeared, a crude rectangular bowl supported by one iron wheel and propelled by a squat hooded slave. His arms were as thick as young oaks and as long as full-grown legs. Heaped in the wheelbarrow were glowing red-hot stones.

The slave dumped the rocks into the pool without

ceremony. They hissed and spit and splashed, and
Baskt fled for the opposite side.

Schraak lifted his face off the ground, using both
hands to smear the slime away from his small beady
eyes, and stared in shocked terror.

Wheelbarrow after wheelbarrow of hot stones was
dumped into the pool until a hot light was cast
throughout the cave and steam loomed like a cloud
on the ceiling.

Trembling, Schraak rose slightly and looked up
over a slick grey shoulder at the Nymph Queen. He
gasped in shock, and a smile jerked on his mushy
pockmarked face. It had a slightly mad leer, and he
laughed in giddy disbelief.

Tiyy, with deliberation, was looking directly at
Schraak, giving him a full view of her face.

The flesh on her broad forehead, and on the firm
balls of her cheeks and small pointed chin, was
brown and smooth and unblemished. There was not
a wrinkle at the corner of either eye, nor did one
crease her full lips. Her rouges were gaudy and thick,
and her bilious yellow hair was luxurious. It stood
straight out from her head in pomaded spikes forming a striking pyramid. Her eyes were a vivid white
and pearly grey. Hostile. Quarrelsome. Playful. The
eyes of a vixen spitfire not yet out of her teens.

"Holy Yang!" Schraak gasped, and again laughed
madly.

She said, "You are brave to laugh," but her eyes
said something else.

Schraak did not notice. "I hardly recognized you,"
he said. "It is a miracle. You . . . you're the Mother
of Desire herself! A goddess! Black Veshta incarnate!" He laughed out of control.

"Stop chortling, worm," she said irritably, "and
watch your friend. The surprises have only begun."

Schraak stopped short at her tone and looked back

at the tide pool. He shuddered so fitfully, he lost his footing and dropped back to all fours.

The sea water above the glowing stones had begun to churn and simmer, then small bubbles exploded on the pool's surface as it began to boil. Baskt was thrashing on the far side, diving for the cool depths, a constant blur of white movement. The boiling became more intense, great bubbles of air exploding on the surface beside the ledge, then spreading throughout the pool.

Again and again the great shark threw his body up out of the water for relief, jaws agape. But there was no escape. His white barrel began to darken, and his teeth dropped from his softening gums. Slowly he rolled over to float belly-up, still thrashing feebly.

Schraak, his teeth chattering, looked up at the Nymph Queen in dumb confusion.

She considered him a moment and parted her fur robe, revealing the trim, tight-skinned body of a voluptuous girl. Except for a girdle of silver chain mail and diamonds, and the short paddle-shaped pendant dangling from it, she was naked. She was still small with short arms, but as pliant as new grass and as round as a dowel. Her breasts were firm balls of flesh as quarrelsome as her eyes. Her belly was flat and hard, descending to swelling hips slightly wider than her narrow shoulders, and her legs were luscious invitations to all that rose above them. Barefoot, brown and dangerous.

Schraak stammered, "I . . . I don't understand! Why . . . why do you torture him? Your infallible flesh is perfection."

"Because he failed!" she snapped peevishly. "What you are now privileged to ogle is the result of my hard labor, not of his! And not yours, you worthless worm! The girl was not among those you delivered to me!"

"But . . . but your wrinkles. They're gone."

"Be still," she said crossly. "That is only because of a lucky accident, and my unusual skills. Whoever the bukko was who selected the Grillard dancing girls, he had an unusual gift of sight. Their beauty and spirit were terribly strong, and fortunately suited to my own. Brazen, vulgar, sensual," her voice tittered, "and shameless. I was able to extract their Kaas from their blood and meat, and use it to restore my beauty, as well as some of my strength. But it is not permanent! It won't last me the year! And it took days of endless labor! Torturous hours of sweating over cooking flasks and stinking potions! None of which would have been necessary if you had delivered the right girl."

Schraak's wide mouth fell open, and his thin pink tongue lolled around inside like a frightened pet.

"Yes," she said as nastily as possible, "you should be afraid. The girl not only got away, but now she knows we hunt her. She will hide now, and make it a thousand times more difficult to find her."

Schraak dropped back facedown to the floor and shuddered.

"Acck! Stop that. It's no use. No use at all." She allowed herself to calm down a little, watching the shark suffer some more, then spoke in a low, husky register.

"I still must have the girl, Schraak. If she is not found, I will not have the power required to fashion a new altar for our Dark Lord . . . and he will be silenced forever."

"Nooooo!"

She nodded. "Yes, and you are as responsible for that tragic possibility as Lord Baskt. Consequently you will receive equal punishment."

Schraak screamed, jumped up and raced toward the entry passageway. But two guards snapped him up and brutally strapped his thrashing body into a tiny chair attached to a long heavy pole. Feeding the pole out over the boiling sea water like a giant ladle, they dipped him, screaming and squirming, down through the rising steam into the bubbling sea water.

Tiyy watched them do this nine times, then ordered the punishment ended. The giant ladle was removed, and Schraak's unconscious body was unstrapped and laid out on the ledge. Then a huge net was thrown around the nearly lifeless shark, and he was hauled out of the water. His flesh, like Schraak's, was cooked and peeling away, like boiled beef.

Tiyy looked at the pair with small satisfaction. This was only the beginning of the pain they would have to endure, and they were not the only ones who would have to suffer.

She shuddered at her thoughts and lifted both hands, running the fingers of her left hand over the little finger of her right. It was smooth and brown and flawless, with an orchid nail that was long and tapered elegantly, the perfect culmination of arm and hand.

She fondled the fatty pad of the fingertip for a moment, then brought the tiny appendage to her lips and kissed it goodbye.

Twenty-three
THE FINGER

Tiyy lay facedown on her bed, kicking her feet with petulant frustration. One arm covered her head, and the other was thrust forward with the hand resting on a pillow. She was naked except for the silver chain mail girdle that spanned the crest of her tight round buttocks, and her muscular curves were oiled. Bright torchlight, reflected by bronze mirrors inlaid in the rock ceiling, played across her glistening sheen, and the leopard-skin spread covering the bed. She smelled of midnight orchids, young men and fear.

She was in her private chambers, a stone-walled room within the castle hung and carpeted with animal hides. Balconies were built off it overlooking the Inland Sea, and daylight and the songs of birds flowed through the open doors. She had been here three days exploring the pleasures of her new body, but now it was time to work.

Her extended hand rested palm-down on a square of white cloth spread over a zebra-skin pillow. It shuddered like a condemned prisoner.

Her three elderly priests stood to the side of the room with their heads together, whispering. Bald and bare-chested, they wore white cotton skirts held in place with black ropes, and elbow-length gloves of a yellow-green fish membrane. Beside them, bottles and vials and bright steel cutting instruments were arranged on ceremonial platters set out on pedestals sculpted like erect male reproductive organs.

Schraak and Baskt, now in his almost human form, stood obediently beside the bed. Their flesh had had three days to heal since being boiled. Schraak's was shriveled, dry and flaking, and he was smaller, a dwarf. The sharkman's natural armor had lost all its subtle hues of blue and violet-pink, and was dark and crusted with thick gnarled scabs. His once huge dorsal fin was now a small hump, like a hunchback's, and his body was thicker, stronger, without grace. The bones of his formerly handsome face were bulging and blunt, and his upper teeth protruded, giving him an overbite that the dwarf could have stood under.

Their expressions said lucidly that each of them had not only had their bodies altered by torture and magic, but their souls. Their pride and intelligence were intact, but their wills had been removed, and their eyes were cold with death and obedience.

A priest picked up a platter containing a row of bottles, and shuffled toward Tiyy. She looked up sharply, glancing over her bare shoulder at the approaching bottles, and moaned like a girl being forced by her mother to wear a tunic that was out of fashion. She again covered her head, and kicked and twisted violently. When she lifted her head, her pyramid of spiked hair looked as if it had been restyled by a pitchfork. She glared hard at Baskt and Schraak as her voice lashed them.

"It's all your fault! If you'd found her, none of this would be necessary."

Schraak and Baskt bowed agreement.

She whimpered petulantly. "You're useless." She turned to the high priest as he stopped in front of her holding out the platter of vessels. She groaned, and shouted at the two boiled men, "You're going to pay for this!"

The pair bowed again.

Fuming, Tiyy turned back to the platter of vessels. They were of translucent green bottle glass and corked. Inside each of them, a little finger severed from a human hand floated in thick liquid that churned of its own accord, as if alive.

"You pick one," Tiyy said testily. "They all look ugly to me." The high priest nodded, and her head snapped up. "But if I don't like it, I'll have you gelded."

The priest, swallowing his wrinkled lips as if to stop himself from replying to her petty outburst, bowed obediently and rejoined the others.

Tiyy grumbled huffily after him, saying, "It better not hurt either."

The high priest did not react. He and the others assembled bottles and cutting tools on a platter, then all three returned to the bed. Two held the platters while the high priest bowed, revealing the three red circles painted on his bald head, then kneeled alongside the pillow supporting the young queen's hand. His assistants extended the platter to him, and he removed a thin steel knife, set it beside the hand.

The priests began to pray, and Tiyy again covered her head with her free arm, trying to block out the sounds. But she couldn't, and looked up, shouting, "Stop it! I've said all the prayers that need to be said. Just do it. Finish it!"

She hid her head again, and the priests dipped their heads, went to work, moving quickly and in harmony.

Using wooden tweezers, the high priest removed a bright yellow Panka tarantula from a bottle and placed it on the vein in the crook of the elbow of

Tiyy's extended arm. He poked at it until it bit her, and she screamed sharply. But she held still. The high priest put the spider back in its bottle, then sat back on his heels watching the arm.

It swelled slightly around the bite, and a yellow-grey jaundiced rash quickly spread out from the bite, reaching for her wrist, then her fingertips.

When Tiyy looked up, her stomach convulsed at the ugly blight on her flesh, and her head teetered sickly. When the nausea passed, Tiyy tried to move her fingers, three times. She could not. "It's ready. I can't feel anything."

The high priest bowed in acknowledgment. Then, in a high-pitched falsetto required of him when speaking to the high priestess, said, "Forgive me, Oh beloved breaker of hearts, for putting my worthless knife into your sacred flesh."

"Aaughh!" she snarled. "Stop that intolerable squealing and talk like a man. There's going to be no more of that nonsense around here. Now cut it! Just cut it, and get it over with."

Instinctively he bowed again, picking up the knife, and one of the assisting priests slid a square of hard black-enameled wood under the white cloth. Holding her hand down with his free hand, the high priest, with a deft cut, made an incision above the knuckle connecting the finger to the hand. A thin red line showed where the cut had been made, and Tiyy's lower lip thrust forward, her eyes filled with tears. She turned and glared at Schraak and Baskt.

"You see what you've done? I'll never be the same again. Never!"

Coolly and swiftly, and using practiced cuts, the high priest removed her little finger and set it on the white cloth, while holding the bloody stump high in the air. An assistant opened a bottle containing a floating finger and removed it. The liquid from the

bottle was heavy and glutinous, and clung to the
digit, which wiggled and squirmed with life. Using
napkin after napkin, an assistant removed the sticky
substance and then ran the finger between his own,
wringing the fluid out of it. The third time he did
this, the finger stopped wiggling. He then held the
new finger in place against the stump. The high
priest felt about the joints of hand and finger, fitting
them as he did, then took a long vampire worm from
the other assistant. It was no thicker than silk string.
He threaded a needle with it and thrust the needle
through the Nymph Queen's smooth brown flesh,
joining the knuckles of hand and finger with the
living thread. The vampire worm promptly began to
attach its body to the living bone and flesh around it.
The high priest then sewed the flesh together with
thin strands of monkey gut which had been treated
with Tiyy's own magic, so that it would eventually
merge with her flesh.

Tiyy, who had watched the entire operation, was
sweating profusely when it was over and shaking
from forehead to toes. When she looked up, the high
priest, who had gotten off of the bed, handed her a
small vial of black wine which she had previously
prepared for herself. She took it in her good left hand
and downed it hurriedly, the black light glowing on
her pouting face.

Immediately her normal healthy color began to
return to her arm, and then spread into her hand.
Before it reached her fingertips, the ugly stitching
around her knuckle was already beginning to disap-
pear.

She held her finger up, watched the last stitch fade
away and laughed with giddy relief. She abruptly sat
up on her knees, holding her hand to her face, and
wiggled her finger, studying it with rapt attention.

Suddenly she frowned savagely, thrust her hand at the priests and shouted, "It's ugly! It's the worst choice you could have made. Look at it! Look what you've done to me. Just look!"

The priests looked.

"I hate it," she screamed. "It's fat and wrinkled! And the nail is square and thick. Arrrgghhh!" She sank back on her heels. "You've destroyed me."

She looked at her finger one more time, then let herself fall on her back, and spread out on the leopard-skin holding her hand as far away from her as possible. Her quarrelsome breasts heaved angrily, and their nipples grew hard and red. Her face was turning the same color, and her eyes were thin and dark. Suddenly she sat up angrily and demanded, "Give it to me."

The priests looked at her, not understanding.

"My finger," she screamed.

The high priest moved toward the now bloody white cloth, and she shouted, "Never mind." She scrambled to the cloth and snapped up her severed finger. She held it against her heaving breasts possessively for a moment, suddenly afraid. Then she raised it alongside the new one and groaned fractiously.

"It's horrible!" She bent her new finger and straightened it several times. "And stiff! Heavy! And too small! It doesn't match the others. Everybody's going to notice! They'll know it's not mine as soon as I enter the throne room." She glared at the priests. "It makes my flesh crawl. It's . . . it's like a stranger has invaded my body. Who did it belong to anyway?"

The high priest started to reply, but hesitated, his face turning pale.

"Tell me!" she demanded. "Was it some filthy

savage? Is that what you've done to me?"

"No, no, my queen," the high priest said quickly.
"It . . . it was a . . . a slave girl."

"I know that," she snarled. "What was she before
that?"

"A . . . a . . ." The priest drew himself up, gathering control. "She had no tribe. She . . . she was a mix
of many tribes."

"Aarrghh! A mongrel."

"But she was young, your holiness. Only thirteen.
That is why it is so small. But this was intentional, so
that it can grow according to the dictates of your own
body. By tomorrow, or the day after, it will be almost
perfect."

Tiyy frowned and sank back, looking from her
original finger to the replacement. "Thirteen," she
mumbled. "Well, all right. I'll wait, but if it doesn't
look any better by tomorrow, I'll geld all three of
you. Now get out!"

The priests bowed, backed up the nine steps
required by ritual, then departed swiftly.

Tiyy drew her legs up under her, and sat looking at
her new finger from all sides. After some of this, she
looked up at Schraak and Baskt, and said, "You've
put me to a lot of bother, do you know that? And
pain!" She held up her new finger. "Not to mention
this . . . this piece of filth! And at a time like this!
When I am looking better than I have in over a
hundred years, maybe even my best!"

They bowed agreement, and she said peevishly,
"Oh, stop that! You haven't the slightest idea of what
I'm talking about. You don't know how I feel. You
couldn't. You're not capable of it."

They bowed again, but she ignored them, and
looked at her former finger for a moment, calming
herself. Then she decided she didn't want to be calm,

and with scalding eyes and a churlish tone, spoke to the two brutes.

"You've tried to ruin everything, and almost have, but that is all over now! Now that I can show myself to my people again, I'm taking charge."

Baskt started to protest, but she cut him off. "Don't interrupt me, Lord Baskt! You're the one who should have taken charge of the army when I grew weak, and strengthened it, rebuilt the castle fortifications, filled our coffers with silver and gold."

"We have gold," Baskt said.

"I know that," she snapped, "but we won't for long! You two are going to spend it. All of it, if that is what it takes." She lay over on a hip and smiled at them with malicious amusement. "I'm sending both of you into the desert, to En Sakalda. The hottest and most miserable spot in the desert, even for lizards, I'm told. The flies and sand and heat there can turn a man into nothing but an itching, pus-filled lump of rash within weeks . . . to say nothing of what they can do to a shark and worm."

Their eyes thinned with terror.

She smiled cruelly and continued, "I need an agent in En Sakalda. An agent of prestige and importance who is well known, like yourself, Lord Baskt. Because soon now, En Sakalda's slave pens will again be teeming with life." Her tone had begun to ring with an authority that was twenty times the age of her flesh. "I have sent out my slavemasters to buy young-girls of high spirit and great beauty, as many as they can. With them, and the new formulas I have concocted, I can sustain myself for years just as you see me now . . . and have strength left over to manufacture all the black wine I will need to put my kingdom back in order."

Their eyes doubted her, and she snapped, "Don't

argue with me. I am telling you a simple fact. As I told you, my powers are not completely or permanently restored, but there is now enough magic in my smallest finger," she held up the severed finger, "for both of you to see the invisible aura of virtue that surrounds this girl called Robin Lakehair. Do you understand?"

They did not.

"Dolts," she said irritably. "All you will have to do is eat it. Then, when you look upon her naked body, you will have the power to see her aura yourselves."

Baskt and Schraak stirred unnaturally, beginning to understand, and their grey cheeks grew hot.

She laughed and waggled the finger at them. "That's right! You would like to chew on me, wouldn't you?"

They did not reply, but their cold empty eyes said yes.

"Well, you're going to get your chance," she whispered crossly, "but you will pay for it dearly. I have instructed my slavemasters to send out word, to every corner of every land, that I will pay handsomely for every girl fitting this Lakehair's description. I'm offering a reward of a thousand crogan to the man who brings her in. But it could be months, even years, before she is found and brought to En Sakalda, months and years for you to sweat and blister in the sun. Eventually she will arrive, the greed and lust of Black Veshta will see to it, and when she does, you will place her little finger in one of those bottles," she pointed at two corked jars on a table beside them, "and her blood in the other, and deliver them to me."

Schraak stammered, "You . . . you cannot mean this, O breaker of hearts!"

"I mean it, worm. In addition to the girl, I want soldiers purchased, enough soldiers to bring the regiments and castle garrison up to strength. And I want that bitch, the Queen of Serpents, found and put in chains. She's more to blame for my problems than any of you. And I want the one called Death Dealer who stole the helmet. I want them all, and you will stay in En Sakalda until the slave hunters you employ bring them to you." She hesitated, then added, "Oh, yes, also have the slavers find and bring the Grillard bukko who picked the girls you stole. He sees something in young girls that I cannot, something which my Kaa hungers for."

Baskt said flatly, "We will die in En Sakalda."

"He's right," blurted Schraak. "Our flesh can't stand heat for any length of time."

"Do not lecture me on your pedigrees, dolt. My magic made you what you are, and it has now altered you so that you will survive the desert heat, painfully and torturously, but nevertheless survive."

She spread out languorously and smiled temptingly, holding the severed finger lightly and running the tip over an erect nipple. Then she laughed and tossed her severed finger on the floor in front of them, saying, "Now eat!"

Baskt hesitated, then snapped up the finger and thrust it into his mouth, biting it in half. He swallowed his piece whole and tossed the remaining portion to Schraak. The dwarf stuffed it into his mouth and truculently began to chew. He had the portion with the fingernail, and it made a small clicking sound when his teeth dismembered it.

"Now leave!" she said fretfully. "The first deliveries of girls should arrive by the time you reach En Sakalda, and I'm sick of looking at you."

Before they were out the door, she was screeching for her servants to bring her her finger-rings and paints. She had to hide her wretched new finger before anyone saw it, and she intended to do it in a

manner that would celebrate her regenerated youth,
by adorning herself like the goddess of demon lust
and creation, Black Veshta. It had been so long since
she had even dared to try, and she was just bubbling
inside to look expensive and savage.

When her servants arrived, she had her nails
redone to match the orchid pink of her cheeks, then
did her nipples in the same color. That was certain to
take their eyes off her hands.

Twenty-four

SLAVERS

The lean dark muscular nomad stood unseen in the
deep shade of a craggy outcropping of red-ochre
sandstone, as erect as his spear. His naked body was
stained with vermilion mud except for his member
and a wide stripe across his face. They were covered
with black tattoos, in accordance with his name. He
was the slave trader Amadak, the notorious Black
Terror of the Wadi Staboulle.

He was the darkness that violated the sun-bright
sands which formed the desert, the Body of Black
Veshta, and his reputation was known to the very
tips of its far corners. But he was obliged to defend it
daily, because he had named himself.

His expression was ponderously grave, and his
pose needlessly majestic for a man no one could see.
But if a man was truly horrible, then he was horrible
at all times. Consequently, the thin white slits of his

desert eyes clearly showed that his mind was actively contemplating magnificently horrific acts of slaughter and sexual depravity, even though what lay before him was a simple job of work.

The outcropping of rock which concealed the slaver thrust bluntly out of a massive sand dune four hundred feet high. At the base of the dune, the sand feathered out onto the wide undulating tongue of flat hard desert that wound between the dunes. The Wadi Staboulle. Hot wind, rushing out of the belly of the desert, was using the narrow depression of the wadi as a road, and sand rode the wind. It glittered like gold in the mid-day sunlight, and slashed and swirled around a huge horse-drawn wagon plodding west.

An oversized, muscled lout wearing a loincloth held the harness of the lead horse with one hand and the leash of a saddled stallion with the other. He was dragging the reluctant animals forward. An older white-haired man, chained to a big-breasted woman, led the other lead horse, and a handsome young man and a girl guided the remaining two. The lout plodded ahead mindlessly, despite the growing threat of a sandstorm. But the others staggered uncertainly and looked about in desperation for some cover to hide within.

The Black Terror of the Wadi Staboulle remained motionless, measuring the two female prey as they came closer and closer. When they passed directly below him, he smiled with great significance and, touching his member, belly and mouth, offered up a silent prayer to sacred Black Veshta for the blessing she was bestowing on him.

The women's plain tunics had been ripped and torn by wind, sand and thorn bush. Only rags and tatters covered their sun-darkened bodies, and his trained desert eyes, even at such a great distance, could see that Bigbreast was at the culmination of womanly beauty and that the girl was at the threshold of perhaps even more wondrous delights of the flesh.

Amadak could not restrain a small smile. Black Veshta's sandy body was delivering forth two morsels of flesh of uncommon beauty, and delivering them to him at the same time her high priestess had offered great rewards for just such beauty. The timing could not be accidental. The Black Terror of the Wadi Staboulle was being rewarded for his hideous acts, and realizing it, his black member came erect, not in anticipation of sensual pleasures or murder, but of gold.

The slaver glanced back through the rocks at the shadows of his men and their camels. They squatted beside their spears, bodies as naked as his, but painted black. They would be ready when the opportune moment arrived. He looked back at the wagon.

The outlanders were coming out of the east. This meant they had not passed a well in two or three days, and had been on the trail for at least five, but probably more. They were undoubtedly lost, as there were no maps of this part of the desert except for the one he carried in his head, and their parched staggering bodies said clearly they were out of water and starving. Weak. They could not withstand his raiders. Nevertheless, the Black Terror waited. In the desert, strength must be used with economy, and soon he would have to exert no more effort than it takes to attach manacles and chains to wrists and ankles.

He looked to the east and watched the black cloud of sand swell, coming faster now, then put his eyes back on the strangers.

Whitehair and Bigbreast had joined the Lout, and

were now talking excitedly, gesturing with alarm at
the advancing cloud. Lout, dragging the horses forward, ignored them. There was a strange red glow
about his face, as if he had a raw rash, but it seemed
to flicker. Bigbreast moved in front of him, blocking
him, and his arm swept her aside as if she weighed
less than the chain binding her to Whitehair. She fell
hard, rolled, and the chain dragged Whitehair down
on top of her. The pair struggled back to their feet, as
Girl ran forward and took hold of Lout's arm,
talking rapidly and pointing back at the dark cloud.
The sand was swirling thickly now, pelting them,
and Girl flinched and covered her face with an arm.
Still Lout pulled forward, and the sandy fingers of
the sandstorm reached for the wagon.

The slave trader remained motionless within the
concealing rocks. The wind, advancing in bursts,
reached up the dune toward him, but he had no fear
of it. He knew the ways of the sand, and here the
wind was his ally and brother. It would be content to
ride the low ground, passing him by. His mind began
to wander over his bloody triumphs to while away
the time, then again focused on the intruders.

Lout had suddenly stopped, and now he made the
horses do the same. This done, Lout slowly faced
Girl, his wide back hiding her completely as the
others gathered around. A moment passed, and a
gust of wind hammered the group, sweeping Girl
away from the others. She tumbled across the ground
covering her face with her arms and calling faintly,
her voice lost in the roaring wind.

Lout dashed after her and plucked her off the
ground. He held her close a moment, then, fighting
the wind, carried her back to the wagon. There he set
her down behind it, and Bigbreast took her in her
arms, protecting her. Lout, with the help of Hand-

some and Whitehair, unharnessed the horses, then single-handedly lifted the wagon and turned it over on its side with a resounding crash that rose above the wind's roar. He herded the group through one of the vehicle's windows into the wagon, then led the horses and his stallion to the downwind side of the upturned vehicle, and forced them down behind it, tying them in place. This done, he climbed to the top of the wagon, opened the door, and the full force of the storm hit him and carried him away.

Lout scrambled for control of his body, but was tumbled and tossed further and further away from the wagon. When the momentary fury of the storm abated, he rose uncertainly, and again the dark cloud swept over him, concealing his muscled body.

A long moment passed during which Amadak could not see either man or wagon, and he smiled, certain the storm had finished Lout for him. But then a frown belted his forehead.

The storm was sweeping through the flat gut of desert like a mammoth, writhing reptile made of sand and wind, and within its blackish-yellow body, a small red glow had appeared. It was plodding against the storm's flow.

Stupefied and mystified, the Black Terror of the Wadi Staboulle watched the apparition until it went out, then bowed with solemn respect, just in case it was a god.

When the last flurries of the storm were battering the wagon, the slave trader led his eight men out of their hiding place. They carried long spears, and led camels laden with manacles, chains and carobwood slave sticks. When the last flurry had passed, and sun and silence again commanded the land, the slavers were surrounding the half-buried wagon.

The Black Terror, gathering all his most terrible

thoughts behind his eyes, advanced until he faced the overturned roof of the wagon. Taking hold of the trapdoor's latch, he suddenly opened it and thrust his head inside, intending to petrify those within with the horrific darkness of his countenance.

What he saw inside was a darkness five times his own size with eyes of fire.

The Black Terror of the Wadi Staboulle took three hurried steps back, shamefully urinating on his own foot, and the darkness came at him. The idea of spearing it leapt from the slave trader's brain, but before it reached his arm, the darkness had pinned his arms to his side and was crushing him against the ground. The black mass smelled of sand and fire and smoke. It seemed to be shaped like Lout, but Amadak had no time to investigate. Pain was leading his mind elsewhere.

His armbone was being twisted out of the shoulder socket. His ribs snapped almost rhythmically. Something hairy forced his head back. His neck made a loud crack, and the pain shot into his spine. His head lolled sideways, and his cheek came to rest against pebbles of flint. His throat was filling with something hot and fluid. It spilled into his mouth choking him, and he spit it out. Blood.

Tasting the red wetness, rage and shame and fury welled inside the slave trader like a storm. He tried to rise, starting with his head, but it refused to cooperate. His neck was broken. The realization clouded his mind and vision, and the world went dark.

When consciousness returned, he heard men screaming, and the thunk and slap of metal eating meat and bone. Grunting howls followed, the kind made by his own men. The clang and clatter of chains came, and the hoofbeats of camels. Then his

vision cleared, and he saw several dead bodies lying
on the ground nearby. They were stained black in his
name, and bleeding from ears and mouths. All
looked as if some wild animal had been at them.
Beyond the bodies, in the distance, his camels raced
off without saddles or waterskins.

Silence followed, then a dark shadow moved over
him, and a hand took hold of his jaw. It turned the
slave trader's face until he was looking into a snarling sun-darkened face with wide, blunt bones and
deep brow. It was Lout. His breathing was loud and
harsh. There was a hot glow in his eyes, and his lips
and teeth were spattered with blood. Without looking away, Lout shouted something, in a language
Amadak did not understand, to someone he could
not see.

The sounds of people climbing down from the
wagon came to Amadak. The slaver, measuring their
different voices as they talked excitedly, counted
four. The sounds of scurrying feet came to him, then
the Black Terror coughed up blood, and it spilled
over Lout's hand. But he did not remove it.

Lout shouted something in a demanding tone, but
Amadak did not understand his language. Then
Handsome appeared, squatting beside Lout. He carried one of the Black Terror's own waterskins and
poured the slaver a drink from it, then spoke to him
in his own tongue, using a tone that carried no
emotion but curiosity.

"In what direction is the river . . . the Staboulle?"

Amadak proudly kept his words in his mouth. He
had served Black Veshta too long to tell a stranger
the secrets of her body.

Handsome asked again, and when the Black Terror still remained silent, Lout growled like the cave
bear, squeezing his jaw. As he did this, Lout's eyes

turned red and smoked. The Black Terror shuddered with fear and spoke as rapidly as possible.

"There is no river. It is dead! Dry! Gone now for hundreds of years. Only the wadi remains! The Wadi Staboulle."

"Where?" demanded Handsome.

"Here," gasped the slaver, spitting blood. "You stand on it."

Handsome looked around and suddenly smiled. "By Kram, you cutthroat, you're right! We've been traveling up a dry river bed all day and didn't know it."

He rose and turned to his unseen companions, talking rapidly in their strange language and pointing off at the dry river banks, and their voices responded excitedly. Amadak coughed up more blood, and this time Lout removed his hand, dropping his head. Then he stood and went away.

The Black Terror listened to the strangers righting their wagon and reharnessing their horses, all the time drinking from his waterskins and talking excitedly. As the sounds of the rolling wagon began to rapidly fade off, he strangled on his own blood and died.

Twenty-five

EN SAKALDA

The wagon bounded and caromed nimbly over the dry river bed, and Cobra hung on to the sideboard and Brown John's shoulder to keep herself from being bounced out of the driver's box. The wheels squealed, the wind whipped her, and her chain did a noisy irritating jig on the seat between her and the *bukko*. But her angularly beautiful face remained reposed as she studied the landscape before them.

The dry river banks on both sides were coming closer and closer as the wagon advanced, forming a funnel that led to a massive mound of black rock some eighty or ninety feet high. At its heights, rays of sun streaked through shadowed columns and crumbling stone walls. At its base, the wadi split in two and moved around opposite sides, indicating this was the spot they were searching for. The junction of the two rivers, the location of the ancient desert skin town, En Sakalda.

Brown John grinned at Cobra and shouted jubilantly, "That has to be it. We're on our way now!"

She nodded, shouting back, "I wish it wasn't black."

"What's that?" he yelled.

"The rock. It looks like the mound of Black Veshta herself." She pointed at the soft rounded flanks of the closing river banks. "I feel like we are being sucked up between her legs . . . to be swallowed."

He laughed. "That, beautiful lady, is not exactly how a man would look at such an eventuality."

She smiled knowingly and slid close beside him, silencing the chain that linked them. Then she put her mouth close to his ear and spoke loudly. "I have to admit that your optimistic male point of view no longer nauseates me, *bukko*, but I do not share it."

His brown eyes glittered youthfully in his wrinkled yet boyish face. "If you think that black doll has cursed us just because I touched it, stop worrying. I once defeated the consort of the Master of Darkness himself, and all I needed was a forked stick."

She laughed, knowing he referred to her, and put a firm hand on his thigh. "Are you telling me," she purred like a cat seeking shelter, "that I have nothing to fear . . . because you are personally going to defend my virtue?"

He arched a white eyebrow, then dipped his head affirmatively with theatrical aplomb.

She laughed again, scolding him with shimmering gold eyes, and said, "You only say that, Brown, because you know I have no virtue left to defend."

Brown John laughed again, lustily whipping the horses forward, and vermilion rose into his blistered cheeks.

Cobra smiled to herself as she watched him. The placement of her hand and her flirtatious humor had been calculated to flatter him and encourage his growing attraction for her. She needed him on her side, and in some way she did not fully understand, she felt the entire group was dependent on him. But despite her calculated flirtations, she could not deny she felt contentment at his touch, and thrilled to his laughter like a girl of twelve. It was as if they were being bound together in some perversely human way, and this she did not understand at all.

When they reached the base of black rock, Gath halted and Brown John reined the wagon up beside him. Robin and Jakar now sat on the roof behind the *bukko* and Cobra. For a long moment, they all looked about warily without speaking.

The mid-day silence was unyielding, heavy. There was no movement of air, creature or cloud. The dry heat reached beneath fingernail, penetrating mouth, nose and ear, and a torpor filled them as they studied the towering slabs of lava.

They formed a multitude of shadows and hiding places, and each seemed to hold a haunting mystery: the impenetrable shadows, the dark boulders carved like chain-links, the strange, voluptuous columns writhing out of the crest, the road winding in supine invitation up into the black body. Somewhere above at the heart of the mysteries was the trail they hunted, the Way of the Scorpion.

Gath shared an understanding glance with Brown John. He flicked the reins, and the group rode up the narrow road with Gath leading. At the top, they rode past crumbling walls and standing pillars, the ancient rotting edifices of some dead race, then through scattered boulders and up a bald rise. Gath suddenly reined up. Brown John started to do the same, but the Barbarian motioned for him to keep coming. When the wagon crested the rise, the *bukko* pulled up, and they all stared in silent shock.

On the opposite side of the rise, spread out on the flat ground which had once supported the ancient skin town of En Sakalda, scattered groups of nomadic tribesmen dozed in the mid-day heat under make-shift tents and lean-tos. About the area were stacked cages, half-built slave pens and piles of carobwood slave sticks. Chains and manacles were heaped beside anvils, where dying fires of dried camel dung glowed. Whitish smoke rose from the fires and lay like a vaporous blanket a few feet above the ground. It drifted languorously on the hot still air, making everything appear vague and ethereal. A stack of occupied cages rose out of the middle of the smoke. They held young girls. At the southern side of the camp, where the surrounding rim of boulders cast the most shade, was a large black tent. A banner dangled limply from its highest post. It was black with three red circles.

Cobra stared at it in shock, whispering sharply, "The banner . . . above the black tent! It is a sign reserved for the personal envoys of the Nymph Queen of Pyram."

Brown John stifled a gasp. "But according to the map, we're still a long ways from her territory! What are they doing out here? In the middle of nowhere?"

"It appears they are buying slaves," she said, her voice tight. "We better ride in and purchase provisions from them . . . so they won't become suspicious."

Gath said quietly, "Bat soldiers."

They looked at him sharply, and he nodded at some rocks rising above the camp site behind him.

A small detachment of armed men, short and covered with fur, were camped on the rocks, perched there like huge flying rodents. Their horses were tethered below the rocks.

Jakar chuckled cynically and said to Robin, "These guys just can't resist you, tart."

"Stop it," she blurted, terror riding her eyes.

Brown John smiled reassuringly at Robin. "No need to be afraid, lass. They can't possibly be looking for you, not here. We'll just ride in, buy what we need and ride out."

He turned to Gath. Both men gave an impercepti-

ble nod of agreement. Gath nudged his stallion with
his boots, started down the incline, and Brown John
moved the wagon after him. At the bottom, a small
group of nomads emerged from their ragged dwell-
ings and warmly greeted the wagon of traveling
players, saluting it in the desert style, touching
stomach, heart and mind.

They were lean, hard, dark men, with the bearing
and pride of those who have bought and sold other
men. Most wore heavy cotton robes, others had only
their hips wrapped. All had daggers with jewel-
crusted hilts hanging from their long necks, and the
richest among them had their long dark fingers
linked with iron chains attached to silver rings inlaid
with red carnelians to ward off the dreaded green-
bellied flies that worked the desert. There were
Kamascene, Bakar, Nubante, Nalik and two or three
tribes Cobra did not recognize. As they crowded up
in front of the horses, several took hold of the
harnesses and shouted to the *bukko* to follow them.

The slavers led the wagon to the back of a large
stone auction block, the top of which rose nearly to
the wagon's door. The nomads were anxious for the
traveling players to use the flat stone block for their
stage, and repeatedly asked when the performance
might begin.

Brown John thanked the slavers for their thought-
fulness and help, but begged off, telling them that his
troupe was too weary from the road to perform. But
the slavers insisted, offering provisions in exchange
for an opportunity to see the two girls dance. To
finalize the arrangement, they brought forth wine
and cheese and bread, handing it up to the players,
and the *bukko* had no choice but to agree. He
promised that his beauties would delight both their
eyes and ears, but pleaded that they needed rest and
food first. The slavers reluctantly agreed to this

condition and returned to their patches of shade to lie down and wait.

The troupe sat in the wagon's shade and hurriedly nourished themselves. This done, Gath remounted his stallion and spoke to Jakar.

"Find out why these slavers are here and who uses the black tent." He turned to Brown John. "I will find the trail."

The *bukko* nodded, and Gath rode off toward the huge boulders rimming the west end of the camp, as Jakar casually strolled into it. Brown John turned to Cobra and Robin.

"You'd two better make yourself beautiful, child," he said, "while Cobra and I see to the horses."

"There is no time for that," Cobra said breathlessly. "We must destroy the map." Brown John started to object, and she added, "I can't explain out here." She took Robin by the elbow, saying, "Come, butterfly, we will need your help," and led her toward the door of the wagon.

Brown John, being linked to the serpent woman by the chain, had no choice but to follow.

When they were inside the lower room of the wagon, Cobra secured the door and shutters. The hard trip had opened cracks in the body of the wagon, and thin shafts of light leaked in, illuminating the room and letting in the faint chatter of the expectant nomads. Finished, she put her eyes on Robin and spoke to her quietly but forcefully.

"Strip to the waist, quickly." Robin hesitated, glancing at Brown John, and Cobra said to him, "Tell her it's all right, and give me the doll."

She extended her hand, and Brown John blustered importantly, "Now just a minute, woman! What are you up to? We can't destroy the map, we still need it."

"Shhhhh," she whispered. "We may be overheard." He scowled, and she added, "Trust me, friend! The only safe thing to do is destroy the doll. It's bringing us bad luck."

"You mean because I touched it?" he said, scoffing at her. "You can't be serious."

"I am quite serious. We are on Black Veshta's sacred ground. She rules here, some even believe the desert to be her body. And we have offended her, so we must destroy the doll."

"That makes no sense," said the *bukko*. "That won't just offend her, that will make her furious."

"No doubt," said Cobra, "but it will also destroy the totem's magic. Now give it to me." She removed a small vial of dark stain and a brush from a shelf, adding, "Before we destroy it, I must copy it." She smiled at Robin. "Go ahead, child, remove your tunic."

Brown John nodded at Robin to oblige, and she quickly slipped out of her tunic as he, looking from Robin to Cobra, reluctantly removed the doll and handed it to her.

"You're going to copy it on Robin?" he asked incredulously.

"Exactly," Cobra said.

She held the doll up to Robin's body as the girl pushed her ragged garment down on her hips, baring herself from belly to throat.

"See," Cobra said anxiously, "she is becoming a woman. The proportions are almost identical."

The *bukko*, flushing slightly at Robin's nakedness, said, "She's grown, all right. But when she dances, everyone will see it."

"Yes," Cobra admitted, "but no one will suspect that a few tattoos on a dusty slattern is a map. Besides, the best place to hide something is in plain sight, correct?"

Cobra, without waiting for his reply, uncorked the vial, sat on a stool facing Robin and began to copy a sign on her belly.

Brown John watched, scowling with suspicion, then said, "Well, it's a dandy place to hide something, there's no denying that. But just what do those signs mean? She's not going to start attracting more demons, is she?"

"Trust me, Brown, please," Cobra pleaded. "They are measurements, distances, that's all. Now please help me. Get some water and a cloth, and wash the dust and oils off her skin. And hurry! Those slavers are already impatient to see her perform."

Brown John obliged, giving Robin the cloth to wash herself while Cobra copied the map.

When Cobra was half finished, drawing the sign of a scorpion between Robin's breasts, the sounds from outside grew louder. They all held still listening. The nomads had begun to gather in front of the stone auction block, and Robin flinched.

"They're already gathering," she gasped.

"It's all right, lass," Brown John said. "It's customary on the road to make the audience wait awhile."

"But where's Jakar?" Robin asked nervously. "Why isn't he back? What if he's found some reason for us not to perform? What if something's happened to him?"

Robin jerked as she spoke, smearing the mark Cobra was drawing, and Cobra snapped, "Hold still!"

"I'm sorry." Robin held as still as a stone.

"Good girl," Cobra purred. "The sooner the map is finished and the doll destroyed, the safer we will all be . . . including Jakar."

Cobra winked at Robin to relax her, then dipped

her brush in the vial of stain and resumed drawing.

When Cobra finished, the crowd outside had grown and become noisy. It was beating small drums and shouting for the entertainment to start. Cobra and Brown John fanned Robin with a blanket to dry the stain, then Robin got back into her ragged tunic. Brown John tied a yellow sash around her waist, and orange and red sashes to her ankles and wrists. Then he held her shoulders as he spoke.

"When you get out there, don't flirt or tease this time. Just be yourself in front of this group, and they will adore you. Slaving is ugly work, and it provides all the lusty pleasures a man can stomach, but little laughter. So have fun! Be the *cutup*, the *knockabout*. You know the parts. Do the opening dance from "Chums" and let them accompany you on their own drums. It will flatter them."

Robin nodded, and Brown John opened the door, letting in bright daylight and a burst of roaring approval from the waiting audience. When the audience whistled and cheered again, the sounds drew her out through the door as if she were on a string. Before her bare feet touched the warm stone of the auction block, she was beaming.

Brown John closed the door behind her and sat down tiredly on a trunk, listening. Outside, the crowd shouted and applauded loudly, and the drums beat out a happy rhythm.

When the noise reached a crescendo, Cobra lifted the hammer she had taken from the *bukko*'s trunk, held the black doll against the floor boards and brought the hammer down hard. She hit it five more times, timing each blow so that the noise was covered by the crowd. Then she brushed the crumbles of stone and dust through cracks in the floor boards scattering it on the ground beneath the wagon.

Finished, she sat down on the stool facing Brown John, and her chain swung lazily between them.

"Feel better?" Brown John asked.

"A great deal better," she said solemnly. "But you look feverish." She smiled knowingly. "It bothers you to look upon her naked flesh, doesn't it?"

"Indeed it does," he said candidly.

"Youth is always a mystery," she said lightly, "and from what I have seen, you are easily seduced by mysteries."

He laughed. "I most surely am. Some are so confounding, I find them irresistible."

She knew again that he referred to her and smiled. He gathered up the chain between them until it was taut, and gave it a slight tug, asking, "If I remove the chain, will you answer a question . . . truthfully?"

"It will depend on the question."

"There is something special about Robin. There always has been, and I am convinced that you know things about her that I don't." His tone hardened. "I must know what they are."

"That is simple enough," she replied in a casual tone. Then she lied, saying, "Apart from her high spirit and extraordinary beauty, she is not special, not to women. But I understand why you think she is. She makes you feel young again."

He listened to the drums and slap of Robin's bare feet on the stone outside, then nodded. "That is true. When I first met her, she did make me feel young. But not now. There's something else."

"You don't feel young now?" she asked behind a skeptical smile.

"Indeed I do. But it's not Robin. It's you."

He pulled on the chain, trying to draw her to him, but she resisted, and their eyes held each other, sober and heated. Then she said slowly, "Don't flatter me,

Brown. It makes me feel strange and weak, and I am
not used to such emotions."

"I am not flattering you," he said.

"Yes, you are," she insisted. "I have seen you
looking at the growing weight at my hips and the
wrinkles appearing on my throat." She hesitated.
"You know I am quickly growing older."

"I suspected it," he replied without concern. "But
I don't understand. It's not natural. It's happening
too fast. When we met, I would have sworn you were
no more than twenty-five."

"Twenty-six," she said, correcting him. "The
Queen of Serpents is twenty-six all her life. It is part
of the contract with the Master of Darkness. But
when you are no longer queen, and only a woman
again, you slowly return to your rightful age."

"Which is?"

She smiled. "That, Brown, will remain a mystery
. . . but we are not as far apart as you might have
thought."

"I was thinking the same thing myself," he said,
white eyebrows arching dramatically. He tugged on
the chain again. She stood slowly, came into his lap,
smiling, and put her arms around his neck. He kissed
her throat, and she stopped him, scolding him with a
regal frown.

"You're forgetting who I am."

"No," he said, with the balls of his ruddy cheeks
burning brightly, "but I'm working on it."

She laughed easily, and her voluptuous body came
against his, surrendering in a dozen places. He
stroked her throat, then her hair. As he did, the play
slowly went out of their eyes, and their lips parted as
their breath quickened. With his eyes on hers, he
removed the chain and set it aside. Then he reached
for her face, and her hands caught his, stopping him.

"Be careful, Brown," she whispered, "I am not who you think I am."

"I'm counting on that," he said.

She hesitated, then let go of his hand, and he placed it at the back of her head, guiding her lips toward his. The trapdoor slammed open in the room above, followed by the sound of feet dropping heavily to the floor. Cobra and Brown John stood abruptly. The feet descended the enclosed staircase, and Jakar appeared, loading his crossbow. His words were controlled but rapid.

"The slavers have gathered here to begin a search for Robin. The Nymph Queen has offered a huge reward for her, and word is being sent to every slave hunter in every land, as far as the eastern border of the Great Forest Basin. It's just the beginning of the hunt that could take years."

"They don't suspect she's here?" blurted Cobra.

Jakar shook his head. "I doubt if they would believe you if you told them."

"Thank the Good Goddess for that," Brown John said, sighing with relief.

"But if they are hunting for her," Cobra said urgently, "they must have some way of identifying her."

"Every girl collected will be brought here and inspected."

"But only Tiyy has the power to identify her."

"How?" demanded Brown John.

"She knows what I told the Master of Darkness about Robin, about the nature of her spirit, and she can see a spirit as easily as you can see a cloud in the sky." She turned back to Jakar, and her voice faltered. "She's . . . Tiyy's not here, is she?"

"No!" Jakar said solemnly. "But that bastard sharkman is."

Brown John glanced with concern at Cobra. "Can he identify you?"

She nodded. "I'll stay in the wagon." She hesitated, then added, "But I don't understand. If he's here to identify her, he must have some way to do it."

"I can't pull her off that stage now," said the *bukko*. "They'd become suspicious."

"I know," Cobra said. She looked at Jakar. "Is there anything else you should tell us?"

He nodded. "They're not just hunting for Robin. Rewards are being posted for Gath, for you," he indicated Cobra, then Brown John, "and for the bukko of the Grillards."

Cobra had to sit down, and Brown John stared in shock.

Jakar shrugged. "I couldn't find out why, but it's getting interesting, isn't it? I have a feeling this Nymph Queen knows more about us than we know ourselves." His eyes laughed coldly, and he bounded back up the stairs. "I'll be on the roof."

Brown John listened until he heard the trapdoor slam, then looked down at Cobra.

"It's the doll," she said. "This is Black Veshta's work."

The *bukko* looked down at his offending hands and forced a lighthearted tone. "She's really touchy, isn't she?"

Cobra looked at him angrily, dumbfounded at his levity. But when she saw his smile, its warmth softened her.

"Is this what it means to be human," she chuckled, "laughing at the face of death?"

He nodded, and said with deliberate profundity, "Laughter is good, but sometimes there are better things."

He took her head in his hands, kissed her full on the lips, then stepped back smiling. "You can blame Black Veshta for that too."

She laughed lightly and shook her head. "If that is all you wish of me, then Black Veshta has nothing to do with it."

He reached for her again, but she pulled away, shaking her head. "Hurry now! Find Gath!"

He hesitated. "You didn't answer my question about Robin."

"I know nothing more," she said, and lowered her voice. "Trust me, Brown. Please."

He nodded and went out the rear door.

Twenty-six

BASKT

The huge sharkman paced inside his tent, cursing the heat and his living armor which he could not remove. The desert was already butchering his body and mind after only three days, and there would be hundreds more, perhaps thousands, before some lucky slaver chanced upon the girl and brought her to him.

With a convulsive growl he cursed Tiyy, then the desert sun. As if in reply, a gust of air parted the tent's flaps allowing a shaft of golden sunlight to cut through the grey gloom and sear the blistered plates of armor at the backs of his legs. He strode to the flaps and whipped them shut. For a moment he stood motionless, helplessly breathing the stench of decay rising from his scabbed armor plates. He smelled like a dead codfish rotting in the sun.

He crossed to a small altar at the back of the tent and stood before it, rubbing his jaw. Lying on the altar was a black doll, an extremely voluptuous version of Black Veshta lolling in supine sexual invitation on a pile of shark teeth. Baskt reached into his mouth, pried out a handful of teeth and tossed their bloody bodies into the box. Then he prostrated himself in front of the altar and prayed to the doll, asking it, as he had five times already that day, for rain.

Finished, he picked up a jar of wine and stood over Schraak, drinking.

The slick little man lay naked and oiled between three shuddering nomad girls chained to his bed. His grey flesh was raw, and his cheeks were a sickly blue. The worm had been drunk or drugged ever since they had ridden into the desert.

Baskt grunted bitterly and moved away. He would have liked to be in the same stupor, but did not dare. He had to keep moving in order to breathe, and the incessant itching would not let him rest anyway.

There was a distant, rolling boom. It had the definite cracking roar of thunder, but he dismissed the notion. He was certain it was the body of the desert bending again under the heat of the sun.

A flash of light again speared through the tent wall, this time using a hole, and a bright whiteness illuminated the deep clefts where his cold death eyes hid. His sharp nose twitched, and the scent of blood reached his brain. A feeding fury instantly leapt through his flesh, and his body spasmodically arched as if it were in shark form. The involuntary movement threw him off balance. He staggered and dropped to all fours, the tip of his pointed helmet aimed at the sandy floor.

His eyes blinked as his mind fought off the scent, and thoughts of going mad dashed around inside his tiny brain until it ached. He was five days' march from any sizable body of water. There was no chance of returning to his shark form, no matter how much he hungered for it. Not in the desert. There was no chance of any kind of relief, yet his mind had suddenly behaved as if he were once more a shark, and his senses had smelled blood, even though he knew there was nothing but the odor of hot dirt on the air.

He listened to his own blood pound the drums of his ears and wanted to scratch in countless places. Every pore, scale and orifice of his body was being violated by heat and sand. His only escape was to think of the ocean, of its wet cold, of its endless liquid-blue space, of the yawning dark green gloom of its depths and of beautiful brown-skinned girls flailing on the surface in a frenzy of fear at the sacred feeding times. A euphoria came over him similar to what he felt when he swam from sea water into fresh water, but then his breath became short, and he had to stand and pace again.

As he moved back and forth, he put his fingers inside his mouth, felt his new teeth rising into place and spit out the taste of his own blood. Even it seemed unusually hot and rancid, and made him thirsty. He went out the back end of the tent and moved to the water barrels standing in the shade. He picked up a wooden bucket and dipped it into the water. He drank deep, trying to fill his entire seven-foot form with one swallow. Suddenly he stopped short. Water splashed over his chest armor as he looked over the rim of the bucket.

Bars of jagged white light were flashing across the

shaded boulders, like lightning, but there was no
lightning in the sky. Another distant, rolling boom
came, again sounding distinctly like thunder. He
climbed up through the rocks until he could see the
far hills. Above them was a dark thundercloud, but
no sign of lightning.

Baskt chuckled bitterly, a low harsh grating sound
without humor. It was a rain cloud, but he had no
hope of it reaching En Sakalda, no hope in anything,
least of all in his prayers. He would have to be
standing in a downpour first.

Shafts of blinding white light suddenly exploded
from the water slopping about the bucket between
his hands, and made him blink and stagger. He
caught his balance, and a shuddering blood hunger
jerked through him. A primordial urge so strong his
entire body began to bend from within, until he was
arched threateningly around the bucket. He looked
down into it, very carefully.

A few remaining scraps of white light shot through
the ripples of the shallow water, then flashed up the
wooden sides and were gone.

Baskt shook the bucket, but the remaining water
sloshed and slapped around revealing no light hiding
within it. He returned to the barrel, dipped the
bucket into it again, came away with half a bucket of
water and looked into it. All he saw was water and a
few dead flies. He lifted the bucket to drink again,
and as it came level with his eyes, white light again
exploded from it. He turned his face away, thinning
his eyes, and watched it out of the corners.

The light was not coming from the water. It was
ricocheting off of its surface, coming from someplace
behind him.

He turned sharply, tossing the bucket aside, and
saw beams of white light spearing out of the smoke at

the center of the camp. It appeared to be coming from the stack of cages within the smoke.

Baskt entered his tent, snapped his sheathed sword from the floor and strode out into the sunlight. He moved straight for the light, stepping over bodies, and through campfires into their smoke, until he faced the stack of cages.

The captive girls were naked except for beads and scraps of cloth. Dark-skinned desert natives, they were young and uncommonly attractive, but there was not a redhead among them, and little virtue.

The sharkman, his body snarling at the blood scent filling it, moved in among the cages, shoving them aside in order to examine each of the girls. Reaching the opposite side of the stack, he looked back and saw that the light was slashing across the girls' frightened faces. But not one of them blinked or appeared to notice it. They only shivered and wiggled with invitation. He pushed through the few remaining cages and stood in the open area beyond.

There the light hit him directly in the face, blinding him. He lifted a forearm, blocking the light, and looked under his hand.

The light was centered in front of a large wagon parked behind a massive stone auction block. It was moving, swirling dizzily.

He thinned his eyes and saw a girl dancing within the light. She moved like a firefly, banging a tambourine with childish abandon, kicking and twirling colorful sashes tied to her wrists and ankles. The light seemed to come from behind her, but he was uncertain. It was blurred by her flashing arms and legs.

Baskt strode forward and stopped behind a scatter of cages, horses and benches. Just beyond them were the backs of a small crowd of clapping slavers, squatting and sitting on the ground below the flat stone. He studied the girl for a long moment, holding the feeding fury within, until he was certain.

The light was not coming from behind the girl. It moved across the small stage as she moved, not following her, but with her. And there was only one answer for this. The white light was pouring forth from her soul, radiating from her body, shooting forth from the naked portions of her flesh.

The sharkman's body shook with a searing jolt of electric pain, then the feeding frenzy balled inside his two bellies like fists, and thrust him forward, spreading his jaws wide. His human mind was gone. Primordial instinct had taken control, and he dove forward, vaulting through the air like a great white shark. He crashed through a cage, dropping his sword, and slammed into a group of tethered horses, scattering them.

When he got back to his feet, the music had stopped and the slavers had jumped to their feet, parting in front of him. But the white light still stood on the auction block. It streaked forth from a small, dark-haired girl with eyes wide and mouth hanging open. There was the movement of a figure on the roof of the wagon behind her, but the light made it indistinguishable.

Baskt found his sword and marched for the stage, with the slavers backing away on all sides.

A crossbow bolt screamed in the air and nailed the sharkman in the left shoulder, half turning him. But he kept moving. He did not feel that kind of pain. He never had.

Without looking at it, he ripped the bolt out and tossed it aside with the plate of living armor that came with it. He leapt onto the stone auction block facing the girl, and a young man jumped down from the roof of the wagon. He landed gracefully, and stood between Baskt and the girl with a sword in his hand. Rage blotted his face, and the light coming from the girl glowed like a halo around him as he charged.

Baskt caught the young man's striking blade with his sheathed sword and turned it. But it came back again, spinning on its own axis with more skill than the sharkman had expected. He fended it off, then slapped it with the sheath, and the blade spun out of his attacker's hand. A scream came from the girl.

Enjoying it now, Baskt stepped in and kicked, driving his foot into the gut of the slight body. The young man flew backward with a grunting gasp, hit the girl and drove her back against the wagon. She half screamed, and gasped. His lithe body tumbled forward, fell to the auction block on its hands and knees.

Baskt kicked the seemingly inert body aside, but as he did, the young man's arms took hold of his leg and tried to throw him. Baskt staggered two steps and drove his fist into the young man's back. There was a gush of air, another scream from the girl, and the young man sank facedown. Baskt raised a foot to crush his head, and the girl leapt on him.

Baskt caught her by the shoulder, shook her until her fight was gone, then set her down. He kicked the unconscious young man off the block, then sniffed the girl, making certain that the scent of blood came from her. It was within the light, just as Tiyy had said it would be.

He laughed insanely, took hold of her by the throat and thigh and held her high over his head, shaking her whimpering body. "It's her! It's her! I've found the bitch!"

Surprised shock, then disappointment creased the slavers' faces. They drew together, chattering among themselves with consternation and disbelief.

Baskt howled with delight and dropped the girl back on the block in an upright position. She staggered under the impact, and he gave her a poke in the ribs that made her gasp with pain.

"You gave me a lot of trouble, slut," he said, "and you're going to pay in kind for it!"

He poked her again, making her double up and hold her stomach, gasping. Suddenly she pivoted toward the door of the wagon, and his arm slashed at her, as fluid as the tail of a shark. The flat of his hand caught her flush on the side of the head. It was a toying blow. But his blood was up, so it was much harder than he had anticipated. She flew sideways, hit the auction block with a pained grunt and rolled off the edge out of sight. All he could see was her radiating light rising behind the rim of the block. Then she reappeared, crawling on all fours amid a flurry of white light. She got about five feet, then collapsed, gasping.

Baskt started toward her, and again thunder rolled through the hot desert sky. Lightning flashed. He hesitated, his eyes on the dark cloud to the south. It had passed over the mountains, and its misted edges were reaching for En Sakalda. More thunder ripped from its dark, heavy body, and lightning cut through it, striking at the ground. Then the cloud covered the sun, and the sharkman felt cool relief as a shadow moved over him.

He unconsciously touched the scabbed armor plates at his shoulder, then strode for the girl, and a darkness blotted out her light. It was made by a man holding a large axe, a Barbarian wearing nothing more than a loincloth and his pride. He was nearly as big as Baskt, and it pleased the sharkman almost as much as the prospect of rain.

The torturous desert had finally provided him with a worthy distraction.

Twenty-seven

THE WILD PLACE

Gath, crouching below the auction block, stared up into the sharkman's cold death eyes and snarled. His muscles swelled, and his burnished flesh pulled over bone and cartilage. Every sinew and nerve told him that he finally stood at the threshold of that world he searched for, and that Baskt held the key.

A smile gathered on his face, surfacing as naturally and inevitably as blood rising in a new wound. It was raucous and untamed, and he realized that there was humor lurking in this world he hungered for. But no mercy, no kindness, no sentiment and no glory, honor or justice. Here the only redemption was the laughter of the strong.

He laughed, low in his throat, and ground his booted feet into the soil, holding the earth between his legs as instinctively as the wings of the hawk hold the wind. His arms hung beside him, loose and dangerous, and his hand held his axe with the same assurance as his arm carried the hand.

There was suddenly no hurry. They were sharing that momentary, menacing truce that rises between beasts of prey when they confront each other.

He lowered his weight to one knee and reached back blindly for Robin, keeping his eyes on the center of Baskt's balance. Feeling her warm bare arm, and her body stirring under it, he asked, "Are you hurt?"

"No," she said breathlessly, "it's nothing." He felt her small hands surround his biceps and tug on it as she pulled herself to her knees. Her breath was hot on his naked shoulder. "Why . . . why is he here? How did he know?"

"I don't know," Gath said, still watching the sharkman. "It does not matter now. Go to Brown John. Quickly!"

"All right," she said. But her hands hesitated, and one touched the hair of his unprotected head. "But . . ."

"Go," he interrupted harshly. "I cannot risk wearing it."

Her fingers trembled against his arm, telling him she knew he took the risk for her, and he felt her lips press into his shoulder. Then they were gone, and the sound of her bare feet danced through the silence. He rose slowly, his eyes and senses measuring the fighting ground, the direction of the sunlight, the bystanders.

The slavers had backed away from the auction block to avoid any bit of gore accidentally thrown up by the impending battle, but not so far that they might miss it. The bat soldiers had come down from their rocks and were perched on nearby boulders with their furry heads just above the smoky drifts. Brown John had carried the unconscious bleeding Jakar to the wagon, and Robin now joined him there, helping the *bukko* load him aboard.

Gath sensed Cobra standing beside his stallion behind him, then he heard her.

"I'm here," she said, a ring of desperation in her

voice that was almost childishly afraid. "I have the helmet."

He shook his head, once, telling her he did not want it. She pleaded, "You must."

By way of reply, he took one stride forward and jumped onto the auction block, landing about ten feet away from the demon spawn. The sharkman betrayed no reaction.

Gath's body was cocked for balance but relaxed. That primordial patience which is the immaculate grace of the hunting animal was flowing through his blood. But he saw no patience in Baskt's eyes, only bravado.

The creature, with noisy growling, two-handed the hilt of his broadsword, whipping it sideways, and the sheath flew off flamboyantly, clattering against the side of the wagon. Before it had time to land on the auction block, he rushed forward, delivering successive overhand blows.

Gath deftly deflected both with the blade of his axe, and his eyes turned red with inner fire, drawing excited gasps of exclamation from the onlookers.

Gath did not hear them. He was at work, charging Baskt with his hands spread wide at the extremities of the axe handle, holding it horizontally like a quarterstaff. The handle took Baskt across the chest and drove him against the side of the wagon. Both demon and wagon groaned in complaint, and the sounds encouraged Gath. Applying pressure, he slowly forced the sharp blade of the axe toward the sharkman's shoulder.

Suddenly the demon spawn's body convulsed, like a whip of solid muscle. The spasm culminated at his chest, which acted like a hammer, and drove the axe handle back into Gath's throat. The impact sent the Barbarian staggering backward, gagging for air.

Baskt followed not far behind, leading with his

face in the manner of a shark, jaws agape, and raising
his sword high over his head.

Gath dropped to a knee, wheezing and clinging to
his axe, and saw armored legs driving for him.
Staying low, he instinctively shortened his grip on
the axe and dove forward, turning sideways in
mid-air. His hip took out one leg, his elbow the
other. Baskt flew forward over the Barbarian's body.
Gath's hip hit the stone block, and he thrust his axe
up at the demon's descending belly.

Baskt twisted fluidly in mid-air, like a fish in
water, writhing away from the blow. The axe sliced
across his belly armor, removed several plates, leaving smears of blood across his chest, and continued
harmlessly into the air.

When Gath rolled upright, Baskt was on his feet
facing him. His heaving belly had already stopped
bleeding, and the bluish-white sheen of new growth
was rising where the armor plates had been, replac-
ing them.

There were hoots of approval and grim laughter
among the slavers, and groans came from Gath's
comrades.

Gath considered briefly the fact that the demon's
armor replaced itself, giving it the respect it deserved, then began a search for the Lord of Destruction's weakness. He worked the sharkman around
until a shaft of sunlight penetrating the gathering
clouds was in his eyes, and tinted membrane descended from the demon spawn's lids, to cut the
glare. No advantage there. Gath then retreated until
Baskt was working with the side of the wagon on his
right. It should have cramped his right-handed
swing. But Baskt took no notice of the wagon's
presence, his sword cutting through the wood as if it
were butter. He tried other tactics, but the sharkman

was oblivious to all of them, and Gath went on the defensive.

As he blocked and dodged and ducked, his blood began to boil in his veins, and the red glow in his eyes grew brighter and brighter. Pain began to burn his flesh inside out. It ate into his brain, but brought no new tactic to mind, only rage and more pain.

They continued to work.

Sparks showered their bodies as axe and sword met solidly. High-pitched tearing howls rent the desert when they sheared across flesh. Gath became drenched in sweat, and it formed puddles in the depressions of the hard stone auction block. Baskt began to fume at knee joints and elbows, and an oily slime surfaced on his fleshlike armor. Its putrid stench of dead fish mixed with the drifting smoke hanging over the camp, and stung Gath's nostrils and eyes.

They worked some more, until Gath's head hung low over his swarthy body. His pride was squirming and swelling in his gut. Then it spilled out, like a contagion. It spread into muscle and bone and to the very ends of his skin and hair, affecting how he stood and moved. It did not straighten him, as normal pride would. It bent him low, like the proud panther. It seared through nerve and brain and blood, and keyed itself to the same guttural pitch of the howl that ripped out of his mouth.

He charged inside the swing of Baskt's sword, and again caught him across the chest, holding his axe handle like a quarterstaff, and drove him back against the side of the wagon. The demon crashed into the splintered wood, and his upper body crushed through it into the interior of the wagon. Then his fluid body once more convulsed like a whip.

Gath anticipated the serpentine blow. He let go of the axe handle just as the demon's chest was about to hammer him, and grabbed Baskt's throat, driving the fingers of both hands under the living neck guard of his helmet. When the blow came, Gath grunted painfully and flew backward, his arms extending. But his fingers, half buried in the sharkman's meat, hung on, and Baskt came flying after him.

Gath hit the stone block with his naked back. The blade of the axe, which had dropped between them, turned on impact and caught against a ridge, momentarily standing upright with the cutting edge exposed. It sheared through Baskt's shoulder armor and penetrated the socket before being wrenched free. The demon dropped his sword, but Gath saw no reaction in his death eyes. This Lord of Destruction felt no pain.

Baskt lay on top of Gath. His upper jaw was raised and protruding, as if it were not attached to his skull. Gath held it off with both hands squeezing Baskt's throat, and the jaws snapped in front of the Barbarian's eyes. Two rows of saw-toothed teeth stood upright in the lower jaw as it swept up to meet the upper. They collided with enough force to remove a forty-pound bite of castle wall, but only fed on strands of stray black hair.

Gath, still holding on with both hands, rolled across the stone block, trying to kick the demon off. But Baskt liked it where he was, and stayed. Still rolling, one of Gath's hands dove for his knife. Its fingers closed on the hilt, and Baskt changed tactics. He wrapped his arms around Gath, pinning the hand between their bodies, and began to convulse, shaking and snapping.

The spiky protuberances on the sharkman's armor, like hundreds of small teeth, raked the Barbari-

an's arms, chest and legs. Pain seared into flesh and
spine. He began to roll in his own blood, and the
moisture sloshed over his pinned arm, making it
slippery. He pulled hard on the knife, and the blade
came out of its sheath. Gath turned it as they rolled,
and used the sharkman's convulsing body to help
him drive the blade deep into the living belly armor.

Feeling no pain, the demon spawn continued to
spasm, and the blade drove in repeatedly. Blood
drained from the wounds, then suddenly erupted in
fountains, and they rolled in that. Locked together.
Howling.

The onlookers stared open-mouthed, stunned.

It was at that moment that Gath felt a surge of
satisfaction shoot through him, a sense of fulfillment
that spilled over him, coming from all directions. He
was immersed in battle, at the core of the chaos and
pain and blood and howling, and he felt a kinship
with this territory as he had felt with no other. Not in
the lair of the wolf, not in the rain forest at the dark
of midnight, not marching at the head of a tramping
army. Here death was the only escape, and the only
release. He had found the world he searched for. It
was that wild place at the center of a battle to the
death, and he was home.

Thunder rolled in the sky above. The ground
below shook. Darkness blotted out the sky. The
sounds of scurrying men and snorting frightened
camels and horses erupted nearby, and a whimpering cry of dread fear. Cobra's. Then cold wetness
pummeled Gath's struggling back and legs. Rain. A
sudden desert torrent was descending from dark
clouds overhead, and its heavy drops filled the air,
blurring all vision.

Baskt, growling with cold satisfaction, and seem-
ing to take strength from the downpour, shook with

renewed effort, stronger and stronger. The pain of
the hundreds of biting teeth numbed Gath's mind.
His grip weakened, and his knife was bludgeoned
from his hand by the Lord of Destruction's twisting
hip. It tumbled across the stone and splashed in a
puddle of diluted blood.

Baskt glanced at it triumphantly, and their bodies
slipped slightly apart. Gath thrashed for release,
tearing at the sharkman's arm, and it came out of the
shoulder socket. Gath discarded the lifeless arm
unconsciously, kicked free and rolled across the
stone, jumping to his feet. Rain pelted his bloody
hide and washed him clean in seconds. But fresh
blood came as soon as the old was washed away, and
he teetered weakly in place, his strength ebbing.

Through the sheet of rain, Gath could barely make
out Baskt kneeling about five feet away. His guts
were streaming from his stomach, and he was
matter-of-factly stuffing them back inside. The fact
that he now had only one arm and hand made the
work slow.

Gath started for him bare-handed. His knee gave
way, and he dropped onto all fours. He pushed up,
then staggered backward. He kept at it, fell off the
auction block and splashed in a puddle at its base.
He flung himself over onto his knees, head low and
wary. Exhausted. Gasping. The blinding rain obliterated everything beyond three feet. Its roaring splat-
ter covered all sound.

A softness pressed into his back. The body of a
woman. It contrasted so sharply with the world he
now inhabited that the pleasure was sublime, ener-
vating. He dizzied at it. Then he heard a grunt of
hard effort, as if someone were lifting a weighty
object, and Cobra's arms and upper body fell heavily
against his back. He knew her curves and scent. She

was heaving something toward his head. He reached up, felt the rim of the horned helmet just as it touched his hair, and stopped it there.

"You must," she begged. "He's too strong. He's getting back up."

Her voice was frantic, suddenly so void of her normal cunning and subterfuge, that it confused him, and he thought for a moment it was Robin behind him instead of Cobra. In that moment he relaxed slightly, and the helmet slid down over his head, imprisoning him.

He rose instantly, sensing the rush of approaching danger, and darkness and blood hunger boiled through his body. Here within the confines of the helmet was a world beyond the wild place. Here battle held no laughter. The last tie with civilization was broken, and he hungered for the taste of frothing blood on his lips.

His head snapped up, and directly above him he saw a massive convulsing darkness dropping out of the rain-filled sky. Baskt.

Gath thrust up with his head through the driving rain, and the horns of the helmet speared up into the descending belly. The force was such that both horns and helmet impaled it, the metal sinking into demon flesh until the flaming eyes of the Death Dealer were washed in blood.

The horns worked into gut and organ, spearing and tearing, then ripped from side to side. Flames blazed out of the helmet's eye slits, incinerating the gore, and an acrid scent of burning fish mixed with the humid air.

Gath's hands caught hold of throat and leg, and crouching low, he drove forward blindly, ramming the sharkman's body against the side of the auction block. His legs kept driving, holding the flailing body

in place. His helmet twisted voraciously. Then the
demon came apart in the middle, falling away in two
pieces, and the helmet bit into the stone.

Gath backed away in a low crouch, leaving the
separated remains of the demon behind. The legs
and hips lay motionless in one puddle of water. The
head and arms and chest thrashed violently in
another.

Gath felt Cobra move up beside him and take hold
of his elbow and shoulder with feverish fingers. She
was trembling, then she gasped.

Fumes were issuing from the demon spawn's gory
chest cavity. Smoke followed, and snapping eruptions of flashing light chased each other within the
smoke. The flashing stopped, and the rain quickly
dispersed the smoke, revealing the upper half of a
great white shark shuddering on the ground.

The rain started to lighten and thin out, revealing
vague figures in the surrounding distance.

Cobra moved in front of Gath, holding his stallion's reins, and looked up at him with the rain
splattering over her white face. "We must leave.
Now! While the rain covers our escape."

He shook his head. "Better they all die."

He moved to his fallen axe and picked it off the
auction block as she followed leading his stallion.
"That won't help," she said forcefully. "Schraak is
here, one of my former servants, and he's seen me."

He turned to her, his eyes thoughtful. Her face was
different, almost girlish with fear and excitement.

Cobra said, "He came out of the black tent while
you were fighting. He recognized me immediately
and loosed his carrier eagles with messages. Before
dark, Tiyy will know everything, and her regiments
will be hunting us!" Her breathing heaved. "Let
Robin remove the helmet, then we must flee."

He hesitated and said, "It's too late for that." He took the reins of his stallion and swung up into the saddle. "Hide her in the wagon. I must not look at her. The helmet is too strong now."

Cobra gasped. "Noooooo!"

He nodded. "The helmet wants her even now. Hide her in the wagon."

Fear blotted Cobra's face, but she controlled it, saying, "I'll hide her . . . you can trust me. She'll be safe."

He looked down at her, and knew he could trust her, but had no idea why.

Moments later he was riding through the blinding rain with the wagon rumbling behind him as they headed out of the camp. Behind them, vague bodies raced about and hollered ineffectually in the surrounding gloom.

Twenty-eight

THE HELMET'S SLAVE

Cobra crawled halfway out of the trapdoor on the roof of the bounding wagon, and looked around anxiously. The bloom of girlish fear was still on her white cheeks, but her intractable will was back behind her eyes.

The rain had stopped as suddenly as it had started, and the brilliant mid-day sun streamed down on the vehicle as it splashed through steaming puddles and raced between walls of rock at the western extremity of En Sakalda. Up ahead was a wooden bridge. Gath galloped across it. His broad back was caked with drying blood, and bits of gore dangled from the helmet's horns.

The structure spanned a man-made channel which separated the island of rock from the main land mass, and linked the two dry river beds which curved around the island. Long ago the two rivers had filled the channel with water, providing a defensive moat, but now it was dry.

Kneeling on the roof, Cobra started to close the trapdoor, and Robin's frightened face popped up out of the shadowed opening. Her eyes were desperate, pleading. Cobra, shaking her head, closed the door in her face, then looked about the roof with vigilant eyes.

Everything, wood, bodies and clothing, was soaked and glittered in the sunlight. Jakar lay at the rear end in a puddle, with one arm tucked against his chest. It looked broken. His other arm aimed his loaded crossbow over the backboard. His hard eyes were on the road, waiting for whoever might emerge from the rocks of En Sakalda. Brown John stood in the driver's box, whipping and shouting at the horses with all the gusto he could muster, as if they had suddenly become the principal players in his greatest production.

Cobra's face made a circumspect smile, then she held still, listening.

A churning roar was rising above the sounds of the wagon. It came from the hills to the south where the center of the storm had been, and was growing louder and louder. It blotted out all other sound. Then a crashing, spilling deluge rushed into the channel. A fifteen-foot-high wall of water, rising in waves and dropping on itself to rise again. A flash flood. Before the wagon had crossed the bridge, the weighty torrent was battering the posts supporting it.

Gath reined up on the opposite side of the bridge and turned toward the wagon with his arm extended, pointing at a trail leading toward gnarled black hills in the distance.

The wagon bounded off the bridge, and the *bukko* pulled on the reins, guiding the horses toward the desired trail.

The trapdoor suddenly burst open, and Robin's head again popped out. "What's happening?" she blurted. "Where . . . ?"

Cobra fell on her, pushing her back inside the wagon and silencing her with a hand over her mouth. Then she turned sharply and looked over the rim of the sideboard at Gath as the wagon swept past him. Her big almond-shaped eyes were desperate with fear.

Gath did not look at the wagon. He had not seen Robin. Nevertheless the eye slits of the horned helmet were smoking and flickering with raw fire, and his swarthy muscles had swollen brutishly. The helmet was still feeding him, not only with its powers but with its diabolical appetites.

When the wagon had left Gath a good fifty feet behind, Cobra pushed herself away from the trapdoor and put her harsh gold eyes on the girl's upturned face, snapping discordantly, "I told you! You must not let him see you!"

"It's always helped him before," Robin protested, her lower lip protruding.

"It won't now!" Cobra shouted. "The helmet has him. You can't remove it now! And it wants you! He told me himself." Robin gasped, sinking weakly to the next rung of the ladder. Cobra nodded fatefully.

"He's fighting it . . . but you've got to help. If he sees you, he won't be able to control it."

Robin shuddered and nodded repeatedly. Then she obediently climbed down into Brown John's room, where she shuddered some more.

Cobra shut the trapdoor and found Jakar's young handsome eyes on her. Their corners smiled with defiant irony. His voice rang with the same sentiment as he shouted over the rumbling, squealing wheels, "It's hell being beautiful, isn't it?"

She grinned, finding his levity strangely relaxing, and shouted back, "Is your arm broken?"

"I hope so," he shouted lightly. "I've always wanted to be crippled." He grinned at his own joke and looked back at the trail.

Chuckling at his self-mockery, she climbed into the driver's box beside Brown John. He was sitting now, and his cheeks were flushed with effort. She patted his arm by way of assuring him she was glad to be beside him again, then held it, and looked back at the bridge.

Gath was walking his stallion onto it, indifferent to the fact that it twisted and shook under him, the full force of the flood now attacking the supporting timbers.

"Has he destroyed the bridge yet?" Brown shouted without looking at her.

"No," she hollered, "he's waiting for them!"

The color drained from the *bukko*'s face, and he looked back over his shoulder at the bridge. "The reckless fool!" he snarled. "He's not only risking his neck, he's risking ours. He should have torn it down!"

"Gath would have," she shouted, "but once again we are dealing with the helmet, not Gath." The *bukko* looked at her, fear hard in his brown eyes, and she added, "He can't resist a fight anymore. The helmet won't let him." She sank slightly in the box, and her voice dropped. "Look . . . see for yourself."

Brown John glanced back again and grimaced painfully.

Mounted bat soldiers were galloping out of En Sakalda. They were shouting unheard in the roar of the flood, and their small horses spattered mud in all directions as they charged for the bridge.

Gath now waited at the center, patient and motionless, even though the bridge was weaving back and forth, promising in every way to fall.

The flash flood had risen almost to the crests of the channel's dirt walls, and was sloshing over the flooring of the bridge. Then a huge wave rose up and crashed across the structure, taking out railings and staggering the stallion. Gath did not appear to notice. He yanked the frightened horse back under control and turned it sideways, blocking the bridge.

The furry, shouting demon spawn thundered onto it and bore down on him with spears leveled.

He waited, bare chest and naked legs glistening wetly in the sunshine. As the spears arrived, he suddenly pivoted in his saddle and swung his axe in a wide arc. With uncanny accuracy, he clipped off short lengths of spear, and their blades fell off just before they reached him. The splintered butts wavered, some gouging him, but most missing altogether. Simultaneously, two spears, which had ducked away from his blow, drove deep into the chest and rump of the stallion.

The stallion reared and whinnied in pain, banging the smaller attacking horses to a snorting, thrashing stop. At the front of the melee, Gath cleaved with his axe and again hauled his snorting, kicking mount under control. Then he plunged into the center of the confusion. There his axe worked to advantage, and the spears were rendered harmless, too long and awkward to wield in cramped quarters.

Several smaller horses were driven into the rush of the flood below, taking their screaming riders with them. The remaining bat soldiers dropped their spears and reached for their swords. Too late. The axe blade ate head and gut, and bodies dropped onto the bridge. Another wave washed over it, carrying off the lamed and wounded and dropping Gath's bleeding, dying stallion to its hocks and knees.

Gath jumped free, and stood in the middle of the mayhem with his body and weapon whirling in place.

Chests and necks and joints were severed, and he vanished behind eruptions of blood and body parts. Then, as suddenly as it had started, the cascading flood fell away, and the bodies of the soldiers and animals crumpled to lie writhing on the bridge around Gath's blood-red body.

Cobra watched with no expression on her face, except for the pride and passion hidden deep behind her molten eyes.

He stood in the middle of the carnage, like no other man had stood before. His stallion had toppled over on its side beside him and was kicking mindlessly at the air. Then another huge wave rushed down the belly of the channel and washed over the bridge, carrying away most of the bleeding, screaming clutter.

Gath, bending low and staggering, fought against the wall of water and held his place, but his stallion vanished amid the deluge. When the wave passed, the Barbarian stood motionless, angrily staring down at the rushing water below. His bloody hands held his axe across his thighs. His chest heaved.

Smoke and fire leapt from the helmet's eyes, crying out his loss. Then the fire died, abruptly, and his body jerked, as if his heart had taken the full thrust of a sword.

Cobra gasped out a sharp scream, feeling the pain he felt at the loss of his animal companion. Brown John looked at her, not understanding, then back at the bridge, and groaned in fear.

The old man gathered the reins in his fists, pulled back hard, and the wagon rumbled to a stop. Then he gathered Cobra in his arms and held her trembling body, as they and Jakar watched helplessly.

The bridge was crumbling under Gath, but he did not move. He seemed incapable. The remains of the railing splintered away, and floor boards appeared to rip themselves free, exploding and twirling into the air. Then part of the main body of the bridge folded up behind Gath, and was carried away in the frothing torrent, cracking and exploding with breaking timbers.

Floor boards and supports started to give way under Gath, and he leapt nimbly away from them, started toward land. He seemed to be in no hurry, as if the helmet could measure the exact extent of the danger he was in. Then the bridge collapsed, and Gath dropped out of sight with it.

Cobra, Brown John and Jakar each shuddered silently, suddenly bereft of all hope. But still they watched.

Pained empty moments passed, then there was a shadowed movement on the lip of the channel, where the ground and the bridge had been joined. Then a figure climbed to safety and started to run toward them. It carried a large battle-axe, wore a horned helmet, and its eye slits were aflame.

"Holy Bled," murmured Brown John, "perhaps

the holy White Veshta is finally giving us some help."

Cobra did not reply.

When Gath reached the wagon, it was starting to roll forward again. In a frenzy of action he stuck his axe in the side of the wagon, grabbed the halter of the lead horse and dragged it forward until it broke into a gallop. Then he leapt onto its back and kicked it into a run, hanging on to the traces.

When they vanished behind a ridge, there was no one following on the back trail, and a maze of lava hills and gullies and trails lay before them. They were gnarled and black, and tangled with sprawling boulders, overhanging shelves and rimrock.

"Beautiful," Brown John shouted excitedly, surveying the waiting landscape. "I could not have planned for a more timely stage."

"It is called the Kaja," Cobra shouted, "the Belly of Black Veshta. The hard ground leaves few tracks, and it spreads for miles and miles. It is said that several tribes have become lost trying to pass through the lava, and that an entire army could hide in it."

"Then a wagon should have little difficulty," the *bukko* howled gleefully, and whipped the horses forward.

Two hours later, the wagon rolled through high hills where green shrubs grew from pockets of earth caught in bowls and fissures lining the black rock. They were no longer in the desert. Grey clouds hung heavily in a grey sky, and cool air blew out of the south.

Following a trail that twisted between concealing walls of lava, they descended a narrow ravine. Gath motioned for Brown John to stop the wagon beside a deep chasm. The wagon pulled up, and the large draft horses snorted and stomped in place, wary of the depths they were parked beside.

Gath, straddling the lead horse, turned in place, putting the still glowing eyes of the helmet on Cobra. "You can find the way from here?"

"Yes. If the sky is clear tonight, I can go by the stars."

Making no reply, he dropped off the horse and cut it free of its traces.

"What are you doing?" demanded Brown John.

When Gath did not answer, Cobra answered for him. "I believe he intends to destroy the wagon and hide it, probably in that chasm."

She nodded at the shadowed depths, and Brown John groaned, "But it's my home. He just can't . . ."

"We must," she interrupted. "It will slow us now, and they will be looking for it."

"We're going to ride draft horses? Without saddles?" he asked in dismay.

"If he can't find better."

Gath remounted the lead horse, and it stomped about, unaccustomed to the freedom. Using the remnants of the severed traces as reins, he quickly brought it under control and rode back to the wagon. He removed his axe from the sideboard and faced Cobra and the *bukko*. Jakar sat behind them, cradling his broken arm and holding his amused curiosity behind his eyes. But they also held respect, and his tone was cordial and grateful as he spoke.

"Thanks for the help back there."

"Yes," said Brown John, "and we're sorry about your horse."

Gath did not appear to hear them. He put his burning eyes on Cobra, and his voice grated. "How did they identify her?"

"I don't know," Cobra replied, "but they did, not only Baskt but Schraak."

He nodded. "You will wait here. I will find horses and saddles, then we will travel by night."

His voice denied any argument, and they nodded agreement.

Gath turned the horse away and kicked it into motion, heading back the way they had come.

"Be careful," Cobra pleaded. "Even you can get lost in these hills." She started to say more, but stopped herself, knowing he was not listening. She sank into the *bukko*'s arms, shuddering, as Gath vanished beyond a ridge of rimrock.

After a moment, Jakar put his eyes on Cobra. "How much further is it?"

With her eyes still on the spot where Gath had disappeared, she said, "Hopefully less than two days . . . but perhaps three."

Brown John patted her shoulders. "Don't worry, we'll get there. He'll be back in no time."

She nodded uncertainly and removed herself from the *bukko*'s gentle hold. In a voice that was low and quivering, she said, "I think now is one of those times when some levity would be very helpful."

They nodded, but said nothing. They were out of jokes.

Twenty-nine

SADDLED HORSES

Gath sat easy on the draft horse, one hand clutching the makeshift reins. He had left the road and now moved through the maze of upended, broken black rock of the lava beds called the Kaja. Cranny, defile, slit, gulch and crevasse offered passage in all directions. Twisting hard passage over black rock and through black shadow. Twenty feet further on, another set of the same choices presented itself. The surrounding rocks limited vision to fifty feet, and sometimes only ten. The low dark cloud cover prevented the sky from offering any sense of direction. No sound offered any information. There was only the squeal of wind through chink and gap and his own sounds. He had been hunting better than an hour and had no idea where he was, but plodded forward steadily. Sure of his direction.

He had surrendered to the helmet.

The headpiece hung low between his shoulders, its hot metal steaming in the grey wet air. The horns pulsed with life, subtly bending and turning like the antennae of some huge bug as they hunted out the nearest danger. His hand responded to each turn, tugging on the reins and guiding the huge horse under arch and down goat path.

He followed a narrow ridge, turned a corner, and a road appeared at the base of a steep incline. He rode down onto it, the clatter of hooves becoming dull thuds as the draft horse moved onto dirt. The tongue of bald ground ran fairly straight for about forty feet in both directions, then vanished behind jagged black rock.

He sat motionless, waiting. The horns pulsed. Suddenly the helmet turned his head, and black smoke billowed from the eye slits. Flames. He turned the horse, and felt it. The vibrations of hooves reverberating in the road. Then he heard them. A group of horses, not coming hard, but steadily. He gathered the traces tight and propped his axe upright on his thigh.

They came around a turn two abreast. Bat soldiers. A patrol of six riders on small horses with long-haired manes and tails. Seeing the smoking, flaming Barbarian, they reined up, chattering to each other. Then two plunged forward, spears in hand.

Gath prodded his mount forward. His breath came in heaving gasps. His blood was hot and the air cool on his sweating flesh. His mind was clouding as helmet dominated man, blotting out sight and sound, forming a tunnel of vision focused on the scent and sound and sight of the living meat coming at him.

The two soldiers reined up, rising in their stirrups and screeching, and threw their spears.

Gath kept coming. Eyes on the furry, leather-clad bodies, yet watching the streaking spears. He turned a shoulder out of the way of the first, and leaned the helmet into the second. It clanged off harmlessly, and he kept coming.

The demon spawn drew their swords and charged. High-pitched squealing rang from their throats, and their four watching comrades added their voices to the unholy battle cry.

The helmet knew the song they sang, and responded with a harmonic howl unnatural in its beauty.

The music chilled the bat soldiers. Sword arms fell slack. Mouths dropped open.

The draft horse slammed into the first small horse, and it went down backward, throwing its rider. At the same time the helmeted Barbarian turned the axe flat, swung it and caught the second bat soldier full in the chest as he galloped past. His hollow, birdlike bones disintegrated on impact, and he was driven out of his saddle. He hit the ground with a slap, the middle of his body as shapeless as a bloody leather sack.

The helmet howled its approval.

The four remaining bat soldiers turned their mounts and galloped back the way they had come. The fifth horse followed dragging its rider, whose foot was caught in a stirrup. The riderless horse continued in the opposite direction.

Gath, his mind briefly clearing, saw the horses and saddles he hunted riding off, and gave chase. But the smaller horses quickly pulled away and vanished around a turn in the road. Gath leaned forward on the draft horse, body loose and pliant, and prodded the animal forward, compelling it with the heat and intensity of his touch and weight. The horse galloped faster and faster, churning up the dirt road, then added more speed. A thundering boulder of meat and bone.

When the bat soldiers saw the huge horse gaining on them, they spurred their small horses hard, drawing blood. But the big horse kept gaining. In desperation, the bat soldiers turned off the road onto a narrow, rocky trail and vanished among the dark jagged terrain.

Gath followed, dashed through gut and gully and reined up on a slight rise. The four mounted bat

soldiers milled in a boxed hollow thirty feet below,
while the fifth lay dying on the ground with his foot
still caught in the stirrup. They were trapped. Two
riders tried to goad their mounts up a steep slope,
but the slippery rock denied them passage. Then,
seeing the huge horse and its rider start for them, the
bat soldiers jumped out of their saddles and scrambled up among the rocks. They tore their flesh on the
sharp rocks, then vanished, bleeding, among them.

Gath walked his horse halfway down the slope
toward the waiting horses and saddles, then hesitated. The helmet was growing hot again, the horns
pulsing. The smell of blood swirled around him, hot
and humid, and his vision once more clouded, his
body heaving for breath. Savage. Animal. Wanting
the taste of the frothing wet redness on his lips.

He leapt off the horse, dashed through the boulders, and the euphoria of the death hunt spilled
through every pore and nerve. The thrill of the kill.

The helmet leading him, he ran down one bat
soldier and pulped him against a flat rock, then ran
down a second and caught him on the horns of the
helmet, threw him into a crevasse. He cornered two
more, their backs against a wall of rock and their
hands empty. Helpless. Craven. Living meat without
a chance or challenge. They were simply more
useless kills. Nevertheless, the helmet howled for
satisfaction, and pushed the Barbarian's body two
strides closer.

The soldiers whimpered and went to their knees,
their eyes and bowels emptying.

The man-pride in Gath snarled and revolted, and
his body came to a stop. His mind demanded control
of itself, defying the helmet's hungers. The metal
steamed and the horns writhed, sending pulses of
desire into the flesh of his body. His pride denied
them, then shame came to its aid, and once again

muscle and sinew, revolted by themselves, contracted, bending his huge frame.

Fighting the helmet, he backed up the slope,
turned and walked away, listening to the bat soldiers
crawl in the opposite direction.

Following a trail of blood left by one of the bat
soldiers, he found his way back to the boxed hollow.
The five saddled horses still milled about, chewing
on short rain-fresh grass growing in pockets of earth.
He tied them in a string, mounted one, and led the
string to the top of the slope where the draft horse
stood idly. He took its traces in hand and guided the
animals the short distance back to the road. There he
looked around for a long moment and realized he
had no idea where he was or in which direction he
should head to find his comrades.

He rode back the way he had come, passed the
dead bat soldier and reined up where he thought he
recognized the gut by which he had first reached the
road. He led the draft horse into the gut and gave it a
sharp slap on the haunch, hoping it would head back
for the wagon. The animal trotted through the gut,
then found another passage back to the road and ran
off.

Gath, his eyes hunting the ground for any sign of
his passage, led the string of horses into the gut. He
found a scraped rock, a hoof print in soft earth, then
nothing, and stopped. Rocks the color of shadows
and shadows the color of rock surrounded him, and
endless natural trails heading in all directions. He
dismounted and led the string forward a few feet,
portioning off the ground in squares with his eyes
and studying each carefully. Finding nothing, he
moved forward and began again. He did this until
the already dark sky grew darker, the daylight dying
behind it, and the truth could not be avoided.

He was lost.

The helmet suddenly lightened, the metal mocking him with laughter. Then it quickly grew heavy again, forcing his head low between his shoulders and making him spread his feet for balance. Smoke and heat showed in the eye slits, and the horns pulsed, sending commands into his body. The helmet was choosing a path to the right between low spreading boulders.

Gath fought it, holding his place, and the metal's hunger increased. It was not danger the metal sensed and wanted to guide him to. Another, stronger desire fed it now. Revenge. It wanted to feed on the creature which had denied it satisfaction and control for so long, and it was pointing the way to that creature. Gath heaved and sweated, holding back, then surrendered to it and started forward. He had no choice, even though he knew it now hungered for Robin Lakehair.

Thirty

LIAR

Cobra climbed up the interior stairwell to the second story of the wagon and asked, "Any sign of him?"

The *bukko*, standing at the window looking out, shook his head. "Not yet." He turned, bringing his boyish smile with him, and said comfortingly, "You've got to relax. We're going to need all the energy we can muster for the trail tonight."

"I should never have put the helmet on him," she despaired. "It was stupid."

"You had no choice."

"I'm not so sure. I was frantic. I behaved like a mindless girl." She threw herself across his bed, hiding her head in her arms. "Oh, Brown, it's so maddening. Once I would have known exactly what to do, and done it without hesitation. Sent an army to help him, or concocted some demon, or poisoned him to quiet his hunger." She lifted her head. "I did that once before, you know. I actually poisoned him. But I've got no poisons now, and no skills to make them. I'm helpless, and alone. And I don't know how to wait. I'm going crazy."

She buried her head again and shuddered the full length of her voluptuous body.

Brown John hesitated, then said quietly, "You're not alone."

She looked across a bare shoulder at him, as if he were a world away.

He stood with his back leaning against the sill of the open window. Outside it was silent and growing dark. Nothing moved. The wall of lava rising above the wagon was black against an indigo sky, and Brown John's face, lit by guttering candlelight, was bright against the darkness. He had obviously been pondering their desperate situation himself, tearing at his hair with his pudgy fingers. But as he spoke again, his voice only carried its normal puckish optimism.

"Robin, I presume, is safely out of his sight, in case he should show up suddenly?"

"Yes," she said emptily. "She promised me she would not let him see one finger." She chuckled hollowly and sat up with her back against the wall. "She's such a simpering fool. She wanted to make me stop worrying, so she assured me that Gath would not only come back, but that we were going to succeed. Not only steal the jewels, but solve all the world's problems with them." She chuckled with humorless ridicule. "Then she went to sleep, as if there wasn't a worry in the world. She's down there now."

Brown John asked casually, "What do you think about the jewels?"

"I don't," she said flatly. "It's pointless if Gath doesn't come back."

The *bukko* smiled carefully and said, "You would make far better company if you could forget that for a while." Getting no reply, he asked, "What do the jewels look like, exactly? Are they ordinary gems, or do they have their own particular qualities?"

"I don't know, Brown," she sighed impatiently. "What difference does it make? There is no point in discussing them now."

"Perhaps not," he said lightly. He sat down beside her, and his brown eyes glittered recklessly. "How old are you?"

"What?" she asked, startled.

"We've got to pass the time somehow, so tell me. How old?"

Thrown off guard, she asked, "Does it show that much? Am I beginning to look my true age, is that it?"

"No," he said, "only more accessible. Now, how old, or have you forgotten?"

"I haven't forgotten," she said candidly, her grey-gold eyes meeting his brown. "I was fourteen when I gave myself to the Master of Darkness, twenty-six when he made me a queen, and I was a queen for twelve years. I guess that makes me thirty-eight, almost thirty-nine."

He grimaced. "That's awful. Nobody should have to be that old."

She laughed with a burst of relaxation, then sighed again and said quietly, "That's not the hard part. I can deal with the added weight and a few wrinkles. But inside I'm mixed up. I have no experience or skills as a mere woman, and when I least expect it, my emotions run wild on me, like I was still fourteen."

"How wild?" he asked, not with a provocative tone, but a deadly serious one.

She hesitated, growing tense, then suddenly turned and sank facedown, avoiding his eyes. Her voice turned low and brutal with self-mockery.

"When he didn't come right back, I was going to kill myself. Really. I'd never felt so full of self-pity. I didn't even think it was possible. It just overwhelmed me and I had to end it." She laughed bitterly, deep in her throat. "But I couldn't find my knife, and it passed."

He smiled, drew a dagger from inside his belt and held it up. It was hers. She looked at it, and again put her eyes on his, holding them this time for a long moment before she spoke.

"You knew!"

"I see things coming sometimes," he said, as casually as if he were discussing someone coming down the road. "Particularly if I am deeply involved with . . . or care for someone."

His change in tone made her hesitate, then she said, "You shouldn't care, Brown. You should have let me do it."

He shook his frowsy head. "Couldn't afford to. After this is all over, I'm going to need a snake charmer, and you have rather unusual qualifications."

She couldn't repress a smile, and shook her head, amused at the timing of his humor.

He shrugged and ran a hand over the boot hiding her scales, then over her calf, patting it gently.

She said, "Brown, I can't believe that a man as wise as yourself is actually making plans for the future at a time like this."

"But this is precisely the time to make them," he said emphatically. "And you should be doing the same. You have a lot of lost time to make up for. Twelve years! The prime of your life!"

"They weren't lost," she said absently. "I was a queen. I had the finest clothes, food, jewels. And an army! Power! Don't forget that, I had everything I wanted."

"I don't believe that," he said softly.

He leaned over and removed a strand of hair from her cheek, looking into her eyes. "Don't, Brown," she purred. "Don't look inside. You'll . . . you'll see things you don't want to see."

"I'll take that chance," he murmured. "Besides, I don't have a choice anymore. I know you've been playing with me, and leading me on, but I don't care."

"I wasn't leading you on. You saved my life! I was grateful, and I don't know any other way to behave with a man."

"I know," he said. "But there's more to it than that. You want to control me, because Gath depends on me. But that's all right too. I don't know what you're up to, why you really want to go to Pyram, but I don't care anymore. Sometimes I think I don't even care about the jewels anymore."

"Brown, don't," she pleaded. "I'll be all right now. You don't have to say that."

"I do," he said, suddenly breathless. He kissed her cheek, and she trembled at the heat in his lips. "I'm going to help you make up those lost years. All of them. One by one. I'm going to show you the other side of every mountain, show you the ways of the rivers and the wind . . . and make you days like you have never had before."

"Don't, Brown, please. I'm . . . you can't. I'm not made for the kind of dreams you dream."

"It's too late," he whispered. "You are their bright cloth now."

He kissed her softly, and she wanted to protest but could not, and surrendered to his touch. There was magic in his lips, a tender soothing magic she had not known existed, and it surged through her. Then she pushed him away, her voice pleading.

"Stop! Please stop!" she gasped. "You don't understand. You can't trust me. I'll let you down. I'll hurt you. And I don't want to."

He shook his head and said it again. "It's too late."

Silence came between them, and a sharp groan came from somewhere outside the wagon.

Cobra sat up wide-eyed and gasped hopefully, "Gath!"

They listened, once more in the middle of the fear and anxiety, but no sound came. They leapt up, and Cobra raced down the staircase as Brown John grabbed up his sword and followed.

The bottom room was empty. Robin was gone.

Cobra moaned and flung open the door, rushed through it.

Outside the wagon they looked up and down the narrow ravine and up at the crests of the lava walls siding it. There was no one, only silence and shadows and darkening sky. They shared a worried glance and held still, listening as a whispering voice echoed up and down the ravine.

"Don't bother with it, it's fine now." It was a courteous, male growl.

"I'm not leaving until I've finished." A girl's voice, full of zeal, and decisive.

"Yes, you are. Now get back in the wagon before he comes back and sees you." Male again, sharp and sensible.

Cobra and Brown John backed away from the wagon, their eyes aimed at the roof.

Jakar sat against the sideboard and Robin was kneeling beside him, wrapping a length of torn cloth around a wand she was using as a splint. The groan had obviously been made by Jakar when she reset the bone.

"You fool!" snarled Cobra. "Get back in the wagon."

Robin and Jakar, momentarily shocked, looked down at Cobra and the *bukko*.

"Do as she says," blurted Brown John. "Hurry!"

"In a minute," Robin said, and started knotting the cloth in place.

"I'll finish," said Jakar, pushing her off, but she wouldn't quit.

Cobra, desperate, climbed up the rungs of the driver's box heading for the couple, as Brown John shouted, "Robin, get back in the wagon."

The girl pulled the knot tight, stood, and the sounds of horses' hooves filled the ravine. Quiet, moving slow, but nearby.

Cobra froze, and the *bukko*, his voice suddenly weak, whispered, "Horses."

Jakar jumped up, taking Robin by the elbow, and pushed her toward the trapdoor. Suddenly she gasped, seeing something beyond the ridge above the roof, and pulled back. Jakar, seeing the same thing, stepped in front of her, shielding her body with his, and picked up his loaded crossbow, leveled it at the ridge.

Lurking darkness filled with the sounds of horses snorting and stomping loomed beyond the lip of the rock. The sounds were growing louder, advancing on the wagon.

"Nooo!" Cobra groaned, and dropped back off the wagon beside the *bukko*. He put an arm around her trembling shoulders and held her close. His sword ready in the other hand.

Where the indigo sky rose above black rimrock, the shape of the horned helmet appeared out of the looming darkness, its eye slits spitting flames. They hissed and grew brighter and brighter as Gath advanced to the edge and looked down at Robin. He was glistening with sweat, bloody from foot to chest, and the wounds he had received from Baskt were charred scabs surrounded by white ash. His huge axe dangled from one hand, caked with drying blood. The other held a lead rope guiding a string of five horses. Small, sturdy animals with fur blankets and black saddles.

Moaning, Robin sank into a puddle behind Jakar, and her loveliness sprawled helplessly, gathering moonlight with bare arms and thighs.

The horned helmet growled and roared at the sight, the axe trembling with impatience inside Gath's bloody grip. His body was hunched low, animal-like, and heaving with hunger. Suddenly tongues of flame spit from the face of the helmet, striking at Jakar, and he staggered back ducking and covering Robin.

Cobra sank against Brown John, her strength gone and her moans inarticulate. "He won't hurt her," Brown John said weakly. "He ..." The *bukko* stopped short, and his cheeks became white.

Gath's body had begun to shudder. Flames and smoke were sputtering from the helmet, and behind him the string of terrified horses whinnied and bolted, trying vainly to escape his grasp. But the Barbarian held on. He threw back his head and howled, and the ground shook beneath his feet. Chunks of rock fell away from the ridge and crashed against the side of the wagon below.

Robin hid her face behind Jakar, and he fired wildly.

The crossbow bolt clanged against the helmet, sheared off into the sky, and the metal roared, spitting shards of white lightning.

Brown John turned Cobra away, not wanting her to see what would happen next. But she resisted, watching over his shoulder with her hands gripping his arm.

Fissures opened in the ground under Gath's heaving weight, ripped down into the hard lava, and huge rocks fell away, crashing against the side of the wagon. Then slowly, like red-hot steel being twisted in an anvil, his body turned away.

Color rushed back into Brown John's cheeks, and his voice whispered encouragement. "That's it, my friend. Just walk away. Whip that filthy headpiece."

Gath remained in place, his back heaving with convulsions, and the ground shook again. Then he walked away, rejoining the darkness beyond.

Cobra, her body still shuddering against the *bukko*, looked up at him. Her face was childish with relief and joy, unable to believe what she had just seen.

Brown John sighed. "Now, I'll bet you're as glad as I am that you didn't stick that dagger in your heart. Just think of all the excitement you would have missed!"

She smiled weakly and kissed his cheek, saying, "I'll go find him. You make sure Robin's out of sight.

We don't dare let this happen again."

He nodded, and she hurried off, found a way up the ridge and vanished through a gut.

She found Gath under an overhanging shelf of rock well away from the ravine. He was on his hands and knees, heaving with flaming convulsions within the dark shadowed recess. The earth and rock beneath the helmet were scorched and smoking. To the side of the rocky shelf, the horses were tethered to a shrub and snorting and stomping with fear.

Gasping with relief, and with her emotions running chaotically through her heart and mind and body, Cobra knelt beside him. Knowing it was useless to speak, she touched his bare shoulder, thrilling at his heat, and the helmet turned slowly in her direction. She ducked away from the flames, felt his hands take hold of her neck and hip, and moaned, "Yes, yes! It's all right. It will cool it."

He drew her roughly under him, and she groaned with pain, the scorched earth searing her clothing and the backs of her bare shoulders. He hesitated, heaving like a smoking mountain above, massive and powerful. Her hands took his, drawing them to her breasts. Her voice had no will but his will. "It's all right. It's all right."

He took her then, quickly but with instinctive tenderness, the force of his weight and searing heat penetrating her flesh and heart. Flames ignited stray strands of her hair, but she did not notice. Her arms went around him, and she held on like the cloud holds the thunderstorm, tears welling from her eyes.

The fury of his passion, the hot metal and the flames took their toll of her clothing and body, but if there was pain she did not feel it. Nor would she recall it. There was only pleasure. But not the heady erotic rapture she had known so often before. This time it had impossible dimensions, was of a size and softness and rapture and contentment only dreamed of by young girls. Never before had a man as powerful and proud and deadly as Gath of Baal walked the earth, nor would there ever be such a man made again, and she held him in her arms.

Tonight he belonged to her.

Thirty-one

NIGHT RIDERS

The string of five riders headed west by north on the Way of the Scorpion. Their bodies were covered with dark robes, and they kept to the low ground, galloping through the concealing gloom of defile and canyon, only crossing moonlit mesa and hogback when the route demanded it.

Three hours had passed since they had packed their provisions on the stolen horses, heaved the wagon into the chasm and ridden into the night. But the string had never lost shape or strength. They rode together, with one destination, one purpose.

Gath galloped well ahead, picking his way through the midnight darkness with his metal head still sputtering flames like a volcanic avalanche. He wore his black chain mail now, and the musical clinks of the metal played lightly among the drumming of hooves on soft earth. Somehow he had mysteriously regained control of the helmet, but he had paid a price. The flames continued to sputter and smoke, and he had lost all ability to speak.

The *bukko* king was second in line, sitting his saddle like a nineteen-year-old braggart soldier in love. Since they had set forth, he had been deliberately displaying his horsemanship by guiding his horse over the most difficult passages, always being careful to suck in his paunch, and never failing to throw spicy glances back at Cobra, a woman young enough to be his daughter, and seductive enough to make a fool out of any nineteen-year-old, particularly one in his middle fifties.

Cobra followed diligently, being careful to acknowledge the *bukko*'s performance. She kept her hood over her head and held her robe tightly about her. Every so often, when the *bukko* was not looking, she would bend forward in the saddle and gasp, as if in pain. But when someone would take notice, she immediately sat erect, and rode on with determination and spirit.

Robin stayed as close to the serpent woman as she could, watching her carefully and with concern. The girl was now so wrapped in black robes that she looked like a billowing bag of felt.

Jakar rode at the tail of the string, with his eyes on the billowing bag. He could not see one soft inch of Robin. Nevertheless he was enjoying the sight of her, and the lighthearted glint in his eyes was now rooted in something more substantial than skepticism.

When the riders broke free of the lava beds, they left the Way of the Scorpion and plunged directly west through thickets of tamarisk and low-lying carob trees. They veered and slashed, tearing their cloaks and scratching faces and thighs, but did not slacken their pace. They continued in this manner for nearly an hour, hiding their movements in every available chink and cranny, and always guided by a distant star Cobra called Veshta's Light. Then the thickets thinned, and they reined up abruptly, still within the concealing growth.

Spreading in front of them were expansive mud flats, dry and hard, as white and smooth as ice in the moonlight, and shattered like a clay plate. In the distance, torch-bearing riders were headed in their direction. The small group watched the torches until they passed by several hundred feet to the north and vanished into the thickets. Spear-bearing soldiers or outlaws. It was impossible to identify them further in the dark. When the sound of their horses faded, Gath led the small group across the flats, using the trail torn out of the dry mud by the night riders.

The first light of dawn was edging into the black sky when they reined up in the bed of a narrow, intermittent stream. Behind them was a shadowy world, a gutted landscape of tabletop mesas, canyons, rifts and fractures. In front of them, a rolling plain rose gently through hazy darkness toward the foothills of a mountain range. The hills were even more gently curved and appeared soft in the dim light. They rose to fully rounded mountains that thrust voluptuously up into the embrace of the indigo sky. They seemed endless, each rising higher and higher. The Breasts of Veshta.

"There they are!" Cobra's breathless voice broke as she spoke, and her smile was weak. Nevertheless it spoke eloquently of her soaring expectations. "All . . . all we have to do is cross those mountains."

They sat exhausted and worn in their saddles, staring at the mountains, more sensing than seeing the faint morning light eat into the darkness around them. If they started into the plain, the sun would be beating down on them before they were halfway across. A moment passed, and Brown John asked the question they were all thinking.

"What do you figure, one more night? Two?"

Except for Gath, they all turned to Cobra. She was breathing heavily. Sensing their eyes, she calmed herself. "If we leave as soon as it's dark, we . . ." She hesitated, wavering weakly in her saddle, then drew herself erect and continued, "We should make Pyram before sunrise tomorrow."

They smiled at that, then held still, watching the plain.

In the distance, a troop of spear-carrying riders, strung out like a writhing black rope, had appeared heading away from them. One of the lead riders held a banner that flapped lazily on the air. It was black with three bright red circles on it, the mark of the Nymph Queen of Pyram.

When the soldiers vanished beyond a hill, Gath dismounted. Brown John, Robin and Jakar did the same, then Cobra tried and fell off her horse. Brown John, Robin and Jakar rushed to her, and the *bukko* held her in his arms, loosening her robes as Robin pushed back the hood. Cobra's hair was charred and burnt short in places on one side of her head, and her neck, shoulder and cheek were red and blistered.

"Holy Bled!" exclaimed Brown John.

"What happened?" Robin asked.

"It's all right," Cobra said weakly.

"No, it's not!" growled the *bukko*.

"Please, Brown," Cobra pleaded, "don't say anything. It's not his fault. And I can rest all day now. I'll be fine by dark."

"But you're badly hurt," the *bukko* said. "You should have said something."

She shook her head. "We couldn't have stopped to rest, and I really will be fine." She pushed the *bukko*'s hands aside gently. "So keep your hands to yourself, you shameless old goat. Robin will take care of me, won't you, lass?"

"Of course," Robin said. "Can you walk? There's a hidden spot just a little ways back that looked like it might be comfortable."

Cobra said she could walk, and they helped her to the spot Robin had spoken of. Then, as Robin privately saw to Cobra's wounds, the men tethered the horses in a depression, watered them and distributed equal portions of water and food for the group, with the exception of Cobra, who was given all her needs required. When Robin finished with Cobra, and the serpent woman fell asleep from the herbs the girl had given her, Brown John asked Robin how Cobra had been hurt.

"I can't tell you, Brown," she said firmly. "Before she would let me attend to her wounds, she made me promise not to speak to anyone about their nature."

"But how badly is she hurt?"

"She's in pain, but she'll be all right."

Not satisfied, he demanded, "Robin, this is the wrong time for you to be keeping your vows. Tell me what happened."

"I can't," she said, "but I will tell you this. Whatever she did, she did it for us."

The *bukko*, seeing he was going to get nowhere, joined Cobra to watch over his bright cloth as she slept.

Jakar and Robin sat together under a concealing shelf of rock, and Gath sat facing the plain behind a rock that looked a little less dangerous than he did. He sat apart from the others in the manner of his dream, by himself.

After Jakar and Robin finished their meal, he casually asked her, "What you said, about Cobra

doing whatever she did for all of us . . . you made
that up, right? To make Brown John feel better?"

She shook her bushy black-red hair. "That's what
she told me to tell him. She didn't want him to
worry, you know, just in case he would blame Gath
instead of the helmet for what happened."

"What did happen?"

"I can't discuss it," Robin said, ending that topic.

He nodded and asked carefully, "While you were
with her, did she look at the map?"

"No. She's exhausted."

Another nod, and he asked, "When did she last
look at it?"

Robin hesitated, frowning as best her smooth
forehead allowed, and said, "I guess it was early last
night, when she gave me this robe to wear. But it was
only a glance. She hasn't really examined it since she
drew it on me."

"That's what I was afraid of," Jakar said, and
leaned back against the rock. "I think she's been
lying. I think she knows the way to Pyram."

Robin started to protest, but gave up and bunched
her cheeks frumpishly under worried eyes. "I was
thinking the same thing. But why did she draw the
map then?"

"Maybe it's not just a map."

"You mean magic signs? Like . . . like before?"

He nodded, once.

"Maybe I should wash it off."

"Maybe," he said, leaving the decision to her.

She thought about it and said, "I don't know.
She's hurt. Hurt bad. And she won't complain about
it. She's very brave, and I don't know why, but I trust
her. And if it is a map, and she does need it, I don't
think . . ."

"I agree," he said, interrupting. "But she's hiding

something, isn't she? You can sense it, can't you?"

She nodded. "I didn't notice at first. I was, well, thinking about you and me, I guess, and wasn't concentrating. But I can feel it now, and the closer we get to Pyram, the harder it is for her to hide it."

"But you still trust her, don't you?" She smiled weakly in reply, and he added, "Well, if you trust her, I trust her."

She smiled at that, then frowned again. "But maybe we should tell Brown John and Gath."

He shrugged. "I'm sure they noticed long before we did."

"But they didn't say anything!"

"Wouldn't be any point. We're going to need her when and if we get to Pyram, and even if she's up to something, well, we still have a chance."

Robin nodded lamely and sat looking off at the mountains with worried eyes.

"Frightened?" he asked.

She nodded without looking at him.

"Good, you should be," he said. She looked at him, suddenly more frightened, and he added, "Whatever he did to her, he can do to you."

She took hold of her lower lip with her teeth, held it briefly, then let go and said evenly, "I know that. I've known it since we started. But he won't. He'll never hurt me, Jakar, believe me."

Jakar smiled at her for a long appreciative moment, then said gently, "Fluff, be careful. Things don't always turn out the way you want them to."

"Are you afraid I couldn't take it if they didn't? Afraid I'd be too hurt?"

"Yes," he said, "I am."

That made her smile, and instinctively she touched his cheek. She started to pull her hand away, but he caught it, stroking her fingers with his. They looked at each other for a long time before she spoke.

"You've changed."

"Yes," he said, "I just noticed that myself."

She grinned. "I guess I'm not going to need any jewels to cure you after all."

"Don't be too sure," he warned with a skeptical smile, then his dark eyes sobered and his voice became intense with passion. "All I can see, all I've ever seen when I look at you, is an incredibly rare jewel."

That melted her, and they gathered each other in their arms, kissing and kissing, like young lovers in the privacy of their hearts, and all around them the world was new.

When the sun was high in the sky, the group still sat in their hiding places, looking across the plain at the Breasts of Veshta. Waiting. They knew they could not move until the light had again died. Then they would cross the open ground, keeping to the shadow-filled valleys and guts between the hills, and ride into the mountains with their movements concealed by night's bountiful darkness. So they waited, silent and patient, each with their separate, yet single, dream.

Thirty-Two

NEW RECRUIT

Tiyy galloped up the mountain road, her dust billowing in the morning sunshine. Impatient. Dirty from a long trail. Leading a detachment of her household guards, a surly bunch wearing leather, steel, dust and violence the way their queen wore her power. Naturally.

The nymph rode bareback, a frothing black and white horse, and was as naked as the animal except for rawhide boots, leather breechclout and sheathed dagger strapped to her forearm. Savage. Regal. Her spiked blond hair flagged wildly and her dark walnut legs wore the trail dust as if it were sprinkled gold.

Reaching her recruiting depot at the heights of the Breasts of Veshta, she reined up hard and dismounted facing Schraak as he prostrated himself in the dirt before her. All around the compound, the border guards manning the depot did the same: at the stables, at the mouths of the many caves pockmarking the mountainside, and on the small parade ground fronting the caves. She looked down at the small man's shuddering body as if he were a hole in the ground.

His drab tunic was torn and filthy, and his body was blistered and heaving with exhaustion. He had obviously raced from En Sakalda to meet with her just as she had ordered him to via carrier eagle.

Without speaking to him, she glanced at a nearby group of prostrate, fearful bat soldiers.

Spotting the officer in charge, she shouted, "Get up, Captain." He jumped up, and she added, "I want armed patrols guarding every trail to Pyram! And I want every caravan, every traveler, stopped! No matter what their credentials. If this Death Dealer is spotted among them, do not attack him, but report back to me here. Immediately! Everyone else is to be killed. Do you understand? No traveler is to reach Pyram alive. And strip the women so Schraak here," she pointed with a booted foot, "can inspect them. I am not taking any more risks. Now send out your patrols!"

The captain saluted and ran about shouting orders. The sergeants instantly repeated them, and the depot burst into noise and action. In moments patrols were riding off in all directions. When they were gone, only the small depot garrison remained and the area became quiet, motionless. All eyes watched the young queen.

She turned back to Schraak. "So, the girl not only eludes me again, but this time her protector kills Lord Baskt. How did this happen, worm?"

"He . . . he was stronger," Schraak said hesitantly.

"What?" Tiyy snapped. "Don't talk like a fool! Get up! Look at me and tell me what happened."

He struggled up. "They . . . they fought. With sword and axe. And the Barbarian was truly Lord Baskt's equal. It was evident to everyone. But when he put on the horned helmet, he was stronger."

"Stronger?" Her tone was incredulous.

"Yes! It's true. I swear it!"

She nodded. "This Barbarian is proving to be almost as interesting as the girl. What else have you learned?"

"Cobra rides with them."

"Cobra?" Her large, sloping eyes were suddenly alarmed. "She's alive? Are you certain? Why didn't your message mention this?"

"I wasn't sure at first. She seemed different. Older. But just before they rode off, I heard her speak and knew it was her."

"So," said Tiyy quietly, feeling a sudden new threat and relishing the rush of excitement that came with it, "Cobra is alive . . . and has somehow allied herself with this brute she had sworn to destroy." She put her eyes on Schraak. "And you say she looked older?"

"Yes. By ten years easily."

Tiyy smiled with churlish malevolence. "Then she's lost her powers! Become a mere woman again! And a foolish, desperate one, at that." Schraak frowned in confusion, and she chuckled. "It is finally making sense why the girl has come here to hide in my domain. Somehow Cobra is controlling her, as well as this Death Dealer, and leading them to Pyram."

"But that would be madness," protested Schraak.

"For anyone else, yes," she said, "but not for the Queen of Serpents. She has always had far more cunning than anyone is entitled to. And with her powers gone, I doubt if there is anything she won't risk." Tiyy smiled knowingly. "She is going to try and steal the jewels. There can be no other answer. It's the only way the slithering bitch can regain her powers now."

"But she could never reach Pyram!"

"Couldn't she?" Tiyy asked mockingly. "If you believe that, then you know nothing about the woman you once served." She looked out over the endless landscape of rounded hills. "She knows every trail in these mountains, even in the dark. So they'll travel at night to avoid my patrols." She turned on the small man. "And if she reaches Pyram, she'll find a way into the castle. She knows of tunnels in the rocks even I have not explored. And the castle garrison is weak, perhaps even too weak to stop this Death Dealer." She nodded to herself. "He must be destroyed! And here! In these mountains. Tonight!" She smiled ruefully at the dark foreboding entrance of the largest cave. "And he will be. Get a torch and follow me."

Schraak hurriedly found a torch, rejoined Tiyy at the mouth of the largest cave and led her inside holding the flaming light in front of him.

Muffled fluttering greeted them and thousands of small eyes peered out of the hovering shadows of the huge cathedral-like cave. Schraak hesitated nervously, and the guttering torch cast moving light over row upon row of bats hanging from the rimstone ledges, stalactites and pillars, knobs and warts. Recruits for the nymph's army of bat soldiers awaiting induction and transformation.

The pair moved deeper and deeper into the meandering cave, tromping on a dark brown powder, millions of years of bat guano many feet deep. The cave grew smaller and smaller, and at the deepest point they crossed over a natural bridge of rock, spanning a stream, and entered a low tunnel. They followed it and came to an interior cave over a hundred feet high. It was silent except for the voices of wind passing through unseen flumes and holes.

Schraak used his torch to light an oil lamp carved out of the rock wall and it guttered to life, casting an orange glow into the cavern. It appeared to be empty. Stalactites hung from the ceiling, but the ground was cleared except for the deep mold of bat manure. At the sides, smaller caves and tunnels opened onto darkness, and at the back, a barred wall caged off a large shadowed gallery.

A door at the base of the cage wall was chained shut. Inside the cage was a throne large enough to seat a pair of well-endowed elephants. It was carved out of stone and inlaid with colored stones in the shape of cyphers and numerals and signs. Pillows, each of them large enough to serve as a bed for a child of six, were heaped on the seat.

The pair stopped before the chained door, and Schraak looked uncertainly from the empty throne to his queen. Her dark cheeks had turned hot under their orchid rouge, and her erect breasts looked suddenly untamed, as if a man would be smart to find a whip and stick before getting in bed with them. He hesitated, peering curiously into the cage and asked, "Is someone there?"

"Yes," she whispered. "Lord Menefret."

He turned sharply, gasping.

She smiled. "Yes. The transformation is almost complete. All he needs is one more feeding."

"But you're not strong enough."

"I have no choice," she interrupted, her quarrel-some eyes turning on him. "This Death Dealer must be found and killed tonight."

"But what if you weaken? He could drink you dry!"

"I am aware of that. That's why you're here. You know my strength is not what it should be, but the others do not. And they must not know. If," she hesitated, "if I do weaken, you must take me out of the cage, and not let anyone see me until I have recovered."

"But it's too great a risk."

She smiled at that and said, "What you fail to

understand, Schraak, is, the greater the risk the greater my pleasure. Now, open it!" Her breathing began to race, and her pointed breasts heaved with budding cruelty. "Open it!"

Schraak set his torch on a rock, hurriedly ran the chains through the grillwork, tossed them aside and swung the iron gate open with a noisy squeak. Tiyy nimbly slipped under the low arch, and he closed the door behind her with a discordant clang.

Slowly, he backed up to a fallen stalactite, and trembled. His grey blistered flesh was slick with slimy sweat, and he smelled of fear.

With swift agile leaps, Tiyy mounted the rocks forming the base of the huge throne and stood facing it. Gasping. Expectant. The front edge was level with her petulant breasts. She took hold of it and muscled her body up, swinging her legs onto the seat. There she stood slowly, peering into the shadows of the gallery. Stretching sensuously, she sprawled on her back among the massive pillows, abandoning herself to their comfort. Against their massive proportions, she looked like a live toy doll.

Removing her mouth harp from her breechclout, she played a haunting phrase three times, then tucked it back in place and waited. Flushed. Body subtly undulating with anticipation.

There was no sound but the faint drip of a stalactite somewhere. No movement but guttering torchlight too weak to penetrate the deep shadows filling the back of the gallery. Then a speck of light glittered on something wet sixty feet above the throne. A pair of small eyes.

Tiyy smiled coyly and said huskily, "Yes, Lord Menefret, it's me at last. Now come down here! Quickly! Today you will feed as I promised you you would feed . . . and tonight you will have powers like none of my lords has had before."

There was a fluttering sound, then the eyes dove forward, and a large bat swooped into the guttering light.

It darted and dove in the air above the throne, its wings flapping, swimming through the air rather than floating. A faint high-pitched clicking came from it, and grew louder and louder as the sound echoed around the cave. It swept through narrow crevices and small loops of hanging stone, passing within inches of jagged rocks in a display of aerial acrobatics. Strong. Proud. Grotesquely beautiful. Then it dove at Tiyy and came to a hovering stop in front of the throne.

A vampire bat.

Its fluttering wings were a full two feet wide and made of thin, almost transparent membrane. Its body was a dark grey-brown. Blunt muzzle hung low between pointed ears and flaming-red eyes. A tiny onyx earring dangled from one furry ear, a black triangle with three red circles on it.

The creature darted off, then back, this time brazenly hovering within inches of the reclining nymph's face. Mouth spread displaying long fangs. Eyes horrid with hunger.

Without flinching, Tiyy smiled directly into the ravenous eyes and whispered, "Patience, my lord. Patience."

The furry vampire bat clicked excitedly, and its dark tongue shot out. There were tiny grooves on its underside and in the lower lip, drinking straws that ran back down the throat.

The Nymph Queen's eyes thinned with desire. Her orchid cheeks pulsed. She stirred languorously beneath the bat, sinking back against a pillow and turning an inviting bare shoulder to its mouth.

The bat fluttered and dropped onto the fleshy perch, its clawed feet holding the nymph's sacred flesh without breaking the skin. Its wings spread wide casting deep shade across her heated face, and fingerlike wingtips embraced her, holding her by neck and hair.

Tiyy moaned slightly, and her lips parted, her breath now coming in sharp gasps.

The grotesque muzzle opened wide, displaying a dark pink mouth filled with sharp teeth, and the upper incisors buried their razor-sharp tips into her earlobe. Tiyy groaned, and her knees gathered up around a pillow, the pleasure of the brutal kiss so great she could barely bear it. Then the tongue lapped the wound, drinking her blood.

A warmth flooded through her and she surrendered to its ecstasy. "Yes! Yes! Drink deep. Tonight you must be strong."

In reply the vampire bat bit deeper. She gasped with pain and took hold of its chest, holding it in check. She let it drink, then gasped, "All right! That's enough." It continued, and she pushed at it, gasping weakly, "Stop. I'm growing faint."

The bat let go, then bit her neck, sucking hard. She shrieked in fear and began to beat at it, shouting, "Schraak! Schraak!"

The small man ran for the gate and fell.

Tiyy rolled across the throne, the bat clawing up ropes of her blond hair and scratching cheeks and shoulders. "Stop! Stop!" she howled, and finally forced him off.

He darted into the air, and shot back at her as she sat up, dropping lustily on a thrusting breast. She screamed and fell back beating at him. Her blows had no effect, and his incisors dipped into a lower swell, drinking ravenously.

"Aahhhhhhhh!" she moaned, and the strength went out of her arms. They fell to her sides like speared birds, and she sank back among the pillows in total surrender. Groaning with pleasure. Thrusting her opulent flesh to the sucking tongue.

When Schraak came through the gate, the spectacle of the vampire rodent embracing his holy queen stopped him cold. All color was draining from her body. Panicking, he started up the rocks, shouting, "Stop! Stop! He's murdering you!"

Tiyy's eyes snapped open, and she blinked uncertainly, her eyes fogged and vacant. Then they focused on her own shoulder. Its dark walnut flesh was turning white.

"Arrrrggggh!" she screamed, and viciously thrust the bat away, rolling onto her hands and knees.

The bat swooped and dropped on her back, driving her forward. She fell off the throne and rolled on the hard ground. When she looked up, Schraak had disappeared. Then he burst back in, thrusting his torch at the bat. It let go of her back, darted aside and up into the blackened shadows, squealing in complaint.

Tiyy stumbled down the rocks, and Schraak gathered her in his arms, then carried her out, kicking the gate shut behind them.

He set Tiyy down against a smooth rock, and the two sat gasping for breath. Her head hung limply, and her exhausted body heaved. A loud clicking sound came from the cage, and their heads snapped up, fear tearing at her tyrannical beauty.

Smoke was swirling high in the gallery, like moving shadows. Flames blazed within their dark embrace, and thunder roared from it, dispersing the greyish-brown clouds. They swirled down over the throne, filling the cage. Gushing sounds and shrieks followed, then the smoke drifted between the bars of the cage, dispersing itself throughout the cave. Slowly, through the thinning smoke, a huge creature could be seen perched on the throne.

Its body was thirty feet high. A monstrous vampire bat with wing thumbs as long as Tiyy's legs, and as thick as sapling oaks. A predator descended from the primordial past, a creature of ten thousand years of breeding and dark magic.

A Lord of Destruction who was also Lord of the Night.

The monster whipped his wings wide, bowing subserviently to the savage nymph, and the force of the wind they created made Tiyy and Schraak gasp for breath. When the wind subsided, Schraak looked fearfully at the creature in the cage, then at Tiyy. Her color was back, and she was smiling.

"This Barbarian cannot protect her now," she whispered.

Thirty-Three

SLAUGHTER

Gath climbed silently down a gash in the side of the cliff. Shadows filled it, hiding his movements except for pins of orange fire thrusting from the helmet's eye slits. Wild fire held in check by the pride of a man. Twice his chain mail tinkled on the night's silence, then he reached the shelf of earth overlooking the lower road and squatted there. Listening. Watching.

He did not hear a sound, or see a sign of anything

that was alive on the road. But still he waited. Murder rode the night the way the winter wind rides through the forest canopy.

He was in the middle of the towering Breasts of Veshta. Far above him, beyond the boulders lining the shadowy crest of the cliff, his four companions hid as they awaited his return. The troupe had crossed the plain and, following Cobra along almost undetectable goat paths, moved high into the mountains without incident. Then the white eye of the full moon came out from behind the cloud cover and cast its cold light on a frightening sight on the road below, and they decided to hide while Gath investigated.

Still hearing and seeing nothing, Gath crawled to the edge of the shelf and looked down at the road. Slowly the light went out of his eyes.

What lay silent on the road was not like any caravan he had seen before, or hoped to see again. There was something disturbingly unnatural about it, something out of place.

Dead horses, baskets and overturned wagons were strewn for fifty yards up and down the road, as if the caravan had panicked and fled in both directions. The gear on the animals had not been removed, and the baskets and wagons had not been pillaged. The dead bodies of the travelers were lying in two neat rows at the center of the debris, as if lined up for inspection. The men were of mixed races, and also did not appear to have been robbed. A few wore robes and turbans, the others wore rags and chains. But they were not separated. Slaver was lying beside slave. The women, however, were set apart, and had been stripped naked. All wore chains, and were healthy and attractive, the kind who normally survive a long trail. Their bodies were bloody, and wore dark wounds.

Gath studied the gruesome scene carefully. As horrible as it was, it was still just a scene of slaughter, and he could not detect what made it appear so unnatural.

He stood, intending to descend to the road, but hesitated, hearing someone descending the gash in the cliff above him. A figure landed quietly on the shelf, and Jakar stepped into the moonlight, nodding in greeting. He held his loaded crossbow with his splinted broken arm. Robin had rebandaged it, and it now served him nearly as well as his good one. Whispering, he explained his presence.

"Brown John told me to take a look . . . in case I might see something you might miss."

Gath took no exception and nodded down at the road. Jakar moved to the edge of the shelf and studied the scene. After a moment, he whispered, "Uh-oh! I saw this kind of madness once before. It seems to amuse certain kinds of savages . . . the heads are on the wrong bodies."

Gath looked back at the caravan, finally understanding where the unnaturalness came from, and they moved silently down to the road. There they advanced to the bodies, and Jakar grunted in shock, "Mother of Death!"

The heads were indeed on the wrong bodies, but that was not where the cruel joke ended. The legs, arms, feet and torsos of the men had been hacked and torn apart, and then reassembled with no effort at getting the arrangement correct. On the contrary, a skillful and successful effort had been made to make the dead men appear as preposterous freaks. Whoever had done the work had had a sense of humor, but it was not the kind that would make a normal man laugh.

A less imaginative effort had been given the women. They were only partially dismembered. Head

matched neck, leg matched hip, and arms belonged
to the shoulders. The women had been healthy,
young and attractive, and in death were cruelly
beautiful.

Jakar moved away, and was sick in a shadow.
When he rejoined Gath, the Barbarian was squatting
beside one of the women, holding her severed arm. It
was almost white. He used it to point out to Jakar
that each of the women also had one severed white
arm, then handed the arm to Jakar.

Jakar took it gingerly, examining it. There were
tiny punctures in the flesh above the veins of the
wrist. He returned the arm to Gath, pointing out the
small holes. "Something sucked out her blood."

Gath's lightless eyes asked for an explanation.

Jakar lifted empty hands. "I don't know what kind
of bite it is, maybe some kind of trained snake. But if
whoever did this is hunting for Robin, then they took
their blood for a reason. Probably to show to this
Nymph Queen."

Gath's eyes asked what reason.

"If her magic is as strong as Cobra says it is, it
could be one of the ways she can identify her."
Jakar's voice was low and hollow with foreboding.

Gath stood and studied the tiny bite carefully. His
breathing was harsh, then it quickened, and the
orange glow came back into his eyes. The helmet was
sensing the presence of danger. He and Jakar quickly
backed into concealing shadows and looked up and
down the road. There was still no sign or sound of
anything living. Gath looked back at the arm, and his
eyes flamed slightly, sending a tremor of fear through
his swart frame.

It was in the tiny bite that the helmet sensed the
danger, and within the shadows of the helmet his
hard eyes tightened thoughtfully.

Never before had the helmet warned him by showing him a wound, but that meant nothing. The headpiece's powers were continually growing as if they had no limitations. It appeared it could see into the future and was telling him to beware the creature which had made the wound. But he could not be certain, and there was no time to seek an explanation. He tore a length of cloth from a dead girl's discarded tunic, wrapped the arm in it and they climbed back up through the gash in the cliff.

They found Robin, Brown John and Cobra where they had left them, huddled under an overhanging boulder on top of the mountain. The horses, muzzled with rags, were tethered in a nearby gully.

Gath and Jakar greeted them silently as they emerged from the rock to stand in the bluish white moonlight, and the Barbarian unwrapped the arm, handed it to Cobra. The serpent woman turned it over and spread the stiff fingers, handling it as casually as she might examine a fresh vegetable. But Robin blanched at the bloody appendage, and had to sit down and hide her face against Jakar's chest. Brown John took no note of this, his eyes intent on Cobra, curious, expectant.

When Cobra found the tiny bite, she lost all trace of casualness, and her hands trembled. She forced herself to explore the tiny wound, feeling its shape with sensitive fingertips, then withdrew her hand abruptly, looking up at Gath and the *bukko*. Her eyes were puzzled and her whisper uncertain.

"It's the bite of a bat."

"You mean a bat soldier," said the *bukko*.

She shook her head. "A bat. And a small one. Tiyy now hunts us with bats."

"Because they can see in the dark," Brown John volunteered.

"Yes," the serpent woman's voice trembled, "but no bat could have killed the owner of this arm." She held it up. "It's been torn out of the shoulder. No bat can do that."

Jakar nodded. "And whoever attacked that caravan down there on the road was not small, but big. Very big. One of the men was torn in two, just above the hips. But the curious part was the girls: they were young, and each one of them had had the blood sucked out of one of their arms, just like this one."

Robin trembled, hiding her head against his chest as Cobra and Brown John looked at the young man thoughtfully, then at Gath. He confirmed what Jakar had said with a nod. They all sat silent for a moment, thinking, and a shadow passed over them, blocking out the moonlight.

They looked up, grateful for the added darkness, and gasped. The darkness blocking the moon was growing larger and larger against the indigo sky, dropping toward them.

Gath jumped up with flames bursting from the horned helmet, and Cobra shrieked, "Look out!"

She grabbed Robin, hauling her roughly under the overhanging boulder. Simultaneously, Jakar and Brown John faced the night sky, crossbow and sword ready, and Gath stepped directly under the descending shadow. His body was cocked and his head was tilted back with the helmet sputtering fire. Then flames spewed into the sky.

The hot light blanketed a monstrous vampire bat with wings easily forty feet wide, and claws and fangs as long and thick as table legs. It continued its drop, its grotesque eyes turning red in the firelight. Then the flames licked its feet and the steel bolt from Jakar's crossbow drilled its leg. Squealing, it darted back into the sky, with its wings flapping loudly, like breakers slapping a hard beach. Bits of the full moon could be seen between them.

Jakar quickly reloaded as Cobra, staring in horror, gasped weakly, "Menefret!"

A whooshing sound came out of the night sky, followed by a blast of wind. Dust swirled into the air, obscuring their vision and stinging their cheeks and hands. Jakar and Brown John backed under the protecting rock with the two women, and covered their faces with their arms, squinting over hands and elbows.

Gath ignored the dust. His arms rippled as he two-handed his axe, his calves cording under browned flesh as snarling smoke drifted from the helmet. It was black and cut with spears of flame which illuminated the sky above him, under control.

The whooshing grew suddenly loud, and the monstrous bat again burst into the burning light, not twenty feet above the Barbarian.

Gath's body convulsed like a bellows, and contracted, blowing flames into the face of the black-brown monster.

The flaccid flesh hanging loose on the jaw of the bat had been drawn up and attached to horny protuberances on the sides of its forehead, so that it now shielded the eyes. But the flames ate into the flesh, and it wrinkled, then crackled with flames, exposing huge wet eyes. They instantly smoked and clouded over as the flames seared them to blind the diving creature.

Gath roared with satisfaction. But the demon spawn did not dart away.

It drove at Gath as if still able to see, its right wing reaching for him like a hand with ten-foot fingers and clawed thumb. The thick membrane crinkled at the joints like thin parchment, and the horny appendages closed around Gath's body.

Gath sank low trying to avoid the hand, and hacked at the lower edge of the wing. The blade bit into fingerbone, cracking it, and the wing twisted and unfolded, causing it to pass above the center of Gath's body. Instead of gripping him, it caught him in the shoulders and helmet, lifting him off his feet and driving him backward. He hit a rock with the back of the helmet and a shoulder, and tumbled down an embankment, clinging to his axe and kicking up dust.

Robin screamed. Cobra leapt up to help, but Jakar and Brown John held her back, and she yelled at them, "Help him! Help him!"

Gath rolled to his feet just past the natural enclosure where their horses were tethered, and the bat darted back for him feetfirst. The claws were as long as the Barbarian's arms.

The horses panicked, snorting and kicking, and two bolted free, running directly across the bat's path. The bat's claws ripped one animal open from withers to shoulder, and carried the other into the sky, then dropped it in three pieces. The creature dove and came swooping across the ground, heading for Gath.

Gath backed away snorting flames, then suddenly charged. He got inside the wings before they could close, and pivoted, swinging his axe. He hammered one wing aside with an ear-shattering clang, kept pivoting with lightning speed and buried the axe into the chest of the bat.

The beast screamed in pain and bowled Gath over, ripping the axe out of Gath's hands. Then it darted skyward, carrying the weapon off. The creature whipped about within the concealing darkness, flapping loudly, then darted back into the moonlight having discarded the axe.

Gath rose in a crouch, flames spitting. Waiting. Hungry.

The vampire bat again swept low across the ground toward him, somehow still able to see. Its wings were spread, filling the darkness on either side.

Gath turned and ran, leading the bat through a cluster of huge boulders. It slowed, having to make sharp twisting turns, and the helmet snarled with satisfaction. Suddenly Gath jammed to a stop, pivoted and dove for the onrushing belly of the demon as it came around a boulder. Its massive wings came sweeping toward him, somehow sensing precisely where he was. Gath's hands grabbed for the body, but it pulled away, and he fell. A wing passed over him, hit the helmet with the crack of splintering bone and caught on the horns. Gath was ripped backward and thrown through the air as the bat swooped back into the sky.

Gath hit the ground with a metallic clang, and rolled over the edge of a steep slope, tumbled down. He thrashed and grabbed for balance, but there was only loose earth to hold on to, and he continued to roll and clang down the slope amid billowing moon-lit dust.

He heard Cobra scream and caught a glimpse of her as she suddenly appeared at the top of the slope. Brown John was with her, holding her back. Then the bat came for him again. Rolling and thrashing down the slope, Gath could not defend himself or escape and the bat's right wing plucked him off the ground as easily as a mother retrieving a fallen doll from the floor of her hut.

Cradled in the furry membrane, and dizzy from the blow of the wing, Gath saw the ground retreating beneath him. He was airborne. His body was held tight, but his feet dangled freely. He heard screaming coming from the ground below: it was growing

fainter and fainter. Ahead, the full moon was growing larger and whiter.

His chest heaved under the painful pressure of the
claws, and he gasped for breath. The claws were
shearing into his chain mail at shoulder and thigh.
He struggled, but it only helped them. He blinked
dizzily and waited, gathering strength. Then he
spewed flames from the helmet. But his head was
pinned, and the fire only scorched the night air. He
roared in frustration.

The mountains, black and round, now looked
small below him. Specks of fire were moving through
them, troops of bat soldiers hunting Robin. Around
him, spreading into infinity, was star-filled sky, a
vast world of air ten thousand times the size of the
one made of earth.

A claw sheared away most of his metal skirt and
exposed his legs, freeing them. He yanked them away
from the reaching fingers and squirmed up inside the
clutch of the furry membrane. He wiggled and
kicked and shoved until his arms and shoulders were
well above the top finger of the wing's grip. He
discarded the clumsy remnant of his chain mail and
padded tunic, leaving himself dressed in boots,
loincloth and helmet, then drew his knife. The
vampire bat somersaulted onto its back in what
appeared to be its feeding position, and the clutching
wing swept him toward its open jaws.

Gath turned the face of his helmet toward the
jaws, and sent flames into the waiting mouth.

The bat shrieked in pain, drawing its human
morsel away from its jaws, and darted down in a
dive.

The Barbarian turned his head away from the rush
of air, but it swept by so fast he could not breathe.
With his lungs bursting, he drove the blade of his

knife into the huge knuckle of the bat's thumb, working it furiously. The knuckle gave a little, then its grip relaxed, and the bat abruptly darted to the side, again somersaulting.

The wing again folded up, drawing Gath toward the waiting mouth, but the movement further loosened its grip, and Gath hauled himself onto the back of the wing, out of reach of the bat's jaws.

The bat dove again, trying to dislodge him. Gath drove his knife and fingers into the wing membrane, tearing it open, then thrust an arm into the wound, seizing a wing bone with it, and hung on.

The bat twisted as it neared the ground, and darted at a mountain. Then it twisted again, avoiding it, and darted along its rock face. Its flapping wings came within inches of the rock, and Gath was raked by the stone. But he was not dislodged.

The vampire bat darted and twisted through the indigo sky, and Gath slowly hauled himself toward the head until a huge pointed ear was within his grasp. Gath got a hold of the bottom edge and waited. The bat somersaulted and Gath used the roll of the creature's body to let himself fall into the ear. There he pulled himself into the narrowest section and hung on.

The bat continued to dart and twist, no more than forty feet above the moonlit ground. Screaming came from the monstrous rodent, but Gath did not hear it. The helmet's hunger was a roar inside him. He gathered his body close to the ear hole, breath and smoke heaving from the helmet, but forced himself to wait.

The bat darted and twisted, driving through narrow chasms of rock and passing between boulders, blind but uncanny with vision. Then it suddenly hovered in mid-air, as if needing time to think.

Gath instantly forced his body in amongst the tangled cartilage of the ear and drove the full length of his thick arm inward. The arm's hand held his knife, and its blade penetrated the eardrum. Gath turned and twisted it, tearing and cutting. Blood washed out of the ear hole, drenching him, but still he cut.

The bat squealed and twisted, darting away from the blunt side of a mountain, then twisted and darted directly for it.

Gath took no notice. He was working.

The bat turned, but too late. It had somehow lost its uncanny sense of direction and distance, and a wing collided with the rocky side of the mountain, breaking with a brittle crack. The vampire bat plummeted.

Gath stopped work, and stared down at the earth coming up at him. The helmet roared in rage, and his body instinctively gathered up in a ball, protecting itself within the membrane and cartilage of the huge ear.

The bat landed headfirst against a boulder with a crunching crash, and the skull exploded on one side allowing the boulder to enter. Gath shuddered at the impact, but hung on. The bat's body stood upright, quivering twenty feet in the air, then toppled over and thudded against the ground.

Stunned by the impact, Gath sat numbed within the protective embrace of the mammoth ear. When his vision cleared, he saw that the skull on his side still held its shape, while the other side had been pulped. The ground was not five feet below him. He wiped his bloody hands on the furry membrane, crawled to the rim of the ear and dropped to the ground. His legs gave way under him, as if they had never stood before, and he sprawled awkwardly.

From the ground, he looked around. He did not know where he was. Then, far off in the distance, he saw vague figures on a moonlit slope of loose earth. He could not tell who they were.

He crawled away from the bones and gore, and held himself up on hands and knees, naked and bleeding. There was no sign of his belts and sword. They had been torn away, he did not know when or where, and he had left his knife in the bat's ear. When he had gathered enough strength, he slowly stood, and a terror unlike any he had felt during the battle shot through him. It was the same fear the helmet had felt when it had seen the small bite on the dead girl's severed arm. Foreboding. Cold. Without remorse. Then he saw the source of that fear.

Hovering against the moon was a cloud of bats, small but numbering in the hundreds. They looked like layers of finely wrought black lace in constant motion, as if they were weaving their bodies together in a flawless pattern. A frantic pattern. Mad.

Gath's body lowered instinctively, and the horned helmet flamed, but the fire was weak, and only served as an invitation.

The bats dove en masse, a blanket of tiny teeth.

Thirty-Four

THE BLOOD TRICK

The blanket dropped over Gath, staggering him. Biting. The bats clawing for a perch on arm, chest, leg, back. Then more descended, mindlessly landing on those already feeding, and their weight bore the Barbarian to his knees. He tore away furry handfuls, crushing them. The helmet's flames charred wings and incinerated bodies, but the frenzied creatures kept swarming and biting.

Far above the action, at the top of the slope of loose earth, Brown John and Jakar winced with horror, and Robin cried openly, her tears spilling on Jakar's circling arms, while Cobra stared helplessly, devoid of tears and color and hope.

"They can't whip him! Not a few bats," Brown John asserted. But his voice lacked sparkle, and the hot spots which normally flushed his cheeks were no bigger than a baby's fingertips.

Jakar glanced off at a distant line of torches moving their way, and said quietly, "We had better get away from here. They know we're here now."

They nodded, but made no move to leave.

Far below, Gath suddenly staggered back to his feet, thrashing wildly and throwing off bats. His bloody body glistened in the moonlight for a moment, then was again covered with the moving black blanket. He went down on his knees, arms flailing.

266

Bits of flame spurted between flapping bodies, then it died to an orange glow.

Cobra groaned in frantic despair and erupted from Brown John's grasp, flinging herself forward. She got ten feet, lost her footing in the loose ground and fell, her arms grabbing at the air. She hit the ground, rolled over twice, and her head came to a stop against a protruding boulder.

Brown John reached her in three strides and gathered her limp body in his arms, cradling it tenderly and stroking her forehead. It was cut and bruised above her left eye.

"It's no use, beauty, you can't help him," he whispered.

She didn't hear him. Her eyes were closed, and her mouth hung open. Holding her close, he looked back down at the moonlit battleground.

Gath was now on his hands and knees, teetering like a dying animal. The bats clung to all sides of him and circled around him, darting at him whenever they saw flesh. The helmet lifted, glowed brightly for a moment, then the light faded and the headpiece dropped between his shoulders.

Robin and Jakar came up behind Brown John, and Jakar tugged at him urgently. "Come on, Brown."

The *bukko* nodded but did not rise. He could not remove his eyes from his friend.

Small and indistinct in the distance below, Gath howled, low and forlorn, and collapsed on the ground. The bats scattered and screeched, those pinned under the body flapping for release. Then they again dropped on him, and heaved and surged like boiling tar on his carcass.

The troupe stared, immobilized with horror. In the silence they could hear the bats drinking, and Robin sagged against Jakar dizzily. He held her close, and suddenly turned sharply.

A line of torches was coming around the side of the nearby mountain at the base of the slope. Riders carried them.

Jakar pulled on Brown John. "Let's go. Now!"

His voice had a ring of authority that shocked Robin to her senses, and as Jakar pushed her up the slope, she pleaded, "Hurry, Brown! Hurry!"

The older Grillard abruptly came to his feet, carrying Cobra in his arms, and took in the situation. "Holy Bled!" he cursed, and ran back up the slope, his short legs pumping in the loose earth.

When the group reached the top of the slope, it crouched in the shadows of boulders, gasping with momentary relief.

The riders, a troop of bat soldiers, had not started up after them, but had circled around Gath's fallen body and were hooting and laughing with delight as the bats, their wings filling the night with a whooshing roar, flew off. Several soldiers dismounted and cast the light of their torches over the fallen bodies of the monster vampire bat and Gath, inspecting them. Two tried to pull off the horned helmet, but it would not come away. So they picked up his body, threw it over a saddle and began to rope it in place.

"He's alive," Brown John whispered excitedly. "He's still alive."

Robin looked uncertainly at Jakar, and he explained, "Otherwise they wouldn't bother to tie him."

She nodded, then shivered as a group of bat soldiers separated from the others and started up the slope toward them.

Staying low and to the shadows, Jakar led the group across the crest of the mountain to the hollow where the surviving horses were still tethered. The sound of the bat soldiers' horses coming their way was growing louder.

Robin moaned. "They'll find us!"

"Maybe not," Jakar said quietly. "Follow me. We'll leave the horses here."

He led Robin through the boulders, and Brown John, carrying Cobra, followed.

Moving swiftly and silently, they found the gash in the cliff and started down. Reaching the shelf of earth overlooking the road, Jakar guided Brown John to a hidden gut of rock, saying, "You stay here." Brown John, acknowledging the young man's authoritative command, slipped out of sight behind the concealing gut with Cobra in his arms, and Jakar turned to Robin. "Follow me, fluff. I'm going to need your help."

Moving with neat, sure-footed steps, Robin followed him to the edge of the shelf, zealous in her desire to help. But when she saw the slaughtered caravan below the ledge, she faltered and turned away, gagging. Ignoring her sick, heaving sounds, Jakar kneeled, studying the bloody tableau below, and his eyes thinned with satisfaction.

Moon vultures were working the two lines of bodies. They were white, with long necks for probing deep into bone cavities, and their necks were red with blood, their crops bulging. The bodies of the slavers and slaves were no longer in an orderly arrangement. Limbs and trunks had been dragged and tossed about by the big birds, and the dead girls, more accessible to the vultures because of having been stripped before the birds arrived, were in total disarray. A tangle of gory limbs, torsos and heads.

When Robin quieted, she squatted beside Jakar, forcing herself to look directly at the scene. She trembled, but asked evenly, "What can I do? How can I help you?"

"It's not going to be easy or pleasant," he whispered. "You finished being sick?"

"I think so," she said, and her voice faltered. "I'm sorry, I . . ."

"Don't be," he interrupted. "I did the same when I saw them." There was a commotion of shouting voices at the top of the crest far above them, and he stood abruptly, bringing her with him. "They've found our horses. We're going to have to hurry."

They scrambled down to the road below, bringing down a small avalanche of earth. The vultures glanced in their direction, but continued to work at their bloody meal. Jakar leveled his crossbow at the nearest bird and fired.

The steel bolt took the vulture in the chest and drove it fluttering and mawking off its gore. The noise startled the others, and they scattered, crying in frustration.

Jakar took Robin's hand, and they hurried across the open road to the bodies of the girls, kneeling beside them. Choking at the sight, Robin averted her head, and shut her eyes tight.

"That's all right," Jakar said, setting his crossbow down. "You don't have to look." He drew his knife. "Give me your wrist . . . I'm going to open your vein."

She looked at him in shock, saw the bodies and gagged again. Quickly turning away, she lifted her wrist to him. He took it, saying, "Listen, fluff, there's not much time to explain, but I think this Nymph Queen has some way of identifying you by your blood. So I'm going to smear it over one of these girls."

She forced a nod, and he guided her wrist to a full-breasted torso, noting the girl's shape paled beside Robin's, and wondering at himself for noting such a thing at such a time. Then he hesitated, and stared wide-eyed, momentarily unable to breathe or move.

Torch-bearing riders had appeared down the road. They were far off, but coming hard. The beat of their horses' hooves was growing louder, and their vibrations could be felt in the road.

Robin opened her eyes, saw the torches and gasped.

Jakar held her arm roughly, so she couldn't move, and drove the blade into the underside of her wrist. Robin jerked at the pain, gasping as blood spurted forth, but did not pull away, and he marveled at her courage as he guided her wrist over the body of the dead girl, drenching it with blood. His eyes shifted to the riders.

They moved around a bend and disappeared behind it, showing no hurry. It appeared they had not seen Jakar and Robin.

Jakar, forcing himself not to do a hurried, inadequate job, continued to spread Robin's blood, and the dead torso began to glitter wetly in the moonlight. Then Robin's body sank heavily against his back, and he turned sharply. Her face was white, and she was gasping.

He cursed himself for taking too much of her blood and, yanking a rag from under his belt, whipped it around her wrist tightly. He tied it off securely, stopping the flow of blood, then guided her to her feet and started across the road toward the shadows of the gash. Noise from the mountain brought him to a sudden stop.

Bodies were coming down the gash. Hurried. Raising dust.

Jakar, holding Robin's trembling body tight, glanced around, suddenly furtive, terrified.

The torches of the riders appeared coming around the bend, only several hundred feet off now.

Jakar hurried Robin back past the gory bodies and moved through the tall grass lining the opposite side of the road, dropped behind it. There he held Robin close.

Her breath came fitfully, but then it quieted, and she whispered, "I'll be all right. It will pass."

He nodded at her brave face and kissed her dirty cheek, again wondering at her healthy scent and the thrilling feel of her warmth. Each sensation stood alone and distinct, and was full of wonder and chance and adventure, and his senses reeled.

The sounds of men descending the mountain were suddenly loud, and they peered through the grass. A squad of bat soldiers, dusty and cursing, now stood on the road. But Brown John and Cobra were not with them, and had apparently not been discovered. The soldiers moved tentatively among the slaughtered bodies, their blunt faces uncertain and wary, then looked up at the sounds of the arriving horses. A troop of twenty bat soldiers pounded to a stop beside the slaughtered caravan. Some of them led trailing horses, and now handed the reins to the squad on foot.

A small man with blistered flesh and wearing a blue skullcap with long pendulous ear flaps appeared to be in charge of the detachment. He was chortling with malevolent triumph, pointing at the dead girls and shouting in a dry, coarse voice.

"There! There! The one with the big dum-dums. Put her in the sack."

Robin cringed, and hugged Jakar tighter, not understanding the small man's language and her eyes asking Jakar if he had somehow identified her blood. Jakar lifted a finger to his lips and squeezed her shoulder reassuringly.

As several bat soldiers began to pick the dead girl up, the small man shouted, "Get all of her, you dolts. I need her right hand."

Robin shuddered and Jakar held her tighter.

The bat soldiers stuffed the torso and severed arm of the girl in a leather sack and slung it over the pommel of their leader's saddle. Chuckling, the little brute patted it as he spoke to it. "You've given me a whole lot of trouble, lass! But you'll behave now."

Several of the bat soldiers grunted with laughter, then one asked the small man if he wanted any of the other bodies. He walked his horse along the row of dead girls, inspecting them, and shook his head. "The serpent queen isn't one of them." He looked off into the surrounding shadows. "She's probably out there hiding someplace, but she's helpless now. Of no importance." He turned to a mounted bat soldier. "Inform your officers that the girl has been found and that I am returning to Pyram with her." He glanced at the others as the squad on foot mounted. "The rest of you will accompany me to Pyram."

The designated soldier saluted, and galloped back down the road, while the small man, smiling with dark triumph, headed west with the troop.

Jakar held Robin tight against him until the riders were out of sight, then whispered, "They're gone. It's all over."

She looked up at him. Her cheeks were smeared with tears and dirt, and he had never seen anything so lovely. "Really?" she asked, and he nodded. She sagged against him, murmuring, "Hold me, Jakar. Please, just hold me."

He held her.

Thirty-five

PIT OF DOOM

Brown John led the now conscious Cobra down to the road as Robin and Jakar emerged from the shadows on the opposite side, and Robin raced into the old man's arms.

"Thank the gods!" the *bukko* exclaimed. "I thought they'd carried you off."

Cobra, her face ashen in the moonlight against her charred black hair, stood uncertainly looking up the road. The torches of the bat soldiers were pins of light in the vast pervading darkness of the night, and growing fainter and fainter. Then they vanished, and Cobra moved slowly alongside the dismembered bodies, studying them. She had regained consciousness in time to overhear Schraak's decision to return to Pyram, but could find no explanation for it. She put her puzzled eyes on Jakar and asked, "What happened? Why have they left?"

"We tricked them," he said evenly. "They think they have Robin."

"Tricked? How?"

"I put her blood on one of the dead girls."

"Her blood?" Cobra's voice lost strength as she spoke. She looked down at the stains of fresh blood on the ground, then at Robin's pale flesh, and staggered in place, her face distending with such horror that it could have been the mother of all nightmares.

The *bukko* moved to her quickly, supporting her with his arms and asking, "What's wrong?"

She had to gasp for breath before she could speak. "Your dream is dead, Brown." Her voice was cold and bitter, and her eyes fixed on Jakar. "That small man leading them was one of my priests. His name is Schraak. Somehow," she gasped, "somehow Tiyy has given him the power to see Robin's aura in her flesh and blood."

"That's what I was counting on," said Jakar.

"And it worked," added the *bukko* enthusiastically. "He thinks he has her."

"He does have her," Cobra said darkly. "Tiyy does not need Robin . . . all she needs is her blood." Their eyes widened in horror, and she added, "She'll extract the power of Robin's Kaa from the blood and corrupt it with her magic, then feed on it. Whatever powers she's lost, she'll regain immediately. But it won't stop there. Now she'll have power over the helmet just as Robin had, power enough to make Gath surrender to it. And when she controls him, she'll send him after Robin."

"It won't make any difference," Robin protested weakly. "He won't hurt me."

"That's right," Brown John chimed in. "Gath won't submit no matter what she does. You've seen how he's fought the helmet. He won't quit now!"

Cobra turned her grey-gold eyes on the *bukko* and smiled. There was warmth in her expression, but no hope. "Brown," she said, "I know you love Gath, and believe me, I know he is an extraordinary man. But he is now held by powers no man can overcome." Her smile sank tiredly. "It's over, my friend. Finished. No amount of words, no matter how filled with humor and hope, can help him now . . . or us."

"I quite agree," Brown John said, "The next scene does not call for dialogue, but for action."

Jakar nodded agreement, saying, "They didn't have our horses with them, so maybe they're where we left them. I'll go find out." He winked at Robin. "You stay here. I'll be right back."

She nodded. "Be careful."

He darted into the shadows of the cliff and started up the gash toward the crest.

Cobra watched him, shaking her head and asking, "Just what do you think you can do, Brown?" She turned to him. "Go to Pyram? Storm the castle with four people?"

"Yes," he said evenly, "and you will lead the way." He smiled knowingly. "You still know it, don't you?"

"Oh, yes, I know the way. But it is useless. They would see us coming for miles. And even if we got inside, we would stand no chance against Gath. The helmet would sense our presence and hunt us down."

"But if we could get to the jewels first, there would be a chance, correct?"

"Brown," she said tiredly, "Pyram is not one of your stages. It's real, and dangerous. The jewels are held deep within its dungeons. We would have to have the luck of the Good Goddess herself to even reach them."

Brown John took hold of her shoulders and grinned. "Then you agree? There is a chance we could reach them?"

"Yes, a chance, but . . ."

"And if this nymph bitch does control Gath, the jewels can free him from her, right?"

She started to reply, and stopped herself, then said, "I don't know."

"You were sure before," he said accusingly.

"I know, but, well . . . maybe I was dreaming, just filling my head with wishful thinking." She turned away, then glanced at Robin. "What about you? If this crazy old man goes to Pyram, are you going with him?"

"Of course," blurted Robin.

"Why?" asked Cobra, her voice flat and hard. "You don't need the jewels. You've already not only cured Jakar of his bitterness, but made him fall in love with you! What do you need them for now?"

Robin blushed. "I don't know if what you say about Jakar is true or not. But that doesn't count, not now. Gath needs us. And we've got to try and help him no matter how small the chance of success."

Cobra moved face-to-face with Robin, studying her, then said bitterly, "You're lying. You want the jewels for yourself! That's all you've ever wanted."

Robin's mouth fell open in shock, and she looked from Brown John to Cobra, gasping, "That's not true! I . . . I . . ."

"Never mind, Robin," Brown John said calmly, "you don't have to explain anything." He turned to Cobra. "There's no need to take your frustrations out on her. That won't help anything."

Cobra stared at him, empty of expression, and sat down on the side of the cliff staring at the dirt. Brown moved to her, but hesitated for a moment before he spoke.

"One more question. Can the jewels free Gath from this Nymph Queen's control or not?"

"I can't promise it, Brown," Cobra replied without looking at him, "but yes, if everything is as it appears to be, yes."

"Then we do have a chance."

"If we can reach the jewels, yes," Cobra said, looking up. "But that's impossible!"

"Perhaps," he said. "But if you will forgive me for saying it myself, I tend to excel at times of extreme hopelessness."

Cobra couldn't repress a grin, and shook her head as Brown John squatted facing her. "Don't shake your lovely head, woman. We stand at the bottom of a pit of doom, so our only recourse is to look up with soaring spirits. It is the only thing that can lift us out."

"You realize, of course," she said, "that you're quite mad."

He nodded affirmatively. "It is a point of honor with me. If there is a cliff, I must jump off it . . . just in case I should chance to fly."

She smiled, and the sounds of horses were heard down the road. They rose, and Jakar rode out of the darkness leading two horses. Robin sighed with relief and raced to greet him as Cobra turned to Brown John.

"You see," he said, "already our luck changes for the better."

"Or for the worse," she said soberly.

He shook his head. "Trust me. I see things coming, remember? And you and I, woman, have only started down our trail, believe me. Our time has only begun."

She hesitated, a madcap rush of girlish hope showing behind her eyes, then her voice surrendered. "Brown, I think you're becoming contagious."

"Oh, yes," he said with a profound grin. "That you can count on."

Thirty-Six

BLACK LIGHT

Clutching her leopard-skin wrap tightly, Tiyy looked over a spotted shoulder with flaring nervous eyes. Thick mustard- and lemon-yellow fumes swirled around her, filling the air in Pyram's underground altar chamber, and her orchid cheeks flamed behind them, blushing her face to the corners of her scarlet lips. She was slick with sweat. Every nerve and sinew strung tight with sensual expectation. A budding goddess in heat.

She pressed back against the shiny obsidian walls, her flat belly convulsing, and spoke in a breathless voice.

"Careful! Careful!"

The high priest and his two acolytes could only nod in reply. They were scurrying back and forth and around a black stone table from which the fumes emanated, making precise adjustments in the apparatus. Their naked chests glittered with sweat, and their bare feet splashed in puddles of it. They were monitoring stills, flasks, tubes of green glass, furnaces and scorching pans joined together in a bubbling maze on the table. Flame pots flickered under the glass instruments, and vapors convulsed through them, spewing fumes from loosely luted joints and elbows.

The high priest added a teardrop of vitriol to a beaker of boiling blood-red liquid, as the acolytes, using spatula and scoop, added powder to a flask and stirred the fires. Then they held still, waiting.

Inside the tubes, the vapors thickened to a yellowish mist and surged toward the bizarre culmination of the apparatus, a bronze tube as thin as a straw. At its tip, a drop of liquid gathered slowly, then fell into a clear-glass vial no bigger than a baby's cup. It was one-third full of a turgid vermilion elixir.

A joint in the tubing near the middle of the maze came loose. Mustard fumes whooshed into the room, and drops of the precious elixir splashed on the table, sizzling.

"Fix it!" Tiyy shrieked.

The three men pounced on the break. The acolytes picked up the hot tubes in gloved hands and fitted the joint together. The high priest quickly coated it with a mixture of clay and straw, then propped the tubing on a stand for added support. They watched it for a moment, and the fumes swirled, continuing through the joint without escaping.

Tiyy relaxed slightly, then turned sharply as a heavy wooden door swung open beside her, and Schraak emerged. A low guttural growl followed the small man out of the door, and Tiyy grinned with a surge of power, knowing the sound came from the magnificent Barbarian she now held prisoner in the adjacent cell. Schraak stopped, facing her, and bowed as he spoke.

"He won't eat or drink, your magnificence. And I cannot remove the horned helmet."

"Leave it," she said breathlessly. "The prospect of a masked lover pleases me."

"Lover?" The worm's eyes were startled. "But . . . but he is not strong enough! The heat of your sacred fire will burn his flesh. Kill him!"

"He will be made strong." The wantonness in her eyes was gaudy.

Schraak was stunned. "You're . . . you're going to feed him the black wine? Make him a Lord of Destruction?"

She nodded.

"But he's only a man!"

"Yes, but a man like no other there has ever been before."

"But he stole the master's helmet! He must die!"

She shook her head, and the bristling spears of her yellow hair shivered. "The master did not mean him to die, but to serve. And he will."

"But . . . but if he wears the helmet while you embrace him, he'll . . . he'll . . ."

"Perhaps," she said, and her voice trembled with a mix of fear and anticipation. "I know the danger. It will be like embracing the master's flame, but soon now, very soon, I will be ready to take that risk."

Shuddering, Schraak looked about the laboratory.

The high priest was gently taping a tube where the fumes inside appeared to be blocked, and they tumbled apart, flowed forward. One of the acolytes was coaxing a syrupy glob of elixir along another tube by passing a dish of fire under it, and the other one, having unraveled a parchment yellow and flaking with age, was reading an ancient word formula aloud.

Tiyy said, "You should pray for their success, Schraak. Because if they aren't successful," she put her scorching eyes on him, "you are going to crawl back into the ground where you came from."

He staggered back a step.

"You failed me a second time, worm. You brought me the carcass of an Ikarian savage, not the girl!"

"But . . . but it was her blood! It had to be!" he stammered. "I saw her aura!"

She nodded. "Yes, it was her blood. The carcass was clotted with it. But did you look at her carefully? Was she the same young, finely made girl you once saw in Bahaara?" He hesitated, and she knew he had not checked the body carefully. "I thought not."

"Forgive me," he pleaded, "I was so anxious to . . ."

"Arrrrggg! If you had used your head, we could have saved hours. As it is we've spent most of the day removing the dried flakes and dissolving them, coaxing them back to life." A flicker of fear passed behind her eyes, and her breath quickened. "If her Kaa is as strong as the serpent queen claimed it was, it will still be alive. But if it isn't!"

The threat in her tone made him groan, and he drew a soft cloth from under his belt, dabbed at the scum gathering on his eyebrows and lips. Then his quavering voice asked, "Is . . . is there enough?"

"Nearly," she said. "The vial is almost full."

He glanced at the clear-glass vial collecting the vermilion liquid, sighed with some relief and turned to his queen. "I'll order the hunt to begin again. The girl will not escape a third time."

"There is no need for that," she said.

His eyes widened, not understanding.

A grin blossomed on her florid heart-shaped face. "Once the Barbarian is in my control, I will send him to hunt her. That way her capture is assured. No one who threatens the master can hide from the horned helmet."

The small man nodded and again dabbed at his face with the soft cloth.

The high priest moved to the end of the table and stood beside the filling vial.

"Hurry! Hurry!" Tiyy growled.

The high priest allowed three more drops to fall into the vial, then closed the spigot. Using both hands, he lifted the tiny vessel and brought it to Tiyy. She straightened regally and shrugged off her leopard-skin wrap, clasping the vial with both hands to her nude body. Her only garments were a sheen of heat and a narrow leopard-skin apron.

Taking a deep breath she followed the high priest to the black stone altar at the deepest portion of the laboratory. They mounted its three circular steps to a cube of shiny obsidian at the top. It measured three feet high, coming to Tiyy's waist, and supported a large ball of black stone which rested in a perfectly matched depression in the top of the cube. Tiyy set her feet apart for balance and held the vial out in front of her, her arms fully extended. The priest wrapped his arms around the black stone ball, gathered his strength and rolled it aside. A shaft of white light, no bigger around than the Nymph Queen's small finger, shot up out of a small hole at the center of the depression. It speared straight up, splitting the darkness like a knife.

The high priest, holding the heavy stone ball against his chest, backed away from the blinding light, averting his head.

Schraak and the acolytes cringed behind the laboratory table.

Tiyy held her place.

The muscles along her arms pulsed and rippled, and her clenched fingers squeezed tightly around the vial, as if it were trying to escape. The shaft of white light had richocheted off a mirrorlike polished black rock set at an angle in the ceiling and descended into the mouth of the vial. There it stirred and heated the elixir, and whiffs of dark smoke emerged from the mouth like fingers of the dead.

Moisture formed around Tiyy's parted lips. Her temples dripped sweat. Her breasts and belly heaved. Her legs corded with muscle, but she held still, fighting to keep the vial in place. Then she wavered, weakening, but still held the vial in the light's path. It churned and rocked inside her grip. Vermilion fumes spewed out of the mouth and flowed up the sides of the beam of white light, coiling around it.

The savage nymph's face flinched with a smile, and she stepped back, cradling the vial against her breasts. The white light bounced off the stone steps, caromed across the room and hit the far wall, exploding in a hundred tiny beams that shot and spiraled through the chamber.

An acolyte was burnt on the cheek. Flasks and tubes were split and cracked. Streaks of fire broke out on the shiny walls where the light passed over it. Schraak took a blow on the hip and fell to the floor groaning and clutching the wound, his grey flesh smoking beneath his thick fingers.

Tiyy ignored the streaking light. She drew the vial to her lips, and poured the elixir into her mouth. She took it in gulps, feeling it burn her stomach. Glowing with pleasure, she licked her lips as power spread like a contagion into her soul.

Schraak, flinching and ducking bolts of light, cried to her, "Stop it! Stop it!"

Tiyy glanced over a naked shoulder, watched a flask explode in a blaze of light, then saw Schraak on the floor pleading with her. One of her acolytes was sprawled unconscious across him, his tunic on fire. She glanced at the base of the altar. There the high priest lay on his back still holding the stone ball in his arms. The white light had hit the ball and driven the heavy stone into his chest, crushing him.

With tyrannical casualness, Tiyy dropped the vial, and it clattered down the steps as she turned and faced the altar. Hesitation flashed across her large eyes as she watched the spear of white light streaking up in front of her, its glow turning her orchid cheeks a pale pink. Then she took a breath and boldly thrust a hand over the shaft of light, about a foot above the hole in the black cube.

The white light came to an abrupt stop against her palm, and the shafts bouncing about the room dissipated, vanished.

Schraak shoved the acolyte's body off, and rose to his hands and knees, staring at his queen with dumb awe.

Her hand had turned to white light, and the light was advancing up her arm. It edged past her elbow and became diffused, mixing with the lustrous walnut of her skin. Then it slowly retreated back down her arm. When it passed her palm, it seemed to flash through her fingers, then departed from her body. For a long moment her hand held steady against the shaft of light still spearing up out of the hole, then trembled with effort, battling it. Her body rippled muscularly under her dark flesh, and beads of sweat trailed down her glossy sheen. A shaft of black light slowly emerged from her palm at precisely the point where the white light hit it. The black light edged down into the white light, forcing it down and down, until the white light vanished back inside the altar stone.

"The ball," Tiyy whispered harshly. "Quickly!"

Schraak and the surviving acolyte came to their feet and hurried to the altar. They hesitated at the sight of the dead high priest, then crouched over him. They took the ball away from his clutching arms and heaved it onto the edge of the altar. Tiyy removed her hand, and the ball rolled into place before the white light could again show itself.

Grinning with giddy power, Tiyy moved to a shelf, almost trotting. She plucked a vial of Nagraa off of it with each hand, glanced back at Schraak's exhausted body sitting on the step of the altar and shouted,

"Get up, you worthless lump. Bring the keys!"

She hurried through the open door by which the dwarf had entered, passed through a narrow passage with earthen walls and stopped short in the open door of a small stone cell facing the Barbarian.

Thirty-Seven

DARK GODDESS

Gath, lit by guttering lamp light, hung lifelessly between chains at the back of the cell. His arms were fully extended and his legs spread apart, with shackles binding his wrists and ankles. They were chained to the side walls so that he was suspended clear of the stone floor. His helmeted head hung between his shoulders, and tiny bites speckled his body, which was pale under its sun-darkened blood smeared flesh.

Slowly the helmet lifted, and the shadowed eyes behind the eye slits studied the savage nymph.

Nearly naked, breathing rapidly and glistening with the heat of some hard effort, she held two vials in her fists. A small slick man came out of the tunnel behind her and stood obediently to her side. He was shaking so badly that the ring of keys in his hand jangled noisily.

Gath growled, low and instinctively, and a smile lifted the nymph's cheeks. She said, "Welcome to Pyram, large one. I am Tiyy, the Nymph Queen, and high priestess of Black Veshta. I presume you have

heard of me?" Gath made no reply, and her eyes
thinned. "I like that. I am partial to proud, defiant
men, and you are easily the proudest of the lot.
That's why you are still alive. I am going to give you a
chance to see who you prefer . . . me or the girl."

Gath pulled on his chains but could summon little
strength, and the shackles cut into wrists and ankles,
causing the drumming pain to throb loudly against
his skull. He became dizzy and his eyes closed, fire
flooding through his brain into his eyeballs. When he
reopened his eyes he knew they glowed with fire.

Tiyy had advanced to within three feet of him, and
her body was flushed, instinctively responding to his
heat with its own.

The helmet tried to turn away from her, but Gath
would not let it, and watched her warily.

"I am amazed," she said quietly, "that the man
inside you still refuses to submit to the helmet. I
would not have believed it possible if I was not
seeing it with my own eyes. But I am glad." Her
words purred with pleasure and power. "I have never
made a Lord of Destruction from a man before.
There was never one strong enough. Until now."

Gath thrashed violently against his chains, flames
shooting from the eye slits, and Schraak had to sit
down to keep from falling. But Tiyy did not move or
flinch, only waited until he sagged helplessly in
place, his chest heaving and dripping sweat and
blood.

Slowly she circled him, holding the two vials in
one hand, touching his arm and back and wrist with
gentle fingertips, then reappeared facing him. His
blood glistened on her thumb. She studied it
thoughtfully and tasted it, then said, "It is written in
the scrolls of the ancients that one day a man will
walk the earth with the power to bring down nations
and raise up mountains, to remake the earth until

north is south and the deserts are blue seas. A man of such courage and strength that where he walks the legends will walk." Her voice became breathless with anticipation. "A man greater than kings and magicians who is made from both good and evil . . . a man whose heart's love is capable of bringing the White Veshta back to life, and whose seed of lust can make the chosen of the Master of Darkness into the Black Veshta incarnate."

He hung silently in place, glaring.

"Do you know what that would mean? Have you any conception of the measure of power such a man could unleash?" She shook her head. "I doubt it. They are beyond even my imagination. But the man I can imagine, and measure . . . and you are that man."

Gath laughed at her, small and bitter and short.

She smiled in reply. "Save your laughter, large one. We will soon see which one of us is right. You, the next Lord of Destruction, or me, the Nymph Queen of Pyram." Her smile sank back into her savagely beautiful face. "You see, I am the chosen of the Lord of Death."

Cold terror ran through Gath's veins, and he thrashed against his chains.

Once more she waited until his strength was wasted, then used her teeth to uncork each of the vials, spitting the corks on the floor. With black light spearing from the vials, she lifted them to his face, saying, "Raise your head."

Despite Gath's efforts, the helmet obeyed, and she emptied a vial into the mouth slit. He gulped and choked, trying to reject the bitter taste, but a heat rushed through him and the helmet took control. It whipped his head about in a frenzy of hunger, then held still as she poured the second vial into him. The helmet jerked and drops of the thick black wine spattered and sizzled on its hot metal. She stepped back, tossing the vials aside, and the helmet leaned for her, its flames licking hungrily at her body.

She laughed throatily. "You see who he wants now, Schraak?" She untied her scanty apron and dropped the leopard skin to the floor. Slowly, flames flickered under her walnut flesh, centering in her breasts and groin, then spread throughout her body until she looked like molten fire sheathed in the body of a woman.

Gath writhed against his chains, reaching for her. Fire consumed his eyes, and he could scent the heady perfume of her youth and heat, but then it became vague and distant, and she seemed suddenly immense, a cloud of undulating flesh that pressed into him. He felt as if he stood atop a mountain, and that the mountain was his own body. It was moving beneath him like quaking earth. Utterly beyond control.

"It's no use, you are mine now." Her voice whispered the words, and the whisper was deafening. Then she snapped, "The locks, worm. Quickly!"

The small man bolted to his feet and unlocked the chains. Gath could feel his mountainous body drop free and land solidly on the floor. The noise and impact dizzied him, and when his head cleared he saw Tiyy's smile as she whispered to the small man, "Don't bother with the chains! Get out!"

The little man did not have to be told twice, and was out the door before she finished, slamming it behind him.

The Nymph Queen undulated like fire, and the mountain moved. Chains rattled through iron loops in the wall, coming free, and clanged to the floor. His arms reached for her, massive hands spanning her waist, and he hauled her violently into his arms, the lengths of chain flailing and clanging against wall and floor. The mountain had more strength than his imagination could have fashioned, and the heat inside it was volcanic. Impatient. Fire wanting to mate with fire.

"Yes! Yes!" she groaned. "Now! Now!"

He crushed her to him, and her legs straddled his hips, the fires merging as she took him standing, in the manner of the Dark Goddess, consuming and defeating him in the manner water defeats the sword.

Then his mind was gone, and there was only bone and muscle and sensation.

Thirty-Eight

PYRAM

The four riders emerged from the hills side by side, crested the ridge together and simultaneously reined up in the shadows of a spreading oak. Their tunics and cloaks had been redesigned by the hard night trail, and were decorated by thorns, dust and sweat. Their faces were vivid with the rouge of exhaustion and drawn with reckless smiles. Mouths were parted, lips cracked, and the lids of their eyes were red against bloodshot whites. But they sat erect in their saddles, as if with one backbone, like actors eager to battle tempest, fire and flood for center stage.

Brown John was in the middle. Cobra was on his right, and Jakar, with Robin riding behind him, on his left.

Seagulls floated against the grey sky overhead, silently working the cool sea breezes. The same breezes ruffled their cloaks, cooled hot cheeks and filled heaving lungs with heady satisfaction.

The coast road waited not a quarter of a mile dead ahead, and a hundred strides beyond it shallow waves tumbled out of a dark blue sea. Scattered shafts of golden light pierced the dark cloud cover, stabbing the seascape. It beckoned like sparkling silver coins scattered on a blanket of blue-black water.

The Inland Sea.

The riders shifted in their saddles, each eager to rush forward and begin the knockabout with bang and outcry, but like seasoned performers, remained in place and studied their stage.

Awed by the immense body of the ocean, Robin sighed. "It's so big . . . so beautiful."

Brown John scolded her with his eyes, reminding her that they were not here to play a scene of awe and wonder, but one of deadly stealth and raw violence, and she nodded her apology.

They rode forward, and the tree cover siding the road thinned like parting curtains exposing bald shoreline, and an ever-widening vista of untamed nature.

The *bukko* had never seen bodies of earth and sky and water of such size or stark contrast. Here was a stage on which gods could roughhouse and war, where goddesses passed like mysteries behind watery veils and sunbeams. He reined up again and sighed with wonder. But no one scolded him, and the others stopped at his sides.

The dark turbulent waters and the verdant greens of tropical growth on the far shore spoke of portentous mysteries, and the black castle standing on the hunched back of the huge grey rock rising out of the sea was a chilling spokesman of imminent doom.

"That's Pyram," Jakar said evenly. "I saw it from
the opposite shore, but there's no mistaking it."

The northern walls and towers were dark ruins,
and tumbled roughly to the south where towers
stood erect amid moats, and valiant and salient
walls. They were topped by crenellated parapets,
their long black bodies hiding whatever monstrosi-
ties might dwell behind them.

The rock supporting the castle was bald at the top,
and descended to thickets of carob bean, cork oak
and wild olive, then to carpets of heather, rosemary
and lavender. Flurries of ravens, warblers and wrens
swept over thicket and brush, and swooped down the
sheer faces of the cliffs past bright patches of snapdragons, periwinkle and broom flowers lining the
runnels in the rock.

The landscape approaching the castle was low and
rugged, and swept in a crescent toward the northern
end of the huge rock. A dirt road turned off the coast
road, wandered through the rough ground and
crossed a shallow bridge of land joining the conti-
nent to the rock. There it meandered up the gentle
western slope toward the southern end of the castle,
and entered it via a port of arms, an outwork which
bisected the valiant wall. Flags waved on the wall,
and tiny shadows moved along it, sentries of the
castle garrison. But the coast road and the road to
the castle were empty tongues of dark dirt waiting
for something edible to suck into the teeth of the
castle.

A fog was drifting out of the Inland Sea. Its
tremulous body was rising in concealing mists
around the base of the sheer cliffs at the north end of
the rock where waves crashed at the mouths of
shadowed caves. Its vaporous fingers probed at the
shore, reaching as far as the coast road and promis-

ing to reach further. Above the castle, the overhanging cloud tumbled on the wind, falling in billowing folds over towers and ruins like a heavy mourning garment.

The *bukko* smiled with patient expectation. "We will wait for the fog to cover us."

They dismounted, distributed the last of their water and provisions, then sat down and watched the fog roll in. When the thick mists reached all the way inland to cover their bodies so they could not see ten feet in front of them, they remounted and moved toward Pyram.

Cobra led them.

Looking warily into the dense concealing fog, Jakar said, "I don't like it. Why should things suddenly become easy?"

"Patience, lad," Brown John said. "We can use all the luck that comes our way."

They traveled the length of the coast road, only passing an ox-cart and driver barely visible in the fog, and turned onto the dirt road. Crossing the narrow bridge of land, they heard distant voices high above on the battlements, but met no one. At the base of the rock, Cobra silently indicated they should turn off, and led the party through boulders to the shoreline. There they hid the horses in a shallow cove, and Brown John and Jakar strapped sword and crossbow to their backs. They crossed the base of the giant rock for nearly a mile, until they were well away from the shore and the incoming waves were drenching them, and stopped.

In front of them, forty feet of sheer cliff plunged into the turbulent surf. Slick shale. Impassable. At its far side, the waves splashed into the darkness of a small cave.

Cobra removed her cloak, raised it in a bundle over her head and moved down into the onrushing water. The others, in like manner, followed. They waded ten feet further along the base of the cliff, then had to swim the rest of the way. At the cave, waves tossed them about, and they were banged against boulders repeatedly before they made the floor of the cave. Scratched and bruised, they crawled into the shallow opening and lay gasping as they watched Robin's cloak, which had been ripped from her grasp, toss fitfully on the frothy waters as it was slowly dragged out to sea.

The cave was wide but only three feet high, and they had to crawl through shallows of ebbing and flowing sea water to dry ground. There they wrung out their clothes, then crawled some more. They moved in the manner Cobra had instructed them while on the night trail, making as little noise as possible. The faintest click or thump of falling shale echoed deep into the dark, sinister body of the rock.

They passed through horizontal tunnels made by sea water and climbed up through vertical ones made by rain water. Vague daylight, drifting in from side tunnels, illuminated their passage from time to time, but most of it was spent in total darkness. Nevertheless, Cobra led the way with assurance.

Brown John smiled unseen as he followed her, his hand maintaining contact with her shoulder. She had told him she had been raised in Pyram, and that as a young girl her constant dream had been to one day possess the sacred jewels. Consequently, she had spent much of her youth crawling through each tunnel and passage until she found the dungeon cell in which the jewels were held. But they had been heavily guarded at all times, and she had never seen them.

Now, as they moved deeper and deeper into the rock, Cobra's pace became strong and quick with growing excitement.

The air became hot and humid, and Brown John and the others began to sweat and gasp. They began a long descent through a narrow tunnel, and at the bottom, a cool sea breeze wafted over them. Here Cobra stopped and turned to Brown John. Her voice was quiet but rough, almost wild with anticipation.

"We're almost there. From here on, the passage is narrow. We'll have to crawl."

The *bukko* passed the word, and they lowered themselves to the moist rock flooring, breathing deeply.

Cobra said, "Hurry now," and began to squirm through a ragged hole in the rock.

Brown John, Robin and Jakar followed.

Puddles of sea water shared the floor of the tunnel with them, and clusters of stinking sea urchin and tiny crabs. They were pinched and bitten, then emerged in a sizable tide pool and stood gasping with relief.

Waves crashed through a tunnel at the opposite end of the pool, their foaming spilling bodies lit by torches guttering in wall embrasures behind the ledge on which they had emerged. It spanned one side of the pool. Through the green water, they could see the whitish bottom of the pool, and a jagged hole in its floor opening onto shadowy depths. An iron-grilled door was positioned beside the hole; it was attached to chains which could pull it over the hole, sealing it. Whitish scrape marks showed in the floor where it had been recently dragged.

Robin shuddered, and Jakar and the *bukko* unstrapped their weapons. The group put their dry cloaks back on and followed Cobra across the ledge. An entrance tunnel opened off the ledge at the far edge. They followed it half its length and stopped, pressing their bodies into shadows.

Torches flickered at the opposite end, and shadowed figures passed in their light.

When the figures vanished, Cobra hurriedly led the group into a side passage. It led to a stairwell, and they ascended it, moving quickly now despite the difficulty. The stone stairs were alternately dark and illuminated by flickering oil lamps set in brass embrasures. The sounds of the ocean grew fainter and fainter far below. At the top, the stairwell opened on a horizontal tunnel. It was low and narrow and undulating, offering no view of what waited at the end.

They followed Cobra through it, almost running now, and it opened onto a large cave with dusty walls of dense black earth rising thirty feet high. Crawl holes pockmarked the curving walls, and the mouth of an arched tunnel was set high to one side. A staircase descended from it, following the curved wall, growing wider and wider, then turned into the cave, ending at its center. The staircase faced a wide polished wall of obsidian blocks. The black rock glittered with flickering orange light from a large oil lamp hanging from the center of the ceiling.

Brown John looked about uncertainly, then at Cobra. Her face was white, and her mouth hung open. She was gasping, teetering in place. Then she staggered to the obsidian wall and moved along it, mumbling incoherently, and frantically exploring it with outstretched arms and probing fingers. When she turned to him, her voice shook with heedless panic.

"It was here! I know it was! The dungeon cell was right here! Behind this wall. But it's been sealed up!"

"Are you sure this is the right cave?" the *bukko* asked.

"Of course!" she gasped. "But it's walled up!"

Brown John, Robin and Jakar shared an alarmed

glance, and edged toward the wall, studying it. Sudden fear had drawn their flesh tight over their jaws, and their bodies were unsteady on feet spread well apart.

"You're absolutely certain?" asked Brown John, not wanting to hear the answer.

"Yes! Yes!" Cobra groaned. "The door was right here!" She pounded the rock wall. "Right in the middle!"

Jakar turned to the *bukko*. "Let's go, Brown. I smell a trap."

The old Grillard lifted a hand telling him to wait. He could not bring himself to agree so quickly. He looked around again, then wished he hadn't. The clang of iron bars rang throughout the room, and they swung around facing the sound. An iron-barred door had descended over the entrance tunnel, blocking their retreat to the tide pool. Behind it stood a small man in a breechclout, oozing fetid slime.

Robin recoiled into Jakar's arms, and Cobra gasped, "Schraak!"

The worm man bowed in reply from behind the bars and laughed.

Cobra staggered behind Brown John and clung to his back, staring over his shoulder in shock and terror. "No. Noooooo!"

"Oh, yes," Schraak said, and lifted a thick finger, pointing up at the top of the staircase.

Their heads lifted, and their eyes widened.

A fog was drifting out of the arched doorway at the top of the stairs and gathering against the ceiling. Then shafts of black light struck through it, and it billowed, filling the ceiling, threatening to fall on them.

The four backed up, holding each other, and bumped against the obsidian wall. Shaking her head,

Cobra collapsed against the *bukko*.

"What's happening?" Robin moaned. "What is it?"

"A trap," Jakar said, as if describing nothing more startling than a stage device. "It's all been a trap. The fog and the black cloud above the castle were put there deliberately, just like the fog we're looking at now, to make us believe we could enter unseen."

"But how?" Robin pleaded.

"Black Veshta," Brown John said in a whisper, and Cobra shuddered agreement.

Robin looked at the *bukko*, trembling with confusion, then looked back up into the billowing fog and screamed shrilly, sinking to her knees.

Flaming eyes had appeared within the dark mist, and now the horned helmet emerged from it. It resided on the head of a huge man clothed only in a black loincloth and boots. The body seemed to be Gath of Baal's, but the carriage was brutish and bent by demonic appetites. Beastly. The Death Dealer as the Master of Darkness had originally conceived of him, as a Lord of Destruction.

Jakar and Brown John both stepped in front of Robin protectively, their weapons ready.

A rough growl instantly ripped out of the helmet, and the beast's body heaved, with the helmet blasting flames through the thinning mist.

Jakar and the *bukko* raised their arms, and the helmet's fire speared down across the room, singeing their garments and flesh, driving them away from Robin. The flames promptly abated, and the helmet hung low between the ponderous shoulders, content to glare down at Robin with impatient hunger.

A slight figure emerged from the fog beside the dark beastman, and leaned lightly against him, supporting itself with a hand on his shoulder.

Brown John knew instantly who it was. The

Nymph Queen. Tiyy. Black Veshta's unholy high priestess. But she was also something more. He could feel it. Her powers were almost tangible in the air, and she had obviously made the fog, ordered it to gather at the center of the Inland Sea and spill out of the sky as if it were an obedient child. Only a deity could do that, and only a deity of dark intent. Black Veshta. The Dark Goddess had been made flesh, and the *bukko* stared in shock and wonder at her.

She was a hoyden, at once both girlishly vital and alluring and as old and dangerous as time. He had never dreamed that pure evil could be so young and charming and desirable. It wasn't fair. Appropriately naked except for a leopard-skin breechclout and a sheen of golden oil on her supple walnut body, she carried her new powers with the same ease with which the mighty oak carries its leaf cover, and the sensual satisfaction on her face was that of the bitch cat who has mated with the lion.

She looked directly at Cobra and said, "Welcome back to Pyram, you slithering bitch. I think I've wanted you as much as I wanted the girl." She laughed with childish mischief and added, "Almost, anyway."

Thirty-Nine

CENTER STAGE

Brown John did not move or speak. He wanted to, but did not know the next line of dialogue, or if it was his to speak. Two of the principal players in his plot suddenly seemed totally out of character, and it terrified him. It was a *bukko*'s nightmare come to life.

Gath of Baal, his trusted friend who was the force that gave movement to the *bukko*'s plots, appeared to have left the cast completely. His body was present, but it looked as if it had been bent from within. There was no trace of the man he knew in its beastlike stance. It stood beside the Nymph Queen as obediently as a domesticated pet waiting to bark or kill on her command.

The nymph herself, of course, was a total surprise. Goddesses were supposed to be regal, and formal, and robed in heavy velvets. But this one was housed in the body of a coltish savage, and there was enough delicious mischief behind her bright eyes to make sin look like the only endeavor worthy of life's trials and tribulations. If anyone doubted this, her brazen nudity would end the argument before it started, and unbuckle your belt as well.

She leaned casually against Gath, her fingers toying with his shoulder as she put two fingers inside her mouth and whistled shrilly like a child calling her pet dog.

Worm soldiers promptly slithered from the shadowed holes pockmarking the black dusty walls. They wore spare leather armor, and their umber flesh was spongy and coated with slime. Dark holes served them as ears and wrinkles as features. Several had short, curved steel blades growing from their wrists instead of hands, while others leveled crossbows at the intruders.

Brown John and Jakar moved side by side, their bodies shielding Cobra and Robin, but all four flinched with horror.

Here and there along the wall facing them the dark earth crumbled apart as something behind them pushed at it. The earth fell away and the heads of huge worms emerged. As round and thick as rain barrels. Slick with slime and coated with dirt. Kival carnivore worms, long believed extinct. Their heads wriggled free, and their scarlet necks spread like hoods below jawless mouths lined with blunt, hard gums.

Schraak laughed behind the barred door blocking the tunnel to the tide pool, and Tiyy sat against Gath's knee, chuckling as she watched her victims wince with fear.

"Come now," she said easily, "what did you expect? That you could walk right into my castle and steal what you like without so much as a struggle?" She chuckled and added, "You're not that foolish, are you?"

Having no answer that seemed appropriate, Brown John turned to reassure the women and found Robin staring at him. Her big eyes were as empty as slate waiting to be written on, as if she, too, were out of character, eager to play whatever role he asked her to play, but with no idea what it was.

He said, "Stay behind us," as if he knew what he was talking about, and glanced uncertainly at Cobra.

She was slumped back against the wall, staring vacantly at Gath. Whipped. Broken. The *bukko* grimaced. Jakar was the only one in character. He seemed to have not only endured the rigors of the quest but grown stronger from them, and in precisely the manner the plot now called for. His smile was right where it always was, but it was suddenly far more resilient.

He winked at the *bukko*. "Why is it that I have the feeling this is not the kind of finish you had in mind?"

Taking courage from the young man's humor, Brown John smiled brazenly at the creatures threatening them. "Not exactly a comedy, is it?"

"Fine by me," Jakar replied easily. "I'm partial to tragedies."

Brown John chuckled, and Tiyy laughed with delight. "By Bled, you did think you could get away with it, didn't you?" She came down the steps halfway with a bouncy stride and sat down, straddling the corner of a step. She leaned forward, arms thrust down between her parted legs for support, and cocked her head like a snappish tart, studying them. Her large sloping eyes carried that confidence only given to women who are certain they will be the most beautiful creature in every room they enter.

The intruders shifted warily as if moved about by the sheer force of her glance, and Tiyy laughed again, loving their torment.

Hating it, Brown John said, "Don't laugh, wench! We're not going to give up without a fight." But the words were spoken by rote, without emotion or conviction.

Tiyy ignored him and put her eyes on Cobra.

"You've put on weight. Oddly enough, it becomes you. But your hair is a fright."

Cobra instinctively put a hand to her tangled, burnt hair and looked at the nymph, momentarily angered. Then the serpent woman's arm dropped and her eyes became wet and thin, hiding none of the bitterness, defeat and misery she felt. Her mystery now seemed to be nothing but a tattered shroud, and it hid no more than her ragged tunic hid, making her look old, bitter and mean.

"Ahhhh!" Tiyy said with a ring of delight. "Your age has caught up with you, hasn't it? As well as your reckless greed." She grinned and looked at the *bukko* as if he were an adorable stray dog, asking, "Now, who might you be?"

"I am Brown John," he said proudly, "the bukko master of the Grillards, and . . ."

"So you're the bukko," Tiyy interrupted. "Well now, that's a welcome surprise. Look!" She arched her back, displaying her high, hard breasts, extended her legs with toes pointed and lifted her arms, twisting slightly so she could be seen from all sides. "This is your work, old man." She relaxed, leaning forward again, her voice intense with anticipation. "Your Grillard dancing girls were perfectly suited to my unnatural appetite, so I welcome you. A man with an eye like yours will be an invaluable addition to my staff."

Brown John was staggered, and the others could only stare in horror.

Tiyy tucked her legs up under her and leaned forward with her elbows on her knees. "Now, let's have a look at you, girl. Let's see if all the fuss has been worth it."

Robin trembled against Jakar's back, and he whispered, "Go ahead, stand up to her. I think she's afraid of you."

Robin nodded uncertainly and came around
Jakar, head high.

Tiyy's eyes thinned, and she uncoiled, slowly
crawling down three more steps, as unconscious of
her movements as a curious cat. She studied Robin,
her head cocking from side to side, as if wary of what
she saw.

"You are worth the fuss," she said flatly. "There's
no doubt of that." She smiled warmly, like an old
chum. "I thought it would irritate me to have to look
at you, knowing that I had to rely on your Kaa . . .
on your magic . . . to make mine fertile. But you're a
delight. In fact, it excites me, knowing our bloods are
joined. You're a rare piece of work, even in rags."

Robin unconsciously ran a hand through her hair.
It had grown on the trip, and the sea water had
washed out most of the dye, so that the torchlight
graced her amber waves with golds and oranges.

"Why do you wear clothes, anyway?" Tiyy asked
fretfully. "If you had any sense you'd go naked, like
you were born to go. Putting on clothes is for fools. A
stupid law made by stupid men."

"It's a good law," Robin said petulantly. "Besides,
it's cold in the forest."

Tiyy laughed easily, then her eyes widened with
sudden recognition, and she said, "You don't know,
do you? You haven't the slightest idea of why Cobra
brought you here? To Pyram?"

"It wasn't her idea," Robin said firmly. "It was
mine. I offered to come, to help Gath with the
helmet."

"Of course," Tiyy said, and put her eyes on Cobra.
"You would have had no trouble making her believe
that." She looked at the others. "But I'll wager the
girl provided little help with the helmet, perhaps
none at all. Am I right?" They shifted nervously, and
she laughed. "I am right, aren't I? And that can mean

only one thing . . . none of you knew what the slithering bitch was up to."

"We knew enough," Brown John said importantly.

Tiyy grunted. "You didn't know anything, and you still don't." She leaned toward Robin, and her smile faded. "Cobra's used you, girl. And you're all going to suffer for being fools enough to allow her to do it."

Robin backed up into Jakar's arms, but the Nymph Queen's eyes and voice followed her.

"Only yesterday, I could not have seen if there was anything more to you than a strong spirit. But now," she nodded with the back of her head at Gath, "with his dark seed planted in me, with the powers of the Dark Goddess housed in my body, I can see everything that hides inside you."

Gasping, Cobra backed against the wall and came to a shuddering stop.

Tiyy took no notice. She held Robin with her hypnotic eyes. They were now laden with the wisdom of a thousand years. Theaters to the underworld.

"What hides inside you does not only make dreams that tame the helmet," she said in a purring monotone, "but dreams for everyone with eyes to see them. Dangerous dreams so grand and noble and pure that they demand imitation . . . and there is no greater threat to my master than that."

Feeling a rush of excitement in his stomach, Brown John glanced expectantly at Robin out of the corner of his eye. But she looked just as she had throughout their journey, worn and frightened and adorned with rags and trail dust. He saw no dreams. Frowning irritably, he looked back at Tiyy.

She now squatted on a step, and was grinning directly at him. "Disappointed, aren't you, bukko?" She chuckled. "Sometimes a primitive gift of sight like yours can see it, or at least suspect it. But you obviously don't. But Cobra saw it and intended to use it." She turned to Cobra. "You see, in order to regain the trust of our master and regain her powers, she had to find some way to control the horned helmet. And the sacred jewels of the Goddess of Light could provide that way. But in order to steal them, she needed the girl." Her smile turned on Robin, malevolent and toying. "Because only a female whose Kaa is pure and strong, who truly seeks the jewels not for herself, but for someone else, can hold them in her hands without being burnt to a cinder. And you, girl, have such a Kaa, and Cobra knew it. Your hands could pick up the jewels and steal them." She chuckled mockingly. "At least Cobra believed they could."

"Come now," said Brown John, "you don't expect us to believe a fairy tale like that?"

"Fairy tale!" Tiyy said, rising like a spitfire. "You call it a fairy tale, when for years it was only these hands," she lifted her hands with fingers spread, "that could control the glimmer of their beauty? Hah! I suppose you thought that a shiftless, lecherous, money-hungry old clown like yourself could steal them?"

Brown John scowled, his best scowl, but no sharp reply came to mind. The best he could do was shift his weight and stand one foot closer to the impertinent young bitch.

Tiyy laughed at him. "You trusted Cobra, didn't you, you old bouse bag? And all the time she was plotting to kill the lot of you."

"That's not true," blurted the *bukko.*

"Be quiet, Brown," Cobra muttered sharply. "In a way, she's right."

Her voice was a bitter hiss, and Brown John stared open-mouthed. Was the hiss some vague instinctive behavior left over from years of demonic living, or was the serpent still there? He had no idea, and aching pain welled inside his chest.

Cobra turned her bitter eyes on Tiyy. "Are you finished playing now?"

"Not quite," Tiyy said impishly. "Since your skill and cunning have brought you this far, I think you deserve a reward before you die . . . so I'm going to let you look at them."

"The jewels?" gasped Cobra.

"Yes," Tiyy said temptingly, "the jewels."

Cobra straightened slightly. "You don't dare," she said, a blush of hope passing behind her grey-gold eyes.

"On the contrary," Tiyy said with wicked anticipation. "I would not miss this for the world."

Forty

THE JEWELS

The nymph looked down at Schraak and nodded. He pulled his slick, grinning face away from the barred door, and scurried back into the shadows of the entrance tunnel out of sight.

Brown John, Cobra, Robin and Jakar looked about uncertainly, not knowing what to expect or where it might come from. The sounds of clanking chains came from the barred passageway, then the grating sounds of metal tearing against metal, and

behind them four of the blocks of obsidian began to
settle into the ground.

They turned sharply and backed away, watching
the slow, grudging descent. Then Cobra, her breath
suddenly heaving with heedless excitement, edged
toward the opening being made by the massive
blocks. The others moved up beside her.

Behind the opening, a timber door joined together
by steel bars was coming into view. Dust filled the
cracks between the timbers and the doorframe, and
the door was set behind it on runners, a sliding door.

The descending blocks of obsidian came to a stop
with a crunching jar, and dust fell away from the
ceiling, landing on faces and shoulders. They
blinked, rubbing the dust away from their eyes, and
stared warily at the door.

Here and there, through tiny cracks between the
heavy beams, bits of brilliant white light streaked
through, reaching across the full depth of the cave.

The group drew away from them, mystified.

"Open it, Cobra!" Tiyy shouted lightly. "You've
wanted to do this all your life! Don't be a coward
now!"

Brown John, Cobra, Robin and Jakar looked back
sharply, their eyes suspicious.

Tiyy stood with legs apart and fists on hips, her
hoyden smile moving on her firm cheeks. A thin
beam of white light was streaking past her, playing
on the wall behind the staircase. She lifted a hand,
caught the beam with the palm and moved it in a
slow circle, controlling the white light and making
the beam swirl and dance.

"Isn't it beautiful?" she said. "You can even play
with it."

Brown John glanced warily at a beam of light
striking the ground beside him, and covertly slid his

hand into the beam. It stung him, and he jumped away, yelping.

Tiyy laughed, and spread her arms. "I'll help you," she said, "so it won't hurt."

She rose up onto her toes, arching and thrusting, and beams of black light emerged slowly and languorously from the palms of her hands. They edged across the room, then came apart in flurries of smoky mist, drifting to the closed door and settling there, slightly darkening the brilliant bits of white light.

Cobra, heaving with anticipation, moved to the door, took hold of the door handle, tried to pull it. It didn't budge. Brown John and Jakar joined her, and together they pulled. The door surrendered a squeaking noise, grated, then slid open and white light spilled out.

They ducked away from the glare, covering their eyes with their arms, and the light billowed into the black cave, mixing with the shady mist to fill it with a bright glow. The astounded group peered over and under arms, watching the light swirl on itself inside the dungeon cell. It seemed to have body, life.

The savage nymph squatted between Gath's legs, laughing easily with her arms wrapped around his thighs. "Go ahead!" she shouted. "Go inside, the jewels won't hurt you now."

The foursome shared a wary glance, then Cobra hurried into the cell and the others followed. Inside the door, they suddenly stopped short, shielding their eyes with their hands.

A pillar of white light stood at the center of the small cell. It rose from a black pedestal to the middle of a black stone ceiling, supporting it. At the very center of the ceiling, white light illuminated the mouth of a narrow shaft, no bigger round than a

walnut. The light billowed in it as if it were plugged
somewhere above. In each corner, thick square columns of black stone also supported the ceiling. The
superstructure on which Pyram's main tower rested.
The column of light was obviously the primary
support. It shimmered with living power, constantly
changing its faceted shape and proportions, and a
nimbus of white light billowed and radiated from its
transparent body. The sacred jewels were not jewels
at all, but a single jewel, a whiteness without flaw or
corruption which was at once both form and formless.

Cobra shrieked at the daunting vision and turned
away, collapsing on the ground.

Recklessly, Brown John advanced on the massive
jewel, his hands moving restlessly in front of him.
Every sense wanted to hold the light, and caress and
fondle it. But even if his heart was as pure and true
as Robin's, his hands could not have. And neither
could any female hands, no matter how pure.

The jewel was impossible to hold. It had no more
substance than an illusion.

Suddenly Brown John backed away.

The pillar seemed to be fading. Then the room
filled with whiteness blotting out all vision, and the
glare blinded him. He staggered back, brushing
someone, but he could not see who it was, and
reached the door. There Jakar stood with his back to
the light, blinking and trying to regain his vision.
Cobra was slumped beside him, wearing an expression that said she no longer had the will to stand
upright. Shielding his eyes, Brown John heard Tiyy
laugh, and there seemed to be no malice in it, only
childish delight. Then fog came tumbling down from
the place where he had last seen her, and mixed with
the light, reducing it to a bright glare. He rubbed his

eyes, blinking. When he could see again, he turned back toward the jewel.

Robin had not come out of the chamber. She still stood facing the pillar of light, spellbound and trembling, her arms floating at her sides. Her head was raised to the pillar, and white light shot through her red curls, turning the tips orange and vermilion and russet. Suddenly the light slowed down, spilled like thick white syrup over her head, and clung to curl and wave, as if the hair were wearing it, as if the light were indeed jewelry.

Brown John and Jakar shared an astounded glance, and the *bukko* nudged Cobra with his toe. She pulled her leg away, not bothering to complain or look up, and he nudged her again. Her head lifted slowly, and as she turned to the light, she gasped.

Tiny beams of light had formed at the center of the pillar, as if the nimbus suddenly had fingers. They probed the air just beyond the form. Suddenly one, two, then a third and fourth shot forth from the pillar and played across Robin's face. Were they hunting something?

Tiyy rose abruptly in front of Gath, eyes aghast.

Cobra rolled to her feet and staggered into the chamber. Brown John and Jakar promptly joined her, and they all stared in a numb stupor.

The tiny beams had gathered on Robin's plump lower lip and gently bounced up and down, caressing it. Then they stopped and held on to the plump flesh. Slowly the lip grew bright red, then pink, then white as the light entered the flesh, seeping into her face until it glowed from within with pink light.

Cobra, dizzy with excitement, staggered, and the *bukko* and Jakar had to hold her up.

Muttering angrily, Tiyy bounded down the stairs until she could see clearly into the chamber, and

came to an abrupt stop at the bottom. Her snarl said
she did not like what she saw.

Flurries of tiny beams were cascading from the
crystalline pillar and playing across Robin's body,
searching bare shoulders, the swell of a breast, a
jagged hole in her tunic at her thigh.

Tiyy turned sharply to the worm soldiers holding
the crossbows and shrieked, "Finish her! Finish
her!"

The crossbowmen raised their pieces, taking aim.

Neither Brown John nor Jakar heard the nymph
clearly, but Cobra did. She flung herself heedlessly
toward Robin, covering the girl's body with her own,
and three steel bolts took her with the loud whap of
metal burying itself in meat. One caught her above
the heart, entering under the shoulderbone, and the
others in hip and thigh.

A fourth bolt missed the target area, hit the pillar
with a flash of lightning and ricocheted around the
chamber, dropping beside Brown John. Its metal was
red-hot and twisted like string. He winced and with
Jakar at his side, positioned himself to protect the
two women, weapons in hand.

Cobra was half bent, her hands clutching the bolt
above her breast as blood spilled between her fingers.
Robin stood behind her, supporting her and looking
about in confusion. "What's happened?" she gasped,
her voice sounding far off, vague.

"Stay behind me," Cobra said with a harsh whisper, and forced herself erect, shielding the girl. "Stay
where you are! Don't move!"

Robin nodded, then groaned with sudden terror.

Gath's body was coming down the stairs in clumsy
loping strides. He carried no weapons, but his hands
dangled at his sides more dangerously than his axe
ever had. Tiyy moved beside him, her small hands

clutching an elbow as if it were a leash, shouting, "Kill her! Quickly! Kill her!"

She unleashed him and stood watching as his body advanced, filling the doorway to the chamber.

Brown John lifted his sword, and Jakar fired.

The steel bolt tore through the Death Dealer's side, but he took no notice and kept coming. The eye slits of the horned helmet spewed flames, driving the white light aside and making it smoke and fade.

Jakar reloaded hurriedly and Brown John thrust with his sword. Gath ignored the bite of the blade on his thigh and jumped forward between them. His thick arms swung sideways, knocking Jakar to one side and the *bukko* to the other.

Jakar hit the stone wall with the back of his head and sagged forward, dazed. Brown John landed on his back, with the air driven from his lungs.

Cobra, shielding Robin with her body, screamed at the massive, beastlike man hovering over her, "No, Gath! No!"

Robin, hiding behind Cobra's shoulder, pleaded, "It's me, Gath! It's me. Robin. Don't . . . don't!"

Gath's body did not listen. Its thick arm swept toward Cobra, bludgeoning her with the back of its hand. She flew sideways, colliding with a black pillar and crumpling at its base. She tried to rise, but sank to the floor instead, and began to bleed on the ground.

Dizzy and blinking, Brown John rose to his feet and staggered toward the beast's back, but fell a good eight feet short of his target. It was two feet further than the still dazed Jakar got.

Gath hovered darkly in front of Robin. She was reduced to whimpering now, unable to move. His flames singed her rags and flesh, and she cringed with pain, moaning. It seemed to encourage him. His

hands yanked her around, violently ripping away
what remained of her tunic, and she screamed. He
drove the butt of his hand into her back, and she
dropped forward, facing the pillar of white light.
Naked. Moaning. Protected by no more than the
flurry of tiny beams of light as they still searched her
body.

He straddled her, bending over with his massive
hands closing about her frail neck, and the helmet's
flames lashed her bare flesh and hair, his own fingers.
The pain made him howl, but he held on, squeezing,
and her body convulsed against his hands like a fish
on the end of a spear, then surrendered and fell limp.

The brute's hands continued the pressure, relent-
less, abandoned to the kill. Suddenly he dropped her
and staggered back, staring.

The tiny beams of light were scurrying together on
her back. Her torso heaved with breath, and she
rolled over. The beams followed her, dashing wildly
about breasts and belly, and came to abrupt stops,
each pulsing and expanding in size and brilliance as
it fixed its beacon on one of the signs or numerals of
the map Cobra had drawn on her flesh.

The white light had found what it hunted.

Forty-One

SURRENDER

Gath did not recognize the girl crumpled under him. His mind was on fire. Hammering his skull. Clouded. Then his mind began to come down off the top of the mountainous body and merge with it. Size, proportion, place came into focus, and he became aware of the billowing white light, the familiar faces watching him, and finally recognized the small naked girl. White light swirled about her, cradling her, and glowed within her, but there was no mistaking her. Robin Lakehair.

Abject shame shook him, then he heard the Nymph Queen shout, "Kill her, you ape!" He turned hard, snarling.

Tiyy screamed and backed up the staircase, her features shocked almost past recognition.

Gath started for her, and the room shook, staggering him. He stopped short, and Jakar and Brown John rose uncertainly, bringing Cobra with them. She was slumped and gasping, her hands clutching the ugly steel bolt protruding above her breast. Suddenly wind howled and sucked at them, and the white light swirled in its grasp, emptying itself from the cave and rushing back toward the huge jewel.

Gath kneeled beside Robin, shielding her from the wind and rushing light, and lifting her gently. She glowed from toes to hair, and her breath came in

short gasps, her eyes closed and lips parted. Their
color was back. His fingers touched her lips gently
and her body became rigid in response. Then her
eyes opened. They were stark with fear, then they
smiled falteringly, and she went soft in his arms.
Tears welled from her eyes, and when she spoke it
was a soft cry.

"Gath."

His body shuddered, stunned. It was only one
word, but her tone said that within that single word
was the entire tale of a man, and it was his tale.

Gath helped Robin to her feet, and Jakar covered
her with his cloak, handing her a length of her torn
tunic to belt it with. As she did this, Gath turned to
Brown John and Cobra. She was pale and gasping,
sagging against the *bukko* and crying with joy.

The room shook again, and they turned toward the
pillar of light.

The wind had stopped. The jewel was no longer
sucking the white light in. It was now centered in the
crystalline body, becoming denser and denser, until
the crystal turned opaque white. Its glow filled the
chamber. Then its opacity faded, leaving a flawless,
transparent pillar. Encased within was the perfectly
preserved body of an ancient priestess.

Her pose was regal, yet kind, and she was muscular, with dark olive skin burnished by the sun. Her
black hair was in wild disarray, uncut in the style of
savages. Her only garments were girdle, halter and
necklace, and they were made of sparkling diamonds.

"The jewels!" gasped Cobra and Brown John.

Gath, Brown John, Cobra and Jakar stared, mystified. The priestess was short and sturdy, her bones
blunt and primitive, unlike anyone they knew. Yet
her features were strangely familiar. They glanced
from Robin to the ancient priestess and realized the

savage priestess looked like Robin. They were almost identical.

Robin realized it too, and staggered into Jakar's arms, dumbfounded.

A wailing shriek came from behind them, and they turned to see Tiyy howl, "No! No!" and spread her arms to send forth dark vapors and destroy them. But there was fear behind her eyes, and she faltered and sank back, lowering her arms, as if confronting an enemy more powerful than herself.

"White Veshta!" Brown John whispered, and they looked once more at Robin.

"Yes," Cobra said weakly. "White Veshta incarnate."

The translucent pillar suddenly cracked open, and fumes came forth from the body of the preserved goddess. Instantly she began to decay. Flesh peeled, bones dissolved, and her limbs went up in smoke until all that remained were her jewels. The pillar itself dissolved into a mist. The jewels fell to the pedestal amid a flurry of white dust and tumbled to Robin's feet.

"Take them," Cobra gasped. Robin looked at her, and she pointed weakly at the jewels. "Pick them up! Hurry! Hurry!"

Robin hesitated, then gathered the jewels in her arms and rose, holding them against her chest. They instantly came alive in her grasp, writhing, glowing, and sparkling with shafts of white light. Where they touched her flesh, they began to merge with it, sinking into her, and she trembled with awe and wonder.

When they vanished within her, the glow behind the eye slits of the horned helmet cooled and faded, revealing the shadowed eyes of Gath of Baal. They stared at Robin.

Again her nut-brown face with its cheeks of budding roses was a theater of soft illusions, and her lips tiny mountains of color, the tissue of dreams. But this time the dreams were rooting inside him, finding sustenance in his blood and bone and muscle, and giving him a strength he had not had before.

His hands took hold of the rim of the helmet and lifted it slightly. The helmet flinched at his touch, twisting away, and the eye slits flamed again. Gath's body convulsed in pain, and the helmet howled and roared, but he held on, righting himself. He shuddered, then the glow behind the eye slits died once more, and the headpiece surrendered.

Gath lifted the helmet off and stood facing his friends.

His thick black hair was again singed and smoking, and his cheekbones, forehead and jawline were burnt raw and rimmed with ash. It made it difficult for him to smile.

Robin raced into his arms and held him, sobbing, "Gath! Oh, Gath, it's true." She looked up into his burnished face. "You're free."

The room shook again and there was a rending crack as dust fell from the ceiling. They all looked up and saw that the stone roof had cracked at the center and was slowly sinking, promising to bury them.

Forty-Two

HOME

The horned helmet in his hand, Gath led them to the door and saw crossbow bolts streaking toward them. He stopped short, deflecting a bolt with the helmet, and shoved the others aside, out of range behind the wall framing the door.

Tiyy stood halfway up the staircase behind her worm soldiers. They were hurriedly reloading their crossbows as she screamed at them, "Hurry! Hurry! Cut them down."

A worm soldier rose up to fire, and Gath threw his helmet. It caught the soldier in the shoulder, crushing his boneless meat, ricocheted off the wall, spitting sparks and flames to blind another soldier, and hit a third, ripping out his throat with its horns.

Tiyy backed up three steps, staring in horror as the bloody headpiece fell at her feet and rolled off the staircase. She gulped a breath and screamed again at her stunned men, "Keep firing."

The worm soldiers let go a volley, and bolts screamed through the air, clanging against the obsidian wall, burying themselves in the wooden doorframe.

Frustrated, the Nymph Queen shouted, "Attack! Attack!"

A half dozen worm soldiers surged toward the open door, hissing wetly, with the steel blades protruding from their wrists weaving in front of them.

Gath stepped out from behind the cell wall into the opening. He now held Brown John's sword in front of him, and Jakar stood behind his shoulder firing his crossbow.

The first worm soldier took the bolt in his face, and it tore through his skull-less head. Still he charged mindlessly, blindly swinging his bladed arms.

Gath's sword took off one arm at the elbow, and still he came, charging past Gath as his arm fell to the floor. It was still alive, like an earthworm torn in two.

Ignoring it, Gath strode into the black room swinging the flat of the blade, crushing instead of stabbing, and his sword ate heartily of the spongy bodies, killing them.

There was a sharp crack within the chamber. Gath glanced back over a shoulder and saw his friends crowding up behind him, their eyes wide with a new terror.

Part of the chamber's black stone ceiling had collapsed into the cell. Streams of dirt and rock were spilling out of the hole, and loud tearing sounds came from the ceiling where cracks were moving in jerks and jags through it.

"We'll be buried!" the *bukko* shouted. "We've got to get out of the tunnel! It leads to a tide pool!"

He pointed at the barred door on the opposite side of the cave. Schraak stood behind it with his arm reaching through the bars, trying to grasp the horned helmet which lay on the floor just out of reach. To the sides of the gate, the huge, hooded carnivore worms were writhing out of their holes.

Gath, raising the sword like a spear, threw it.

The blade took one of the huge worms in the head,

and it recoiled, began to writhe and whip its head about trying to dislodge the unwanted pain.

Gath glanced up at Tiyy. She stood near the top of the staircase surrounded by worm soldiers. Gath's eyes glittered dangerously, and he picked up two large stones, one in each hand. He ducked a cross-bow bolt, then flung the rock, crushing a huge worm's head.

He used five more rocks, crushing the worms or trapping them in their holes, then threw a handful of small rocks at the crossbowmen on the staircase. The speed of the rocks was such that they drilled the spongy bodies and came out the opposite side. Panicking, the worm soldiers raced past Tiyy, vanished through the arched door at the top of the staircase.

Gath retrieved the helmet and stood in the middle of the cave, lowering it over his head. Before it touched his neck, flames and black smoke roared from the eye slits.

Tiyy turned to flee and the cave shook, threw her down. She rolled over the side of the staircase onto the floor of the cave.

Gath moved for her, but hesitated as the cave again shook.

Shrieks of breaking, tearing stone came from the dungeon cell, and Brown John, Cobra, Robin and Jakar surged out amid swirling clouds of dust. Behind them falling rocks and dirt were filling the cell.

Tiyy jumped up, nimbly darted halfway back up the staircase, and cracks opened in the wall siding it. The arched doorway at the top of the stairs had collapsed, and dirt and rubble were spilling down the stairs toward her. She jumped back to the floor and hesitated.

Gath could sense her only ten feet away, but his

back was to her, and he was occupied, driving the last of the huge worms into its hole with the flames of the helmet.

The nymph raced to the barred door blocking the passage to the tide pool and shouted, "Open it! Open it!"

Schraak stood in the shadows behind the barred door, trembling and shaking his head.

"Open it!" the nymph screamed.

The small man backed up a step, still shaking his head, and turned, plunged into the passage out of sight. Tiyy brought her fingers to her lips and whistled shrilly, twice.

A horrid scream came from within the passage, then Schraak reappeared beyond the bars. He was not walking, but was being propelled backward by some huge darkness filling the passage. He screamed again and again and came into the flickering light. He was clinging to the moist spongy head of a monstrous worm five times the size of the others. Its body was so thick it was scraping off chunks of rock from the sides of the passage. The legendary Anababis, the ancient carnivore worm of the primordial underworld and the guardian of Pyram's dungeons. Black Veshta's favorite pet.

Tiyy slid to the side of the barred door, and Schraak was driven against it. He screamed and flailed, then came through the bars in large wet chunks of wormy flesh and fell into the cave in seven pieces.

Robin screamed, and hid her face against Jakar's chest. The young nobleman held her, but could not hold the color in his face.

The worm kept on driving and the barred door burst free, clanging on the floor of the cave. Then the creature stopped with its massive featureless head beside its master, and Tiyy stroked it lovingly. In response, the worm spread its wrinkled face wide, opening its mouth until its gums touched both floor and ceiling of the passageway.

Tiyy jumped nimbly over the lower teeth, landing barefoot in a splash of slime. She glanced around ropes of saliva hanging from the roof of the creature's mouth at Robin as she lifted her head.

"We'll meet again," Tiyy said matter-of-factly, then plunged into the pinkish-grey throat and vanished in its shadows, the splat of her running feet echoing behind her.

Forty-Three

INDIGESTION

The giant worm dropped its mouth closed, dislodging enough saliva to fill a washtub, and plugged the tunnel.

Gath looked around the cave.

Rubble was spilling in from the dungeon cell and deep cracks in the wall behind the staircase, and dust swirled, filling the black cave. Robin, Jakar and Brown John coughed and choked as it gagged them, settling thickly on hair, eyelids and shoulders. Cobra was now unconscious in the *bukko*'s arms, and bleeding on his chest.

Brown John answered the question in Gath's eyes before he could ask it. "It's the only way out." He nodded at the giant worm. "You've got to get us past that creature."

Gath nodded, glanced at Robin's hope-filled eyes as they watched him, and rushed into the dust swirling out the cell.

Working almost blindly, he found the timber door and kicked it down. He ripped and twisted at a timber, and it came away from the debris wearing a large rusted hinge. Holding it in both massive hands, he advanced out of dust and stood face-to-face with the worm. Black smoke spewed from the helmet's eye slits and the red glow reappeared within it.

The worm's wrinkled face jerked and opened slightly, spreading webs of slime across thick blunt teeth.

Gath lowered his head, and flames erupted from the eye slits. They seared the worm's face, and its spongy grey flesh puckered like the skin of a fig, the wet slime sizzling and steaming. Instinctively the creature writhed backward, cramming its shapeless head inside the tunnel, and spread its jaws. Saliva as thick as rope was strung between its teeth.

Gath swung the heavy timber, hammering the teeth with the rusted hinge, and three broke off, making an opening as wide as a door. He swung again, and the worm spit out a gob of saliva large enough to bathe in. The congealed liquid slurped around Gath's legs, and he slipped, plunging forward out of control into the mouth, and it closed with a wet slap.

Inside the worm's mouth, Gath rolled forward, slipping toward the digestive tract and barely hearing Robin's faint scream outside. Still holding the timber, he wrestled it sideways, jamming it against the sides of the worm's throat, and came to a sudden stop. Gathering his balance, he found he was knee-deep in guck, barely able to move his legs. He spewed flames around the interior of the worm's mouth, and the instinctive creature writhed and again opened its mouth, trying to eject him with its convulsing body.

Gath held his ground, took hold of the timber and ripped it free. Then he thrust it up, this time jamming it vertically between the mushy jaws. He kicked at the base of it until the timber was firmly stuck in place with the creature's jaws spread wide, and looked outside at Brown John.

"Come on! Hurry!" The three words were one harsh yell.

Brown John and the others hesitated, unable to accept for a moment the nature of the passageway offered to them. Then the *bukko* shouted, "Let's go," and stepped through the gap in the worm's teeth, carrying Cobra. Robin and Jakar followed.

Gath proceeded into the digestive tract of the worm, spewing flames around its gummy interior, and it flinched and convulsed, opening the passage wider. The others followed rapidly, scrambling and dodging in an effort to avoid the sting of digestive fluids, and choking on their putrid gases.

Every time the walls of the worm's interior convulsed against Robin, a glittering diamond would appear on her flesh emitting beams of white light which burnt and repelled the offending flesh.

Near the middle of the worm, the tract began to narrow, and Gath had to crouch low, pushing and shoving, as well as burning away protruding glands and growths. Suddenly the helmet sensed a threat up ahead, and he charged forward, shouldering the meat aside.

Just short of the end of the tract, the savage nymph goddess was on her hands and knees hacking an opening in the side of the worm with her knife. Flashes of guttering torchlight were slipping through the cut she had already made, and splashing across her slick body.

Gath's legs churned forward, the horns of his helmet chewing up the narrowing sides of the tract, his knees banging it aside.

Tiyy glanced over a shoulder, her large, sloped eyes bright with reckless daring, then dove into the cut up to her hips and came to a stop. Stuck. She wiggled and squirmed violently, and began to slip through.

Gath dove for a kicking ankle, and it vanished through the cut. Growling, he jumped up, holding the roof of the tract away with his back, and pulling apart the sides of the small hole Tiyy had made. He turned the eye slits on the sides of the hole, and flame erupted, burning the hole wider and wider and weakening the surrounding flesh. Then he ripped the hole wide enough to serve as a second mouth, and held it open.

When the others reached him, Jakar took Gath's place, and the Barbarian dove through the hole, leading the way. The hole opened on the vertical staircase, and he dashed down it with the others following.

As they descended, the rumblings within the surrounding rock walls grew loud and threatening, and the stairs shuddered under them, shaking loose clouds of rock and dust. Reaching the bottom of the vertical shaft, Gath plunged through the short side passage into a main cross tunnel. It was still lit by torches, and there were sounds of running feet from the interior opening.

"To the right," the *bukko* shouted.

Gath did not need to be told. He was already headed that way, following the helmet's instincts.

He burst out of the tunnel onto the ledge siding the tide pool, and saw Tiyy perched on the edge. She was naked now except for the sheathed dagger on her forearm, and glistened with slime and blood. She dove like a flying arrow out over the swirling pool, arched at the center and plunged down into the frothing ocean water.

Gath dove in after her, touched bottom and saw her slicing through the greenish waters into the dark sinister hole in the white floor. He swam for the hole, and black light shot up out of it. It spread quickly, filling the pool with an inky darkness, and his hands groped blindly before taking hold of the edge of the hole. He could see nothing. The black light had subdued the helmet's powers: its glow had gone out, and it could no longer sense anything. His mind and body heaved with frustration, but it was Gath of Baal's frustration, not the helmet's. He bunched his legs under him and thrust himself toward the surface.

Erupting from the center of the tide pool, he gasped for air and saw Jakar standing knee-deep in sea water at the tunnel leading to the ocean. He was waving and shouting for Gath to come that way, but the sounds of the swirling water and roar of the surf echoing through the tunnel covered his words. Gath swam for the tunnel, and Jakar vanished into it.

Reaching the tunnel, Gath climbed into it, and a wave tried to drive him back. He stood with his legs set apart and body low, and the weight of the wave battered thighs and chest. Then its force was spent, and the incoming water lowered, allowing him to wade through it.

He found the others waiting on a wooden dock twenty feet down the tunnel, where it widened into a huge cavern that reached through the base of the mountain for a hundred feet then opened onto the Inland Sea. There a dark fog lay just above the white-capped blue-black water. The sounds of frightened gulls were shrill, and the crashing waves were loud as they spilled into the cave. Rocks broke away from the rim of the mouth and crashed into the churning sea. The cave itself shook and rumbled, and dust swirled from the roof, clouding the air.

Through the haze, Gath could see that the dock
ran the length of the cave to its mouth, where it
joined a pier which reached out another three hundred feet into the dark sea waters. A blood-red barge
bobbed up and down just inside the mouth. A dozen
bat soldiers were loading it hurriedly, while others
were untying it from the dock. Twenty feet this side
of the barge, more bat soldiers lay half buried under
a rubble of rock. It had spilled out of the mouth of a
tunnel opening off of the dock, and dust and more
rubble were now joining it.

Gath turned to the *bukko* and hesitated. The old
man still held Cobra. She was barely breathing now.
Her face was chalky against his blood-stained tunic.
Gath looked into Brown John's eyes. There was no
humor or reckless plots behind them now, only pain
and panic.

"The nymph got away," Gath said, because there
was nothing else to say, and charged down the dock
toward the barge. After two strides the helmet was
roaring and spewing flames.

When the bat soldiers saw him coming, there was
no doubt in their minds that the flaming demon
spawn, their sacred queen's newest Lord of Destruction, wanted the barge exclusively for himself. So
they jumped into the water and swam for the Inland
Sea. Those who were not certain that the only thing
he wanted was the barge did so very swiftly.

When Brown John and the others boarded the
barge, Gath manned both the port and starboard
oars as Jakar took the rudder, and the craft pulled
away slowly from the dock. The *bukko* huddled with
Cobra on the raised command deck at the center of
the ship, and Robin searched hurriedly through the
baskets of provisions and stores of arms and armor
loaded by the bat soldiers, hunting for a knife and
firepot so she could remove the crossbow bolts from

Cobra's flesh and close her wounds.

A flurry of small rocks and spilling dirt fell on the barge as it passed under the rim of the cave mouth, then the lumbering craft floated clear, and the massive, hunched rock supporting Pyram growled in complaint at their departure.

Gath took no notice, his huge body bending and pulling on the oars. Cording. Glistening.

The barge plowed into the incoming surf, riding over wave after wave, then broke free and headed out to sea under the concealing roof of fog.

Forty-Four

TWADDLE

The blood-red barge was halfway across the Inland Sea when the fog began to burn off, and the huge grey rock supporting Pyram appeared behind the thinning mists. It was rumbling and shaking, and the vibrations churned up the surface of the sea, causing the awkward craft to dip and bob. Then the black castle shuddered at the heights of the rock, and its three central towers began to sway.

On the command deck of the barge, Brown John held Cobra's unconscious body close as he looked back at the impending spectacle. Robin had removed the crossbow bolts from the woman's body and closed the wounds in hip and thigh with fire. But the wound in her chest could not be closed and continued to bleed.

Robin, shamed and frightened by this failure, now squatted beside the *bukko*, her big eyes also on the shuddering castle. Her arms were stained with blood and ash up to her elbows.

Gath stood motionless beside the banked oars on the aft deck, and Jakar stood beside him, holding the rudder steady, as they also watched.

The castle's black towers weaved, then suddenly collapsed inward, and clouds of dust erupted under them. The walls of the castle shook and also fell inward, sucked down by the towers, and vanished behind billowing banks of grey dust that rose toward the overhanging cloud.

Pyram was dead.

Brown John nodded with approval, but it was imperceptible. In less than a month, the Master of Darkness had been driven back into the underworld and silenced, and now the source of his demon spawn was destroyed, and the sacred jewels of White Veshta, which had provided the magical powers to create his demons, had been taken from the dark sorceress. But the *bukko* felt no joy.

Despite his and Robin's efforts, Cobra had not revived and he could feel her growing cold in his arms.

He held her close, warming her with his own heat, until the barge ran ashore on the southern coast of the Inland Sea. There he carried her to the edge of a forest with trees taller than any he had ever seen before, and laid her in the shade at the foot of one. Its bark was soft and red, and its needles were thick on the ground.

While Gath and Jakar unloaded the weapons, armor, clothing and provisions, the *bukko* and Robin made a bed of needles and laid Cobra on it, covering her with blankets. Robin raced into the forest, with Jakar following to guard her, and moments later returned with herb leaves clutched in her hands, and a full waterskin slung over Jakar's shoulder. They sat beside Cobra, and Robin slowly fed her sips of water, then bits of herbs, first chewing them slightly to soften and moisten them.

Brown John watched the girl do this for a long time, his brown eyes heavy, no longer wearing a trace of vitality or optimism. He felt Cobra stir, and a smile lifted his cheeks. Robin shared a hopeful glance with the *bukko*, fed Cobra some more herbs, and she stirred again, opening her eyes. They blinked with a vague expression, then hardened with fear.

"It's all right," Brown John reassured her. "We're safe. Pyram is destroyed . . . and Robin wears the jewels."

Cobra glanced at Robin, and the girl pushed back the collar of her wrap, her fingers lightly touching her neck. A glow rose from her nut-brown flesh, and sparkling diamonds briefly appeared around her slender throat, then faded back into her body.

A smile flickered at the corners of Cobra's mouth, and she whispered, "I . . . I had no idea. I only thought you might be able to hold them." Panic suddenly creased her face, and she turned to Brown John, her voice cold with fear. "Gath? Where's Gath?"

"He's here," Brown John said comfortingly. "He's all right now. He's himself again, and he controls the helmet."

She smiled buoyantly, gasping with relief, and tears formed in her eyes. "Show me," she begged. "Hold me up."

Brown John lifted her slightly, and the tears fell from her eyes, streamed over her swelling cheeks.

Gath stood twenty paces off amidst the loot taken from the barge. He had found and put on a ragged leather tunic, a belted sword and a pouch and dagger belt. The horned helmet was tied to his hip, and he was sorting among a collection of spears. Sensing their eyes on him, he looked up. Seeing Cobra awake, he straightened and a smile moved his burnt cheeks. He selected a spear, dropped the others and moved toward his comrades.

Reaching them, he stopped, facing Cobra, and she asked, "You're . . . you're free? Truly free?"

He nodded, and she sank back against Brown John whispering, her voice too weak to make her words intelligible, but her tone overflowing with euphoric joy.

Gath asked her, "What would you like to eat? Venison? Rabbit? Turkey?"

She smiled up at him, and her purr came back into her voice, stroking him. "I'll eat whatever you kill, Dark One."

He nodded and started off, then stopped and looked back at her. His slate-grey eyes clouded as a confusion of emotions passed behind them. Memories. Suspicions and sensual pleasure. Deceit. Violence. Hate. Then trust and gratitude filled them unlike any the *bukko* had seen there before. Sober with regret and guilt. A moment passed before he could speak, and when he did, the words did not come easily to his lips. Nevertheless, they came.

"Forgive me," he said. "You are a true and honorable and brave friend. I owe you my life."

Then he turned and strode into the forest.

Cobra watched the shadowed foliage where he had disappeared until she had no more tears of joy to cry. Then she laid her head back, with her cheek against Brown John's palm, and closed her eyes. Some time passed before she spoke.

"Brown," she asked timidly, "can . . . can you forgive me? For all the lies?"

"Of course," he assured her. "It was my fault. I

knew you loved him. It was foolish of me to think you might have, you know, changed your mind. I'm old enough, I should have known better."

Her eyes opened and said, "I'm glad you didn't." She shuddered with a chill and sank back against him, her eyes closing again as she whispered, "Hold me, Brown. Hold me."

"I'm right here," he said, pressing her close. For a long moment he sat stroking her burnt hair and cheek, then he continued, "You knew from the beginning, didn't you? About Robin?"

She nodded. "I saw how strong her Kaa was when she was a prisoner of the Kitzakks."

Brown John, Robin and Jakar shared a thoughtful glance, and the *bukko* asked, "And you planned everything, didn't you? You knew just what you were doing every step of the trail. You knew the way to Pyram all the time, but you wanted the map so you could copy the signs on Robin."

"No," she whispered emphatically, and looked up into his eyes. "I knew the way, and I knew the legend said that the signs were somehow involved, but I didn't know how. I . . . I was just hoping that somehow things would work out. It was crazy of me. Stupid and reckless. And I would have given up a dozen times, but you wouldn't let me." She smiled warmly. "It wasn't me, Brown. It was you. You were my bukko. You picked the stage, and you set the plot, not me. And with your flattering eyes and magical twaddle you compelled all of us to play it as it deserved to be played." Her voice weakened, and her whisper barely had breath. "No, Brown . . . it was you."

She reached to touch his cheek, and her arm lost strength, dropped lifelessly beside her.

Robin moaned, hiding her face against Jakar's chest, and he held her as she heaved with sobs.

The *bukko* closed Cobra's eyes, then kissed her softly on her lips, lingering there.

She was still in his arms when Gath returned carrying a dead buck over his shoulders. It was dusk, and Robin and Jakar had found clothing and weapons, and built a fire in the open beside the tree. They stood beside it now, silent, watching Gath. He noted the firelight glistening on Robin's tear-stained cheeks, then set the buck beside the fire and joined Brown John. He did not speak until the *bukko* looked up.

"I will dig her grave," he said. "You will tell me where."

The *bukko* nodded in reply.

They buried Cobra where she died, under the tall tree with the red bark. The grave was deep, and she was laid on a thick bed of needles so her passage to the other world would be made in comfort. Earth covered her, and then heavy stones, so that the animals would not dig up her bones and carry off her Kaa.

When this was done, Brown John stood alone beside the grave until night came. Then Robin joined him, took hold of one of his hands in both of hers, and they stood silently together. After a long moment, the *bukko* hugged Robin, then turned to move back to the fire. Robin gently stopped him.

"Brown," she said, her tone curious but respectful, "there's something I don't understand. Why, if she knew, didn't she tell us?"

"Because she knew what that savage nymph knew. Only a woman with a strong and virtuous Kaa, who only wants the jewels so they could help someone else, can touch them. And she was afraid to tell, fearing, if you knew you had that strength, that the knowledge might corrupt you and ruin everything."

"Oh," said Robin. "But she could have told you!"

"No," he said. "She had been the Queen of Serpents too long . . . she could trust no one."

Robin nodded uncertainly.

"I know," he said thoughtfully, "that it seems strange that a woman of such deadly cunning could believe in the legend, and trust it. But she was desperate to save Gath, and she had nothing to believe in, except what she had believed in as a child."

"She wasn't born a serpent?"

"No. She had a childhood just as you did, at least until she was fourteen, but she never had a chance to grow up. In fact, for the last few weeks, deep inside, in her heart . . . she was that child again. Wildly and helplessly in love."

"I don't understand," Robin said.

"You don't have to," the *bukko* replied, his tone kind but firm. "Someday, perhaps, I'll explain it to you. Not now."

Robin smiled. "I shouldn't be making you think about it, should I? But there's just one thing, then I won't talk anymore. What am I going to do with the jewels? I mean, it's wonderful and all that, and very flattering. But I'm not a goddess! You know that. I'm a dancing girl."

"I know," he said casually. "That does present a problem, but we'll work it out."

"You'll help me?" she asked, excited by the prospect.

"Of course," he said, "I'm your bukko! That's what I do."

She smiled as only she could smile, and raised up on her toes, kissing him on the cheek. Then, with sober gratitude, she said firmly, "She was right about you, Brown. You talked us through the hard times, all of us, even Gath. We would have failed, wouldn't even have tried, if you hadn't helped us all. And I won't have you thinking different."

He chuckled at that, and the boyish glint came back into his eyes. "You may be right," he said firmly, "and it's proud of it, I am. I admit it." Then he felt his voice change, and he asked himself as much as he asked Robin, "But can those that help others, help themselves? Answer me that."

Forty-Five

WALK AWAY

Jakar led them south through the forest of red trees. He had traveled in this land, and was searching for a trade road which he remembered headed east. By following it, they hoped to reach the vast desert which lay to the south of the Great Forest Basin.

After a day on foot, they came across a village built among the branches of the trees, one of the many belonging to a tribe of savages Jakar believed were called Ikarians. They traded meat Gath had killed in the forest for a cart and a mule, obtained vague directions and continued on their journey.

On the second day, they reached a savanna and found the road Jakar searched for. The Way of All Coins. It was a merchants' road that stretched all the way from the Endless Sea in the west to the Kitzakk Empire in the east.

Following the road southeast, they crossed the savanna in one day, came to the northern edge of the great desert and turned east. After five days they reached the massive dry cataracts that marked the border between the desert and the forest. They headed along the cataracts for the better part of a day, and came to Wowell Pass, the first trail heading north into the forest basin.

It was dusk when they arrived. The orange light of the sun was spilling across the flat desert to the southeast in long radiant bars, and striking through the drifting clouds that hovered over the heights of the deep stone chasms, turning them to glowing golds and oranges and pinks. Through the openings in the clouds, they could see the huge shelves of rock that descended to the basin, the stepping-stones of the gods.

They stared at the vista long and hard, with weary relief on their trail-darkened faces. They all knew that at the base of Wowell Pass, only two days away, was the Valley of Miracles and Rag Camp. Home.

They made a night camp behind sheltering rocks, and Robin set about preparing a feast to celebrate. In their travels, she had secured a skin of desert wine, various herbs and a vial of olive oil, and Gath had speared several plump desert hens. Insisting that, since the men had done the work of hunting, she would prepare the feast by herself.

By the time she was applying the last garnishes to the meal, the sunset was only a glow in the western sky, and Brown John, Jakar and Gath were waiting obediently, sitting together on the ground a good twenty feet from her fire. Gath rested against a rock beside his helmet. Jakar, the bandages now removed from his healed arm, sat facing him, massaging the weakened muscles. Brown John sat to one side between them, with his legs drawn up under him.

They were travel-filthy but relaxed. Silent. A-mused as they watched Robin scurry about basting her roast and setting out the foods on large dry leaves which served as plates. When the *bukko* spoke, it was in a tone exclusively for their ears.

"She doesn't look much like a goddess from here, does she? Bustling about and sweating like a tavern wench."

Jakar and Gath grinned, and Jakar said, "You've got your work cut out for you, old man. She's going to need the very best now. Rich robes. Acolytes. Rituals. A golden temple. A priesthood! To say nothing of a whole damn theology."

"Who says that's my job?" Brown John said behind a mild scowl.

"She does," Jakar said casually. "She's already decided you're going to be her high priest."

"Arrrghhh!" said the *bukko*, accepting the fact but hating it. "I always hated priests. Nothing but a bunch of nasty old men taking advantage of pretty little virgins. Pompous, arrogant, vile beasts every one of them. I never met one that wasn't a poseur and a snob." He grunted with distaste. "Well, that's not the way it's going to be with us."

"Us?" Jakar lifted a wary eyebrow.

"Yes," insisted Brown John. "You're in this up to your neck, young man. If I'm a priest, you're a priest! And since you're so educated and experienced with the ways of this world, you're going to see to it that we don't get carried away with ourselves . . . and get too fancy."

"No more holy quests?" Jakar asked sardonically.

"No," the old man said emphatically. "I've had enough of grand schemes to last a lifetime. We're going to keep it simple now, so ordinary folks can appreciate her."

Jakar chuckled. "I see, we're back to baubles and beads, and tambourines and drums."

"Exactly!" said the Grillard, ignoring Jakar's sarcasm. "Nothing nasty, there's no call for that. But she's going to have to put on some weight! And you're going to see she does. You can't have a skinny goddess, not these days."

"Is that a personal or theological observation?" inquired Jakar.

"It's a practical one. She's just too damned beautiful. She'll frighten folks off."

"You mean . . . she has to be made more accessible."

"That's right!" Brown John said emphatically. "So the little boys' eyes will go wide, and so the little girls will dream they can grow up to be just like her."

Jakar chuckled warmly, shook his head in dismay and stood. "I think I have heard this plot before," he said. "If you'll excuse me, I'll see if she'll allow me to help now."

Jakar joined Robin at the fire and she smiled, sighing with exhaustion, then handed him her knife so he could cut the meat, giving him a quick kiss in the process.

Brown John chuckled and turned to Gath. "He's all right. He never faltered on the trail. Never once lost his humor. In fact he gained a good deal."

Gath nodded. "And he's right. You're going to be busy, old man. Religion is hard work."

The *bukko* thought about that and sighed. "I'm sure I will be, and thank the gods for it. I want no time to think . . . or remember." He sat silent, looking at the ground, then looked Gath in the eyes and smiled with one cheek. "But we have had some times, haven't we?"

Gath smiled.

Brown John did the same, then lowered his voice and said carefully, "You really are free, Gath. You have no more obligations to anyone here, and the road from here to Rag Camp is safe. There's no need for you to go any further . . . if you don't want to."

Gath nodded, but said nothing.

"The way I see it," Brown John continued, "with that helmet, you can go just about anyplace you want to now. And be just what you've always wanted to be, the lord of wherever you choose to stand."

Gath again made no reply, but their eyes held each other, and understanding passed between them. They knew they were linked by a friendship, the sum of which was greater than either of them. It was strong, bound together like mind and muscle. But the time had come for separate trails. Both had wounds to heal, and the younger man had to prove himself without his mentor to guide him.

Brown John said, "Don't misunderstand me, friend. I'm not trying to talk you into anything, but I've got to say this, because I've never been certain just what there was between you and Robin. And I'm not suggesting there should be. But if you leave again, the chances are Robin won't be there waiting for you when you get back. She may be a goddess, but she's a woman first, and she's ready to make life."

Gath glanced at Robin and Jakar, watching as they smiled and touched each other at each chance, and said, "I know."

He turned to the *bukko,* and his eyes said he had made his decision.

Brown John said, "All right, I'm the last man to try and stop you from going. But there is something I do know, and it's something you should know. Somehow, in a way far beyond my understanding, the two of you, despite what happens between her and Jakar, even if they have a dozen children, are bound together. Maybe it will only be in legends told around campfires, but it's a fact. I can sense it. The feeling's been there since I first saw the two of you together. And it wasn't just the power she had over the helmet. It's much deeper than that."

Gath hesitated, then again said quietly, "I know."

The *bukko* smiled in surrender. "But not even knowing that changes anything, does it? At least not now. You just won't be tied to anyone . . . not even me?"

The Barbarian shook his head.

"I understand," Brown John said quietly. "But let me give you one last word of advice." He glanced at Robin, saw she wasn't listening and continued in a whisper, "Don't say goodbye. Just walk away. It will be easier on her . . . because she's still torn inside between you and Jakar, even though she may not act it."

Gath nodded agreement, not bothering to say he had come to the same decision several days earlier.

The next day, when the first light of morning touched the distant horizon with its cool grey light, Gath was up before the others. He belted his plain sword around his simple homespun tunic and tied the helmet at his hip. Then he walked quietly through their camp to the corner of its sheltering rock, and looked back one last time.

Brown John slept fitfully beside the fire, his breathing unsteady and his face torn with frowns born of sad dreams. Robin slept nearby in Jakar's arms, for the moment at peace with herself and the world.

Gath backed around the rock, then turned and walked away.

When the sun had reached the middle of the sky, he was well into the desert, striding down Amber Road heading south toward the ruins of Bahaara, the former desert capital of the Kitzakk Horde. There was no glory in his stride, no triumph, and his face was hard, bitten with determination.

On the road ahead new worlds awaited him, and within them would be that wild place which was his home. Perhaps there he would find the land in which he had been born, his tribe, his family. Contentment. Then again, perhaps it lay behind, in the smile beneath a crop of red-gold hair, just as his heart said it did. But his trail was set. It was written in the sands of time, and he had done the writing. He now traveled the Endless Trail of chance and adventure, and he was walking it in the only manner his pride allowed.

Alone.

THE BEST IN SCIENCE FICTION

THE BEST IN FANTASY

THE BEST IN HORROR

THE BEST IN SUSPENSE

BESTSELLING BOOKS FROM TOR

MORE BESTSELLERS FROM TOR